Deadly Ethics

Deadly Ethics

DEATH MAY NOT BE THE END

Gerard Michael

Marilyn Keenan

Marimac Publishing

This book is dedicated to all of the ethical healthcare workers who
provide a safe environment for healing, and for their courage and
dedication during the Covid pandemic.

I would also like to acknowledge all of the everyday heroes
who stand up to injustice.

Preface

The night is darkest just before the dawn.
I encourage you to read beyond the darkness
so that you may find the light.

If you can reach beyond the depravity that humans sometimes exhibit,
you will find heroes, selflessness and kindness.
I prefer to believe that this story is more about the latter.

Contents

Copyright iv
Dedication v

About The Author 276

1

❧

Prologue

The story you are about to read is fiction. The places and characters were created in the mind of the writer. That is not to say the events depicted can't or haven't happened. Mary Shelley's Frankenstein and Bram Stoker's Dracula are good examples of fictional stories that are not likely to be realized. It's the human condition that makes this scenario possible.

Monsters do exist, just watch the evening news, or pick up the morning paper. They're not the ones hiding in our childhood closet, nor the ones lurking under our childhood bed. They don't hide behind hideous make-up as portrayed on the silver screen. They are among us, hiding in plain view.

They can be our neighbors, family members, clergy, police, or educators. People we have been taught to trust. A trip to the local grocery store, a jog through the park and even walking home from school have resulted in unthinkable crimes. What drives these behaviors will be examined and debated forever, just as they have been since the beginning of time.

The depravity of man is well documented throughout history. Because we choose to ignore or deny it, will not make it any less real. Our story takes place just after the arrival of the new millennium, in a setting that we trust, at a time when trust was in short supply.

As with villains, heroes are also hiding in plain sight. Everyday people who rise against the injustice in the world, unafraid to challenge those who have a stronghold on the weak and the vulnerable. The proverbial battle of good against evil.

Chapter 1

"Code Blue, Room 3313; code blue room 3313; code blue room 3313" the half startled, half anxious voice wailed over the intercom. Overhead, the thud of hastened footsteps responded to the alarm. The area within and around room 3313 is fast becoming pure chaos.

The bed belonging to, and still occupied by the victim's roommate is now resting in slip-shod fashion in the corridor to allow access for the multitude of healthcare professionals that make up the emergency response team. Some wear street clothes while others don surgical greens, all are gloved up to the elbow.

Commands are flying, responses and vital signs are being aired simultaneously so that it appears that everyone is talking and no one listening.

It's 7:20am, the nursing staff has just finished report, that time at the change of shifts designed to ease the transition from one staff to another. Key events of the previous watch are rehashed for the new arrivals. In room 3313, the time of day has no bearing. All of time is reduced to the next 4 or 5 crucial minutes in which decades of cumulative knowledge would need to focus on this one brief battle against death.

There were half a dozen nurses already present when Dr. Shand arrived. One nurse, standing on a footstool to achieve a height advantage was applying external cardiac massage, deep chest compressions, while another white coat was supplying precious little oxygen to the patient using an Ambu bag.

"Fill me in," said Dr. Shand as he placed his hand on the patient's groin, trying to palpate the femoral artery. "A little deeper on those compressions. I want to feel a pulse down here! Let me have 1 mil of epi, and 40 units of atropine." He pushed the meds through the IV line. "Follow that with 20 ml saline flush please. And let's get a tube down her. Call for a stat portable chest x-ray and we better have a respirator standing by. Patient's name?" said Dr. Shand as his fingers walked between the rib spaces on the left chest wall. Selecting his spot, he pierced the skin in one quick plunge with a 6-inch needle. At the other end, the syringe held 20 mg. of sodium bicarb. He drew back slightly on the syringe, "bull's eye" he exclaimed as deep red blood swirled into the bicarb. He had hit his target, the heart.

"Patient is Gail Lockwood," said a voice from behind him. Marti Short, the charge nurse for 3 East had just returned with updated notes. "33 year old white female admitted 2 days ago with thrombosis of the left leg. Ultrasound done yesterday found a half-inch clot just proximal to the trifurcation. Heparin therapy and warm packs have been ongoing with good results. Last vitals at 0400 today were fine."

"OK. Thanks Marti." Let's get that ET tube in so we get some proper ventilation," Shand repeated as he looked up at the cardiac monitor. "Hey, we've got something here! Stop compressions!" Three, four, five seconds pass. "She's fibrillating. Let's try to cardiovert her. Paddles please. Clear!" This quieted the crowd a bit. CLICK..THUD. one one thousand, two one thousand, three one tho.." Alright. Sinus rhythm baby! Not great, but it's there."

The ET tube went in easily. Gail Lockwood's skin color had gone from deep purple to ashen, not normal but certainly better. With the patient maintaining her own cardiac rhythm and the respirator aiding her breathing, the team sat back to observe and reflect.

While others talked quietly or went about their business of note taking and cleaning up, Dr. Shand kept silent, drifting off into a semi dreamlike state. Farther and farther away until the incessant beeping of the monitor was just a dull, background noise, barely noticeable.

John Shand wanted to be a doctor for as long as he could remember. While most kids in high school and college were testing the waters, he stayed focused. John enjoyed having fun as much as the next guy, but he knew how difficult it was for an American student of modest financial background to get accepted to medical school. He also knew that if he made it, he couldn't burden his parents with the financial responsibility. His diligence and fortitude were about to be tested, again.

"Dr. Shand? Dr. Shand!" As if passing through a time tunnel, John Shand abruptly emerged from his daydream. "She's losing her rhythm," said Marti. "Oh shit!" exclaimed John. "Alright, let's do it again. Paddles!"

This time John Shand and his team of medical magicians could not pull off the trick. Gail Lockwood, age 33 died of cardiac arrest just 24 short minutes after the code was called. "Marti, if you don't mind, bring the death certificate to the physician's lounge. I need some coffee...oh and I need her chart and contact her attending and fill him in. One more thing, get permission from the next of kin for an autopsy.

With that, John Shand left room 3313, but in his wake left a small piece of his heart and a good size chunk of pride.

The conversation in 3313 continued but on a much softer scale. "Let's get her cleaned and wrapped and shipped down to the P.O." ordered Marti. The morgue was in a very public area near the cafeteria. Instead of a sign on the door that read "Morgue," the impact was lessened by the title Post Obitum.

If there is a silver lining to every cloud, in this case it would have to be that Gail Lockwood died on the day shift, much to the disappointment of others...

Chapter 2

Maury Slater was late again. He could count on one hand, the number of times he actually made it to the time clock by 7:30am over the last 12 years. He was habitually late, however, no one complained if the card was punched by 7:36. The hospital allowed a punch 6 minutes early or late without penalty and without paying overtime.

The time was now 7:32. Maury raced his new Nissan 300ZX into the parking garage, squealing the tires on the turns. Just a couple of year ago he could pick a spot in the lot and be at the clock by 7:31. In an effort to increase revenue and employee morale, the hospital decided to build a parking garage. Maury didn't see any advantages. It took longer to park, and one could grow old waiting for the elevator. But then, Maury was a bit simple minded.

Maury decided to take the stairs. Down to the first floor, through the glass enclosed tunnel, through the main lobby, down one more flight, past the cafeteria toward the finish line. As he reached the clock, his fingers flicked up the line of timecards making a sound like a baseball card in the spokes of a bicycle tire. He found his, yanked it out of the slot and slammed it into the clock. He closed his eyes as he removed the card. Opening one eye he yelled loud enough to turn a few heads "yes!" Now that he was officially on time, he would leisurely stop at the cafeteria for a cup of coffee on his way to the ward.

A couple of first year nursing students were sharing stories about their evenings when Maury entered. "Hey Denise, look what the cat dragged in" one of them said just loud enough for him to hear her. "Hello Maurice" whispered the other in a sexy, breathy voice. Maury ignored her. "Hey Maury, did you get lucky last night?" Again, he ignored the statement. Maury hadn't been "lucky" in quite a while although he really didn't care. He considered most women airheads and was unable to tolerate conversation with them.

"Mister Slater please call extension 300, Mister Slater 300" announced the nasally voiced operator. "*That lady needs a nose job*" Maury said to himself as he walked toward the phone. The students watching this simultaneously exclaimed "what an asshole" and then roared with laughter.

Maury found a phone outside the cafeteria and dialed 300. "3 East, Ms. Jansen"

"Lynette? Is that you?" asked Maury.

"Where the hell have you been Slater? It's 7:45 already!" "Yeah, sorry Lynette, I was in Personnel filling out a tax form" he lied.

"Well get up here" she fumed, "I need you to make a run to the P.O."

"Okay Lynette" he said with a sudden excitement in his voice.

"And Maury, no jerking off on the way."

Maury backtracked past the time clock to the other end of the hall. The morgue door would be locked but with any luck, someone would be in the autopsy room, which was the unmarked door next to it. Inside, the two rooms were connected by an interior door so that bodies could be moved from cooler to the table and back without the need to access the public corridor. As Maury approached the door, he knew someone was there...he could hear the bone saw.

Maury gave the door seven or eight hard, loud knocks to ascend above the sound of the saw. Within seconds, the door opened to the sound of the blade slowing itself to a stop. "Hello Mr. Slater, come on in." It was Dr. Seike, the Chief pathologist. "What brings you here?"

"I need the cart doc, someone up on 3 bit the dust and I was already in the basement and didn't want to go upstairs to get the key."

"Understood" said Seiki. "Help yourself and just let yourself out the other side Maury" "Will do doc."

It looked like the doctor had just cut through the ribs. His assistant, Jim was garbed in a disposable surgical suit and safety mask. The mask was raised and in one ungloved hand he held a breakfast sandwich. Jim was about 5'11" and weighed close to 260 pounds and not much of it was muscle. His friends called him "Slim Jim." Apparently, there wasn't much that slowed Jim's appetite including the smell of burning human flesh.

Maury grabbed the cart and headed toward the elevator. When he arrived on the third floor, he stopped at the nurse's station to get a copy of the transportation certificate and the key to the morgue just in case it was locked when he returned. He read the death notice...Rm 3313, 7: 31am..Age 33, female. Maury's heart began to race. Upon arrival at 3313, Maury found 2 nurses straightening up the room. Nurse Janzen walked in right behind him. "It's about time Maury! What took you so long?"

"I had to get the cart, Lynette, and I was held up for a few minutes." "What a bitch," he thought. "Always embarrassing me in front of the other staff." She developed this habit shortly after he asked her out and she laughingly declined. Maury wasn't homely but he wasn't overly handsome either, fairly tall and slim, but not thin. His downfall was that he did not possess an ounce of cool. His hair was old fashioned, his clothes looked like they came out of the charity bin, and he had an eighth-grade mentality. The only thing cool about Maury was his car, a new Nissan 300ZX, fully loaded, T-bar roof, great stereo and a color that was not white and not gray. It looked like the underbelly of a shark, sort of pearly. You wouldn't see this color twice in a lifetime. The question on everyone's mind was how an orderly could afford such a sweet ride.

"Everyone ready to lift," said Lynette. "One..two...three..go!"

"How much did she weigh?" asked one of the nurses?

"About one twenty-five alive but they always seem to gain weight when they die" Lynette answered. Maury put the cover on the cart and backed it into the corridor. With the cover on, it looked like a typical linen cart, no bumps, or lumps. "I'll go with you Maury," said Lynette.

"Oh no, that won't be necessary" Maury blurted out, "I'm sure you have a lot to do with the shift change and all and besides, I think Dr. Seiki and Jim are still in the P.O., they can help once I'm down there."

"Okay, you're sure?" asked Lynette. "Just be sure to return the key when you're through." "You've got it Lynette." And off he went to the elevator. He could feel his heartbeat quickening and now he could also feel that familiar sensation of an erection mounting.

Chapter 3

John Shand sat on an old vinyl sofa in the doctor's lounge. Weathered from years of abuse by young residents and interns from nearby universities. After long days at the college, they would supplement their meager student stipends by moonlighting in the emergency departments at nearby hospitals.

Every night of the year from 7PM until 7AM, newly licensed MDs training to be surgeons, pediatricians, urologists, gynecologists, and a variety of other medical specialties would hone their skills on unknowing patients. If you were lucky, your symptoms would coincide with the course of study of that of the physician on duty. If not, you could be in for a long night of consults and testing.

To be fair, some of these young people were naturals and would go on to become well known in their respective fields. Others, you would swear found their degrees in a box of Cracker Jacks.

Now, on this couch where these poor slobs caught a few winks between cases and if fortunate, found the periodic company of a willing student nurse, John sat, arms folded, head back and eyes closed, reliving the last hour of his life in fast forward.

"Don't dwell on the less successful situations you may encounter but relish in the triumphs" John could hear one of his many proctors quoting, always careful to avoid the word failure. But John couldn't just dismiss the fact that a person just a few years younger than him expires for no apparent reason.

Every step, every procedure seemed perfectly logical. He could not find one "what if" as he replayed the incident. Still not satisfied, he would allow his mind to rest until the results of the autopsy were back. He turned his thoughts toward more pleasant things.

In 1992, John was a senior at Union College in Schenectady, New York. Being in upstate NY in the summer was fine, actually more than fine, it was perfect. Mostly moderate temperatures and humidity and a world of exploration at your fingertips.

Less than an hour by car could place you swimming or hiking in the Adirondacks, studying early American history through seventeenth-, and eighteenth-century homes and museums or visiting Revolutionary War battlefields. Or as John often did, travel a mere half hour to Saratoga for a concert in the open amphitheater of Saratoga Performing Arts Center.

SPAC drew big name contemporary entertainment. John would take a blanket, a wine skin and perhaps a couple of joints if he had them and find a place to sprawl out on the vast grassy area. Lawn seats were dirt-cheap and although the visibility wasn't as good as having a seat inside, the action all took place outside.

Being surrounded by 20,000 other blanket dwellers had it perks. There was never a shortage of alcohol, weed and scantily clad young women willing to share these items and more. Inhibition ran low and love was in the air and often on the ground as well. John loved his young life.

But summer would end, and fall would arrive bringing with it the falling temperatures and falling leaves. The most colorful time of year would in a matter of a few short weeks transition to a world void of color. The gray hues of fall would force John inward.

He would hit the books hard now, striving for the GPA that would secure a spot in medical school. A 3.7 and the right connections may get him into a state school or a foreign medical college, but he would need a 4.0 to make it to one of the good ones.

Studying occupied just about all of John's waking moments. That was until John's roommate Greg convinced him to stop long enough to spend an evening out at the Kampus Kafe enjoying a few beers and a pizza. The café was just across the street from the front gate of the college.

Inside, it was predictably decorated, several small tables with red and white checkered table clothes, four seaters in the middle of the room and 2 seaters against the walls. The exception was the 2two rounded booths on either side of the entrance.

In the rear, a walk-up counter on the right and restrooms on the left. Near the entry to the restrooms was a small, elevated platform that served as a stage for local musicians, usually Union students.

As John and Greg passed through the front door, they were immediately struck by the drastic change in temperature. The sudden warmth coupled with the exquisite aroma of baking pizza and other delectable menu items stimulated John's endorphins to the point of euphoria.

He hadn't felt this alive in months. The place was about a quarter full, with most of the customers occupying seats in the back of the restaurant.

"Where to" John asked, gazing around,

"Why don't you grab that table for 2 over there and I'll get the first round of beer" Greg replied. John did as he was instructed and secured the table. Greg appeared moments later carrying 2 draft beers in frosty cold mugs, which were melting quickly.

As Greg sat down, John could see a couple of young ladies entering. Just as they had done, the ladies stopped just inside the door and perused the possibilities. Suddenly, Greg stood up, "hey Wendy, over here!" he shouted as John realized everyone is the place was looking at him.

As the girls approached Greg said, "You girls want to join us? We'll get a bigger table."

"Sure, why not?" replied one of them.

"John, grab a couple more beers for the ladies and meet us up front."

John responded as told and delivered the goods to one of the rounded booths right by the entrance.

As John approached, Greg began the introductions. "John Shand this is Wendy Hogan and uh...."

"Sara Wallace" the other girl chimed in, obviously not an acquaintance of Greg.

"How do you do Wendy? Sara?" John said shaking each of their hands. They were seated boy, girl, boy, girl around the booth so that John was directly across from Sara.

Although Wendy had the better body, John just couldn't take his eyes off Sara. John guessed she was about 5 feet 5 inches tall and probably carried 5-10 pounds more than she would like but her face was gorgeous. She had deep blond hair that almost looked light brown in the indoor light, cut short but very feminine.

Her eyes were sky blue with tiny specks of green and brown. She had high cheekbones and although her teeth were not perfect, she had a smile that was genuine and lighthearted. Her skin seemed perfect, light complexion with rosy cheeks, perhaps from the cold. She wore just enough makeup, expertly applied, to add a touch of color.

"Do you and Wendy share some classes?' John inquired of Greg.

"Just one this semester but we're both business majors" John really didn't hear an answer but turned his attention directly to Sara. "And how about you? What's your major?" The nervousness obvious in his voice.

His palms were sweating and that reminded him of elementary school where they were forced to learn square dancing as part of gym class. The boys all hated this, they would much rather play baseball or dodgeball or pretty much anything but square dance. Boys on one side of the gym and girls on the other, the gentleman would ask one of the girls if they "could have the pleasure of the dance."

Of course, all the pretty, popular girls went quickly, and John was often left with limited choices. It seemed like he always ended up with the same partner, Jenny, a sweet girl with sweaty hands. The poor thing was forced to wear gloves. But even then, John was a polite, sensitive young man and Jenny was delighted to be paired with him. Here he is 20 years later and could finally empathize with her.

"Education" Sara said for the second time before John tuned back in. He felt foolish and could feel the blood rush to his face.

"I'm sorry, that's great. Elementary or secondary?"

"High school, I think. I love children but I don't know if I could be with 25 of them all day and then go home to my own, besides, I would really like to specialize in Math or English, probably English" she elaborated. "And what about you John?"

"Well, if all goes well, I hope to go on to medical school when I finish here next year." "That's super! A doctor, I don't think I could stay in school that long."

"I know, I guess maybe I'm just a glutton for punishment!" John joked.

After another round, and a lot more small talk, John and Greg walked their friends to their dorm. John asked Sara if he could call her sometime and she assured him she would be delighted. After a gentle, lengthy handshake they said good night and John returned to his room. He couldn't believe how much his outlook could change in a matter of hours.

He knew his studies had to be the priority, but new feelings were awakened in him tonight. John called Sara the very next day. Cupid's arrow made a direct hit on John's heart and Sara's as well. The next several months flew by in an instant. Sara understood the essence of John's studies and never interfered. In fact, it was Sara who would keep him on track when she felt he was beginning to drift.

A full year would go by before they made love. While the sex was somewhat clumsy, the love they felt that moment would stay with them forever.

John and Sara both graduated cum laude. John was offered entrance at Albany Medical College and accepted. The college was a mere 10 miles from Union and both John and Sara were getting used to upstate New York.

Sara landed a teaching job in an Albany suburb and so they decided to marry that summer and begin their life together, he the student and her the breadwinner. The next several years were hard ones. They had little time to spend together but the time they did have, they cherished.

They didn't enjoy love in the fast lane so they would avoid the temptation for a quickie. They would wait for a day off and spend the entire day in bed. No more clumsiness, there lovemaking was rich and rewarding.

John finished medical school and his internal medicine residency at AMC. A hospital in High Falls, NY had offered him a low interest loan and a part-time job as a house physician, so he and Sara headed west from Albany to establish a new home.

Eight years had passed, and it was time to begin a family. John had a good practice and some money in the bank. Not for lack of trying but their efforts were to no avail. Sara would make a great mother but.......

John drifted back from his daydream, back to the reality of his current situation and the imagery of the doctor's lounge. The thought hadn't crossed his mind before but suddenly he wondered if Gail Lockwood was leaving children behind. John struggled to find the fairness in life.

Feeling a bit rested, John left the lounge to get a start on his day. Morning rounds, chart documentation, lunch and then perhaps a quiet afternoon just handling the routine bullshit required of the house physician, a position he held two days a week usually Monday and Thursday.

For the most part he enjoyed the job because it paid well, and it allowed him a couple of days out of the office. The hospital also paid a portion of his malpractice insurance, which was substantial. The downside of the job was being on call both nights after he left the building.

He was usually awakened several times during the night. Most often, he could handle the situation over the phone but there were times when he would have to leave the warmth of his bed and wife and venture out into the cold and dark of night. All in all, it wasn't such a bad job. At least not yet.

Chapter 4

As Maury approached the morgue, he noticed the absence of noise from the adjoining autopsy room. "They couldn't possibly be finished already" he thought. He put the key in the lock and turned it until the tumblers gave way with a thud that he could hear echoing on the other side of the door. He opened the door and reached for the light switch before entering.

Maury didn't mind coming to the morgue; in fact, at times like this he enjoyed it, as long as there was light. Once the light was on, he proceeded inside pulling the cart behind him. The room was basically empty. The left wall was end-to-end stainless steel with handles that gave the appearance of an ice cream truck. In all, there were six small doors and one very large one. The large door was a walk-in cooler that held up to three carts or stretchers side by side. That allowed for a total of nine bodies to be stored at one time but for as long as Maury could remember, he had never seen a full house.

It generally took two people to lift the body from the cart to the drawer. Maury decided to just leave the body on the cart in the big cooler. This would also save Seiki some work when it was time to begin the post. But before Maury would leave, he would spend a few minutes alone with his new guest. He walked over to the door of the autopsy room and opened it.

To his surprise, neither Jim nor Dr. Seike was there. The corpse still lay on the table cut from stem to stern and partially eviscerated. "Strange" he mumbled to himself as he closed and locked the door. Even though the situation didn't feel right to him, Maury was happy that he was alone.

The body of Gail Lockwood was wrapped in a sheet of milky white plastic that allows one to see the shape of the object beneath it but not transparent enough to actually see through. Maury reached out with one hand and touched her breast.

He could feel the warmth of her flesh even through the plastic and he was now sensing a raging hard on rising in his pants. He swiftly moved his other hand and was now kneading both breasts roughly. He wanted more. He wanted it all, but he couldn't. Not now. Not at this time of day.

If it was later in the afternoon, he could punch out and stay without fear of being caught but Dr. Seike and Jim could return any minute. He couldn't settle for less than touching her naked flesh. He hastily but carefully unwrapped the heavy plastic shroud. Then, as if performing a strip tease, he started at her feet, then her legs. His breath was escaping him, and he could feel his heart racing inside his chest. He unveiled her pelvis and stopped for a moment. He ran his hand up the inside of her thigh. Her legs were too close together, preventing him from reaching his target. He settled for rubbing her reddish-blond pubic hair while he uncovered the abdomen, chest and then neck. He stopped again and lowered his head to her breasts. He licked and sucked wildly, first one, then the other. Back and forth he flew like a mad man his hand desperately trying to get to her mound, but he couldn't part her heavy legs.

He could feel the pressure building in his groin. He freed one hand from her body and brought it down on his own throbbing cock. He rubbed himself through his pants. Harder, faster, faster until...lightheadedness, warmth and wetness were all he could sense. He didn't move for what seemed like several minutes. Then, as suddenly as it had arrived, his ecstasy was gone. Replaced by the fear of being caught.

Quickly, Maury re-wrapped the body, opened the cooler door, drove the cart in and slammed the door shut behind him. He stood, back against the door, heart pounding in the emptiness of the morgue. He never saw her face. Off to the lavatory to clean up. He was grateful for lab coats.

While in the bathroom, Maury thought back to his introduction to necrophilia.

Chapter 5

After repeating two lower grades in school, by the skin of his teeth, Maury received his high school diploma. It was a school credit diploma, the non-regent's version for New York State schools.

The curriculum included courses such as gym, ceramics, remedial reading, and shop. Anyone with half a brain and a drop of enthusiasm was pushed toward the regent's program with hopes of feeding the university system. Maury found himself in the small minority of kids who the system gave up on. He was unprepared for most significant paying jobs, so he settled for a position as traffic director for a local funeral home.

It was a lousy job. Adverse weather and irregular hours were the norm, but they bought him a suit, paid him minimum wage, and treated him decently, so he stayed. Eventually, he became a junior assistant. More hours and same pay but indoors. He would help set up rooms, stock supplies and caskets and occasionally make a body run to the local hospital or nursing home.

At first, it gave him the creeps, but he gradually got used to it and it wasn't long before he found death fascinating. After a couple of years, he was promoted to assistant, many hours but a little more money. This position allowed him to assist with the preparation of the bodies.

The owner and director of the home, Harold Mease, took Maury under his wing. Apparently, Harold saw something in Maury that others had missed. Not having any sons of his own, Harold became close to Maury and allowed him to live in the apartment above the shop.

On many occasions, a call would come in the middle of the night to pick up a body at a home or accident scene, which unlike the hospital required immediate removal. Harold and Maury would share this duty by taking call on alternate nights.

Early one morning, around 3 am, Maury was awakened by noises coming from downstairs. He went down to the main floor and looked around the three viewing rooms. Everything seemed normal.eH

He paused to listen again and sure enough, he heard the noise.

It appeared to be coming from the basement. The basement door was ajar. Maury proceeded cautiously and quietly down the lower flight of stairs. About halfway down he paused to listen. He heard heavy breathing and moaning coming from the preparation room. He continued his descent.

The basement was dark except for a thin shard of light coming from the partially opened embalming room door. He picked up a piece of galvanized pipe he found leaning in a corner of the cement wall. He reached the door and peeked in through the crack. His heart was pounding and his own breathing extremely labored.

Maury was astounded to find Harold Mease, bare ass up in the air, pounding it home to some chick right there on the embalming table.

"Why would anyone bring a girl here to have sex with her"? Maury thought. "How about a hotel"? "Or even the office upstairs"? He had overcome his fear and now Maury found the scene playing out in front of him exciting, making him hot.

The girl was laying on her back with her legs hanging over the sides of the table. Harold was grunting and moaning but the girl was silent. The humping became more intense, and Harold gave a final loud moan as if he was in pain. Harold's body now laid limp on top of this girl, his knees shaking.

Maury started to turn to make his exit and avoid an embarrassing situation when he saw the girl's flail arms drop to the sides of the table. He was all too familiar with the appearance of her extremities. This girl was dead. Maury turned to flee, but in his haste tripped over a toolbox on the floor and fell with a crash. He picked himself up and started for the stairs when the room got suddenly brighter. He stopped to find Harold standing in the doorway.

Chapter 6

Jim returned to the morgue about five minutes ahead of Dr. Seike. Although he found it extremely peculiar to be asked to take a break this early in the morning, and particularly in the middle of an autopsy, he would never consider questioning Dr. Seike. The doctor complained that he suddenly developed an excruciating headache and suggested the twenty-minute break so he could take some aspirin and lie down in the doctor's lounge.

Jim offered to stay behind and pick up a little, but Seike was adamant that he go to the coffee shop. He even gave Jim a couple of dollars to cover his refreshments. Never before could Jim remember the doctor paying for anything. Even when they would work through lunch and would need to send out for food, it was Dutch treat.

Jim was washing a few instruments when Seike's familiar knock came at the door. He hurried over to open it.

"Thank you, my good man," Seike quipped, adding a little bowing gesture. "Shall we return to our endeavor Jim"?

"Yes sir. Is your headache better?"

"Oh yes. Completely. Thank you."

"Well, I'll need to get me some of them." Jim said under his breath, or so he thought. "They're all the same Jim, may as well buy the cheap ones!" That comment didn't surprise Jim at all. Seike was nice but he was tight.

"Where did we leave off Jim?" said Seike rhetorically. Jim played the game.

"You completed the kidneys, spleen and the liver."

"Ok then. The aorta, vena cava, gall bladder, bowel and urinary bladder all look fine. Let's just grab the pancreas for weight and specimen then we'll move on to the chest.

How about a blade Jimmy?" Jim had the scalpel in his hand, anticipating the next move. Jim wasn't scholarly but he did possess a good deal of common sense, which is why Seike kept him on. That and the fact that Jim Larkin was the hardest worker he had ever known.

With the pancreas removed, weighed, and dissected for observation and specimen, Seike was preparing to extricate the heart. In his gloved hand, he held the essence of life and the evidence of death.

"This is It, Jim. No matter what else fails in the body, a creature is still alive until the heart beats it's last."

Seike now spoke into the microphone hanging above the table.

"Pericardial sack is intact without evidence of hemorrhage or infarction. All entering and exiting vessels appear intact with no signs of sclerosis or narrowing."

He clipped the vessels leading to the heart with speed and agility and removed the heart from the chest. Placing it on the scale, he said.

"External survey reveals normal size and weight for the patient's body type and age." He moved to the counter and placed the heart on a cutting board, which angled ever so slightly toward the stainless-steel sink. As he sliced into the heart with a butcher's knife, deep crimson, near black blood, raced to the sink where it blended with the swirling water before disappearing down the drain.

"Nothing here Jim." He explained as he held the heart, which was now cut every which way to expose all four chambers.

"It looks like we'll need to open the head. Do we have the family's consent?"

"Have it right here doc." Jim replied.

Dr. Seike took the scalpel and starting behind one ear etched a deep cut around the ear, across the middle of her skull then over and behind the other ear. He then pulled up on the skin and carefully pared between skin and bone as if he were skinning an animal. With the flesh and bone now separated, he pulled the flap of skin, hair, fat, and muscle down over Gail Lockwood's face until the shiny, pinkish-blue lining covered the eyes and nose.

"Alright Jim, hand me the bone saw...

Chapter 7

"Mr. Mease! I uh...I'm sorry...I was just on my way...I heard some noises and I thought maybe. I thought you were, you know uh...shit. Listen I didn't see anything ok? I'll just get back upstairs and forget all about..."

" Maury!" Harold cracked abruptly. "Stop stammering! It's all right. I know what you saw and I'm sure you think I'm crazy or weird or something, but I'm not. Come in here and we'll talk."

Maury held his ground, reluctant to follow. "Please Maury?" Harold pleaded. "Just a short talk. I think you owe me that. He was right. Maury cautiously followed Harold back into the embalming room. Harold stood on one side of the girl while Maury had his back to the work counter on the other side.

"Maury. What do you see here?" Maury didn't answer. "Come on. Tell me what you see?"

"I see a dead girl." He said every so softly.

"Aside from life-or-death Maury, what do you see?" Harold answered for him, "I see a girl. Just a girl! Take a look." Maury looked the body up and down. "Do you think she's attractive Maury?"

He guessed the girl was in her early twenties, short dyed blonde hair, good makeup job. Further down, his eyes fixed on her breasts, so firm that even lying down, they stood straight up. Her abdomen was flat, and her skin was flawless. Further down now, a small patch of hair between her legs that gave away her natural color, brunette.

Her legs were still spread open revealing soft, moist pink lips. He couldn't focus. He was feeling very faint, dizzy...too much happening. He closed his eyes for a long moment. Mease gave him the space.

"I guess she's attractive." He muttered with his eyes still closed, trying to stop the room from spinning.

"Of course, she's attractive!" Harold confirmed. "She's only twenty-two and in great shape! Not a mark on her body to even insinuate death or trauma."

"How did she die?" Maury inquired.

"Overdose. Barbs, I guess. They found her a little too late. DOA at the emergency room. Damn shame." Harold said with true compassion. "But you see Maury, she is gone. That is, her soul is gone and what's left is a beautiful body, a mere vehicle for the soul.

Look at it this way, when you were a kid just discovering your own sexuality, didn't you ever look at a girl in a magazine and wish with all your might that the girl in those pictures could materialize into flesh before you?" Harold continued without pausing for a response.

"Did you wish the girl was moving, breathing, talking? No! That made no difference, all you wanted was five minutes with that flesh, to do whatever your heart desired. Now don't get me wrong," Harold continued, "sex with a live girl can be great but sometimes you just don't feel like playing all the head games. Am I good enough? Big enough? Does it feel good for her? Can I make her cum? Sometimes you just want to screw without all the emotional baggage. Do see what I'm saying here Maury? Do you follow me at all?"

"This can't be making sense." Maury thought to himself. "It's wrong. It's just plain wrong."

"How about this?" Harold started again. "Did you ever wish you could put a girl to sleep? Or maybe hypnotize her and take advantage of her? It's sex without inhibition! Who gets hurt? No one.

"My God, he is making sense." But a sleeping girl and a dead girl are two different things." Maury said, with a little more energy now.

"You're right." Said Harold. "The difference is that the sleeping girl will wake up. That's it. Look Maury, it's not like you killed her or that you are responsible for her death. You are simply borrowing her lifeless flesh for which she no longer has use. She can give pleasure in her last physical act on earth. Do you think she would mind?"

"I don't know, it still sounds pretty weird to me." "Of course, it does Maury but after you think about it a while, you'll see that I'm right. The soul is gone and what is left is the centerfold transformed into the flesh. Your wildest dream, come true. I'm right." Harold concluded.

"Come on, what do you say you help me move her into the cooler now Maury?" "Ok boss." Maury answered, his mind now in another place. A place far away. Searching the past, present and future for the ramifications of this night's happenings.

"One more thing Maury, the body only stays flexible for 2 to 8 hours before rigor mortis sets in. All the muscles will begin to stiffen. After 24-72 hours, the rigor passes, and they become flexible again. However, the body also starts to organically break down by then. It may longer be a pleasant experience."

After the body was covered and placed in cold storage, Harold turned back to Maury. "You understand the essence of silence in this matter, don't you Maury? After all, I would hate to lose you as an employee. Besides, after thinking about this for a few days, you will see this as one of the benefits of the job. I'll see you in the morning my friend."

Maury locked the door behind Harold and returned to his apartment above the viewing rooms where he consumed beer after beer until sleep stole the night away......

"Hey buddy! You almost done in there or did you fall in?" Maury flew out of the past and slammed into the present to find himself locked in the stall of the men's room holding tissue paper to his penis. "How long have I been in here?" He wondered. He got his answer when he tried to pull the paper away.

Chapter 8

Sleep was brief for John Shand. The hospital had called three times during the night, all medication problems. Can't find the order for this one, so and so is having a reaction to a drug, Mrs. Jones would like something to help her sleep. Even without interruption, John would have found sleep difficult.

It was unlike him to dwell on a patient of his, but this Lockwood case had a hold on him. He couldn't explain it, but something seemed amiss. Within a few hours, he should have the results of the autopsy performed late the previous day and still in progress when he left the building. For now, he would concentrate on showering and breakfast and then a long day of office hours.

John had been into his office routine for about an hour when the call he had been waiting for came from Kyle Seike. "Peg, I'll take the call in my office." He told his receptionist. "Try to entertain these patients for about ten minutes, would you?" He closed the door to his office, sat back in his big black leather chair and picked up the phone. "Dr. Shand here." He spoke.

"Hello John, Kyle Seike. How are you today?"

"Just fine Kyle. Hey thanks for getting back to me so soon. I owe you one."

"My pleasure John. I'm afraid I don't have much news for you though. The autopsy proved inconclusive for cause of death." Seiki explained apologetically.

"Are you sure Kyle? No coronary or clot?"

"Heart and lungs were fine John aside from the minor contusions caused by CPR."

"How about the head Kyle? Maybe you should take a look."

"Already done John, no sclerosis, no emboli, no evidence of CVA."

"How about hematology and micro, Kyle? Anything there?"

"Micro was all normal and aside from a few samples we sent out to the state crime lab, hemo was ok too."

"State crime lab?" John quizzed. "What sort of tests?"

"Just a couple of drug related tests that we can't perform here. It's grasping at straws but if there was a wrong administration or overdose of a drug, they should pick it up." "When will we know Kyle?"

"We should have the results in a week or two."

"Ok Kyle. I guess we wait. Thanks again for your help."

"Any time John. Oh, and John, don't hold your breath. I don't expect to hear anything positive. Have a good day, John."

"Thanks Kyle, you too."

John placed the receiver back in the cradle and leaned back in his chair. He gazed over at the several certificates hanging on his office wall. Seven framed documents, each signifying a higher level of academic achievement. "What does it all mean?" he asked himself.

"When a healthy woman in her thirties dies without a single clue as to why, it makes a mockery of the medical profession and it's education system." John felt it gnawing at his ego like a cancer. Silently, slowly but surely, little by little, John Shand was being consumed.

Chapter 9

Myrna Shapiro was a typical middle class Jewish woman living in this part of upstate New York. Her husband Mel made an honest living operating a small delicatessen in town. Myrna and Mel had two grown daughters who were finally off on their own leaving them to relax and enjoy their middle years. Although they hadn't stock-piled a huge savings, their home was paid for, they had helped their daughters through college and Mel was able to reduce his hours at the deli.

Mel played golf once or twice a week with a few of his cronies and Myrna was an avid jogger. That is until she twisted her knee in a pothole on the side of the road.

Myrna was admitted through the emergency department with a torn cartilage. She underwent an arthroscopy the following morning to confirm the diagnosis. Ordinarily, a small meniscal tear can be surgically removed during the endoscopy but because of her current level of physical activity, her surgeon had decided the best prognosis for a full recovery lied in surgically opening the knee. Her doctor assured her she would be home in a day or two and back to jogging in three months.

Mel stayed by her side until she was wheeled away to the O.R. He paced nervously in the surgical waiting room until the doctor came out to assure him that the surgery went as expected and that Myrna was doing just fine. About ninety minutes later, Myrna was delivered back her room as promised. Tomorrow, Mel would take his bride home and care for her as she recovered.

Mel arrived early the next morning to find that Myrna had developed a post-surgical infection. A minor setback, he was assured, and Myrna would have to remain an additional three or four days. She was started on a regimen of intravenous antibiotics and should begin to feel relief in a matter of hours.

Mel stayed with Myrna until her lunch tray arrived. He had a few errands to run and planned to meet a friend for a little lunch of his own. He told Myrna he would see her later in the afternoon and instructed her to take a nap after lunch. "I promise. And don't rush back. I'm not going anywhere on this bum leg."

Mel leaned over the lunch tray and kissed his wife. For the first time in what seemed like forever, he noticed the true color of her eyes and made a mental note to pay more attention to the subtle, important things in his life. "I love you" he said and brushed her hair back tenderly away from her face.

Myrna's nurse arrived just minutes after she finished her lunch. She checked the I.V., took her pulse at her wrist, and then checked the dressing and confirmed a femoral pulse on the affected leg. She told Myrna everything looked good and asked if she needed anything. Myrna assured her she was fine but a little tired.

She had promised Mel she would nap and now she really felt ready to fulfill that promise. The nurse lowered the head of the bed and left the room. "Sleep tight Mrs. Shapiro."

Myrna was dozing in no time at all. She was practically in a sound sleep when the door behind her slipped open. "Mrs. Shapiro" a voice whispered. "I need to add a little more medication to your I.V." Myrna didn't bother turning over, she just nodded her head, eyes still closed. This was a common occurrence and instilled no need for alarm. *After all, this was a hospital, and one should not expect to get any real rest here.*

Myrna hadn't been cared for by a male nurse during this visit, but she was used to men caring for her during previous stays in the hospital. She really hadn't formed a preference. Everyone here treated her nicely.

The male attendant pulled a small syringe from his lab coat pocket. Locating the piggyback site on the IV tubing, he removed the cap from the needle and inserted it into the tubing. Using one hand to pinch off the proximal tube to prevent backflow, he began to administer the medication by depressing the syringe with the other hand. He released the pinched tubing and opened the flow to max. The clear medicine raced toward her arm.

After two or three seconds, Myrna's eyes shot open, and she started to mutter. "I feel strange...." she tried to say but not recognizing her own voice. She couldn't feel her lips. She tried to move her arms, but nothing happened. She couldn't move at all. She began to panic and then realized that she wasn't breathing. "What is happening?" she screamed inside her head. Her eyes stared straight ahead. She couldn't move them. She could see the call button within inches mounted to the bed rail. "If only I could reach it" she said to herself.

Myrna felt her face flushing and her eyes were getting a bulging feeling. Her vision was clouding over from not blinking. Outwardly, her skin was changing from pallor to purple. She now knew she was suffocating. She understood what it would feel like to drown. A billion tiny black dots were now floating in front of her eyes. She could just barely make out a face in front of her. A face she had never seen. He was saying something to her, but she could only hear a loud buzzing in her ears.

The face faded as did the panicky feeling. Her thoughts turned to Mel and the girls. "I love you, Mel. Give the girls a kiss for me....in her last fleeting thought, she turned her spirit to God.

Chapter 10

The logbook for the morgue was kept at the front desk in the main lobby. Anyone wishing to sign a body in or out was required to make an entry in this book. For the past several years, Maury had made it a habit to check the book twice daily. First thing in the morning and again just before leaving in the afternoon. Not too long ago, the receptionist had asked Maury about this ritual. He responded by saying he needed to always know the capacity of the morgue just in case a patient should depart during his shift. She bought the explanation and hadn't questioned him again. Everyone knew Maury was a few cards short of a full deck and she felt it was better to leave well enough alone.

Today, as Maury fingered through the log nonchalantly, he was pleasantly surprised to find a recent entry:

IN: #4122Name: Shapiro, MyrnaAge: 53

Date: August 4Time: 14:33Signed: T.A. Johnson

Comment: HOLD FOR POST

OUT: Date: Time: To: Signed:

"Fantastic" Maury thought to himself as he closed the book and handed it over to the receptionist. "Thanks Hun. See ya tomorrow." He casually walked away, turned the corner, and reached for his cell phone. From his rear pocket he pulled a little black book. The book was three quarters full of entries. "Perfect timing" he whispered as he thumbed through the pages.

Every entry in this book was written in a simplistic code. Certain characters were missing from the name and the phone numbers were all letters. Next to the phone entries were another set of digits, in most cases two numbers, a hyphen then two more numbers. He rode the wave of each page with his index finger. Up one page and down the other until he stopped at this entry:

WLMN IGQ KBEN 40-65 TM

He cradled the phone between his ear and shoulder and dropped a quarter in the slot. His fingers, flying with nervous excitement dialed the number. One ring.... two...

" hello" a gentleman's voice answered.

"Greetings Mister W., this is the P.O. man. Are you interested today?"

"What do you have?" the gentleman asked.

"53, very fresh."

"And size?" "Uncertain, but satisfaction guaranteed or full refund."

"Price?"

"The usual. A double." Maury said.

"What time?"

"5 PM OK?"

"Affirmative."

"Very good. Thank you, Mr. W, I'll see you at 5 then." Maury hung up the phone and checked his watch. 3:15. His shift ends in another 15 minutes. He would have about an hour to kill before coming back.

Maury knew no one would be in the morgue after 4:00pm. And the body wasn't going anywhere until it was posted the next morning. He had his routine down so well that he had very little fear of being caught. He headed back upstairs to finish his shift. "Only the fourth of August" he thought. "This could be a very good month."

Chapter 11

By the time the nurse returned to check on Myrna Shapiro, she was long gone. The revival attempt led by Dr. Ingraham, another house physician, was over before it began. When Dr. Ingraham arrived at the code scene, he determined that irreversible death was already apparent and called off the code.

Richard Ingraham was a retired OB/GYN physician. He joined the staff as a part time house physician just 6 months ago. He also held a similar part time position at Memorial Hospital just 10 miles away. He has been there since his retirement from private practice two years prior.

Although well-known and reputable, being the busiest obstetrician in a two-hospital town had taken its toll forcing Ingraham into early retirement and adding 10 years of wear on his 56-year-old body.

Myrna Shapiro's death was viewed by Ingraham as unfortunate but certainly not extraordinary. An autopsy would be ordered but only because the death was un-witnessed and there was no obvious cause. Had it been his decision, he would have opted to drop the whole review.

Dr. Ingraham's trademark was a cigar, very expensive and very pungent. A habit he picked up in residency at a time when every young doctor is searching for his niche. That something that sets them apart from the crowd. For some it's a new hairstyle. Others prefer a Porsche or Jaguar. For Ingraham, just a cigar. It was his way of saying "I don't care what you think." He was self-assured and cocky.

About the only time Ingraham would be seen without the cigar was during a delivery or performing surgery. Otherwise, the two were inseparable. More offensive than the smell itself was the half chewed, saliva-soaked remnants he would leave lying around the O.R.

Richard Ingraham was very good at telling you exactly what he was thinking. Although his reputation qualified his capabilities, his tact left a lot to be desired. It was not uncommon for him to bring a patient to tears through humiliation. From being overweight to having hairy legs or underarms, Ingraham would tear you apart.

His family was just the opposite. His wife Marilyn was attractive, personable, and not snobbish at all. She acknowledged everyone. As a volunteer in the hospital, she was known and loved by all, despite her husband. Together they had three handsome, well- mannered and very athletic sons. They were fortunate enough to inherit their mother's personality and her good looks. They had the self-esteem of their father but applied it in a much more positive way. This was undoubtedly their key to the athletic accomplishments.

Now, in the quiet of the evening, Richard Ingraham would sit in the doctor's lounge and complete the death certificate much the same as John Shand had just two days before. The difference is, Ingraham would sleep tonight.

Chapter 12

Maury had spent the last half hour at a burger joint just a few minutes from the hospital. After punching out at 3:30, he returned to the morgue, which he had left unlocked by placing a piece of cellophane tape over the latch. Once inside, Maury removed the body of Myrna Shapiro from the cooler so that she would warm up and be a bit more pliable. Once things were in place, he left to grab a bite.

It was now ten minutes before five and Maury was standing just inside the basement door where deliveries are made to the cafeteria. He knew there wouldn't be any deliveries this time of day and that the only danger of being caught rested with the night watchman while making rounds. Stuart, the night security guard was very punctual, almost rigid in his tasks. Just the opposite of Maury.

Maury had staked things out for quite a while before launching his lucrative venture. The delivery door was checked at 4:45, a routine that seldom if ever varied. A few more minutes and Mr. W would arrive. Maury checked his pockets for all the necessary supplies. In one pocket he felt two rubbers and the tube of lubricant. In the other pocket was a wad of money, ten's, twenties, and fives just in case Mr. W needed change. More than once, Maury would have gotten stiffed had he not been prepared with the correct change. He knew that you can't cry foul to the police when you get shorted by people renting corpses.

Maury could see his client pulling his late model Park Avenue into the loading dock parking area. He waited until the client was at the door before he opened it. Quickly and quietly, he let him in. "Let's go Maurice." He spoke. He was dressed in a $500 suit and Carrera sunglasses. "Plenty of time W. The next round will be at 6:45. If you can't finish by then, you should try live people again. And one more thing, don't ever call me Maurice."

The two men completed the short walk around the bend and down the corridor to the morgue. As was customary, the body was set up in the cooler room, on the cooler stretcher. Maury would lock and sandbag the stretchers wheels so that it wouldn't move or tip over.

"How do want her my friend? Front or back?" Maury knew that some were front humpers and others were back stabbers. W could go either way.

"On her back please."

"Well let me just get her legs apart for you and I'll be on my way." Maury got on one side of the stretcher and pulled out on her knee. It was a little stiffer than he expected. There was also a 3–4-inch fresh scar on her knee. "Hey how about a little help here?" he said. "I guess she's not as fresh as you thought." W said. "Yeah sorry. I guess she was gone awhile before they found her." Maury laid out a rubber and the jelly.

Myrna's legs were hanging over the edge of the stretcher. "Do you have a little pillow I can use to prop her hips up a bit?" Maury looked around. He found a blanket and rolled it up. "Here, help me lift. There you go. I'm just going into the adjoining room here. You have fun now!" Maury exclaimed as he left. He made a point of never closing the door all the way so that he could hear and catch a glimpse of the action. That's also why he carried a second rubber.

Chapter 13

John Shand was tying up a few charts in his office when his secretary came in. "DR. Shand, the hospital's calling on line 2." "It's not my turn Peg!" John snapped, sorry the moment he said it.

"Dr. Ingraham is on call."

"I know John, it's Marti Short. She says it's important."

"Ok Peg. Hi Marti" John said, his hands and mind still busy writing notes in the charts. "Sorry to trouble you Dr. Shand but I'm a little concerned."

"About what Marti?"

"Well, you remember Gail Lockwood?"

"I can't think of anything else lately Marti." He said remorsefully.

"Well today a patient on the fourth floor died for no apparent reason. The nurse made her routine round and meds check, and she was fine. A couple of hours later and she was dead." There was anxiety in Marti's voice.

"Alright Marti, it's ok." John consoled her. "Probably just coincidence. Who was the attending?"

"I believe Dr. Ingraham was here." Marti answered.

"Ok. I doubt this is anything to worry about, but I'll call Dr. Ingraham tomorrow at Memorial. Thanks for the call, Marti. And Marti, try not to worry."

Although John was still upset about the Lockwood affair, he doubted there was any connection to this new incident. He was determined not to let this get the best of him. Was determination enough?

Chapter 14

Alex Winfield was revered by his peers in the healthcare field. At a time when the vast majority of hospitals were experiencing rising costs and diminishing revenues, City Hospital was an exception. While other hospitals were announcing layoffs and the closing of services, City Hospital was setting benchmarks for efficiency and positive cash flow.

Winfield was well respected and had earned his reputation as a leader. At the same time, he was not well liked and had few true friends. City had a history of good staff retention and when necessary, excellent recruiting statistics, but was it because of or in spite of Alex? At times he could be quite personable, but he also had periods of extreme behavior and unreasonable expectations. One thing everyone agreed on was that Alex Winfield never fully let down his shield.

Born Allis Weinfeld in 1930 in Germany, he was the second son of a Jewish tailor. Along with his parents and his older brother Sigmund, they lived a modest life in the second-floor apartment above the store. Allis and Siggie were raised by parents devoted to their religion and to hard work. Mr. And Mrs. Weinfeld worked the store all day and sometimes well into the evening. Allis couldn't ever remember seeing his mother asleep and often wondered if she really did.

Allis and Siggie had many friends in their predominantly Jewish neighborhood. They would spend their days in school, studying hard (which was expected of them) but in the afternoons and evenings they were strictly children. They would run and play games with the other children until their poor mother would lose her voice screaming for them to come home to bed. Many a summer's day would find them swimming or fishing in the nearby stream. But that was yesterday.

Allis was now 10 and it was a different Germany. His father had recently been taken away for questioning by the SS and hadn't returned. His mother decided to take Allis and Siggie, now 12, to visit a cousin in Austria.

The Nazi soldiers were everywhere, making escape across the border very difficult. They wandered from town to town with little more than the clothes on their backs and a small sum of money Mr. Weinfeld had been able to stash away. They all looked very frail, but the boys never complained, fully aware of the gravity of the situation.

They hadn't been the first family in the old neighborhood to have a father disappear. There was plenty of talk and it was assumed he had been moved to a work camp to support the military efforts.

It was becoming more difficult to move within a village, so they stuck to the outskirts. Food was nearly impossible to come by and they sustained themselves by finding apples and berries, sometimes half eaten or rotten along the paths. They never ate more than one meal a day. After nearly two months they found themselves near the Austrian border. They had taken refuge in a deserted barn.

The barn had been vacant for some time now, a spoil of the war. They had created a small makeshift fireplace and used a rusted cast iron kettle to boil water. There was a working well not too far from the barn. They stored what food they could find under a floorboard.

The Nazi's finally caught up with them. It was late afternoon and they heard footsteps and talking outside. Mrs. Weinfeld motioned for Allis to hide under the floorboard with the food and water. Allis did as he was told. She whispered to him to stay there for as long as it took for the soldiers to move on. "I will surrender myself and when they are distracted, Siggie will make a run for it."

"Why can't I go with Siggie?" Allis whispered.

"You will be easier to catch in a pair. Please do as I say. When it is clear, move toward the Austrian border and hide there in the mountains. When it is safe, we will all meet up in Austria and we will then find your father. God be with you Allis" With that she laid her hand on the floorboard. She had no tears left to cry.

Allis could hear her through the floor instructing Siggie to wait until they are busy with her, then run as fast as you can." Run with the wings of angels." She told him.

From beneath the floorboard, Allis could hear the soldiers interrogating his mother. Siggie was hiding, waiting to make his break. They were inside now, searching the barn for others. Allis could hear things being thrown around. Now there were footsteps. Right above his face. He tried to pretend he was playing hide and seek with his friends. The next few minutes would haunt him the rest of his life.

The footsteps and the voices grew more faint.

"They're moving away." He thought. "It's working." Then he heard his mother's sweet but broken voice. She was singing. Yes, she was singing a lullaby she sang to calm then down before bedtime. Tears flowed from his eyes uncontrollably. The voices were growing dim now, his mothers' song, disappearing on the afternoon breeze. They were leaving.

He could hear Siggie rustling in the hay.

"Allis?" Siggie whispered. "I am going to follow Mama. Wait here and I'll come back to get you. Lay still my little brother and I will return." Allis heard the barn door creaking as it opened. His brother's footsteps now pounding the earth as he ran off. Fainter and fainter.... almost gone. Then he heard the crack of the rifle. The footsteps stopped. Allis closed his eyes. He would never see his family and he would never cry again.

Alex opened his eyes. The surrounding of his office brought him back from the past. He hadn't been there in quite a while. He would only allow himself to go there when he needed to draw on strength to face an issue. Right now, Alex has a hospital to run.

City Hospital was strong. He made it strong. He knew that his future resided in his financial strength and that relied on the success of the hospital. Money is power. Money is strength. The strong do not hide beneath the floor. It was nearing 6:30pm and Alex Winfield would pull his thoughts back to the future and would soon eat his one meal of the day.

Chapter 15

Stan Waloman was really taking his time with this one. Maury, watching and listening from behind the steel door was getting a little nervous. "What is taking so long?" He wondered aloud. Usually, by this time Maury would be ready to explode himself but it was nearly 6:30 and he knew the security guard would be coming soon.

"Hey, Mr. W? What's the problem in there? Christ! It's almost 6:30 and we're going to get our asses caught if you don't hurry." Waloman didn't answer but just climbed off Myrna Shapiro's body. Sex with dead people was getting old and just didn't do it for him anymore.

The first few times were exhilarating. Knowing it was wrong, knowing you were being watched, having to pay for it. But as time went on, it lost its' appeal. He knew this would be his last time.

"W. Pull up your fucking pants and let's go!"

"I'm coming already!" Waloman said, moving toward the door. Maury rushed in as Waloman came out. While Stan gathered his clothes, Maury cleaned and wrapped the body and put her back in the fridge. When he came out, Waloman handed Maury the two hundred dollars and they both walked out without another word.

Maury never suspected this would be the last time for Waloman. Neither suspected they were being videotaped.

Chapter 16

When a death occurs in any hospital in New York within 48 hours of admission, the hospital is required to notify the Health Department. Alex Winfield had just made that call for the second time in 3 days. This time, the NYS Department of Health was sending an investigator.

Winfield also called a special meeting of the Leadership Team to discuss the issue. This team consisted of the Chief Financial Officer, the vice presidents of Public Relations, Nursing, Operations and Human Resources as well as several department Managers.

Alex opened the meeting by confirming the rumors of the two

suspicious deaths and announcing the pending investigation. "I'm convinced these incidents are coincidental and that the hospital will be cleared of any wrongdoing." He said assumingly. "Business as usual." That's all that was said about the deaths before he turned the floor over to Barry Miller, CFO.

CEO's may look like they run the show, but the CFO takes responsibility for the financial success of a hospital. Or so Barry thought. "All the grief, none of the glory" was his favorite expression.

"The financials through the first half of the year are off a bit." He said parentally. We are currently down 12% on the revenue side and I'll show you how that breaks down in just a second. If you look at the graph on page 2 in your handouts, you'll see that we're actually down 15% on the inpatient side but up just a little on the outpatient revenue. Balancing that all out, it we still show a deficit of about 12% overall." Even in good times Barry could make it sound like the sky was falling.

"On the next page, you'll see a breakdown of our expenses. Pretty much in line with what we budgeted and considering our higher-than-average census, pretty darn good." "So, what does this all mean?" "Well, it looks like we're getting hurt by Diagnosis Related Groups. If you look at this line here," he was pointing to his own copy of the report, "you'll see that our average length of stay is up significantly.

We projected 4.9 days per admission but we're realizing almost 6.2. When census is good, we need to turn the patients around faster to make a profit." Alex could feel his anxiety rising. *DRG's are the fucking Nazis of healthcare!*" he swore to himself. Barry continued, "let's look at this DRG for a cholecystectomy.

A patient comes in to have his gall bladder taken out. We get paid a fee based on the diagnosis of just a little under $3000. We estimate that patient will be here 3 days. Let's say we do it and send the patient home the next day. We still get paid the 3 grand.

The converse is also true. The patient develops complications and stays 6 days, we still get $3000. We could have had 3 different patients in and out of that room getting paid for 3 different DRG's. The net impact is a potential loss of $3000 to $6000." There was some rumbling now going on in the room.

"So, what are you saying Barry? We should send these patients home before they're ready?" Charlene Kuchar blurted out from the back of the room. "Of course, not Charlene but getting defensive won't fix the problem either!" "I'm not defensive Barry but man, my nurses are working their asses off to take care of these patients. Many of them are a lot sicker than they used to be." Charlene rifled back. And she was sounding defensive.

"Look Charlene, these are the rules. We can't change what the insurance companies are going to pay us. We need to work smarter, harder. We need to work with the doctors to make sure they're discharging their patients when it's appropriate.

You know yourself that there are still social issues driving length of stay. Mrs. Smith is ready to go home but her daughter left town for a few days so Dr. Jones is keeping her here until she returns and can care for her mother. It happens and we pay the price.

Alex could feel his security slipping away. For 20 years he has managed a black bottom line. He would not, could not let this year be any different. *"I will not be the one the wolves bring down!"* He promised himself internally. He could sense himself drifting back again. He couldn't remember the last time it happened to him twice in one day. He would allow it but only for a brief moment. Just long enough to sense his own torture. *"There it is."* He closed his eyes. *"I will not go back in that hole. I will not...*

"Here's the key." Barry was in control again. "If we can manage the length of stay, we can turn this around. But it's going to take all of us." "Beep beep," the intercom interrupted. "Mr. Winfield, the gentleman from the department of health is holding on line one for you." "Thank you, Kathy. I'll be right there."

He sat for a moment, and no one said a word. "Thank you, people. I trust you will take a look at your areas of responsibility and see what you can contribute to correcting this temporary setback. Charlene, you will need to make yourself available to this investigator today. I'll have Kathy call you when I'm finished with him."

She nodded agreement and everyone stood to leave the room. "Barry, I'll need to see a length of stay report by physician ASAP." "Already working on it, Alex.

Chapter 17

Bob Kline had just returned from a 2-week vacation to Hawaii. He had left the pharmacy in the hands of his qualified assistant, Mark Hilton. Bob was a stickler for everything. He drove people nuts. A place for everything and everything in its place was Bob's credo. Most people thought Bob was an asshole.

"Mark. Please bring me the purchase orders for the last 2 weeks along with the dispensary log and current balance sheet. Just lay it on my desk if you would and I'll have a look right after I grab some coffee." Bob didn't wait for a response. He never did. He just barked and assumed it was happening.

Bob was still in vacation mode. He was wearing khaki pants and a flowered shirt. On his way to the cafeteria, he ran into Pietro, one of the housekeepers whose responsibilities included the pharmacy. "Pietro my man!" Bob yelled out.

"Ola!" Pietro responded.

"No, no that's aloha my friend."

"Yeah, whatever Bob. What's shaking?"

"Oh, I have to tell you about my trip man, it was wild!"

"Come on, You Bob? Wild?" Pietro thought to himself.

"Listen, I wasn't in Hawaii for 5 minutes and I got a babe out of her shirt!"

"Get lost Bob, you went with your wife. Right?'

"Well, yes I went with my wife but listen to this. I'm getting off the plane, right? And you know, those girls come at you with those flower leis? Well, I bend over because she's a little shorter than me, and my glasses, which were on top of my head..."

"You mean your bald head."

"Yeah ok. Funny. My glasses fall off and the bow catches right in her cleavage. I'm freakin, right? So now I'm spasing a little and I reach down to get my glasses just as she's pulling away. Well, you know, those tops don't have any straps!! I tug on my glasses and here comes her top along with them. Wholly shit! What a rush man."

"Yeah, it sure sounds it dude," what did you do?"

"I just froze, man. I mean I just freakin froze!."

"Well, what happened?"

"This girl turned and ran like hell, leis and tits flapping in the breeze! Then my wife came over and pulled me away toward the terminal."

"Geez, what a story dude. Hey, listen, I gotta go before I get my ass in some serious trouble with the boss. Take it easy dude."

"Yeah, ok Pete, I'll catch you later."

"Not if I can help it." Pietro said under his breath. "What an asshole!"

When Bob returned to the pharmacy, the paperwork was waiting for him as expected. He took a quick look at the numbers, and everything seemed to jive. He couldn't have been more wrong.

Chapter 18

Doesn't it seem like we just did this one?" Jim asked Seike.

"Similarities Jimmy. Both females, both unexpected, both dead. That's it. Every case needs a fresh new look, Jim. If we try to make comparisons out of the gate, we compromise our ability to be unbiased. We must look for everything and look for nothing. Anywhere in between creates potential for error."

"A little more than I bargained for." Jim thought as he walked to the cooler to get the body. Opening the drawer, he pulled back the plastic shroud to expose the feet. He found the toe tag and verified the name and number. "This is the one. Myrna Shapiro."

"Let's get her up on the table Jim." He pulled the cart to the side of the autopsy table. Long, narrow, and shiny, the autopsy table looked like a buffet cart at an all you can eat, Chinese restaurant. The sides were elevated and angled up and out. The bottom was perforated to let the fluids run under the body to the drain.

Overhead were ceiling mounted lights similar to those used in the operating room. Suspended from the ceiling was a voice-activated microphone hard-wired to a recording device in the office. There was an identical microphone mounted over the dissection counter. Right in the middle of the table was a flexible, retractable hose with an adjustable spray head for washing things off.

Seiki helped Jim slide the corpse onto the table. When they got her there, Seiki stopped and stared for a few moments. "Something wrong Doc?" Jim asked.

"Probably not. I'm just a little curious about the position of the legs. You see how they are both retracted to roughly the same degree?" Jim Looked closely now. There was something peculiar about them. "It's unusual to find the legs retracted unless the person was found that way several hours post expiration." He wasn't really directing this at Jim any longer. Jim knew that once he got in a trance-like groove, Seiki wouldn't hear an acknowledgment even if he made one.

Myrna Shapiro's legs were in a modest frog position. Hips rotated out, knees flexed out and the soles of her feet facing each other. Kyle referred back to the death certificate. "There! You see Jim? It says here that she was discovered in her bed, on her left side. She was found at least an hour after she passed."

He stopped again, just staring at the woman. "Conclusion? Either she died with a pillow between her legs or, her legs were put this way afterward. Now I don't see anything in her chart that would indicate an order had been placed for a support between her legs but, considering she had knee surgery, some sort of cushion would have been appropriate. Well, enough about that. Let's find out what killed her Jim."

"Give me a blade and start the water my friend." Jim handed the scalpel to Dr. Seiki who wasted no time making his Y incision. Shoulders to sternum, and sternum to pubic bone. "Let's get a blood sample from the heart Jim, and a CSF from the spine."

"You got it, Doc." Jim said as he headed for the supply cart. He was extraordinarily chipper this morning.

Arriving at the large, wheeled, covered utility cart against the wall, Jim noticed a small hole in the wall just above the top of the cart. "That's odd," Jim thought. "I've been using this cart for years and have never noticed that hole." The hole was about ¾ inch in diameter and very clean. Jim grabbed the supplies from the cart and headed back to the table.

Seiki had already exposed the inner abdomen by removing part of the omentum and was beginning his evisceration. "No evidence of an internal bleed here Jim. First glance looks pretty normal. Let's remove and weigh the organs." Kyle took the better part of a half hour to carefully remove and weigh each major organ.

"Ok Jim, hand me the syringe for the spinal sample." With the abdomen empty, Kyle had easy access to the spinal cord. He hit his target with the skill of an Olympic archer and withdrew about 5ml of the clear fluid. Jim passed him a sterile container into which he injected the sample. Jim sealed the tube and set it aside.

"Hand me the saw Jim and we'll open the chest." Jim obeyed. The small saw started its high-pitched whine. Seiki made a large square cut through the sternum and ribs. Jim helped him remove the plate. Beneath lied the pleural and pericardial sacs. One membrane covering the heart and one covering the lungs.

"Jim, let's have the other syringe." This time Larkin handed him a large, 30cc syringe with an 18guage needle. In no time, Seike had pierced the heart and obtained a large sample of deep red blood. Jim set the tube next to the one containing the cerebral spinal fluid.

"Shall I label these now Doc?" Jim inquired.

"No leave them for now. I'll label them and deliver them to the lab myself when we're finished here."

Another hour went by before Kyle finished his work. Had the family given permission to open the head, it would have taken longer. "Nothing obvious here Jim my boy. Swollen peri-aortic and inguinal lymph nodes from the infection. Otherwise, pretty clean. That's two in a row that I haven't been much help on." His voice sounding a bit humble. "Hey

Doc, you can't win them all. If these people had been a little older, we wouldn't even be doing posts on them. People do die for no reason sometimes, right Doc?"

"Yes, you're right Jim. We won't lose any sleep over it, I guess. Why don't you finish up here and I'll prepare the sample for shipment to the state crime lab"?

"Sure thing Doc."

As Jim cleaned up, he looked back at the hole in the wall. He prided himself on his attention to detail. How could he not have noticed it before?

Chapter 19

It was almost lunchtime before John Shand had a chance to call Dr. Ingraham at Memorial. He didn't think it was necessary in the first place, but he had promised Marti. Ingraham was admitting an ER patient when he got the call.

"Dr. Ingraham? John Shand here." "Hello John. What can I do for you?" "Well Richard, I really hate to take up your time with such foolishness but." he was interrupted.

"Listen John, It's no trouble at all. What's on your mind?"

"It's about the death on your shift yesterday. The young woman."

"Yes John, a real shame. What can I tell you about it?"

"Richard, are you aware that I had a similar situation just a couple days ago?"

"Yes John. I did hear about that."

"Richard, did you find anything unusual? I mean, do you think the two could be related somehow?"

"The Shapiro woman was a post-surgical infection. Probably died from sepsis." Ingraham was concise.

"You really think the infection was that systemic?"

"Well John, in and of itself, it probably wasn't enough to kill her, but it may have aggravated an underlying ailment like a bad heart or something." John detected some defensiveness in Richard's voice and didn't want to push his buttons.

"Look Richard, I'm not pointing any fingers here and I certainly hope I'm not coming across as such. I'm just a little troubled by the timing of these events."

"I understand John but listen, you can't take these things to heart. The post was scheduled for this morning. Why don't you give Kyle Seike a call in a little while? Maybe he'll have some answers for you."

"Alright Richard. Sorry to have troubled you." They hung up. Apparently, John was more concerned than his colleague and perhaps Richard was right. He's been in this business a long time. He probably knows from experience that you can't become so involved with your patients. Maybe he was over-involved and that's why he burned out at an early age.

Right or wrong, a leopard can't change his spots. He sat by the phone, deep in thought about medicine, about the fragility of life and about love...

The last time John had any real time off was about 6 months ago. A three-day weekend in the Adirondacks with Sara. A little place they had found one summer while dating. A small, beautifully secluded lake, just one of hundreds in the Adirondacks. Built around one side of the lake were a series of log cabins. The site was family owned and operated and the variety of style of the cabins gave clues as to how many generations ago the business began.

The cabins were close enough together so that you didn't feel alone, yet far enough apart to afford the privacy one desired. The current owners, Frank, and Sandy and their two teenage sons cared for the grounds and buildings as well as the campers. They no longer served meals in the family farmhouse as had Frank's parents, but they still invoked a real family atmosphere.

John and Sara didn't mind being the only campers there without kids, but it did heighten the realization that they were getting older and were still childless. That summer, they spent their days swimming and fishing in the lake, hiking and socializing with the other guests. The evenings brought with them the tender passion that they desperately needed. With the sounds of fish jumping and frogs croaking and the glow of the bright summer moon spilling through the screened window, there was nothing between them but the night.

After making love again for the first time, they would curl up in the wicker swing in front of the fireplace. John in his flannel shorts and t-shirt and Sara in one of his worn Union sweatshirts and nothing else. They would stare, mesmerized by the flickering fire. Perfectly still now, nothing left to say. Sometimes, they would drift off to sleep right there in the swing. John would wake up and carry his love to bed.

In the morning, they would wake to the sounds of children laughing and splashing in the water at the beach. They each silently hoped that the magic they shared last night would bring little noise makers of their own.... John's phone was ringing. He sped through the time tunnel in his mind back to the present. It was Sara on the other end. They talked about making time to go back to Minnow Lake.

Chapter 20

Spider was running a little late. Of course, that wasn't unusual for health department inspectors and particularly for Spider, especially when he had a road assignment.

"I made some toast for you to take with you." Spider's wife proclaimed unenthusiastically. "Thanks hon." An equal lack of emotion. "Mary Webster had grown accustomed to her husband's habits. Used to them but not happy about them.

"Why can't you get out of bed the first time I wake you up? For crying out loud, you're worse than the kids! Same shit, different day." She thought. "What time tonight?" Spider knew what she meant. "I don't know, forty-five minutes to get there, first day of an investigation, it will probably go long then another forty-five to get home. Maybe fifty-five with traffic. I'm guessing 7:30? 8:00? Don't hold dinner for me." "Do we ever?" Mary mumbled. She didn't really care. Her life was so mundane all she ever looked forward to, was sleep.

Spider kissed his wife. "Bye dear. I'll see you all later. Goodbye kids!

I love you!" "Bye daddy, love you too." They all said in unison. Greg "Spider" Webster started his routine day, off to a routine investigation. He manually lifted the garage door of their modified Cape Cod and eased into the driver's seat of his late model Hyundai Sonata. He backed out the drive and began winding his way through the twenty-year-old neighborhood he called home.

After a quick stop at the Dunkin Donuts shop, he would jump on the interstate and head toward Utica. City Hospital was located in High Falls, New York. Less than an hour from his home in Clifton Park, this would be an easy commute for Greg. Just a few minutes south on I-87 would lead him to I-90 west, bringing Greg right to High Falls.

Known collectively as the New York State Thruway Authority, I-90 and I-87 were toll roads connecting New York City to the Canadian border north and south and Buffalo to Boston east and west. Greg enjoyed traveling the thruway, especially west bound. The roads were well maintained and although heavily monitored by state troopers, traffic was usually allowed to flow at a moderate clip. The posted speed was 65 mph, but the average speed was closer to 72. The best part of thruway driving was the view. The interstate wound its' way through much of the Mohawk River valley. At times within feet of the river itself but at other times, the road climbed to majestic heights offering an eagle's view of the entire valley and villages and towns that sprouted along the river's edge.

Greg spent many hours traveling this stretch of road. He used it often for work of course but his fondest memories were drawn from his treks between his childhood home and college. The beautiful scenery coupled with the quiet, steady hum of the engine had Greg in a lucid yet dream-like state. For a reason he could not comprehend, Greg felt a nervous excitement surrounding this journey.

Chapter 21

Maury Slater woke up in a sweat. It was a full hour before the alarm clock was set to go off. He was confused. Typically, he reset the alarm at least three times before truly becoming awake. He had been keyed up since getting home from the hospital last night.

He wasn't sure why he felt so uneasy, he had sneaked his way inside the hospital a hundred times before and never once felt this nervous. Was he getting older? Losing his nerve? Perhaps it was just because he came a little closer to getting caught but he didn't think so.

He remembered feeling like this one other time. It was a long time ago. He felt like the floor he was walking on would suddenly disappear and the earth would swallow him alive. Pulse quickening, breath labored.

He was eleven years old. He was entering adolescence and had no real male guidance. His father had died in a car accident when he was just a toddler. His mother had never remarried and was doing the best she could raising Maury by herself.

He was well adjusted and had many friends. The neighborhood boys were coming of age. Most of their time was spent playing baseball and football but some of them were beginning to realize there were more differences between boys and girls than what kind of toys they played with.

Maury would sometimes wake up with a hard penis. He couldn't ask his mother what to do and having no one else at home, he relied on the limited knowledge of his friends. The boys were at various stages of their sexuality, and it made for some interesting conversations.

Mike Lomanski was twelve but had 3 older brothers. For lack of anyone better, he was the local authority on all things sexual. He told Maury these "stiffs" were nothing to worry about. "They can actually be good for you." Mike told him. "My brother say's you need them when you get older, but he really didn't tell me why.

He said I would find out soon enough. I do know that when you have one, it will sometimes just kind of explode!"

"No way!" Maury said. "How do you know if it's going to happen to you?" "Well, I'm not sure, but Tommy said it's happened to him." "Tommy? Really?"

"Yeah. He said he can make it happen whenever he wants." "Let's go find him!" Maury suggested.

The boys went to Tommy's house just down the street. His mom said he was out back. Maury and Mike looked around back, but no one was there. The door to the upstairs apartment was open. "Hey Tommy?" Mike called out. In a moment, the door upstairs opened, and Tommy shouted down. "Hi Mike. I'll be down in a second. "After a few minutes Tommy came down along with another friend, Gary. "What's up?" Mike said. "Hey Tommy, isn't it true that you can explode anytime you want?" Tommy's face turned beet red. "Jesus Mike, you gonna tell the whole world?" "No man, just Maury here. He's been waking up with a stiffy.

Tommy looked at Gary. Gary shrugged his shoulders. "Alright." Tommy said. "Follow me." Up the stairs they went, all four of them. The stairs ended in just one room. Tommy's older brother used to stay there before he went in the service. Now it looked like a junk storage room.

Tommy and Gary reached under the bed and pulled out some magazines. They laid a stack on the bed and the boys started fingering through them. Maury was amazed to find book after book filled with pictures of naked women.

"Wow!" He exclaimed. "Where did you get all these?" "Howie left them behind for me when he joined the Navy. He said I may need them. "Your brother is so cool!" Mike said.

After a few minutes, Tommy said "Do you want me to show you what I do?" No one spoke. Tommy stood up and unbuttoned his jeans. He slid them down and pulled up his shirt a little. His penis was already hard. Maury could feel his own starting to stiffen.

Tommy turned a few pages of the book. He landed on one of a lady who looked like she could have been his mother's age. She was wearing black stockings and high heel shoes but nothing else. Maury had seen pictures of semi-nude women before, but this was different. This woman was spreading her legs and she looked different down there than he could have imagined. It was pink and wet.

Tommy was holding his penis in one hand like a baseball bat. He pulled on it over and over again. Soon he was moving it faster and faster. Maury's head was spinning. "Should I be watching this? Should I join in?" No one else was. They were all just watching intently. "I'm not feeling right." Maury said and he ran for the stairs. He ran home without looking back.

When Maury reached his house, he opened the door and flew into the bathroom. He was frightened but stiff all the way home. He knew no one would be there this time of the day. Locking himself in, he gave it a try. Nothing. It felt alright but no explosion.

It would be weeks before Maury would find what he was looking for. It was August. The entire week had consisted of one humid day after the next, not typical for upstate New York. He woke up with an erection, a common occurrence now. Maury tried again.

He had been stroking it now for several minutes. It was hot and Maury was sweating profusely. He kicked off the covers and lay naked on top of the sheets. The room seemed extra bright. The morning sun was still low in the sky and penetrated his window like a knife.

He was dizzy. Was it the heat, the extreme light or his hormones raging inside him? He felt as though a freight train was approaching. "Is this it?" He wondered. He was a little nervous but deep in thought. His eyes closed tightly now, sinking well within himself. He envisioned the naked ladies in the magazines. The bodies were the same, but the faces were people he knew, classmates, neighbors.

The train was thundering more loudly now, the bed shaking. "What will happen?" He couldn't stop now. He was frightened but he had to go there. Would this train carry him away in a level of pleasure he's never known or run him over? His hips were thrusting, his hand moving faster. "it's here...it's almost here.... the heat, the sweat. He could fell a cool draft now coming from behind him. Faster, faster...here it is.......

Maury let out an uncontrollable choked moan. His legs were tight, his hand and abdomen felt wet. For a brief moment, he felt an extreme sense of relaxation. The realization of what had transpired closing in on him. "Tommy was right!"

His muscles were relaxing, trying to get back to normal. He was swimming in emotions he never felt before. The train had arrived. Maury opened his eyes. The room as bright as before. He turned slightly to face the cool draft behind him, his wet, flaccid penis still in hand. For an instant, his heart stopped. The train had arrived...and Maury was standing on the tracks. His mother stood in the doorway.

Chapter 22

He entered the fire exit staircase off the administrative corridor and quickly climbed past the second-floor entrance and paused when he reached the door to 3 West. He peered through the wire reinforced fire safety glass while catching his breath. The traffic on the floor seemed about right for this time of the day.

The early morning rush of nurses completing orders left by doctors making their rounds was over. Many patients would be off to the O.R. or medical imaging. Except for a possible physical therapist or dietitian, most patients would be in their rooms resting.

He had stopped at his locker before coming up here to gather his lab coat and necessary supplies. His target today is in room 3110 located across from the elevator. He had been following this one for a couple of days now. The patient had recovered quickly from the pneumonia that brought him here, but the CT exam had revealed a more serious underlying condition in the chest. He knew these things often took weeks to fully identify let alone treat. This situation called for an intervention.

He checked his pocket once more and was reassured to feel the syringe. A deep breath and he pulled open the door. He stepped into the hallway and briefly looked left and right, no one of significance in either direction. He headed to his right toward the bank of elevators. When he reached them, he paused for a moment and then approached the door to 3110. This was a semi-private room, and his patient was in bed B, near the window. He would need to sneak by the patient in bed A without being seen.

The curtain was mounted on a ceiling rail and was partially closed. This was typical and provided the patient with a little visual privacy from passersby in the hall. As he entered the room, he grabbed the curtain and pulled it with him as he passed by, surrounding the patient in bed A.

His objective was lying face up, dozing. The television was on, playing a rerun of I Love Lucy. The speakers were part of the call handset attached to each bed so that each patient could adjust the volume independently.

He walked past the window toward the IV pump. He reached into his pocket and withdrew the syringe. When he pinched off the IV line, the pump's alarm started to ring. He silenced the alarm immediately but not before the patient woke up.

"Who are you?' The patient asked. Without directly facing the patient, the killer answered "I'm doctor Slater. I'm a lung specialist and I've been asked by your doctor to have a look at you. No need to worry now, I'm just giving you a little medicine to help your breathing." With that said he again pinched off the tubing and inserted the needle. He pushed on the plunger, released the tubing, and opened the line. "Dr. Ingraham didn't tell...." the chatter stopped. The patient's eyes became fixed on the man in the white coat. Trying to ask another question but the breath wouldn't come. Pressure now rising in his face, trying to reach out but nothing happened. He was dozing again now, feeling the pneumonia coming back....

Returning the empty syringe to his pocket, he walked past the closed curtain and back into the hall. The elevator door was opening, and a young couple stepped out. He quickly walked past them, onto the elevator and pressed the close button. He took the elevator all the way to the basement to avoid any traffic in the main corridor. He then took the stairs back up to the locker room. After carefully locking his lab coat and empty syringe in the locker, he went to the restroom right there inside the locker room. When finished he went about his regular business.

Chapter 23

"Can I help you?" The woman behind the information desk said with a welcoming smile.

"I'm sure you can. My name is Greg Webster and I have an appointment with Mr. Winfield."

"Of course, Mr. Webster, his office is just around that corner to your right, second door on the left."

"Thank you." Greg said and turned to walk away.

"Mr. Webster sir?" he turned back. "You're going to need a visitor's ID badge and if you don't mind, please sign the logbook." Again, a big smile.

"Certainly, my dear. Thank you."

Greg was impressed already. He had met one person but formed an image of friendliness and security. "*This may be a pleasant assignment.*" He thought as he turned the corner. "*Let's see, second on the left. Here we are.*"

The door to the administrative suite was open. To the left was a small conference room. Straight ahead was an office and to the right sat a very attractive young woman.

"You must be Kathy?" Greg extended his hand.

"I am. And you are Mr. Webster."

"You may call me Greg if you like." "Thank you, Greg, but in front of Mr. Winfield I'm afraid it will have to be Mr. Webster." She said rolling her eyes a little.

"Understood." He said in a whisper.

"I'm afraid Mr. Winfield stepped away from his desk for a moment, Mr. Webster, but you are welcome to wait in his office. I know he's expecting you and should return any moment."

"That would be nice, thank you."

"Could I get you some coffee or tea perhaps?"

"No thank you dear. Long drive this morning and I've had too much to drink already, if you know what I mean." Kathy offered a comprehensive smile.

"Well the facilities are just down the hall to the left should you need them."

"Good to know. Thank you."

Greg entered Winfield's office. It was a good size and nicely furnished. A moderate size desk, small loveseat, and chair on one side, and a conference table and chairs that would accommodate 6 comfortably on the other side.

The walls were somewhat sterile. A couple of framed diplomas and a few historical pictures of the hospital, but no family photos or personal effects to be found. Experience had taught Greg that he could learn a lot about a person from the way they decorate and maintain their office. He didn't expect Alex Winfield to be warm and fuzzy. Greg helped himself to the single, cushioned chair across from the desk and continued to glance around.

"Mr. Webster is waiting in your office sir." Greg could hear Kathy say.

"Thank you, Kathy. Please hold my calls and ask Charlene Kuchar to come down in about fifteen minutes or so."

"Yes sir."

"Mr. Webster? Alex Winfield," he said holding out his hand. Greg stood up.

"It's a pleasure Mr. Winfield." Greg noticed the firmness in the handshake. "I'm sorry we need to meet under these circumstances. I'm sure we'll have this figured out in no time and I'll be out of your hair. Let me begin by saying how impressed I am with the friendliness of your staff. I don't recall ever feeling so welcomed, so soon."

"Thank you, Mr. Webster. We're fortunate to have some very good people here and after all, it is their job."

"Please, call me Greg, and it may be their job, but I think they enjoy it."

"Yes perhaps." Greg was thinking he was right on about the warm, fuzzy stuff.

"Greg, we reported two unusual deaths in two days. Obviously, we're confident both cases are coincidental and unavoidable. In each case, the patient was post-operative. We have a strong record of excellent quality and have received full accreditation from the JCAHO since I've been here. We hire competent staff and follow a process for continuous improvement."

"I'm sure you run a fine organization here Mr. Winfield. I don't expect to find anything out of the ordinary. I will need to review the charts and speak with some of the key people involved."

"Of course. I have asked our Director of Nursing to coordinate your time with us today. She should be waiting outside." Winfield opened the door. "Kathy is Charlene here?"

"She's on her way Mr. Winfield."

"Please send her in when she arrives." He closed the door.

"Alright Greg. Charlene will give you anything you need. I will make myself available to you as well. Just call Kathy if you need me.'

"Thank you, Mr. Winfield. I'm sure we'll be fine." Alex showed Greg to the door. When it opened Charlene had her hand raised, ready to knock.

Chapter 24

Charlene had secured the charts for Gail Lockwood and Myrna Shapiro and handed them to Greg Webster.

"We keep high profile charts, those requiring investigation or that we anticipate may be litigated, in a special safe in Medical Records."

"I've seen that before,' said Greg. "It's fairly common practice." Without speaking, Charlene guided Greg to the unoccupied conference room next to Alex Winfield's office.

"I'll be fine here for the next hour or so. Is there a number where I can reach you?"

"Sure." She wrote the number on a piece of paper and handed it to him.

"Thanks Charlene."

Charlene left the room and Greg got down to business. He liked to start at the end and work his way backward. He opened the chart belonging to Gail Lockwood first. The death certificate listed the age, room number, attending physician, family physician, pathologist, cause of death and final disposition. Greg took out a yellow legal pad, drew a vertical line down the center of the page and began jotting down a few notes. The left side of the page was for findings and the right side was the "to do" section.

He printed the name of the attending with a note to get a phone number for him. BJ Shand, that name seemed familiar to him. He kept going. 33-year-old female. Thrombosis of the left leg. "Could be what killed her." He thought. "Breaks off and moves to the heart or brain, maybe the lung." "Don't jump." He reminded himself. He slowed himself down and began to methodically pick apart the record.

He took about 40 minutes to get through the chart. He had compiled three pages of notes and a half page of follow up tasks. He turned to a fresh page of note paper and opened the second file. Myrna Shapiro. Age: 53. Cause of death: Possible sepsis, cardiac arrest. Attending: Richard Ingraham. Pathologist: Seiki. It was looking like Seiki was the common denominator so far. This may be the appropriate place to begin his interviews.

Chapter 25

Jim Larkin enjoyed days when no posts were scheduled. It gave him a chance to clean the storage units and order supplies. When he ran out of busy work, he would lend a hand in the main lab by processing incoming orders for the techs. Today he was going to check out that hole in the wall. It had been bothering him since he first noticed it yesterday.

After punching in and getting some breakfast to go in the cafeteria, Jim unlocked the door to the morgue. The fluorescent bulbs hummed when he threw the switch. As the lights came up to full brilliance, he let the door close behind him. He set his coffee and sandwich on the counter and headed straight for the supply cart.

When he approached, he looked up for the hole. He stood breathless, facing the cart. He could not believe what he was seeing. The wall where the hole had been, was as solid as the rest. No hole, no missing paint, no discoloration. He questioned himself. "I know I saw it there yesterday."

He closed his eyes for a moment. Reopening them only confirmed his prior findings. He took hold of the cart and pulled it hurriedly away from the wall. Perhaps the hole was lower than he thought. He moved it straight out, a few feet from the wall and walked behind it. Nothing.

Jim slowly looked around the room in a panoramic fashion. *"Was the cart moved?"* No, he knew exactly where the cart had been, it had been there for years. *"OK. Maybe it was a shadow.* Something on top of the cart casting a round, perfect shadow on the wall. *Could happen."*

He felt the wall now. Running his hand over a large area, he felt no difference in the texture or temperature of the paint. He slid the cart back into place and leaned back against the counter. He picked up his coffee and breakfast sandwich and took one last long look at the wall. In a room where most things are black and white, true, or false, dead, or alive, Jim felt that nothing was certain anymore.

He finished his breakfast and began taking inventory. Opening each cabinet, taking a quick look, and jotting down the supplies he needed. He didn't know he was still being watched, this time from a less noticeable vantage point.

Chapter 26

John Shand was in the middle of morning rounds when he heard the code blue come over the PA. He left his patient on the second floor and darted up the stairs to 3 West. When he arrived, the code team was assembling. The nurse who had found the patient had begun CPR and was joined by the members as they arrived. The patient in bed A had been moved to the hallway.

As John approached the bed, he noticed the horrific deep pallor of the victim's skin. He placed a hand on the inside of the femur to check for a pulse. The skin was cold. This patient had been gone awhile. "How long?" he asked anyone.

"Eight minutes." The nurse in charge replied.

"When was the patient last seen alive?"

"About an hour before we found him."

"OK. I'm calling it. Official time of death is 09:35." The team stopped chest compressions and bagging. "I want the chart and the nurse who found him and the last person to see him alive in the lounge in 30 minutes."

The team started to break up. As they gathered their tools and personal items and began filing out of the room, John took a closer look at the patient. The eyes were open and stared directly ahead. The corneas were dry, but he could see some petechial hemorrhaging. He parted the blue lips and shined his flashlight in the victim's mouth. Nothing obvious. The skin, aside from the color appeared normal. No bruises or wounds except for the I.V. entry sites.

John reached across the body and turned it toward him. He could hear air escaping from the patient's chest. He leaned over the turned body and checked his back. The skin was a little darker due to blood beginning to pool but otherwise, no marks. He rolled the patient back and covered him with his bed sheet. Backing away, John looked around the room. Nothing out of the ordinary.

John was leaving 3110 and saw the victim's roommate lying in the hall. He approached. "Excuse me Mr. ...." He delayed while looking at the patient's wrist ID badge. "Schuler. Mr. Schuler. I'm doctor Shand and I'm sorry about your roommate. How long have you been rooming together?"

"Hello doctor, I came in last night around 10:30 but Joe there had been here a few days."

"Did you get to speak to Joe at all?"

"You mean today?"

"Well anytime. Today, last evening."

"We briefly spoke this morning.

His curtain was drawn when I came in last night."

"How did he seem this morning?"

"Gee I thought he sounded fine. He said the pneumonia was clearing up and he felt much better. I mean, I'm really surprised, you know, that he uh..." John didn't make him finish.

"Did he eat his breakfast, have a bath, see his doctor this morning?"

"Well breakfast came around 7:30 and I guess he ate ok. Didn't look like much, a little juice, toast and coffee or tea maybe. Probably better off you know, food's not much to brag about here."

"I understand." John smiled. "How about any visitors?"

"Didn't see any. Joe said he didn't have much family around. I don't know if he was married, he never said."

"Do you recall the last time a nurse came by?"

"Well, one brought the breakfast and then one came in to wash us up around 8:00 or 8:15, I guess. I went into the lavatory and washed myself, but they didn't let Joe out of bed by himself yet."

"Anyone else come around?"

"There was one more person, a male. I didn't see him because he pulled my curtain closed as he passed by.

"Was this man a doctor?"

You know I think he was...yes, I'm sure he introduced himself as a doctor."

"Do you remember his name?"

"Oh boy, my memory isn't what it used to be doc. Let me think a minute." Silence.

John tried to be patient. He looked at his watch.

"Boy, it's right there you know, on the tip of my tongue. I think it started with an S. I know it sounded a little like my own name. Same number of syllables, I think. I can't get it doc. It may come to me later."

"Do you know what they talked about?"

"Gee, I try to give them the privacy and all, but these rooms are pretty small. I did hear Joe ask who he was. Then I heard the alarm go off." "Which alarm?"

"The one on that pump thing."

"You mean the IV pump."

"Yeah, that's it. Darn things make a racket. Anyway, this doctor said he was asked to come here by his other doctor and that he was gonna give him something to make him breathe better. The alarm stopped and that was it."

"What do mean, it?"

"I mean the doctor left."

"Nothing else was said?"

"No that was pretty much it."

"Mr. Schuler, you have been a big help. I want to thank you for your time. Perhaps I'll see you later."

"OK doc, later it is. Hey wait! "John stopped in his tracks. "Later, later. That's it! Isn't that the funniest thing?" "What's that?"

"His name. It was Slater."

"Good job Mr. Schuler. Your memory's not so bad after all. Is it?"

John left the room and headed back to the second floor to finish his rounds before going to the lounge. He pulled out a little note pad and wrote down Dr. Slater.

He didn't know anyone by that name, but he didn't pretend to know every doctor who visited this hospital. It could very well be someone from out of town. He could do a search on the NYSDOH website from the lounge. He made a mental note to do that.

Chapter 27

Maury was in line at the cafeteria when he got the page. His friend Lynette was calling. "Are you always on break Maury?" He just listened. For some reason, Maury was just not in the mood to fight today. He had a rough night and waking up early and stressed didn't help. "Maury, I need to you to bring the cart to 3110 pronto." Maury's demeanor changed quickly.

"What do you have, Lynette?"

"Does it really matter? You'll know when you get here." She hung up.

It may not matter to Lynette, but it sure did to Maury. This could be a good week. The last one didn't go so well but here was a chance to redeem himself. He went back to pay for his coffee and left the cafeteria.

The morgue was right down the hall. If someone was in there, he wouldn't need to go to the main desk to get the key. He rattled the handle, He knocked on the door and placed his ear to it. Nothing. No sound coming from inside. He threw his coffee in a waste can and headed up the stairs to get the key.

Lynette was exiting 3110 when Maury arrived. "He's by the window." She said and kept walking.

"*He*?" Maury thought to himself. "Shit!" Why the fuck does it have to be he?" He was suddenly back in his state of depression.

Maury left his cart outside and went in to check out the situation. The room was still a mess. This one obviously didn't go quietly. He moved enough stuff out the way to get his cart through. He elevated the bed to stretcher height and brought the cart up close. Using the sheet underneath the patient, he rocked the body back and forth, first legs then upper torso until the body slid into the recess of the cart.

He placed the canvas top on and pulled the rig back into the hallway. Maury headed toward the elevator. He wished he hadn't thrown his coffee away.

Chapter 28

"This is a fickle business." He thought. *"How did he even get here?"* Maury thought about his time with Harold Mease. Once he was over the shock of catching Harold in the act the first time, they began to bond over it. Maury learned to look up to Harold. He was a great father figure, something Maury missed out on.

They would have frequent long talks about the business and about necrophilia. Harold had some great stories based on his escapades with the unliving. Maury found many of them to be very stimulating, some becoming fodder for his own future explorations.

"Hey Hal" Maury remembered asking him one time, "how did you get involved in all this? Did it come with the job?" Harold took a moment, thinking about where to begin." I didn't come with the job for me. For me, my curiosity with necrophilia brought me to the job. You see Maury, you and I are more alike than you may think.

My father and I were never close, He was a real man's man, hunting, fishing, bowling and whatever else kept him out the house and away from my mother. I had very little interest in sports and as a result, he and I grew apart while my mother and I, well, we really bonded. She was a very loving woman and pretty to boot.

My mom took the time to teach me things. I learned how to cook and sew. I would watch her apply her make-up and she would explain the art of color and shadow to me. She didn't dress up for dad, no, he would never notice, but she did like to gussie up a bit before getting together with her girlfriends. They would meet once or twice a week at each other's homes for sewing club or to play Po-Ke-No. Every once in a while, they would splurge and go play Bingo at the church hall.

Some days, as I was on my way out of the house for school, I would walk by Momma's bedroom door and catch her getting dressed. I don't know if she knew I was watching although it happened often enough my guess is she knew I was there. I would get this funny feeling watching her pull on her stockings, real slow like, making sure they were smooth all the way up, careful not catch a nail and create a run. I got really excited when she raised her slip to attach the stockings to her garter belt."

Maury felt his own excitement as Hal was reliving his own story. "A few times, I remember walking by just as she was putting her bra on. She would hook it in the front, swing the clips around to the back and the slowly and gently lift each breast into the cup. She may not have known I was there, but it seemed she always turned sideways while she did this which gave me a perfect view. Our eyes never met. Anyway, I'm making a long story out of this and still not answering your question. I apologize."

"Nothing to apologize for Hal, I'm enjoying the story." Maury was also getting hard, but he wasn't about to tell Hal. "I guess I learned about sex that way, from my mother. Hell, Daddy wasn't going to explain any of that for me, he probably that I was queer anyway." Harold gave a little chuckle and Maury laughed along.

"The years went by, mom and dad divorced but mom and I kept the house going. I went to school during the day and worked in a grocery store afternoons and weekends. Mom still had her outings with the girls, in fact, she picked up the pace and was quite happy. Probably happier than ever. I started to realize that having no partner is better than having a partner that doesn't care, or a partner that you don't get along with. Certainly better than an emotionally abusive partner."

"I still watched mom as she dressed, and she still didn't show any sign of knowing. In my heart, I knew she was doing it for me. It was her way of showing me what I needed to know without making me feel embarrassed or guilty about it."

"After dad was gone, she slept with the bedroom door open. Sometimes I would check in on her while she slept. She always wore these short nightgowns that were loose around the neck and made of very thin material. There were times, especially when it was warm, that she would be on top of the covers and her nightgown would be pulled in a way that would expose one or both breasts."

"I would stand by her bed, just inches away and stare at her naked breasts." I was about seventeen years old by now, and really feeling my hormones building inside me. I couldn't touch her. I knew it was wrong and I didn't know what she would do. If she was hurt or embarrassed, our relationship would change forever. I couldn't risk that. But I loved her, and she excited me. I couldn't control my feelings. There were times that I would grab a handful of tissues, and standing by her bed staring at her breasts, I would pull my pajama's down and masturbate. God, it felt so good, and I swear that while I was doing this, her nipples became erect."

Maury was ready to pull down his own pants and beat off right there, but he would wait.

"So, life continued that way for several years. I knew I was different and that I was not going to fit into a regular job and a regular married life with 2.5 kids. I looked into vocational programs through the local community college, and they offered one in mortuary science. I did some research, and I spent a few weeks one summer as an intern with a local funeral home. I was hooked and the rest, as they say, is history."

"But that doesn't explain the sex with the dead." Maury said.

"No, it doesn't. We're getting there. I went to mortuary school, got my associate degree, and became a licensed undertaker. When you're in the business, you hear stories. It's difficult to tell which ones are true, but if you hear them enough, you know that there must be some level of truth."

"I worked for a funeral home about 45 minutes from here for about 3 years before I bought this place and started Mease Mortuary. It wasn't too long after, that my mom passed away. She had sold the house and moved in with me so that I could continue to care for her, and her for me. The rule at the time was that funeral homes must have residents occupying the same space. That is why most mortuaries are in old houses with attached apartments."

"That's why you had the space to rent to me." Maury stated.

"Exactly. Now mom had been ill for a while, and during this time, we became closer than ever. She was very forthcoming about her love for me and her appreciation for me bring there for her all these years. The playful teasing continued but neither of us acted on it, probably for the same reason. Neither of us wanted to disappoint the other."

"When mom passed, I called the local coroner right way. He was here in a matter of minutes and pronounced her. With a history of recent illness and my witness of her death, the was no cause for an autopsy of course."

"Mom was still lying in bed, in the same position as she had died just 45 minutes prior. The coroner had left, the house was quiet. I locked the doors, placed the phone on answering service, removed my clothes and crawled in bed next to my mother. I placed my arm around her waist and snuggled up against her. For the next 30 minutes, I cried while holding her."

Maury's eyes were tearing. Maury didn't share similar feelings for his own mother. They did not have this kind of relationship.

"As I held her, I told her how much she meant to me. I thanked her for her kindness, her commitment to me. I told her what a privilege it was to belong to her. How happy she made me. I joked about her provocative teasing that had been going on for years and how I knew that she knew. I thanked her for teaching me about love and life, about clothes and color, about womanhood, about manhood."

"When I was sure I had said all I needed to, all I wanted to, I told her I was going consummate our love and send her from this life to the next, a happy woman." I will not share the details with you, Maury, but I will say that it was beautiful, and real, and life changing. My mother was as perfect as I always knew she would be.

I couldn't swear to it, but I believe my mother went to her resting place with a smile. And I, I will never forget her."

"Maury. Maury. Hey, Maury!" He felt a punch to his shoulder.

"Ouch, Jesus! What's the deal?"

"Maury, you dink. Are you going to take this guy down or what?" Lynette was yelling at him.

"I was waiting for the damned elevator for crying out loud!"

"Yeah? Well maybe it would come if you pushed the button, you idiot!"

Chapter 29

Greg had his list of questions ready for Kyle Seike. Charlene had arranged for the two of them to meet over lunch. Alex Winfield had told Seiki that the DOH would have an investigator here today. Kyle had assured Alex that the cases were clean.

Kyle was already in the lab conference room when Greg arrived. "Good afternoon Mr. Webster, I'm Kyle Seike."

"Nice to meet you, Dr. Seike. Thanks for taking time out of your busy schedule to meet with me today."

"No trouble at all. As you can imaging, we're all very concerned about these cases and we won't be able to rest until we're given a clean bill of health, if you'll pardon the phrase."

"Well, I can tell you that from my initial chart review, most everything seems to be in order. Unless you can tell me otherwise, I think we're looking at a couple of circumstantial deaths. While tragic, most likely, unavoidable."

"That's good news." Kyle said. "How can I help you?" Kyle liked this guy. Very laid back and polite. Not the usual distant, threatening personalities he was accustomed to in his previous dealings with state agencies.

"I just have a few questions to ask. My review indicates a few similarities of the two cases. The first, both are female and secondly, they were both fairly young. Were there any abnormal findings common to both patients, doctor?"

"None that I could find. Gail Lockwood, the first woman, had a confirmed venous thrombosis of the leg. It stands to reason that the sudden, unexpected death of a woman her age, with her diagnosis, succumbed to a secondary clot. At autopsy, there were minimal signs of asphyxiation, which would coincide with a major clot in the pulmonary artery. However, I didn't find the clot at dissection, nor did I find an area of infarct in the heart.

Now it could be that it happened so suddenly that the heart stopped almost immediately so that an infarct would be indistinguishable. There was a mild to moderate contusion to the anterior wall of the heart from chest compressions during our efforts to resuscitate."

"Doctor, I noticed you opened the head as well. What did you find?"

"Yes. When we reached a dead end in the torso, we decided to give the brain a look. Everything appeared normal on gross examination. There are still a few slides to go through but everything to this point checks out."

"How about her chemistry and serology?"

"Well, some shifts in her electrolytes from previous known levels but we attribute those to the meds given to revive her. Things like elevated sodium and glucose and of course diminished oxygenation."

"Toxicology?"

Yes of course," Kyle answered. "We sent a sample to the crime lab but have yet to receive the results."

"Right. That was the New York State crime lab?" Seiki nodded agreement. "Let me see if there is anything I can do to expedite that. No promises of course, they're always dealing with a backlog, but I do know some folks over there and I may be able to pull a few strings."

"Great!" Seike said with an obvious lack of enthusiasm. "How about the second patient doctor. Myrna Shapiro."

"Now Myrna was a bit older but still in very good shape. She was one day post-surgery if I recall."

"That's correct." Greg confirmed.

"Well pretty much the same findings. It appears that she died suddenly as well. Similar findings to the first patient. A lack of oxygenation as well but no visible sign of clotting."

"Were there any changes in the skin? Any bruising, sores, puncture wounds, that sort of thing?

"No, nothing like that. There was one peculiar finding though with Mrs. Shapiro."

"Really? What would that be?"

"Well, I noticed when we first unwrapped her that her legs were in an odd position."

"Odd? How so?"

Her legs were bent at the knees slightly and externally rotated. A slight frog position if you will. I thought that perhaps she was given a support of some sort to keep her legs apart at the knee while she rested on her side. I didn't see an order for such a device however in her chart."

"Perhaps it wasn't an order at all but something the nurse did to satisfy the patient's request?" Greg threw out there for Seike.

"Perhaps Mr. Webster. Yes, I'm sure you're right. At any rate, the two are similar in their findings, no conclusive reason for their deaths."

"Could the bending of the legs be related to rigor mortis doctor?

"Excellent question, Mr. Webster. I thought about that too, and I suppose it is possible, but the body was kept cool which should prolong the onset of rigor for several hours. I also didn't find any signs of rigor in other regions of the body; we usually see it begin in the eyelids and neck but that all seemed fine."

"Dr. Seike, I really do appreciate your time today and I have just one last thing. I need to include some biographical data on each person I interview. Would you mind answering a few personal questions?"

"Not at all Greg."

"Great. Let's start with education. Can you tell me where you got your degrees?"

"Of course. Undergraduate, B.S. in Science from State University of New York at Plattsburgh. MD from the University of Vermont and I did my residency in pathology at Albert Einstein in Philadelphia."

"And how long have you been here at High Falls?"

"Probably too long." He joked. "I came here right out of residency so that would be nearly 30 years ago."

"Well, you must really enjoy the area?"

"I used to Greg. No offense to you, but it's not what it once was thanks to our state government."

"How do you mean, doctor?"

"I mean New York is the most taxed state in the nation." Between the state taxing me and the federal government cutting reimbursement, each year I have to work harder to generate the same revenue."

"But don't you think that's true all over?"

"To a much lesser degree, Greg."

"I suppose you're right. Well listen, I've taken enough of your time. Have a great day and if I think of anything else, I'll track you down."

"You're welcome, Greg." Suddenly, Kyle didn't think as highly of Greg as he did at the outset of the conversation.

Seike was disillusioned with New York and with healthcare in general. He was getting older and working harder. This wasn't the life his father lived as a physician in downstate New York. His father had provided a beautiful home for Kyle and his mother. They were treated differently. Being the family of a physician in the 1950's brought honor, favor, and privilege. His father was treated like a king in their upper-class community.

Kyle loved the life he had as a child and young adult. Even when he first got out of medical school things were different. The prestige was still there. Now he felt like a pawn of the system. So many rules, everybody watching, it was not the practice of medicine anymore. It was business.

The insurance companies follow the lead of the federal government so when Medicare enacts reduced reimbursement, private payers follow suit. In the good old days, the hospital would offer a salary to the pathologist but now, he was his own company. He contracted with the hospital to provide services, but his revenue was based on his own billing and collections. He worked or he starved, it was that simple.

Not adverse to hard work, he found other ways to generate income. He knew that as the game changed, the survivors would find new ways to play it. Kyle Seike was a survivor.

Chapter 30

Jim Larkin moved about the morgue checking his supplies. His untimely sense of his surroundings forced a hasty relocation of the surveillance equipment, but it looked like it was all for the better. This new vantage point offered not only a broader view of the area, but the lofty placement prevented obstruction by the movement of the people in the room. The newly added sound feature provided a whole new level of entertainment.

The watcher could hear a knock on the door. Jim moved to the door and opened it. "Good morning, Slater." Jim said.

"Really? What's so good about it?" Maury fired back. Jim just let it go. He had seen this side of Slater before.

"Here, let me help you in the cooler with that." Jim grabbed the front end of the cart and steered it toward the entrance. "What do we have here?" Jim asked.

"Beats me. Some old guy bought the farm I guess."

"And where did you find this old guy Maury?"

"3 west. He died about a half hour ago I guess."

Yes, this location was going to work out much better. Better sight, new sound, a little more expensive, but well worth it. Jim would never stumble across this hiding place. With the old hole being repaired, Jim would be left to forever question his own mental stability. It was only mid-morning and so much had been accomplished. The rest of the day would be a breeze.

The inspector had added an interesting twist to the plan, but it was anticipated, and it couldn't be allowed to throw the program off track. Suspension of the work while the state was here had been considered but, in the end, seemed to be an unnecessary delay. In fact, there was no reason this plan shouldn't keep right on rolling. And it was going to.

Chapter 31

It was nearly 1pm before John finished his rounds. He skipped lunch and headed directly to the lounge to get some work done. He needed access to the internet in order to do his search for Dr. Slater. The lounge was empty when he arrived. Most of the medical staff would have finished rounds and headed back to their offices by now.

The computer was all booted up when John sat at the chair. Like all the physicians on staff, he fought the advancements of computerization at the hospital. What started out as hatred was now a passion. He quickly realized that the world became a much smaller place with the introduction of the World Wide Web. He also found that he needed to rely less and less on others.

John typed in www.nysdoh.gov and hit the enter key. The home page came right up. A few more keystrokes and he was perusing the alphabetical list of all physicians licensed in New York. He was quickly moving down the listing of S when a knock came at the door. "Come in." John said, his eyes never leaving the screen.

"Good afternoon. Doctor Shand?" the voice said from behind him. He felt a familiarity with the voice, but he couldn't place it. He turned to face the door.

"Yes, I'm doctor Shand. How can I help you?" John and Greg stared at each other for a moment without speaking.

"John Shand? The Union College John Shand?"

"That's me. Wait a... Greg? Greg Webster! Wow, is that really you?"

"John, it's great to see you again. I've often wondered where you ended up. I knew you went off to medical school but then I lost track of you. You look great!"

"Thanks Greg, so do you." What brings you here?"

"I'm an investigator for the department of health John. I'm working on a couple of cases here and you were next on my list. Man, you really look great! I mean, you haven't aged at all.'

"Greg, I feel like I've aged a hundred years in the last week. I'm really stressed about these deaths. I was involved as house physician in two of the three."

"Did you say three John? I only have two on my list."

"The third happened this morning. Perhaps I shouldn't lump this one in yet because they haven't done the post. I suppose it could be perfectly legit, but it was the same set of circumstances. The patient was showing signs of improvement and there was no warning of impending doom."

"Yes, that seems to be the course." Greg confirmed. "What are your thoughts John?"

"I don't know Greg. I've never really come up against something like this. I suppose it's just coincidence. They just seem so young, and they should have responded better to resuscitation efforts. I have a gut feeling there's more to it."

"John, do you think you want to see more because you're taking it too personally? I mean, you obviously care about your patients and it's always tough to lose the young ones."

"I know Greg, but these were house patients. Not ones I see in my office. I hadn't even met them before the codes."

"I see your point, Greg. Tell me about Gail Lockwood."

"She was the first. When I arrived, she was in full cardiac and respiratory arrest. Her color wasn't good, and her eyes were already glazed over. She had been there a while before being noticed. That tells me she didn't have any warning. The call button was within reach but never used. Wouldn't you think she would have pain or shortness of breath before going into arrest?"

"Well, you're more the expert John. You tell me?"

"I guess I am telling you. My experience tells me there should be some warning signs and there weren't. Not in any of the three cases."

"John, was there anything unusual or out of place when you arrived on the scene? Think of the way the room looked, the staff who were present, any family or visitors hanging around. Anything at all?"

"Well, it's pretty hectic at a time like that and you really don't have time to notice. I don't recall any family being there, at least none that I spoke to. I guess I didn't notice anything suspect."

"Did the record look intact and up to date?"

"Yes. I spent a good deal of time going through the chart and everything seemed to be in order. I really can't put my finger on anything. It's just a gut feeling."

"Well, ordinarily I would say go with the gut feeling. I usually do, but I do agree with you that the chart looks perfectly in order. Now the second patient, Myrna Shapiro, you were not the attending."

"That's correct. Richard Ingraham was on duty that day. I received a call from one of the nurses asking me to talk to Ingraham to see if there was any correlation. Apparently, she had a gut feeling as well."

"Which nurse was this?

"Her name is Marti Short. She is a supervisor on 3 and a fine nurse. She's been here as long as I have, maybe longer."

"And your conversation with Dr. Ingraham, were you able to draw any conclusions?"

"No. He believed it was coincidental. I guess he's probably right."

"It's looking that way but hey, let's not jump ahead of ourselves. I spoke with Kyle Seike earlier today. He's leaning in that same direction. He still needs to do some micro and of course he hasn't received the results of the toxicology. I told him I would see if I can move that along a little."

"Do you think tox will show anything Greg?"

"I doubt it. It's a long shot at best but certainly worth a look. With toxins, you usually have some warning signs and death is not typically this sudden. I mean there have been cases of food poisoning and delayed reactions to medications or anesthesia, but the patients show symptoms and at the very least have definitive signs at autopsy."

"That's what I thought too."

"John, what about this case this morning? I haven't been informed about that one yet. I'm assuming Mr. Winfield isn't even aware."

Well, there are some differences here but mostly similarities. Sudden death, no warning signs. Patient was admitted for pneumonia and was responding fairly well. He was eligible for discharge but was being held for some tests and a pulmonary consult. The follow up C.T. scan demonstrated a potential mediastinal mass."

"Do you think the patient died as a result of the mass?"

"I guess the post will tell us for sure, but I wouldn't think so. Not that fast anyway. But then again, if the mass ate through a vessel he could have bled or thrown a clot."

"Did you notice anything unusual with this one?"

"Not much. I called the code off right away because it was obvious the patient had been gone a while. I don't suspect any neglect or wrongdoing there, I just think some time had elapsed since anyone saw the patient. I did interview the roommate in this case. I'm not sure why but he was sitting in the hall, and I thought I would ask a few questions."

"Do you remember his name Greg?"

"Actually, I do. His name is Schuler. Nice guy. Now this is a little peculiar. I asked if he was visited by anyone this morning and he said a doctor came to see him. He didn't see this guy, but he heard him. He also said the alarm had gone off on the IV pump. That's nothing unusual of course, they go off all the time."

"What did Mr. Schuler hear this doctor say."

"Let's see, he told him he was there at the request of his regular doctor and that he was going to give him some medicine to help his breathing."

"Sounds like it was the pulmonologist."

"Well, that's what I thought at first, but I checked the chart and there wasn't a progress note entered by a pulmonologist or any other specialist for that matter. In fact, just before you arrived, I was surfing the DOH website to find this guy."

"How do know who to look for?"

"Mr. Schuler said this gentleman introduced himself as Dr. Slater. I'm not familiar with a Doctor Slater on the regular medical staff but that doesn't mean he doesn't exist. There are plenty of physicians from surrounding areas that have courtesy staff privileges, and I wouldn't know them. But anyway, I thought I would check out the website for any Slaters in the area. If that failed, I would search for pulmonologists to see if any names came close just in case Mr. Schuler was off a little."

"Great thinking John. Do you have time to take a look right now? I would love to know what you find."

"You mean you want me to do your job for you!" John joked.

"You got me John. Still quick on the uptake I see."

John brought the screen back to life with a shake of the mouse. The page was still in the S. He scrolled down Sh, Si, Sk, Sl, Slater. There were 6 Slater's in the directory. He looked at the mailing address.

Slater, AnnaGastroenterology Buffalo, NY

Slater, JeremyFamily PracticeIthaca, NY

Slater, LawrenceImmunologistMontauk, NY

Slater, Michael Family Practice Cohoes, NY

Slater, PeterPulmonology Utica, NY

Slater, SusanObstetricsNew York, NY

"I only see one that may fit the bill." John said.

"Peter." They both said it at the same time. "Male, pulmonology and he's close by." Greg said as he scribbled the details on his pad.

"I'll do a little research on this guy, starting with the medical affairs office here at the hospital. Let's see if he's on the staff. If so, I think I'll pay him a visit. He can't be more than 45 minutes from here. I'm also going to follow up with Mr. Schuler and the nursing staff on 3 west. John, you can reach me through Winfield's office if you need me. I appreciate your time and it was great to see you again!"

"Hey, you too Greg. Where do you call home these days?"

"I'm down in Clifton Park about halfway between Saratoga and Schenectady."

"Well listen, Sara and I would love to have you for dinner tonight. I'm sure she would be delighted to see you again."

"Oh, I appreciate it John but perhaps some other time. I don't see myself getting out of here anytime soon and I promised Mary I would be home tonight."

"I understand Greg. We'll make it another time then. I'll find you if I think of anything else. Let me know how you make out with Dr. Slater."

"Will do John. Have great afternoon!"

John relaxed back in his chair for a moment. He felt better knowing that Greg would be investigating the deaths. It was a great surprise to see him again and he wished he could have brought him home to see Sara, but one win was good enough for today. He closed out the internet and opened the stack of charts in front of him. If he didn't get back to work, he wouldn't be going home tonight either.

Chapter 32

"Jim, I'm afraid we're going to have to pull some overtime tonight." Seike announced. "I just received a call from Administration, Winfield wants this one done today. I guess he's a little nervous with the DOH hanging around."

"It's ok with me doc, I could use the extra pay and I don't have much to do this evening so take all night if you like."

"Well, I sure hope it doesn't take all night but thanks anyway. Let's roll this guy out here and see what we have. Shall we?"

Jim went in the cooler and pushed while Seike pulled the cart toward the table. "Ready when you are Jim."

"On three. One, two and three." They pulled together in one quick movement. Jim unwrapped the body while Seike gowned and gloved. On the counter in front of him was the chart.

"Joseph Brighton, age 56, admitted with pneumonia. Died this morning, no witnesses. Have you ever seen a streak like this Jim?"

"Not droppers like this. We've had many a run of multiple deaths, but I can't remember this many unanticipated ones."

"Alright, let's have a look around before we open him. Extremities look ok. Some tape still on his left arm where the IV was. Some redness around the IV site. Legs look ok. Let's roll him Jim."

Jim grabbed his shoulder, Seike took his legs, and they rolled him toward them. "Hold him up there Jim so I can go around the back and have a look."

Jim held the victim on his side while Seike walked around the table to the other side. "Some pooling in the lower back and buttocks. A four inch scar from previous surgery is noted in the central lower lumbar area otherwise unremarkable. Ok Jim, let's let him down." Seike walked back around the table.

"Alright let me have a blade and we'll begin." Jim had the blade already in his hand. Seike could do this without saying a word if he wanted to. Jim knew the procedure inside and out and could anticipate his every move.

"Making the customary Y incision." Seike said for the microphone.

He started the knife at the left anterior shoulder and drew it toward the lower sternum. When he arrived, he drew the blade straight down to the navel without ever leaving the skin. He then made the cut from the right shoulder to the sternum. He pulled the chest flaps back cutting away at the connective tissue to release the skin.

With the flesh now out of the way, Jim reached for the saw. Seike took the saw and cut through the ribs on both side of the sternum. He handed the saw back to Jim and pulled an 8 inch by 8 inch piece of sternum and rib out to expose the mediastinum. "The lungs look ok from here. I want to locate this mass they were looking for." He reached in and moved the central portion of the lungs aside. "Jim, grab a hold of that side and pull it back gently. That's it. Here it is right at the base of the trachea. There is a firm mass measuring roughly four centimeters long by 3 centimeters wide and encompasses the trachea. We will pull out the lungs intact and dissect the tumor then." Speaking to the microphone again.

"Jim, we'll have a quick look at the abdomen before we begin the evisceration. I don't think this tumor killed him. I think it would have over the next several months, but it is not restricting the airway and it doesn't appear to have invaded any vital tissue yet. If anything, he may have had some difficulty swallowing because it looks like it may have been putting pressure on the esophagus."

There was a knock at the door. Jim grabbed a towel and walked over to it. Using the towel, he opened the door a crack. He instinctively said, "we're in the middle of a post, you'll have to return later."

"I understand but I was hoping to watch a bit of this one."

"And who are you?"

I'm Greg Webster, special investigator for the department of health." Greg opened his wallet to show his identification.

"It's ok Jim. Let Mr. Webster in. Good afternoon, Greg. You're welcome to join us. You'll find a gown and gloves in that cabinet over there. The masks are right here and there is some deodorizer over here if you need it. Sometimes a drop or two inside the mask will cover the foul odors."

"Thank you, Dr. Seike. Don't let me hold you up. I'll just hang out in the background here."

"Fine Greg. Make yourself at home. Say hello to Mr. Webster, Jim."

"Hello Mr. Webster. Sorry I gave you a hard time."

"Not at all. You followed proper protocol. Kudos!"

"Thank you, sir." Jim said, smiling under his mask.

"We've really just begun here Greg, but this one looks to be more straight forward than the others, at least from a pathology perspective. Have a look here." Seike said, pointing to the open chest cavity. "We started here in the chest. I've removed the sternum and proximal ribs to have a good look at the mediastinum. The chart said something about a mass so I thought this would be an appropriate first step."

Greg was now standing across the table from Seike. "If I push the heart over a little and Jim, if you could just pull that right lung over once again, you'll see this purplish-grey tissue surrounding the trachea. This looks to be a malignant tumor. It's impossible to tell without looking at a specimen under the microscope but the irregularity of it leads me to believe it's cancerous."

"So, there you have it!" Greg said.

"Not exactly, Greg. This would certainly have killed the man eventually, but it didn't necessarily kill him today. We'll know for sure in a minute, but I don't see any outward evidence that this tumor has invaded any critical organs."

"So, you're saying you haven't found the cause of death."

"Not yet, I'm afraid. I was just about to remove the abdominal viscera to have a better look. Jim, the scissors please." Jim handed Seike the scissors and placed a stack of medium sized stainless-steel bowls next to the patient. Seike raised and pulled the yellowish, fatty omentum up over the chest cavity and began clipping at tissue. His hands were very fast.

After a few minutes, He set the scissors down. "Jim, I'm going to remove the entire abdominal viscera in one package. Can you bring the large cutting board over please?" Jim turned around and grabbed the board that was resting next to the sink. He laid the board across the patient's upper things.

"Ok now Jim, we're going to get our arms under the organs until our hands meet in the middle. When I say, lift and slide the package onto the board. Greg, if you wouldn't mind just steadying the board for us."

"Not at all." Greg moved toward the lower end of the table and held the back edge of the cutting board.

"One, two and lift!" Jim And Dr. Seike lifted the organs out of the body and on to the board. "Very good. Thank you both. We can now take this over to the sink and have a look." Greg noticed a sudden foul smell and coughed a little.

"Wish you had taken the deodorizer now Greg? That smell is from where I cut thought the bowel at the lower rectum. You'll get used to it in a minute or so." Greg found that hard to believe but he would manage.

Jim carried the board over to the sink while Seiki and Greg followed. "The advantage of doing it this way versus removing one organ at a time is that you can view the anatomy in its' natural arrangement. Sometimes when we remove the organs individually, we cause trauma to surrounding tissue. We'll have a look at the front first and then we can flip the whole thing over."

Seike spent the next 20 minutes explaining in great detail everything he was looking at. Greg was fascinated. He had seen autopsies before but was never allowed to be this closely involved. After all was said and done, they were no closer to a cause of death.

"Let's leave this for a moment Jim and check out the chest again. We'll do the weighing and dissection later." They moved back to the table where Seike skillfully removed the heart and lungs. Holding the heart in his hand he showed Greg the vessels leading to and from the muscle.

"You can see here in the aorta that this man had a good deal of calcification." He tapped the artery with his forceps and Greg could hear the tick, tick, tick. This man was a smoker."

"You can tell that just from looking?" Greg asked.

"Yes. The lining should be shiny but pliable. This hardening is caused by nicotine."

"I would expect it to be black." Greg said surprised.

"Well, you can get some really black stuff in the lungs, but the arteries typically become white and brittle like this. In fact, it can become so brittle that they can actually break during trauma. We've seen it here before haven't we Jim?"

"Many times, doc."

"We'll have a look at the inside of the heart in a moment. Let's check the lungs. Here, you can see on the surface of the right lung, some discoloration from where the tumor was resting against it. It would have eaten its way through eventually." Seike then grabbed a big knife and made a longitudinal slice the entire length of the lung.

"You can see the three unique lobes of the right lung here. Definitely a smoker. Now, if we had an infarct caused by a clot, we would see a gross difference in the color of the tissue. I don't see any here."

He performed the same procedure on the other lung with the same findings. Kyle grabbed the heart and moved to the sink. On the way, he placed the organ on the scale briefly to weigh it. Jim looked at the meter and wrote down the weight. Seike lifted the heart again and laid it on the cutting board.

"First we look at the exterior for signs of infarct. If blood stops flowing to the heart the un-oxygenated tissue will begin to necrose almost immediately. All I see is slight bruising from external chest compressions."

He again picked up the large knife and sliced through the heart on an angle to reveal all four chambers. He pointed out the atria and ventricles, aorta, vena cava and pulmonary artery. Everything checked out.

"Well Greg, this case looks no different than the others I'm afraid. I'll do the sectioning and we'll draw for toxicology but unless we find something in the head, we're at a dead end, no pun intended."

"Ok, so we now have three unexplained, sudden deaths in as many days. I'd say that's a lot of bad luck for one facility. Listen, I appreciate you allowing me to sit in on this. I sure learned a great deal and I'm sure it will help me do my job here and in the future. I'm going to disrobe now and meet with some other people."

"It was our pleasure, Greg. I'm sorry we couldn't be more conclusive."

"Not your fault, I'm sure. When do you think you'll have the results of the specimens?"

"We should have some results for you in a couple of days. Can I have them mailed or faxed to you?"

"No, I have a feeling I'll be back. There's no way I'll finish today. Can I pick them up when I return?"

"Sure, I'll ask the secretary to have copies ready for you."

'Thanks so much."

"It was nice meeting you Mr. Webster." Jim said.

"The pleasure was mine Jim. Have a great day."

After Greg had washed up, he stepped out into the hall. There may be just enough time to meet with some of the nursing staff before they leave but first, he was going to get some coffee in the cafeteria. He wondered why the cafeteria was always so close to the morgue.

Chapter 33

Mark Hilton was coming out of the grocery store when his cell phone rang. "Hello."

"Hello Mark." The voice said slowly. Mark recognized the voice and he hesitated before he spoke. "Mark, are you there?"

"I'm here."

"Mark, I'm going to need some supplies and I'll need them soon. I trust you have some in stock?"

"I believe I do." He said reluctantly. "It may take a day or two. The boss is back and it's going to be a little harder to get it out without being noticed."

"I understand, but I am in a bit of a hurry. By the end of the day tomorrow would be best."

"I'll do what I can. Same place?"

"Yes. You still have the key, I assume."

"I have it. By the end of the day then."

"Very good. The envelope will be waiting."

Mark heard the call terminate. This whole thing was making him a little nervous and he wished he had never gotten involved. He didn't need the money anymore, but he couldn't risk this idiot following through with his threat to expose the dirt he had on him. He would surely lose his license and without that, he would lose everything. His wife certainly wouldn't understand even though he was doing it for her and the kids. Pharmacy was the only thing he knew how to do. It was the only thing he had ever done.

He would have to continue the game for now. Perhaps this guy's needs would dissipate, and the issue would resolve itself. Mark didn't know what he was using this stuff for, and he didn't care. He didn't even know who he was. The less he knew the better. It was going to be tougher now that Bob was back.

Chapter 34

"Administration, this is Kathy, how can I help you?"

"Hi Kathy, it's Greg Webster. I was hoping to meet with Mr. Winfield before he left for the day."

"Of course, Mr. Webster, let me just check his schedule." There was a moment's pause. "He does have an appointment out of the building at six o'clock. Would you be available at 5:15?"

"Yes. I promise I won't keep him more than 30 minutes."

That's fine then. I'll put you on his calendar for 5:15. I will be gone by then, but the door will be open. Help yourself to a seat by my desk and he'll come out to get you."

"Thanks Kathy. Enjoy your evening."

"You're welcome, Greg and I'll try."

Greg hung up the phone in the small room within Medical Records that was now his office. He was surprised there was even a phone in here. It wasn't much bigger than a closet, yet it housed a small desk, phone, copier and one chair. He wasn't complaining though, he had been in worse. At least this offered some privacy.

He pulled out his note pad and tried to make sense of his handwriting. It had been a long day. When he arrived this morning, he was certain he would have the entire project wrapped up by now, but he was realizing that John Shand was right. He shared the same gut feeling. He had no evidence to indicate foul play, but something was amiss.

The interview with Marti Short didn't reveal much. The notes were complete. Nurses had checked on both Gail Lockwood and Myrna Shapiro in a timely, ordinary fashion. No unusual meds were ordered nor were there any changes in medication. When asked why she contacted Dr. Shand, she said that after the second death, she was concerned that it might be more than coincidental. He asked if she had any evidence to back that up and of course she didn't.

He spoke with the staff that cared for Myrna and they all denied using a device or pillow between her legs as Seike suggested. He looked at the timing of all the events from med administrations to response times for the code blue. He even checked the morgue logbook for entries. Everything was handled quickly and appropriately.

He called on Mr. Schuler and verified the story John had given him. This was the one lead he still needed to follow. He thought he would have time today, but it will need to wait for tomorrow. He made a note to call the office and reschedule his appointments. He would need to be here at least one more full day. He would drive directly to Utica tomorrow and try to track down Dr. Slater. When he was finished there, he would return to the hospital and try to wrap up.

It was good to see John again, "sure is a small world." He told himself. John looked happy. He knew that he and Sara had become a thing in college, but he quickly lost track of them and had no idea they were married. He never asked about kids. He made a mental note to ask John tomorrow.

He thought back to the night John met Sara. That little café near Union. He couldn't remember the name of the other girl. He never had a real date with her, but they did share a class for the rest of the semester. John seemed very happy. He wished he could say the same. At one time he was very happy, and he wanted to be again, but things had changed. Maybe he changed. He couldn't be sure anymore.

Was it the job? He spent a lot of time away from home. Or was it the home that justified spending many late nights at work? Mary worked for the state as well. They were introduced by a common friend and appeared to hit it off right away. They were both numbers people, she, an accountant in the tax department and he used his degree in business in the Comptroller's office. That was before he moved over to the health department.

When the kids came along, they decided she would stay home with them. He had the better paying job, and she had the better temperament. He thought that she now regretted that decision. He did feel sorry for her but how could he make it right now? The years she had sacrificed were gone, water under the bridge. Even if she returned to the workforce now, she wouldn't get those years back. Would she always hold him responsible?

He knew he wasn't going to get anything done thinking about the past. It was almost 5:05. Greg threw the note pad in his briefcase, turned out the lights and closed the door. In less than an hour, he would be on his way home.

Chapter 35

Lorena Nunez was lying in bed with her head turned to the side. Just a foot away her beautiful new baby girl lay asleep in her bassinette. She couldn't believe Maria was really hers. She had never really had anything she could call her own.

"Ms. Nunez?"

"Si." I'm Lorena Nunez." She said softly in broken English.

"Ms. Nunez, I'm Mrs. Donovan from Patient Intake. I would like to speak to you about your financial responsibility and payment options if I may."

"Yes, please sit down."

"I'm sorry I don't speak Spanish; will you be able to understand me alright?"

"Yes. I understand better than I speak.

"Will you understand me?" she replied.

"Well, let's give it a try. According to your registration information, you are currently uninsured. Is that correct?"

"Si. I mean yes. I have sent the paperwork to the county, but they haven't approved it yet."

"You list your employer as Ace Cleaners, is that correct?"

"Yes. If I still have a job." The boss told me I need to be back in three days, or he cannot hold the job for me."

"How long have you worked there?"

"Only three months." I moved here from New York three months ago."

"Lorena, is the child's father here?"

"No. He left me when I was still in New York. I have a cousin who helped me come here."

"Do you live with your cousin?"

"Si, but they told me I need to find a place of my own once the baby comes."

"I see. So, you have no home, no money, no job, and no insurance." That sounded worse than she wanted it to. Lorena's eyes welled up with tears.

"I'm sorry. I tried to get the Medicaid, but it takes so long. I thought I would have a better chance here than in the city. I don't want my daughter to live like I've had to." She was bawling now.

"Lorena, I don't want you to worry. We can help you. I am going to help you complete the forms for insurance and food stamps and I will work with the county to find you housing. There are people here who can help you, Lorena." She put a hand on Lorena's shoulder. "You get some rest now and I will have someone come back in the morning to get things started. It may take a few days to get things arranged. We may need to keep you here until we have everything set up."

"That's ok. Everybody here is so nice. I don't mind staying." Mrs. Donovan stood up and headed toward the door. "Your baby is beautiful." She said. "Congratulations!" She walked out the door and headed toward the nurse's desk.

"Hi Doris, Ms. Nunez in 4115 may be with us a while. It looks like she is going to be a social admission for at least a few days or until we can find a home and food for her."

"Great, another one living off our taxes. I'll note the chart and tell the doctor."

"Hey Doris? Thank God it's not you in her situation." She turned and walked away.

Lorena regained her composure and stared lovingly at her daughter. "I promise you will have a good life, or I will die trying."

Chapter 36

Greg arrived at Winfield's office at about 5:10pm. The door to the administrative suite was open but the reception area was empty. He moved down the corridor toward Alex's office, bypassing the set of chairs Kathy referred to. He poked his head into Winfield's office but that too, was empty although the desk lamp was on.

The door next to Winfield's was locked. The sign next to the door read Conference Room. He could hear voices from inside the room, but they were very faint, as if the people inside were whispering. He figured Alex was in there, so he headed back toward Kathy's desk to have a seat. He no sooner arrived when he heard the door opened. He turned to see Alex walking out. He closed the door behind him.

"Hello again, Mr. Webster. "

"Good evening Mr. Winfield, I know you have another appointment so I will make this as brief as possible."

"Just a dinner affair I'm afraid, I can afford to be a few minutes late. These things rarely begin on time." He said somewhat disgustedly. Greg was learning more about Alex all the time. He was rigid, punctual, very brusque and just a little uptight.

"Well, what I have won't take long unfortunately. You see Alex, I'm sorry," Greg caught himself, "Mr. Winfield, I don't have much to report."

"It's alright Greg, you may call me Alex if you wish. And I would think not having much to report is a good thing."

"Well, ordinarily I would agree. Are you aware that there was a third death today? A man in his fifties on the third floor."

"Greg, I have been in and out of meetings since I left you this morning. I usually check the roster first thing in the morning and again before I leave for the day. I like to know the census so that I'm not surprised when I receive the phone call at home telling me we are at capacity. I like to have a plan in mind if called upon. Do you consider this death suspicious as well?"

"I really have no evidence to consider any of the deaths suspicious but you're either having the worst run of luck I've come across or something strange is going on. Your mortality rate is going to hit the roof this month."

"Well naturally I'm concerned about that as well. With all the consumer groups scoring us these days, an increase in mortality can chase admissions away quickly. I'm gravely concerned, and I was hoping you would be able to clear it up. Greg, tell me you have more than "bad luck" to go on here."

"What I'm saying is that I have nothing concrete. But three deaths in as many days, all with no clear indication of what killed them? For all I know, it could be airborne, waterborne or food related. I watched the autopsy on this last gentleman. Dr. Seiki did find some pathology, but he didn't think it was life threatening. At least not yet."

"So, are you telling me we should contact the CDC? Create a panic? I have 1600 employees that count on their jobs here to survive. One word about some mysterious disease on the loose and were talking massive layoffs!"

"Alex, I'm not proposing we call the CDC. Not yet. I'm saying that I'm uncomfortable enough to keep this case open for a while. I have a lead or two to follow up on tomorrow. It's not very promising but it's something. Let me start there. We keep a lid on this thing for now. If I come up empty and no one dies without cause in the next couple of days, I close the case."

"That sounds reasonable Greg. Sorry for the guttural response."

"Hey, nothing to be sorry for. You have a difficult job and I understand fully. Go to your dinner and enjoy yourself. I'll be back around mid-morning. I'll check in with you at the end of the day."

"I'll be here. Thanks, Greg. Goodnight.

"Goodnight, Alex."

Greg left the office. With any luck, he could still be home by 7pm.

Chapter 37

The ride to work was anything but typical for Maury Slater. Although he lived just 15 minutes from the hospital, he was already a half hour into the trip. Lucky for him, he awoke early again this morning. He had heard about people sleeping less as they got older and wondered if this could be happening to him.

The construction crews were out in force today, taking advantage of the fair weather to resurface Commonwealth Avenue. Commonwealth was the main artery running east-west through High Falls. Traffic was redirected to Route 5 which ran parallel about four blocks to the south.

Maury caught the red light at the intersection of Route 5 and Forrest Street. Ordinarily, getting caught in traffic irritated the hell out of him but he was well ahead of schedule today. He glanced over to his right and saw it. The big white colonial was hard to miss with the burgundy awnings and well-manicured lawn.

Mease Mortuary had been home for Maury for nearly five years. His life had certainly changed because of his history with the place. There was a time he thought he would stay there forever. He was comfortable living in the home and he and Harold had traversed the issue created that night in the preparation room. They had in fact become closer because of it.

Maury thought about that situation for several days, just as Harold had suggested. At first, he wanted to quit and just leave the environment all together. He soon realized he had nowhere else to go so he avoided Harold as much as he could, took a couple days of vacation and thought. He thought about everything Harold had said that night and he fought with every fiber in his being not to buy into it. He thought about his adolescent years, his friends introducing him to sex, and he thought about his mother standing there watching him the first time he had an orgasm. The more he debated with himself, the more he believed Harold was right. No ties, no emotions, and no bullshit afterwards. Pure sex.

He remembered telling Harold his decision. They had just returned from the cemetery. The back of the hearse needed vacuuming, so they were working in the garage.

"Harold? I would like to talk about what you said the other night." Harold didn't speak but directed his full attention to Maury. "I've thought a lot about this. At first, I was sort of horrified, or at least I thought I was. I think I was more surprised than anything. Anyway, I don't think you're weird. I think you're a good man and I appreciate everything you've done for me. He waited for a response. Harold looked him straight in the eyes for several seconds.

"Son, I knew, or I hoped anyway that you would come around once you had time to get over the shock. In retrospect, I should have told you about it before you had a chance to catch me in the act."

"Well, I don't think that's something you want to go telling folks if you don't have to, I mean, I surely wouldn't."

"No, I guess not but I think of you as my son, and I should have trusted my instincts. I thought you would be ok with it."

"I'm not saying I'm ready to try it myself, but I guess I'm ok with you doing it. And you don't have to worry about me ever saying anything to anyone. I swear."

"Well, I certainly appreciate that Maury. In fact, I know how hard you've been working here, and I think you're entitled to a little jump in pay. How does that sound?" Maury thought for a moment.

"It sounds like you're buying my silence but lucky for you, I can be bought!" They both laughed and Maury stuck out his hand. Harold took it with both of his and squeezed tightly. Maury could feel the bond between them strengthening. They went about their work in the garage, chatting about just about anything, the tension between them now gone.

The light turned green, and Maury pulled away slowly. "Things change, life goes on" he whispered to himself. The next few years at the funeral home were the best years of Maury's life. He and Harold never spoke about the incident again. Maury was very careful about going down to the prep room unannounced. He knew Harold still had a fling occasionally, but he didn't believe Harold was aware of his own activities.

Maury resisted the temptation for a while. He was ok with the idea but just wasn't ready to jump in. That ended one evening when he was called to pick up a body at a local nursing home. It was a Saturday. The mortuary was empty and deserted. The body belonged to Claire Hempstead, a 57-year-old woman who had been a resident of the facility for a couple years. The only next of kin listed was her 88-year-old mother, also a resident.

Maury was confused by the youthful age. He was accustomed to retrieving bodies in their seventies and beyond. He returned to the mortuary and wheeled the body into the prep room. She was wrapped in white plastic and zipped in a black body bag.

Maury removed the bag and unwrapped her slowly. He hated this part, particularly when they came from the hospital. He never knew what to expect. Accident victims could be shocking, no matter how many times he saw it. Patients who were autopsied, were stitched stem to stern, the viscera typically stuffed into a bag in the abdomen. The more thoughtful pathologists would place a colored string around the carotid and femoral arteries to assist the embalmer.

As Maury peeled away the plastic, he was pleasantly surprised to see a clean, well-maintained women who looked younger than her years. Her skin was pale and taught. He guessed she weight about 130 pounds with auburn hair. She had larger than average breasts that still looked very firm. Maury stared at her for a long time.

When he first began in this business, he stared at every body for a long time. At times, he would swear the body moved. His mind would reassure him that it was not possible but for a brief moment, it would freak him out.

After several minutes, his mind rested. He wasn't sure why a young woman like this was in a nursing home. She looked perfectly normal to him. He moved to the side of the gurney and reached out a hand. She wasn't as cold as he expected. Certainly, warmer than the ones from the hospital where the bodies are almost always placed in the cooler before transporting. He ran his hand up the side of her abdomen. It was so soft and without a single blemish.

No husband or children listed, he wondered if Claire had died a virgin. As his eyes and hand moved around her belly and up toward her chest, Maury could sense his excitement. He instinctively looked around the room. He knew no one was there but he walked over to the door leading upstairs and closed it.

He returned to the body and pondered his next move. Was he really going to do this? He placed his hand back on her abdomen and swiftly moved up to her chest, resting for a moment between her breasts. He gently moved his fingers toward her left breast and held it softly for a moment. The skin was soft but the tissue beneath was firm. Her nipple was soft and pink. He cupped her a little harder fully expecting her to flinch. She just lay there, motionless. Harold was right.

Maury was beginning to feel liberated. He was in full control. He didn't have to worry about doing something wrong or being humiliated. He was beginning to throb. His heart was racing, and his breath was quick and shallow. He looked around the room for something to lay her on. He found a foam pad and a blanket on a shelf and spread them out on the floor.

Getting her on the floor would be easy but lifting her back up would be the hard part. He wasn't worried about that yet. He removed the rest of the plastic and placing one arm under her knees and the other under her neck, he moved Claire to the floor. He pulled his arms out from under her. She was lying flat on her back, her head turned to the side and her eyes closed.

Maury stood up and unbuttoned his shirt. He was moving quickly now. Once his shirt was off, he unbuckled his belt while kicking off his shoes. In no time he was standing there in the prep room stark naked. That alone increased his excitement. He knelt down next to Claire and shifted her body to allow room for his knees. He bent over and placed his mouth on her breast. His tongue was swirling around her nipple feverishly.

He never felt so sexually free. He brought his teeth together and bit her nipple. Not a single complaint. He kissed her up the neck and then down to the other breast. His hand was moving down her leg.

He rubbed the outside of her thigh, crossing over to the inside and then pulling outward. Her leg moved with very little effort. He sat back again to kneel by her side. Her right leg was bent outward. He repositioned himself at her feet and worked both legs outward until she was spread at the crotch. Her legs wanted to spring back.

He found a couple of sandbags that they use to combat rigor, and placed one on each knee, keeping the thighs open. He was now staring at her pussy. He placed a hand on each side and pulled her labia apart. He could see her vagina glistening. He reached down and wet his fingers with his own juice and rubbed it on her opening.

He positioned himself in front of her, his knees against her buttocks. He grabbed his cock and placed the head between her lips. He moved it up and down a few times until he felt he would explode. *"Not yet!"* He told himself. He leaned forward on one arm and with his other hand, guided his prick into her vagina. It slid in easily. He moved slowly at first, enjoying the tightness of his surroundings. He was lightheaded.

He looked at her face for the first time and wondered if she was enjoying this. He was moving faster now, his eyes closed. His knees were beginning to hurt from the hard floor beneath the thin pad, but it added to the pleasure.

He was rocking up and down giving it to her fully. He was about ready to explode when he saw his mother standing in the doorway. "Not again!" He thought. "This can't be happening! Let me be, you stupid bitch" He screamed inside his head. He opened his eyes and saw that it was his mother lying there. He jumped back on his knees looking at her face. He was going to finish this.

With extraordinary strength, he quickly rolled Claire on to her side and toward her belly. He pushed her upper thigh as high as he could and placed the head of his penis at her anus. "Take this you cock sucker!" He pushed as hard as he could and penetrated her ass. "Take that! Take that! How does it feel mother? Take that you bitch!"

Maury could feel his ejaculation right down to his toes, pulsating over and over again. He was still pumping with his eyes closed. When the pulsating stopped, he opened his eyes and rolled the body back. It was Claire. He looked over his shoulder to the door. There was no evidence of his mother.

Maury reached the parking garage. As he pulled in, he thought about that first encounter and realized he was better because of it. It forced him to confront his fears. His mother never showed her face again.

Chapter 38

Greg Webster arrived at the entrance to Mary Higgins Hospital in Utica at 8:30 AM. He felt like he hadn't slept at all. He left High Falls shortly before 6pm with every intention of going straight home. Once on the road, he knew he needed time to review the day's events before walking into the confusion he called home. The kids would still be awake, and Mary would be pissing and moaning about him being late.

He decided to end the day the same way it started, at Dunkin Donuts. He stopped at the rest area between High Falls and Amsterdam. He called Mary to say he was still on the job and would be leaving soon. It was easier to lie.

Greg tried to find a common link between the three deaths. He had promised Alex Winfield he would call off the investigation if he didn't find anything by tomorrow. He had only two stones unturned, Dr. Slater and the toxicology results. As he sipped his coffee, he jotted a note to call the lab. His best hope right now lied in this Dr. Slater. He would have been the last one to see Joseph Brighton alive.

He went down his list. The record review indicated that the level of care was appropriate in all cases. The posts, all done by the same pathologist corroborate. No signs of environmental concerns or causes. He could have the air handling system checked out but without reasonable cause, Winfield would protest. He pulled out the death certificates.

Two females, one male, all under age 60. One routine surgery, one thrombosis and one pneumonia. No link there. Two had family nearby.

No indication that they knew each other. All random. He continued to compare the certificates lying side by side. He looked at the disposition. "*Now that's funny.*" He thought. All three were released to the Mease Mortuary. "*Probably nothing. This town may not have more than one funeral home. "Nothing. I have absolutely nothing.*" He realized he said that aloud. He put the papers back, finished his coffee and headed home.

Greg was now standing at the information desk at Mary Higgins Hospital. He hadn't been here before but then there were many hospitals he had never been in. A middle-aged woman in a pink coat greeted him. "Good morning, sir. How may I help you?"

Greg took out his identification. "Good morning, ma'am, I'm Greg Webster from the department of health, I was wondering if I may speak to someone in Medical Affairs."

"I'm certain you may Mr. Webster. If you would like to have a seat over there, I'll find someone who can help you."

"You're so kind. Thank you, dear." Greg moved to the sitting area and picked up a copy of Time magazine. It was actually a current issue. He leafed through the periodical, skimming the pages but not really recognizing what he saw. His mind was elsewhere. He couldn't remember being stumped like this before. Most of the cases he had been involved in were pretty self-evident. Most involved medication errors and most of those were caused by illegible handwritten orders.

"Mr. Webster?" The receptionist called. Greg closed the magazine and stood up. "Mr. Webster, this is Mrs. Brown, she's going to take you to the Medical Affairs Office."

"Hello Mrs. Brown.'

"Good morning, sir, would you follow me please?"

"Mrs. Brown, I would follow you anywhere." He joked. The elderly Mrs. Brown blushed a little. Greg could be charming when he wanted to be.

It was a short walk to the Medical Affairs Office. A young lady greeted them at the door. "Hi, I'm Stacia. Can I help you?" Greg paused a moment. This girl seemed too young to be employed and that made him feel very old.

"My name is Greg Webster. Stacia, I was hoping to ask you a few questions.

"I'm sorry. Who did you say you were with?"

"Oh, pardon me, I'm with the department of health. I'm conducting an investigation and I need some information on a doctor you have on staff here. His name is Slater, Peter Slater."

"Yes. Peter Slater is a pulmonologist. Is he in some kind of trouble?"

"No, not at all. I just wanted to speak with him for a moment and I was hoping you could help me find him."

"Of course. He has an office in the medical complex across the street. I believe he is in suite 212 but let me check." Stacia bent over her desk and retrieved a manila folder. She opened to a roster of the medical staff. "Yes, it's 212."

"Would you have a listing of his other affiliations in the manual?"

"Do you mean other hospital affiliations?"

"That's right."

"I would list them if the doctor made us aware of them. Let's see...I have him listed as being on staff at Genesee Hospital, across town."

"Do you see anything for City Hospital in High Falls?"

"No, nothing here for High Falls. Sorry?"

She read the disappointment on Greg's face. "You've been a great help Stacia. Thank you and enjoy your day."

"You're welcome Mr. Webster. Can you find your way out?"

"Yes, I'll be fine. Thanks."

Greg found his way back to the information desk and thanked the ladies once again for their help. He exited the lobby and could see the medical office building directly across the street. It took just a minute to cross the road and enter the building. He checked the directory in the foyer and confirmed that Dr, Slater was in suite 212. He found the staircase and climbed them two at a time.

When he exited the stairwell, 212 was staring him in the face. He entered and approached the reception desk. The woman behind the desk was on the phone. Greg looked around the office. While his back was turned the woman said, "Can I help you?"

"Yes, I was wondering if Dr. Slater was on staff at City Hospital in High Falls."

"No, I'm sorry, he works here at MH and at Genesee."

"Has he ever had privileges at City?"

"I've been with him since he started practice and to my knowledge he has never worked at City."

"Thanks for your time."

Greg left the office. He was down to one lead, the toxicology results.

Greg sat in his car and started it. He grabbed his cell phone and dialed the office. "Hi Christine, it's Greg. Can you give me the number for Russ Lang at the state lab please?"

"Sure Greg, hold on." He waited. "That's 518-555-3200 extension 117."

"You're a sweetheart Christine! Thanks."

Greg dialed the number. "Toxicology, Lang."

"Hello Russ, Greg Webster here."

"Well Spider, it's been a while. How are you man?" Not many people called Greg "Spider" anymore, but Russ was one of them.

"Hey, I'm doing well Russ. I can't complain. Actually, that's not true. I have my back to the wall for a change Russ, and I need a favor."

"Sure Spider, what can I do?"

"I'm looking at a few cases in High Falls and I'm waiting for the results of some tox screens. They would have come in say, in the last 3 or 4 days."

"Wow, we wouldn't ordinarily get to them for another week or so. You know how it is, always backed up."

"Yeah, I know, and I hate to ask but this is really important. Do you think there is any way to move them up a bit?"

"Can you give me 48 Spider?"

"48 hours? Sure Russ, that would be great!"

"You've got it my man. Where do you want the results sent?"

"My office would be fine. I'll be back there by then."

"May I ask what you're looking for?"

"I wish I knew Russ. I wish I knew."

Chapter 39

Nora Hilton rolled over to snuggle with her husband. She didn't know exactly what time it was, but it was still dark outside, and her husband was not in bed. This was becoming far too routine, and she was concerned. Several months ago, she would have been able to comprehend his restlessness, but things were better now, yet he seemed worse.

Mark was in the shower when Nora entered the bathroom. "Trouble sleeping again?" She asked.

"Good morning, babe. I'm fine, go back to sleep. I just thought I would get an early start."

"Mark, I'm worried about you. What's going on?"

"Nothing really." He tried to sound convincing, but she knew him better than he knew himself. "I was awake so I thought I would shower and get a jump on the day, that's all."

"Honey, it goes well beyond sleepless nights, and you know it. Don't you think I notice it at the dinner table? Jesus, even the kids are noticing that you're not really here. I thought things were better now. We're getting caught up, the calls have stopped, and Ella is just about back to normal. We have a lot to be thankful for."

She was right of course. Things were better, most things anyway. After many months of constant stress not knowing whether Ella would survive, things have finally settled down. Mark made a promise to his daughter that she would get better, and he was prepared to do everything in his power to make it happen.

The illness sneaked its way in, literally in the middle of the night. Nora had tucked Ella into bed. Mark came a few minutes later, right on schedule, to read her a bedtime story. She was only three, but she knew exactly when the page needed to be turned. He would try to trick her sometimes by changing the order of the words or improvising the story. It didn't work. She knew these stories by heart and Mark looked forward to bedtime even more then Ella did.

She was fine when he turned out the light and kissed her goodnight. By morning she was on fire and her color was terrible. They called the pediatrician immediately who advised meeting him in the emergency room. They administered an antibiotic and fever reducer, which brought Ella around almost immediately. Mark and Nora were relieved but not for long.

"The antibiotic will cover her for a while, but I'm concerned about what's causing the fever." Mark had known Dr. Ashton for several years. He was on staff at City Hospital and Mark knew him professionally long before Ella came along. He trusted him. "Her cervical glands are swollen which by itself, is common with many infections. What concerns me is the noticeable enlargement of the axillary and peri-aortic nodes. Now this can be found in systemic infections, but I think we need to run a few tests to be sure."

"What else could it be, Bill?" Mark asked although he already had a good idea. "Look, I don't want to speculate. It's probably nothing and before we get all worried, let's keep her overnight and see what the tests show. Fair enough?" Nora loved his bedside manner and felt reassured. She offered a smile and a nod of her head. "Thank you, Dr. Ashton."

"I'll see to it that your needs are taken care of while you're here. Mark, you know your way around, see to it that your wife is comfortable."

"Ok, doc."

The next 24 hours seemed like weeks. Ella was subjected to a battery of lab and imaging tests. Aside from a few silent tears following the needle stick, she approached each new test inquisitively but unafraid. Bill Ashton arrived at Ella's room early the next morning to find Nora in bed with Ella and Mark curled up in a chair, all sound asleep.

This was the part of the job Bill despised. "Good morning, Ella." He whispered while he rubbed her arm gently. Ella stirred a little but wasn't fully awake. Nora and Mark on the other hand were both on their feet in no time at all. "Good morning, Mark, Nora. Please, sit back down for a moment. Mark tried to prepare himself and Nora gripped his arm tightly.

"Ella is showing signs of leukemia. The early lab results confirm this." No matter how many times Bill would give this speech, he would never get better at it. Mark was stunned. Tears welled up in both their eyes. "Now, before we go too deep on this, you have to know that it's still a stage one which means we caught it very early. The prognosis is very good. "

"What does that mean Bill?" Mark was whispering as if to prevent Ella from hearing.

"Early detection and prompt treatment can result in a success rate approaching ninety percent."

"What sort of treatment?" Nora asked.

"Initially, chemo and/or radiation. At some point down the road, she may need a bone marrow transplant. In the meantime, she can live a mostly normal life and so will you." I would like to ask Dr. Simonson, a pediatric oncologist from Utica for a consult with your permission. I think he is the best in the area."

"Of course, Bill, whatever you think."

"He will be much better equipped than I to discuss the treatment options with you."

"Ella can be discharged this afternoon and go home. Make sure she gets plenty of rest and plenty of fluids. She can eat whatever she feels like, and she can play in small doses when she is up to it. I'm going to write a script for some medication that I would like her to continue on at home. The nurse will bring everything you need at the time of discharge."

"Do you have any questions right now?" There was silence as Nora and Bill stared at each other. "It's ok. It will take time for this to sink in and then the questions will come. Call me anytime day or night. My exchange will take your number and I'll call back as soon as I can." They both nodded their heads.

"You need to trust me on this. Ella will be fine and so will you. It's going to take time of course, and you will be tested. Stay the course and support each other. That's my advice. Now, if you will excuse me, I will get the wheels turning." Bill turned and walked out. He believed Ella would be fine, but he knew what lay ahead for the Hiltons and it wasn't pretty.

Mark turned off the shower and opened the curtain. "Honey, it's just been a little unnerving at work lately. You know, really busy and people getting on my nerves. I guess I'm easily flustered these days."

"I understand Mark. I feel the same way sometimes. Like I've been through the wringer. Maybe we need some time away, all three of us."

"I don't know honey, we're just back on our feet, I don't want to squander money, you never know when we'll need it again."

I'm not talking anything fancy or expensive, maybe just a couple of days at your folk's camp, you know, a change of scenery."

That actually sounded pretty good to Mark. If he could pull off the delivery today and collect his gratuity, they could afford a little time away. That is if Bob Kline would let him have the time off.

"I'll request the time today dear, good idea." Nora could feel her husband coming back albeit ever so slightly, but it was better than nothing.

Chapter 40

Lorena Nunez had finished her breakfast, nursed the baby and was washing up when the pain started. It lasted just a few seconds, but it was enough to make her double over. When it resided, she stood upright and placed her hand on her abdomen. She was certain it was normal post-labor symptoms and brushed it off.

When she came out of the lavatory, she was startled to find Estelle Sanchez sitting by her bed. "Buenos Dias" senorita Lorena. My name is Estelle, and I am an enrollment specialist here. Mrs. Donovan has asked me to help you complete the necessary paperwork for assistance."

"Si, she said you would be coming. I am so grateful; everyone here has been so nice." She was getting emotional again.

"Now don't you worry; everything will be alright. This isn't New York City; we won't put you and your baby out on the street. It will take time though. Is there anyone here who can provide shelter for you, even if for just a few days?"

"My cousin is the only family I have here. He said I could not return with the baby. I don't blame him though; he has all he can do to feed his own children."

"I'll see if we can push DSS on this one. Until then, you will remain with us. Let's get started on the paperwork, shall we?"

Stella pulled her chair closer to the bed and she and Lorena began the arduous task of applying for welfare.

Chapter 41

Alex Winfield sat behind his large oak desk going through his morning ritual of checking the census. They were nearing capacity, which meant he would need to call physicians soon to ask them to discharge patients. He perused the list, checking for admission date and calculating the current length of stay. He always looked at the ones who were here the longest, first.

There were always a few patients awaiting placement in nursing homes. They could be there for weeks at a time. There were some truly sick or injured patients who had justifiably long stays and there were many who hung around longer than necessary because the doctors had no incentive to push them along. It was the hospital that lost money on these admissions. The doctors were held harmless. But the ones he hated the most were the ones who were there for no good reason other than they had no better place to go, the social admissions.

"If these people only knew what true pain and sacrifice were." He thought to himself. "They are weak and lazy, and their troubles are self-inflicted, and each generation is worse than the one they follow." He could feel the anger building up inside as he continued down the list. *"Here's one, Nunez. Maternity ward. Normal delivery two days ago. She should have been gone yesterday!"* His blood was beginning to boil. He picked up the receiver and dialed maternity.

"Maternity, this is Jan, can I help you?"

"Yes Jan, this is mister Winfield. I'm calling about Nunez in 2414. Is there a reason she didn't go home yesterday?"

Jan and the rest of the nurses were accustomed to this kind of questioning. If it wasn't Winfield, it was Barry Miller. They all kept very close watch on the census.

"Why yes mister Winfield. Ms. Nunez doesn't have a home. She has no relatives in the area and no place to go. On top of that, she is now complaining of lower abdominal pain.”

“No home? What does that mean? She came from somewhere, didn’t she?”

“Yes sir. She came from New York a few months ago and was staying with a cousin but she is no longer welcome there. We have completed the forms for DSS and should know to what extent they can help her within a few days.”

“Another blasted social admission!” He made it sound as if it were Jan’s fault.

“I’m afraid so sir.”

“OK Jan. Thanks for your help.”

“You’re welcome, sir.”

Winfield slammed the phone down just as Kathy pushed open his door. “Mr. Winfield, Greg Webster is here to see you.”

“Give me a couple minutes Kathy. I’ll ring you when I’m ready.”

“Very good.”

“That son of a bitch from the health department. He better have good news for me the little bastard!” He said to himself after Kathy left the room.

Winfield sat back and took a few deep breaths. He needed to regain control. He closed his eyes and envisioned the floorboards of the barn above him, the stillness, and the shallow breathing, calming him down now. He was strong and in control. Neither this little prick from the state nor a teenage, homeless whore was going to get in his way. “I am in control. I am in control. I am in control.

He picked up the phone. “Kathy, please show Mr. Webster in.” He hung up without waiting for a reply.

“Good morning, Greg.” Alex said, faking a smile. “I trust you have good news?”

“Hello Mr. Winfield. In the absence of any substantiated bad news, I guess the news is good for you. I have nothing in my possession, nor do I have any knowledge at this time to justify continuing this investigation. The few leads I did have led us down a dead-end trail.”

"Well, that is good news Greg. I was certain from the beginning that you would find this hospital free of any wrong doing." He sounded smug and Greg resented that.

"Wrong-doing or not, the fact remains that three people are dead and no one can explain why. I wouldn't call that a banner week in the annuls of City Hospital. Would you?"

Winfield was taken aback by Greg's sudden boldness and passion. He may have underestimated this guy.

"I don't mean to sound callous Greg; I empathize with the victims here. But if I took it to heart every time a patient died in my hospital, I would have caved in a long time ago. Someone here needs to deal with these issues without prejudice, or pity and if that comes across as "matter of fact" to you Greg, you're just going to have to deal with it. I cannot afford to take it personally. I have a business to run."

Greg relaxed now and carefully thought about his next move. He could simply apologize for being crass, thank Winfield for his time and trouble and be on his merry way but that didn't feel right to him. In fact, nothing felt right about this situation. No, he wasn't backing down on this one.

"I am awaiting toxicology results from the lab. I am keeping this case open at least until I receive them. I will get out of your hair for now Alex, but if the tox results even hint at foul play, I'm setting up camp here until I find the reason for these deaths and if that seems over the top to you, *you're* just going to have to deal with it. Thanks for your time and I'll be in touch."

Greg grabbed his briefcase and headed for the door without so much as looking back. Winfield rocked back in his chair. "Who does he think he's fucking with here?" He was steaming inside. "I'll teach this bastard a thing or two. I'll get on the horn to his superior and have his ass fired for inappropriate behavior, the little cocksucker. We'll see how he likes that!" He had lost total control now. This mild mannered half-assed investigator had beaten him at his own game. He knew Greg had the upper hand and he knew he couldn't follow through on any of his idle threats. Complaining to the health department would bring their wrath upon his facility. They would be here in full force, reviewing every chart, policy, and procedure. No, he would need to calm down, regain the upper hand. He could only do that by over-cooperating.

By the time Greg reached the lobby, he had broken a sweat. He couldn't remember a time, other than at home, that he took the upper hand like that. He had always known that the department would support him. After all, most of the other investigators acted that way all the time. The department didn't want them to be pushovers. He was shaking a little but felt good about what he did. He gathered his thoughts for a moment and set off to find John Shand. He may not hang around the hospital too much longer but he sure as hell wasn't ready to drop this case.

Chapter 42

Mark Hilton was feeling better about his situation since talking to his wife this morning, but he was still nervous about the task at hand. It wasn't the first time, but it was still very much against his nature. Mark considered himself an honest man and would never think about stealing if he wasn't desperate.

He had seen himself clear some time ago, but his contact wasn't ready to quit. He could just refuse to do it, but he was warned about what the consequences would be in no uncertain terms. He couldn't risk being exposed. He needed his job now more than ever and if he were caught, it might mean jail time in addition to losing his license. He would surely lose his family.

It was difficult to do anything with Bob around. He was hyperactive and never stayed in one spot for more than a few minutes. He would wait until he left for his morning break before making the switch. Until then, he would keep working on the inpatient orders, looking busy. Mark thought about the first time his client made contact. It was shortly after Ella became ill. She had been to several specialists and a treatment plan was laid out. The chemo and radiation would be done together, a system that was showing good results elsewhere. One week Ella would undergo daily radiation for five days and the next, chemo for 4 straight days.

Mark's insurance through the hospital paid the majority of the bills but just the co-pays alone were breaking them financially. Between chemo and radiation visits, oral medications and antibiotics, Mark was dishing out nearly $500 a week. He would gladly pay a hundred times that amount to keep his little girl alive, but he didn't even have the $500.

About two weeks after treatments started, Mark received a letter at work labeled "personal and confidential." It was not postmarked and came in an inter-office envelope. It appeared to be from someone in the organization. He opened the envelope when no one was around. It was a small notepad size paper, torn at the top as if someone had ripped of the header. In all capital, printed letters it read:

MARK, WE ALL NEED HELP FROM TIME TO TIME. I CAN HELP WITH YOUR MONEY ISSUES. CAN YOU HELP ME? IF YOU WANT MY HELP, SAY SO ON THE BACK OF THIS PAPER, PLACE THE PAPER BACK IN THE ENVELOPE AND PLACE IT IN THE TRASHCAN IN THE MEN'S ROOM OUTSIDE THE CAFETERIA AT 2PM TODAY. THIS IS A ONE-TIME OFFER. AS A TOKEN OF MY TRUST, I'VE INCLUDED SOMETHING TO GET YOU STARTED. DON'T LET ELLA DOWN.

Mark looked back inside the envelope and found two new one-hundred-dollar bills. His first reaction was to call security and report this incident, but he would then have to turn over the money. It was nearly 10am and he had until 2pm to think about it. Just before 2:00, Nora called to say they wanted Ella to begin a new drug regimen. The medication was still experimental and not covered by insurance. The two-week supply would cost $900, out of pocket. The decision to entertain the secret offer had just been made for him.

Mark simply wrote: "I'm listening." On the back of the paper and stuffed it back into the envelope. At five minutes before 2pm, he excused himself to use the lavatory. When he arrived, someone was using the lone urinal. Mark moved to the sink and washed his hands until the other party flushed the toilet and moved to the sink as well. Mark then went to the urinal. When the guy left, Mark zipped his pants, pulled the folded envelope out of his pocket, and placed it in the trashcan. He moved a few crumpled paper towels over the top to disguise it a little.

Mark left the restroom. He thought about staying close by to see who would be coming at 2pm but there was no place to hide. It was a busy corridor this time of day and he would certainly look out of place just standing by the lavatory door. He decided to go back to the pharmacy.

The next morning, he had another letter, marked the same way. It read: I'M GLAD I CAN HELP. I WILL CALL YOU WITH IN-STRUCTIONS AT 10:15AM. WHEN EXTENSION 1123 RINGS, BE READY TO ANSWER IT.

Bob Kline was predictable. He took his morning break between 10:00 and 10:15 every morning. He was gone when the phone rang. "Pharmacy, this is Mark." There was silence on the other end. "Pharm.." he was cut off.

"Good morning, Mark." The voice was male but soft and not one he immediately recognized. "Mark, I want to help you help yourself. You have financial needs and I have, let's just say medicinal needs."

"I'm still here." Mark replied.

"I need several vials of Propofol."

"That comes in 50 and 100 milligrams." Mark was trying to keep his end of the conversation as matter of fact as possible in case someone was listening.

"500 milligrams will do for now, 50 or 100 ml vials are fine, but I need 500 total."

"I can see what we have in stock. How soon do you need that?"

"I need it ASAP Mark."

"I see. And where does that get delivered?"

"Men's locker room, second floor. You will receive a key to the locker in tomorrow's mail. Deliver the goods at the end of the day tomorrow and there's an extra couple hundred for you. What do want for this product Mark?"

"The list on that is two hundred per 50 ml."

"An envelope will be waiting in the locker. Enough for 500 ml plus your bonus."

"Ok doc, I'll do the best I can."

"Ella and Nora thank you Mark."

He hung up. Mark was spooked. This guy seemed to know a lot about him. He had to work here. He had a locker; he knew the telephone extension and he knew when Bob took his break.

Mark was thinking about how he was going to deliver the goods without someone finding the shortage. He thought he knew the answer, but he wasn't sure he could pull it together in time.

Mark did find a way and he did pull it together by the end of the day. That seemed so long ago now but it was just a few weeks. Here he was filling this order again. He was fortunate that part of his responsibility included checking for and disposing of outdated drug. The hospital policy was to pull anything with an expiration date three months into the future. That minimized any chance of an outdated drug being dispensed to a patient, so in essence, the drugs weren't expired at all.

Mark would go around the hospital checking all the med cabinets and medication vending machines, replacing the drugs in question. He would then return to the pharmacy and dispose of the drugs. Anything in plastic or cardboard went to the incinerator. Meds in pre-packaged syringes or multiple dose glass vials were flushed down the sink and the containers disposed of as ordinary trash.

Today, he hoped he would find a few vials of Propofol ready to outdate. He may need to extend the criteria to 4 or 5 months to meet the quota. Once he pulled the stock, he would reorder replacement amounts. He was pretty sure even Bob wouldn't catch on right away.

Chapter 43

Greg arrived at the physician's lounge only to find that John wasn't scheduled to work. As much as he hated risking running into Alex Winfield again today, he worked his way down the staircase to the first floor. He peeked his head into the administrative suite. Kathy was sitting at her desk and Winfield's door was closed. He felt better.

"Kathy, I was wondering if I could trouble you for Dr. Shand's office and home telephone numbers. It appears he is not on the schedule to work here today."

"Of course, Mr. Webster, it's no trouble at all. Let me just pull it up here...the office is 555-6500 and his home is 555-8790, both in area code 518. She was writing the numbers on a Post it Note as she spoke. She handed Greg the note.

"You're the best Kathy! So efficient and accommodating."

"That's my job." She said with an honest excitement to her voice. But Greg couldn't help thinking that it was Winfield she was echoing. Very precise and without feeling, everything is the job.

Greg grabbed the note and headed toward the door, "oh," he paused, "could you tell me how to get to his office?"

Kathy gave him directions and he headed out once again. John's place was only about a mile from the hospital and Greg found it without difficulty. It was a two-story home converted to office space, in a residential neighborhood. Like many small upstate cities, the inner city was mostly residential with a small downtown section. Most of the major commerce had moved out to the highways years before, leaving main street with a couple of cafés, a bookstore and too many vacant store fronts.

Greg found a place to park in the street right outside John's office. He climbed the few steps up to a big wrap around front porch, decorated with white wicker furniture and many live plants. It had all the charm of a New England bed and breakfast. After looking around for a moment and peering through one of the large, leaded glass windows, Greg let himself in.

The inside was just as quaint as the porch. Scatter rugs covered immaculate but original hardwood floors. The woodwork was ornate but painted white. Greg had no doubt that it, too, was natural oak at one time. It was a center hall colonial with the staircase straight ahead as you entered. To the left was a small waiting and registration area and to the right was a very spacious second waiting room. There were about six patients waiting to be seen.

Greg worked his way over to the reception counter and introduced himself. He could see the girl behind the desk become stressed when he announced he was from the health department. She asked him to have a seat and she would get the doctor right away. "No hurry really." Greg assured her but she hustled off anyway. He helped himself to a chair and picked up a recent copy of Yankee Magazine. He felt like he was in a Norman Rockwell painting that sprang to life. He was just inside the front cover when John walked into the waiting room.

"Good morning, Greg! What brings you here?"

"Good morning to you John. I'm sorry to be bothering you at the office here. I tried to catch you at the hospital but when I found out you wouldn't be in today, I asked for your address. I won't take but a minute."

"It's alright Greg, we can talk a while. Come on back to my office."

They walked beside the staircase toward the back of the house. Once they cleared the stairs, the corridor opened to exam rooms on both sides. In the back, there was a small kitchen, lavatory, stat laboratory, and his office. "Linda, could you bring two cups of coffee when you get a chance? How do you take yours Greg?"

"Cream, one sugar, thank you."

"Thank you, Linda."

John put his hand behind Greg's back and guided him into the office.

"Have a seat, Greg." John went behind the desk and sat down. He could barely see Greg through the stacks of charts waiting to be completed.

"Sorry about the mess here. Things pile up on the days that I'm at the hospital and this is typical of what I walk into the next day."

"It's ok, as long as they're taken care of by the end of the day, I won't have to site you." Greg joked. They both laughed for a moment.

"What's on your mind Greg?"

"I'm pretty much finished at the hospital John, and I want to give you an update." John listened with a concerned, concentrated look on his face. "I'm afraid I don't have much. That doctor in Utica, Dr. Slater, checked out. No affiliation with City Hospital. The records at the hospital were reasonably intact and there didn't seem to be any breach of procedures.

I didn't find any common ground between the three victims. excuse me, patients. You really can't have a victim without the crime I guess."

"What about the toxicology?" John said.

"I called in a favor, and I hope to have something tomorrow. That's a good two weeks ahead of schedule. Until then, I have nothing. Well, nothing except possibly getting fired, if Winfield calls my boss."

"What do mean, fired?" John asked.

"You know John, I really don't like that guy so much. I mean I've worked with all kinds of yahoos and never gave it a second thought, but this guy is different. He's cocky and arrogant and...."

"And heartless?" Greg interrupted.

"Exactly, heartless. The man has no soul, John. He was speaking of the deaths as an inconvenience of doing business! If this guy has the balls, pardon my language, to act that way in front of a man inspecting his facility, how ruthless must he be ordinarily?"

"He's very cold Greg. There is no doubt about it. Do you suspect him?"

"I didn't before, but I sure want to now! I have no suspects John, no suspects, no clues, and no evidence, that anything improper has taken place, but after speaking to him, I have a gut feeling that something isn't right."

"I share your ill feeling, Greg. I've seen plenty of death and although I can't be callous about it, I have accepted it. I cannot accept these. What did you say that may get you fired?"

"Well, I know it won't get me fired. I'm pretty tame compared to most investigators. I told him that if I even suspect wrong-doing, I'm going to camp out in his hospital until I find the problem and if he couldn't deal with that, too bad."

"Good for you Greg! I'm sure there are many at the hospital who echo your response."

Greg hung his head and lowered his voice. "I feel like I've failed somehow. I feel like there is something obvious that I'm missing."

"Greg. You can't take this to heart. Sometimes, you do the very best you can, and it still isn't good enough. Perhaps after you've backed off for a day or two, you'll develop a new perspective."

"I sure hope so John. I sure hope so. Hey, you need to get back to work. Thanks for the coffee. I would like to look you up again once I have the tox results. Maybe we could do lunch?"

"Sure Greg, that sounds great. I'm in the office again tomorrow but back at the hospital on Thursday. You know how to get a hold of me now. Don't be shy."

"I won't John. I'll call as soon as I have something. Thanks again."

"It was good seeing you again Greg."

They shook hands with the solidarity of two soldiers who shared a battlefield. When they released, Greg turned and walked down the long corridor, and out on to the porch. He stood for a moment trying to absorb the tranquility of his surroundings. He thought about going back to the office, but it was a pretty decent day and he opted for a leisurely drive home.

Chapter 44

The killer checked his locker. It was only 2pm but he was hopeful that Mark was able to deliver early. It wasn't there. It could be another three hours before it arrived, and he felt himself getting anxious. This one would be risky, but it was necessary. He wasn't quite sure yet how he was going to manage this one. The location called for different tactics than he had employed in the past.

He removed the wireless PDA device from his locker and went into the restroom. After locking the door, he placed the earplugs in his ears and powered the unit. He selected the live feed option and at once had access inside the morgue. It was difficult to see much detail because of the small screen but he could make out enough to know that Jim Larkin was there all by himself. The exam table was empty, the room was clean, and Jim was reading a book. He often read toward the end of the day, especially days when there weren't any posts. "Don't worry Jim," he said silently, "You'll have some work to do soon enough."

He knew the health department had been nosing around and he fully expected it. He also knew that the only way he would be suspected was if they actually caught him in the act of administering the drug. He had spent months monitoring the day-to-day activities and planning his approach. It wasn't as easy as he had first thought but it was necessary none the less. He was desperate to improve the bottom line and he had exhausted all other options. The idea had actually occurred to him a few years earlier, but he needed time to sow some seeds before actually implementing a plan. So far, he was on task. It would be easier of course if he didn't have another job to do. Between this and his real job, he worked around the clock some days.

He turned off the device, removed the earplugs and cracked the restroom door. Seeing no one, he left the lavatory, put the device back in his locker, concealed it under some clothing and closed and locked the door. He had other business to tend to but would return after 5pm to check for the delivery. The cash was already in the envelope, inside the locker. With any luck, he would complete his next act before dusk tonight. It would be another long day.

Chapter 45

John arrived home a little after 7pm. As usual, Sara had supper waiting on the stove. She tried to wait for him to get home so they could have dinner together but half the time, she just couldn't. Her days at school started pretty early and she had the first lunch period so by noon, she had already had two meals. At first, she tried snacking on something until Greg arrived, but she soon found she was gaining weight. Now, more often than not, during the week, she would eat alone before he arrived.

"Good evening, dear," Sara said without any negative inflection.

"Hi honey, sorry I'm late. I guess you ate already, huh?"

"Yeah, my stomach was turning inside out by 5 o'clock but I'll sit with you while you eat. You can tell me all about your day." Sara knew from the beginning that being a doctor's wife meant little normalcy of life. She accepted it and embraced it and she genuinely liked listening to his work stories. She would share teaching stories as well and he would gracefully listen, but she learned long ago that blood and guts were much more exciting than ABC's.

"Well, it was pretty much a typical day. First day in the office after the weekend so a lot of walk-ins and a deluge of phone calls. I didn't cure any cancers or deliver any babies on the wicker couch, so I guess it was a real regular day. Well, with the exception of a visit from the health department." That caught her attention.

"The health department?" The nervousness in her voice was obvious.

"Nothing to worry about. I told you about Greg Webster being at the hospital, didn't I?"

"Who's Greg Webster?"

"I guess I forgot to tell you. I know I told you about the somewhat suspicious deaths."

"Yes, that I remember."

"Well, the investigator for the health department shows up and it's none other than Greg Webster!"

"That name sounds familiar but..."

"Ok, think back to Union, our first date. Actually, before our first date."

"Oh! That Greg. The pizza place, right?"

"That's they guy. He interviewed me in the lounge yesterday and then stopped by the office today on his way out of town. He's going to call me for lunch in the next day or two. Would you like to come along?"

"No, you fellows go ahead. I'll just be in the way."

"You certainly won't be in the way."

"That's ok, but perhaps you can bring him home for dinner! That is if you can make it home yourself." The line oozed sarcasm.

"Funny, very funny. I'll ask him."

"Great. So, what did he say about the deaths?"

"Well, he said he's stumped. He has no evidence, no clues, and no leads."

"You see, like I told you John, all coincidental. You were beating yourself up over something you couldn't control."

"I wouldn't say I was beating myself up Sara. I was concerned and perplexed, that's all."

"Call it whatever you want, all I know is you didn't sleep for two nights."

"This is true," he admitted.

"Anyway, he's about ready to call it quits but he has the same bad feeling I do that something isn't right. But, if the toxicology comes up clean, he has no choice but to close the investigation."

John finished his dinner and carried his dirty dishes to the sink. Sara took them from him and started washing. "Go relax, I'll be in shortly." John stepped into the family room and took his usual position in the recliner. They both knew that he would be asleep in less than a minute. It would only last fifteen or twenty minutes. He was used to catnaps and would feel refreshed after this short siesta.

Sara watched him drift off as she worked on the few remaining dishes. She thought about their life together, how perfect it was, or would be if they only had a child or two. She couldn't imagine loving anyone more than John. He was perfect in her eyes. He was hard working, caring, compassionate, handsome, undemanding, and loyal. But most importantly, he loved her just as much and he let her know.

They tried to conceive since John had finished with school. After a few years, they went to a fertility specialist. Neither John nor Sara had any obvious problems. For some reason, they were just incompatible. "It's so ironic," she thought, "that two people can be so perfectly compatible in every way except for that." After so much time trying, she consoled herself by thinking that God had given them the perfect love and that they shouldn't be greedy. They had even talked about artificial insemination but decided that it may go against Gods wishes. If it was meant to be, it would happen without artificial, human intervention.

As she watched John sleep, she felt even more sorry for him than she did for herself. "He would be a great father."

Chapter 46

Greg decided to take Route 5 home instead of the Thruway. The state highway ran just about the entire width of New York and passed through every village and cornfield on the north side of the Mohawk River. It was mid-morning so he thought the commute shouldn't be too slow.

He wasn't too far from High Falls when he decided to stop for another coffee. He was feeling a bit hungry as well, so he chose a little diner right on the highway. The breakfast crowd had already come and gone, and the place was empty except for a couple of older ladies in a booth, and man, probably the driver of the rig parked outside, at the counter. Greg took the seat at the counter nearest the cash register. A perky little waitress appeared out of nowhere.

"What can I get for you today?" She seemed to be in high gear still, even though the morning rush was obviously over.

"Could I get some French toast and a couple slices of bacon, and a coffee please?"

"Regular or decaf?"

"Regular would be fine, thanks."

Before he even finished saying the words, a cup and saucer appeared, and the coffee was pouring. "This girl is a pro," he thought. As soon as the cup was filled, she disappeared. Greg took a moment to look around the diner. He felt sure it had been around a while, probably forty years or more. The paint and décor were fresh, but the counter, stools and booths looked original. The red vinyl was cracked in places and the tables were trimmed in steel that was rusting in spots.

Greg found a newspaper folded next to the cash register and opened it up. The front page declared it as the High Falls Tribune. He was certain this small town didn't have its own paper. It was pretty light, and he felt certain he must only have the first half but another look at the front page verified he had it all, all sixteen pages. There were a couple of national stories on the front, along with the major local news. Today's big story was the town's purchase of two new snowplows.

He leafed through the pages, reading just the headlines. For every half page of news there was an equal share of advertising. When he reached page nine, right in the center of the paper, he paused. It was the Obituary page. He read down the list of names, eight all together.

Smith, Lester: age 82 : High Falls

Porter, Ruth Ann: age 91: Summit

Willowbee, Hanna: age 78: High Falls

Lockwood, Gail: age 33: Herkimer

Shapiro, Myrna: age 53: High Falls

Hickman, Paul: age 76: Fort Plain

Cruthers, Alice: age 80: Pennington

Brighton, Joseph: age 56: High Falls

There they were, three of the eight were part of his investigation. He looked at the ages of the deceased. People seemed to live a long time around here, except for the ones on his list. Joseph's obituary said he died after a brief illness. Gail and Myrna both said they died suddenly. Three of the others died either at home or in a nursing facility, which meant a total of five died at City Hospital. Of course, the other two wouldn't seem suspicious because of their age. At the bottom of the Obituary column, an add caught Greg's attention:

This page sponsored by the caring professionals at

Mease Mortuary.

Greg's eyes moved back up to the individual notices. Six of the eight bodies were reposing at Mease Mortuary. This included Lockwood, Shapiro, and Brighton. He thought about it for a minute and then shrugged it off as coincidence. His first hunch was probably right, "it's the only funeral home in town."

Greg folded the paper just as his breakfast arrived. He was suddenly very hungry. It may have been the aroma or perhaps it was an idea brewing that sparked his appetite. He may not be done for the day after all. In fact, he had a good mind to turn his car around and head back to High Falls.

Chapter 47

Greg was sitting in his car with the engine running. He was debating whether to continue on home or return to City Hospital. If he waited a day or two, he would have the results from the toxicology tests but if he went back today, he could get a jump at reviewing all the deaths that occurred at City in the last year. He didn't know why he didn't think of this before. "Just because the recent deaths were reported doesn't mean there weren't more that were overlooked or just plain ignored.

Greg fastened his seat belt and put the car in drive. When he reached the end of the parking lot, he made his decision. He turned left, heading west once again, back to High Falls. He couldn't wait to see the look on Winfield's face, when he asked him for the records for every patient that expired in his hospital over the last 12 months. Greg had a few other questions for Alex as well. He couldn't remember being this hell-bent to get to the bottom of an issue before and he felt alive, inspired.

Greg picked up his cell phone and dialed home. Mary answered.

"Hey honey, it's just me, it looks like I may be late again, in fact, if it's going to be too late, I may just stay out here somewhere for the night."

"Why Greg? What's up?"

"Well, this case just got a little more complicated, that's all. There's something going on here Mary, but I haven't been able to figure it out yet. I was on my way home but decided to turn around and dig a little deeper."

"Ok Greg. Do what you have to do." He knew she was upset. It wasn't that she missed him, she just missed having him around to distract the kids for a while.

"I'm sorry Mary, I know it's been a long week already, but it is my job."

"Fine, I said!" He knew he wasn't going to console her.

"I'll call when I know whether I'm staying or not."

"Don't bother Greg, if you're not here by the time I go to bed, I'll assume you're not coming, and I'll lock up."

"Ok Mary, whatever you say. I'll talk to you later. Goodbye."

"So long." She hung up.

Greg was definitely not going home tonight. Mary had just made that decision for him. The first thing he needed to do was secure a hotel room. He had passed a Holiday Inn on the way out of town and would stop there on his way to the hospital. A night away from home would be a nice break and he was looking forward to it, although most of his time may be spent reviewing charts.

Chapter 48

It was still well before five o'clock when he checked the locker again. He wasn't ordinarily this anxious, but this particular job was going to be more difficult, the timing was crucial. If he waited until five, the floor would be humming with visitors, obstetricians and pediatricians making their rounds after finishing up office hours. It was either now, or he would need to wait until well after eight o'clock. He put his key in the locker and pulled it open. He was pleasantly surprised to find the package holding five vials of Propofol. Administered for its intended use, each vial would supply anywhere from five to twenty doses but in his case, each one was good for one patient only. He also noticed the envelope was gone.

He removed one vial of the drug and a 50 ml. Syringe and placed them in his lab coat pocket. He then quickly closed and secured the locker and moved to the restroom. He had been very lucky not to be seen in the locker room thus far although even if he were, he doubted anyone would really question his presence.

He closed the door to the restroom and removed the medicine and syringe. He removed the metal tab covering the rubber plug, uncapped the needle and pierced the rubber stopper. Turning it upside down he injected air into the bottle to create positive pressure and began withdrawing the drug. When finished, he carefully recapped the needle and placed everything back in his pocket.

He returned the empty vial to the locker, secured it, and walked out of the locker room. He had verified the location of the patient just before coming here. She was in room 4416, four east, the maternity unit. He would have to act quickly and be very careful not to be seen. He had his lines all ready. He had actually become comfortable in his role, knowing what to say to gain access to the patient.

He moved quickly down the second-floor corridor toward the east stairwell. Without making eye contact with anyone in the hall, he reached the door and rushed through it. He took the stairs two at a time, up two flights. He was a bit winded at the top and rested a few seconds on the landing. When he caught his breath, he opened the door and took a quick look in both directions. There was some activity at the nurse's station to his left but the hallway to his right was quiet. He passed eight or nine rooms before he came to 4416.

Every room in maternity was private, only one patient to a room. He wouldn't need to worry about the patient in the next bed. He knew from the admission data that Lorena Nunez had no immediate family in the area so the chance of her having a visitor right now was slim. He was also aware that in this hospital, babies were allowed to stay in the mother's room around the clock. That added a potential complication. If the baby was fussing, a nurse passing by may stop in unannounced.

He reached 4416 and ducked inside the door. He grabbed the curtain and pulled it along with him.

"Ms' Nunez?" He said quietly, "I'm doctor Slater. How are you feeling today?"

"Hello doctor. I'm feeling a little better now."

"That's great Lorena. Doctor Ingraham asked me to have a look at your abdomen. He said you were having some discomfort." He had obviously done his homework.

"Si, the pain was worse this morning, but they gave me something and it seems to be working a little." He was looking at the bassinette next to the bed. The baby was sleeping.

"You have a beautiful little girl there. Congratulations!" The baby was on the side opposite the IV pole.

"Thank you. She is a gift."

"Aren't they all? I'm going to put the head of the bed down so I can have a look at your tummy, ok?" He didn't wait for a response. His hand was on the button, lowering Lorena' head. When the bed was flat, he pulled back the sheet, raised her gown and pulled the sheet back up to her navel.

"I'm just going to press a little, tell me where it hurts." He moved his hand around and applied pressure in different areas. "Someone is going to have some fun with this body later." He thought to himself. When he reached her lower right abdomen, she winced.

"So that's where it hurts?" He removed his hand. "Did doctor Ingraham order a CT scan?"

"I think it's scheduled for tomorrow." Lorena said.

"Good, I'll check on that tomorrow then. Right now, I would like to give you a little medicine. It's an additional antibiotic to ward off any possible infection."

"Will it hurt the baby? I'm nursing her."

"No need to worry about the baby Lorena, and I promise it won't hurt. I'll just go right into your IV tubing over there."

He moved around to the other side of the bed as Lorena watched. He took an alcohol pad from his pocket and swabbed the IV port. He was careful to turn off the alarm on the pump this time before he pinched the tubing.

"Here we go, you won't feel a thing." He began pushing the drug. He needed to go fast enough to get immediate results, or the patient might be able to cry out for help, but if he went too fast, he risked blowing the vein and it would take much longer to have the desired effect.

Lorena felt cold and warm running in her vein at the same time. "That feels strange." She spoke. She suddenly wanted to look over at her baby, but she couldn't move her head. She wanted to scream but the air wouldn't come. "A deep breath, I need a deep breath." She tried as hard as she could to pull in air, but it was no use. She wanted to move her arms, to strike out at this maniac but nothing worked. She felt the pressure building in her head, behind her eyes.

The room was becoming dark, and she noticed a thousand tiny flecks in her eyes. A buzzing in her head now, there was no sound coming from outside. She thought about her little girl and about the promise of a new start here. She knew that dream was gone. "Who will take care of my baby?" Panic turned to emptiness as Lorena's brain began to shut down.

He removed the needle from the tubing, carefully recapped it and set it in his pocket. He walked around the curtain this time, keeping it closed. He moved quickly into the hall and toward the stairwell. In a moment, he was gone.

The security guard noticed the alarm on his panel for the second time in just a few minutes. The stairwell doors on maternity had recently been wired to prevent child abductions. The doors were problematic in the beginning, so the staff was accustomed to not taking them seriously, but the second alarm was worth investigating.

He called Maternity and informed them of the alarm. They didn't seem too concerned either but agreed to check it out. A nurse aide walked down the center of the hallway giving a quick glance in both directions. She didn't notice anything obvious and briskly returned to the desk.

It would be more than an hour before Lorena would be found. It could well have been much longer if a nurse hadn't responded to the crying baby.

Chapter 49

Greg left the Holiday Inn where he had just secured a room for the evening. Returning home tonight was not an option after his call with Mary earlier in the day. He was on fire now, a feeling he hadn't felt in a long, long time in either his professional or personal life and he wasn't about to have it extinguished by his wife's negative attitude.

He pulled into the parking garage at City Hospital and found a parking space next to a sporty looking Nissan. Greg got out of his car and looked at the Sonata sitting next to the sharp, sleek new roadster and realized his life was passing him by. Perhaps it was just the new-found adrenalin talking. He turned and headed toward the stairs with a walk he didn't recognize.

He was going to check in at the information desk, but he didn't want to ruin the element of surprise. Instead, he walked straight to the administration suite. Kathy was sitting at her desk when Greg walked in.

"Good afternoon, Kathy, I'm here to see Mr. Winfield."

"Of course, Mr. Webster, let me tell him you're here."

"That's ok Kathy, I'll tell him myself. Thank you."

Greg turned and walked toward Alex's office. Kathy had an alarmed look on her face. Greg reached the door, which was partially opened. He could hear Winfield speaking but he pushed the door open anyway. Winfield looked up to see Greg standing at the door.

"I'll call you back in a few minutes. Something has come up." Alex set the phone in its cradle and stared at Greg; his hands folded under his chin as if he were deep in thought. Greg made the first move by taking a seat on the small sofa.

"Alex, I'm going to need to see the records for every patient who has expired in your facility in the past twelve months. In addition, I may need to speak with every staff member involved in the care of those patients and I'll need that closet in medical records to work out of. It may be a few days or a few months, I don't know for sure."

Winfield didn't move a muscle. He wouldn't allow himself to show Greg even an ounce of intimidation. "I see," he said. "Have you found something that renewed your interest Mister Webster?"

"Let's just call it a hunch for now Alex. I'll keep you informed of any progress that I make. How soon would that room be ready for me?"

"I'm sure it's available for you now if you need it. I'll call to facilitate it. By the time you walk over there, it will be ready."

"I appreciate it, Alex."

Alex nodded and offered a phony smile. Greg stood up and left the office. He blew by Kathy and gave her a little wink. His confidence astonished him. As he walked down the hall toward Medical Records, he felt as though he was walking on air. This project had become a new drug for him, and he liked it.

His mind was ablaze with formulating priorities. He would begin with requesting the chart for every patient that expired. Then he would look at the autopsy report if one was done and conduct interviews with staff involved in the care of the patient and processing of the body.

He figured it may take the better part of two weeks to complete this part of the investigation. He would need to call the office and get approval for this type of detailed survey. He didn't think he would have a problem. Tomorrow would be soon enough to find out. Right now, he was headed to the cafeteria for some more coffee.

As he turned down the corridor leading to the dining room, he heard the code blue being paged.

Chapter 50

Greg stopped in his tracks. He was probably over sensitized to the situation, but he couldn't help but think this was going to be another unexplainable episode. He knew he couldn't interfere with a medical emergency, but there was nothing to stop him from hanging around the room while the code was going on. He turned on his heels and headed for the elevator.

Inside room 4416, the all too familiar scene was playing out. Richard Ingraham had just arrived, running from the third floor. He was out of breath. "What now?" He said as he entered the room not knowing if it was the mother or the baby having the problem.

"Young female, a few days post-partum." One of the nurses said.

"Who found her?" Ingraham said as he opened her eyes and shined his flashlight in one eye, then the other.

"I did," said another nurse. "The baby was crying, and I was just passing by. I stopped to see if everything was all right. She was lying there staring straight at the ceiling. I called the code right away."

"Well, you can stop compressions and respiration. She's gone. Her eyes are unresponsive to light, and I'm guessing her temperature is way down. Somebody stick a thermometer in her."

Another young girl came forward. "Orally or rectally?" She said nervously.

"I don't think she's going to hold it under her tongue. Do you?"

Ingraham replied sarcastically. The girl blushed a bit as a couple of assistants rolled the patient away from her. It took only a few seconds for the digital probe to register.

"Can this be right?" She said, "it says 95.2 degrees."

"Sounds right to me." Said Ingraham. "My guess is she's been gone close to an hour. There's no hope now. I'm calling the code. Official time of death is 16:31."

Greg had been standing outside the door for a few minutes now. He watched as workers, pushing a variety of emergency equipment filed out of the room. Richard Ingraham noticed him as he came out. At first, he didn't place him and the two just looked at each other. Then it struck.

"Hey, you're the guy from the state, right?"

"That's right Dr. Ingraham, Greg Webster."

"Webster, right. I remember now. Good timing Mr. Webster. I don't know what the hell is going on around here, but something smells fishy if you know what I mean."

"I'm afraid I do doctor. Can you tell me what just transpired?"

"Walk with me, Webster. Anita! Yelled Ingraham. "Please bring the chart on this young lady to the lounge for me."

"Right away Dr. Ingraham."

Greg followed Ingraham to the elevator. The doors closed and Ingraham started.

"The first couple didn't trouble me. I assumed they were coincidental, but I've been doing this a long while now and I have never in my entire career had this many patients die this way."

"What way is that doctor?"

"With total lack of warning or expectation. Christ, these people are long gone before they're even found and reported!"

"Is that what happened here? "

"Greg, this girl had been gone an easy hour before I arrived. I'm good but I'm no magician."

"Doctor, can I meet you in the lounge in a few minutes? I need to have a look at that room before they clean it up."

"Sure. I'll be there, take your time."

"Thanks."

The elevator opened and Richard got out. Greg pushed the close button and then level four. The elevator seemed to move painfully slow. Finally, it stopped, and the doors opened. He ran back to 4416. People were moving about, trying to clean the room. The body was still there.

"My name is Greg Webster. I'm with the department of health and I need you all to give me a few minutes before you clean up, please."

"May I see some identification please?" Asked one of the nurses.

"You certainly may." Greg pulled his wallet from his back pocket and showed her his NYSDOH I.D.

"You won't mind if I verify your presence with administration, would you Mister Webster?"

"I would be delighted. And by the way, excellent job! I wish everyone was as conscientious as you." The woman nodded and left the room, unimpressed with the compliment. Greg now had the room to himself.

The bed was pulled out, away from the wall. All of the other furniture was either removed from the room or pushed against a wall. The patient was covered in a sheet. He moved to the side of the bed and grabbed the top of the sheet. He slowly pulled it down to expose the face. "My God!" He whispered to himself. "She is just a baby herself."

He pulled the cover back over her ashen face and stood there, looking around the room.

The IV pole was on the far side of the bed. The lines had already been removed from her arm. In the far corner, he noticed a wastebasket. There was a box of disposable gloves on the windowsill. He removed two gloves and stretched them over his hands.

He moved to the wastebasket and began moving things around. There were gauze pads, foil packets from alcohol prep pads and a few round cotton pads that he didn't recognize at first. He picked one up to have a closer look.

His memory finally kicked in and told him they were breast pads. Mary had used them when she was nursing the babies. It had been a few years since he had seen one.

The center of the breast pad was slightly discolored, obviously from breast milk. He didn't have any plastic bags with him, so he grabbed a couple of paper towels from the lavatory and wrapped them around the pad. He then placed the pad in his pocket. He moved around the trash but didn't see anything else of interest.

He moved to the IV pump. He had seen them before of course but every manufacturer had their own look. He wondered if it was the alarm that prompted someone to look in on her. He would try to remember to ask that question later.

There were no medications piggybacked into the main IV solution. He glanced around the room once more, and then left. He didn't want to keep Dr. Ingraham waiting. He stopped at the nurse's desk to thank them and to let them know he was finished. He walked back to the elevator and pushed the down button. It arrived and the doors opened. Alex Winfield greeted him once again.

"I didn't know you were a part of our emergency response team Greg. Can I offer you a ride?"

Chapter 51

"I wasn't in the room during the code. Do you really think I would compromise the care of a patient?"

"What I think Mr. Webster is that if you want to travel above the first floor of this hospital, you had better obtain prior approval." Alex said calmly.

"Look Alex, we can do this by the book, or we can find out what is really going on here. And by the way, although I would like your permission to have open access to your facility, I don't require it. The law is clearly on my side here. In fact, the regulations state that if you or any member of your team attempt to be an impediment, I can have you temporarily removed."

"All right. You made your point Mr. Webster!" Winfield was outwardly agitated now, and this pleased Greg. "I want to know what is going on as much as you do. "

"Do you really, Alex? Are you sure you want to know?"

"Of course, Greg, why wouldn't I?"

"I don't know yet Alex, that is what I'm here to find out, and in order to do so, I need your full cooperation."

Alex paused a moment as the elevator doors opened. He motioned for Greg to exit first. He held the door for some visitors to get in. When the doors closed, he said "what do need from me?"

"I want the staff to know I'm here and that you expect their full cooperation. I need carte blanche access to all your staff and all areas of your facility. I promise I will not interrupt procedures, delay schedules, or invade patient privacy. And, if and when the time comes, I may need to bring in the CDC, local police, or FBI."

"The FBI? Are you crazy Greg? All I need is a few guys running around in blue jackets with FBI written across the back and my patients will run for the hills!"

"Alex, get a grip. If, I said and that's a big if, I find evidence that suggests criminal activity, this quickly becomes a police issue. I can't control that."

"Do you really think there is criminal activity behind these deaths Greg?"

"I certainly hope not Alex but right now, anything is possible, and nothing can be ruled out. I am going to visit with Dr. Ingraham, would you like to come along?"

Alex thought a minute and then declined.

"You go ahead. I have other things to do, like get you presidential clearance to my hospital," he said sarcastically.

"I will be here for a while tonight," Greg said, "in fact, I think I will be staying right here in town for a few days. I'm going to write down my cell phone number, if you should need me, feel free to call.

If another death occurs, I absolutely want you to call me right away. I also want the staff to know that every time a death occurs, that room needs to be treated like a crime scene. With the exception of the emergency response team, no one enters the room without permission. Housekeeping doesn't clean and the body is not removed until I say so. Okay?"

"I've got it Greg."

"Thank you, Alex. I know this isn't easy for you and I appreciate your help."

"I don't think you have any idea, Greg." He sounded dejected.

Greg watched as Alex Winfield walked away, the life sucked out of him. For the first time, Greg did feel a little bit sorry for him.

When Alex was gone, Greg started down the hall to the physician's lounge. When he arrived, Richard Ingraham was talking on the phone. He stood outside, waiting for the conversation to end. Ingraham looked up and saw Greg waiting in the hall. He waived him in.

"Very good Kyle, give me a call if you would when you have your results. Ok, you too. Good night."

"Come in Greg. I was just speaking to Kyle Seike. He has agreed to do a post first thing tomorrow."

"I would like to be there." Greg said.

"I'm sure Kyle would welcome the company."

"Great then. Dr. Ingraham, what's your take on this?"

"Greg, I would like to believe these folks died from natural causes or complications from surgery."

"But do you believe that?"

"We just found a nineteen-year-old girl dead in her bed. Aside from a little abdominal pain, she was symptom free just two hours prior. While it's not unusual for some post-partum bleeding to occur, there was no outward signs of that happening here. I'm afraid I find her death just a little puzzling."

Greg didn't say anything.

"That being said, I don't know what else to blame it on. If it were environmental or food borne, we would see similar issues with staff or visitors. We eat the same food, drink the same water, and breathe the same air."

"That's true. Good point." Greg replied. "Unless someone in dietary was targeting just inpatients."

"What do you mean Greg/"

"Well, isn't it possible that the food for tray delivery could be tainted during plating or just prior to delivery so that the general population wouldn't be affected?"

"Sure, I suppose it could." Richard agreed, "That would explain why it's manifested in one patient at a time. But wait, if it were the food, say poison, wouldn't we see vomiting or abdominal pain before death?"

"Usually, but not necessarily. There are some poisons that don't cause vomiting and are potent enough to work quickly." Greg continued.

"But Greg, wouldn't that show up in the toxicology results?"

"It would if we had the toxicology results back. It will be another day or two before we have them, but what about the stomach contents of the other victims? Surely Dr. Seike would have taken samples. I'll make a note to ask him at the post tomorrow."

"Dr. Ingraham, you were involved in a couple of these deaths and John Shand attended the others. I would like to be able to sit down all together to discuss this. What's the best way to do that?"

"It's difficult Greg because we cover opposite shifts, when he's off, I'm on and vice versa. I suppose we could see if he would be willing come to the hospital tonight."

"Great idea! I'll give him a call right now." Greg pulled the cell phone from his pocket.

"You had better use the land line Greg. Cell phone use is restricted inside the hospital."

"Right. Got a little ahead of myself."

Greg picked up the desk phone and looked through his cell for the number.

"Speed dial 222." Richard said.

"I'm sorry." Greg questioned.

"Press the speed dial button and then 222. We're all in there."

"Got it. Is that his office or home?"

"Office is 222, home is 223. It's five o'clock, he's still in the office."

Greg dialed the office. After two rings it was answered.

"Dr. Shand's answering service, may I help you?"

It wasn't what Greg was expecting and he hesitated.

"Hello?" The voice on the other end said again.

"Hello, I thought the doctor was still in the office."

"I'm sorry sir, the office closes at 5pm."

"I understand, well I guess...." Richard took the receiver from Greg's hand.

"Hazel, Dr. Ingraham here. Please put me through to the back-office number."

"Yes Dr. Ingraham."

He handed the receiver back to Greg and smiled.

"Hello." A female voice he remembered.

"Hi Linda? This is Greg Webster from the department of health, is John still in the office?"

"Are you kidding, He'll be here for a while yet. Let me see if I can get him to come to the phone."

"Thanks Linda."

Greg looked at Ingraham. "Still there." He spoke.

"Surprise, Surprise." Richard returned.

Greg was on hold for a moment before John came to the phone.

"Dr. Shand."

"John, it's Greg Webster."

"Hi Greg, I thought you left."

"I came back. Listen John, there's been another death. I'm here with Richard Ingraham and we were wondering if you could meet with us tonight, here at the hospital."

"Who was it this time Greg?"

"A nineteen-year-old maternity patient John. Same vague circumstances."

"I can be there by seven. Where shall we meet?"

"I have a makeshift office in medical records, it's not big but it is private. I'll also have access to the charts from there."

"Ok Greg. I'll see you around seven."

"Thanks John." They hung up.

Greg looked at Ingraham, "I'll be there at seven." Richard said.

Chapter 52

Maury had just arrived home when his cell phone rang. He was somewhat startled. It wasn't often that he received calls. He looked at the caller ID, UNKNOWN CALLER.

"Hello?" He said apprehensively. "Mr. Slater, this is Dr. Seike, I hope I'm not troubling you. I realize this is unusual, l but I have a request."

"Sure doc, what's up?"

"Maury, I am going to be doing a post very early tomorrow morning and I need your help. I'm almost certain I left the morgue door unlocked. I would return myself but I'm already well out of town. I was hoping you would run by the place and be sure it was locked up."

"Well, I guess I could, but you could just call security."

"No, I'm afraid that would be too much of an embarrassment for me to admit that I left that poor young lady's body unattended."

He had Maury's attention now.

"Well, I guess I could help you out doc. How old was she?"

"Just her late teens my friend, a real shame, so good looking and all. Well, if you could see to it ASAP, I would certainly appreciate it."

"It would be my pleasure doc; you just enjoy your evening."

The doctor hung up. Maury couldn't believe his luck. He could certainly use a little cash, but it was getting late. He would need to make a contact and get to the morgue before the security guard made his evening rounds. He pulled out his black book, looking for the right client. Not seeing her first, he would need to find someone with a broader range of taste in the physical attributes. He may even have to offer a slight discount.

Maury thumbed through the coded pages. He was looking for anyone who preferred young women. He also had limited time. Most of his clients were out of towners, some of whom would travel hours to have sex with one of his prospects. He needed someone local.

About halfway through the "L" section, he found what he was looking for. Josh Leremy. He dialed the number.

"Hello."

"Mister L, this is the PO man. Are you interested?"

"What do you have?"

"Teen, attractive, no wounds."

"Color?"

"Not sure but I'm willing to offer a discount and full refund if unused."

"What's the deal?"

"Two large but it has to be between 7:15 and 9:00 tonight."

"That's short notice. One fifty and I can be there."

"One seventy-five and she's yours."

"I think I'll pass."

"Ok, ok, you drive a hard bargain. One and a half."

"I'll be there by 7:30."

"Done. See you then."

Maury grabbed his keys and headed for his car. He would have some time to kill before his client arrived, but he needed to secure the door from the inside before the security check. He was also anxious to see his prospect.

Chapter 53

Kathy was getting ready to go home for the evening when her phone rang. She thought about letting it go to the switchboard, but Alex was still in his office, and he might come out to find her gone. It was quitting time, but Alex would never understand that, and she would pay the price tomorrow.

"Mr. Winfield's office, Kathy speaking."

"Hello Kathleen, I'm glad I caught you." Kathy knew who it was, but he never called her Kathleen at work.

"Yes sir, how can I help you?"

"It's to do with your visitor, Mr. Webster. I need to know what he thinks he knows. Can you help me?"

"What do you suggest?"

"Try to get close to him, he seems to like you. Ask a few leading questions. Perhaps he will ask you some in return. He looks like the type that would think aloud, unlike other State inspectors."

"I'll see what I can do." Kathy was careful not to use his name.

"Please do, and Kathleen, don't be afraid to dress and play the part."

Kathy had to think about this. Is this really what he wants? Can she do it? It seemed a bit out of her wheelhouse.

"Okay, I'll do my best."

"I'm sure you will. Goodnight."

Kathy didn't reply before she heard him hang up.

Chapter 54

Greg left the lounge and jumped on the elevator to the first floor. He had worked up an appetite since breakfast and thought he would grab some dinner while waiting for his meeting with Shand and Ingraham. He chose the chicken parmesan and a salad and headed for a table in the far corner of the room. The dining room was nearly empty even though it was dinnertime. He guessed the large space would be nearly full at lunchtime when the majority of the staff was working.

From his distant vantage point, he could see people entering and leaving and although he hadn't a single clue of what he was looking for, he thought an investigator should be aware of his surroundings. He thought about calling home but decided against it. Mary made it clear that she didn't require a call. He may do it later just to say goodnight to the kids. Right now, he wanted to focus on where this 7pm meeting needed to go.

Perhaps if he just let the doctors talk, they would tell him what he needed to know. That would be a good start, but he needed to have a list of questions ready. He needed to establish a pattern. If these deaths were related, there would certainly be similarities. Food, drug, air, and water were the obvious ones. He could request copies of the dietary orders tomorrow. The last meal would be the important one. The pharmacy orders would all be in the chart and air and water quality could be tested.

Greg was playing question and answer inside his own head. They were all found dead with no previous complaints. Only one was successfully resuscitated, the first, Gail Lockwood and only for a few short minutes. All were women, with the exception of one. The ages varied widely but none would be considered old. Only one occurred each day. Some were in private rooms and others were not. All but one had insurance. Not all were married. They all had IVs at the time. They were on different floors and different units. He doubted they had the same shoe size or color eyes. Now he was getting crazy.

He wondered what the personal circumstances were for each patient. If they were targeted, was there a common financial, social, or religious reason? Would he need to interview the family? Could he interview the family without launching a formal criminal investigation? That would certainlyHe

seem premature and would most likely impede the chances for a quick resolution.

It occurred to him that he needed to research the health department archives for similarities to other cases. If he came up empty, he could access the review cases from other states. He had his laptop with him and planned to do that as soon as he got back to his hotel room.

Greg was tired of thinking, and he didn't feel he was being all that productive anyway. He decided to have a walk around the hospital. He still had his visitor's pass clipped to his lapel. He figured he would begin at the location of the first death and follow the pattern. But first, while he was on the ground floor, he would have a look around.

He exited the cafeteria and headed left down a long corridor that went past the laboratory on the right, the morgue further down on the left and straight ahead was the exit to the loading dock. He went into the lab, entering the accessioning room.

He couldn't see anyone upon entering but an alarm sounded, not the kind of alarm that would startle you but more of a doorbell type. The room was small, with countertop along the entire periphery. There was a central drop off tank just inside the door. On the counter to the left, a cooler waited next to a small centrifuge.

To Greg's right was a computer terminal. Straight ahead, the doorway opened to a huge room with several doors on the back wall that appeared to lead to smaller workrooms. It seemed to be a standard layout for hospital-based laboratories.

Greg was impressed with the cleanliness of his surroundings. He had been in many labs but couldn't recall seeing one that sparkled like this, a testament to the staff. As he progressed into the large area, he heard the door behind him open. A young lady, in her late twenties he guessed, looked a little surprised to see him there. Greg turned to face her.

"I'm sorry if I scared you, my name is Greg Webster and I'm with the state health department."

The girl's face became even more serious.

"I'm Loretta. I should call my supervisor to let her know you're here."

"That's not necessary Loretta, I'm not here to survey the lab. I'm doing some investigative work and had a few minutes to kill so I thought I would have a look around, but you may be able to answer a few questions for me."

"I'll do my best. Would you mind if I just get this stuff started while we talk? I'm the only one here right now, the other tech is at dinner."

"Please, go about your business." Greg insisted.

"Is it common that the doors remain unlocked while no one is in the lab?"

"I wouldn't say common, but it does happen., especially when we're short staffed. If I were going to leave for any length of time, I would lock up, but I was just in the ER for a brief moment."

Greg understood. She was probably gone for more than a moment, but it would be a big deal to lock all the outside doors. He guessed that due to the twenty-four-hour operation, the doors to this lab were rarely, if ever, locked.

"It's ok Loretta, I get it. Do you have any idea why I'm here?"

"Does it have anything to do with Lorena Nunez?"

"What do you know about Lorena?"

"Just that she was very young and that they called a code earlier today. I understand she didn't make it."

"Who told you that?"

"Why? Is it not true?"

"No, I'm afraid it's true, I was just wondering how word gets around so fast."

"Well, anytime a code is called, people start to ask questions. Also, just before the change of shifts, Lenore, that's the girl I replace, drew Lorena."

"You mean she went to get a blood sample?"

"Exactly. Her doctor had ordered a WBC to rule out appendicitis."

"What time would that have been?"

Loretta moved to the computer and filled in a couple of text boxes. A screen appeared that listed the details of the collection and results.

"It looks like the draw was at 15:15. The sample was assessed at 15:22 and the results were released at 16:08."

"That's about an hour before the code was called. *Lenore may have been the last person to see Lorena alive.*" Greg said aloud but really speaking to himself. He pulled out his pad to take a few notes. He was getting confused, every body's name began with L.

He wrote:

LORENA......VICTIM

LORETTA.... EVENING TECH

LENORE......DAY TECH.... NEED INTERVIEW

"Loretta, will Lenore be working tomorrow?"

"Let me check. The schedule is right over here." She led him back to the front room where he originally entered.

"Yes, Lenore will be here at 7am tomorrow." Greg was listening but was more intrigued with the schedule posted on the wall. "This schedule is for the entire month, right?"

"Yes sir."

"Do you think I could have a copy of that?"

"It will take just a second."

Loretta pulled the tack holding the schedule to the board and raced off to the far end of the room to the copier. She was back in a matter of seconds.

"Here you are."

"Loretta, you have been a big help tonight. I hope the remainder of your shift goes well."

"Thank you, Mr. Webster." Loretta was obviously pleased that she was helpful.

"Goodnight, Loretta."

Greg let himself out. He knew what his first step would be tomorrow. Every department must post a schedule like this. He needed them all. From these he could develop a list of the employees who may have had access to the patients shortly before they died. Perhaps they could help put some of the pieces of this puzzle in place.

Greg was turning back toward the cafeteria when he heard a door behind him close. He spun around but didn't see anything. It had to be either the exit at the end of the hall or the door to the morgue. He started walking. As he approached the morgue door, he thought he heard sounds inside, but they were gone now. He paused a second and then knocked on the door. No answer. He tried to turn the handle, but it was clearly locked. He waited another moment. Nothing.

He stepped away slowly and headed toward the exit door. There was a sign that said:

DOOR ALARM IS ACTIVATED AFTER 5PM
EMERGENCY EXIT ONLY

Greg figured he would give it a try, if security came running, he would ask to have the morgue checked. He grabbed the long bar and gave a push. He didn't hear anything but that didn't mean an alarm wasn't sounding somewhere else. He stepped out onto the loading dock, holding the door open. He looked around and could just see the brake lights of a vehicle reaching the end of the drive. He couldn't discern color or model and when the car reached the main road, it turned left and disappeared behind the building.

Greg looked around at the loading dock and then stepped back inside. It must have been someone leaving via the loading dock door. They probably stepped through the door just as he was exiting the lab. When he turned around, he was staring eye to chin with one of the biggest men he had ever seen in person.

Chapter 55

Maury could still hear voices in the hall. He recognized the deep voice of the security guard, the other was unmistakably male, but unfamiliar. His nerve was shaken by the knock on the door just moments ago. For a brief second, he was considering opening the door and justifying his presence by telling of his call with Dr. Seike but if it were the security guard, he would have asked why he wasn't called. He would also make sure the door was locked when they left and that would ruin Maury's business plans. He made an instant decision to remain quiet. Now he stood with his back to the wall just to the right of the door.

He was listening as hard as he could but couldn't make out the words. His mind was racing, preparing his next move. He had options, none of which he considered as strong. He could crawl beneath the prep table, which was elevated several inches off the floor to facilitate cleaning. It might work, but his first choice was going into the adjoining room. There, he could either lie on a cot and cover himself with a sheet or his least favorite plan, slide himself into an empty drawer in the cooler.

Maury moved himself closer to the adjoining room, careful not to make any noise. He stood still, barely breathing for what seemed like an eternity. The handle rattled a couple of times. Finally, he heard the voice moving away from the door. His pulse was beginning to slow down. This was much more than he bargained for. All he wanted was a few minutes alone with the product before his client arrived and to make sure the door was locked from the inside before the guard made his rounds. He barely achieved the latter.

He may still have his chance. The voices had been gone a few minutes. He opened the door to the cooler room, passed through and closed the door behind him. Once the door was securely closed, he switched on the light. There was one body on a cot out in the open and two drawers were labeled. He knew the freshest victim would be in the open. The evening orderly was shared between many departments and wouldn't have the time or assistance to load the body into a drawer.

Maury's nervousness was once again returning to excitement. The small body was neatly covered in the white, plastic shroud. He was standing at the head end of the cot. Slowly, he moved his hand over the plastic, looking for the seam. Sometimes the seam was taped closed but usually, it was just tucked under the body. He found an open seam just under her left shoulder.

Maury tugged at the plastic until it loosened along the top half of her body. She was still covered but the material was now loose. He picked up the edge and peeled it down off her face. She was obviously dark skinned, probably Italian or Latino. Seiki was right, she was a very pretty girl. He pulled more of the plastic until her shoulders and breasts were exposed. "Wow!" He said quietly. "What a set on this young mama."

He didn't waste any time. He leaned over her head and grabbed both breasts. They felt heavy and cold. He knew he would need to wheel her out into the prep room right away so that she could warm up a little. He put his own desires aside and opened the door. Once propped open, he wheeled the gurney out of the cooler. He had about thirty minutes before Josh arrived. She was still going to be cold.

Chapter 56

The very large man he had met in the hallway near the morgue escorted Greg to the security office. Although Greg explained his presence, the guard felt a need to "gather some information for the record." Greg understood. Although it was nearing seven o'clock and he didn't want to be late for his meeting with Ingraham and Shand, he felt it was better just to go along than to ruffle any feathers.

The security office was on the first floor as well but the opposite end of the building. The office was small but well-furnished and Greg was surprised by the amount of surveillance equipment. "Do you monitor the entire hospital?" He asked the guard.

"I'm really not at liberty to say." He replied seriously.

"Look mister...Belden," Greg said while staring at his name badge. "Let me explain why I'm here."

"You already told me, you're with the health department."

"Yes, but I'm here to investigate some recent deaths of patients in your hospital. You may be able to assist me by answering my questions."

"I'm afraid I would need to refer you to my supervisor for that." Greg was once again finding himself getting frustrated.

"Fine. Let's call him."

"Well, I can't call him right now, it will have to wait until tomorrow."

"Alright, if you want to play that game fine. I'll just have Mr. Winfield call your supervisor tomorrow. Now tell me what you need from me so I can get out of here. I have an appointment with some people here who prefer to help me and I'm going to be late."

Greg gave him the routine information he was looking for. He knew this guy was just flexing his muscles. When Greg stood up to leave, he said, "You're not going to harass me every time I show up on your camera are you?"

"Only when you open a secured door Mr. Webster." He was obviously referring to the loading dock incident.

"I opened that door not more than 30 seconds before you arrived. You couldn't have possibly responded that quickly." Then it hit him, he wasn't responding to Greg's opening of the door but to whoever left just before he came out of the lab. "Do you have a security camera on the loading dock?" No response. "I know." Greg said. "Never mind, I'll ask your supervisor tomorrow. Thank you very little." He said as he walked out the door.

Now Greg needed to find his way back to Medical Records. He was running late so he asked the first person he came across for directions. When he arrived, John Shand was waiting for him, but Ingraham hadn't arrived yet.

"Hi John, thanks for coming. It's good to see you again."

"My pleasure Greg, well maybe pleasure isn't the word, but I want to find out what's going on."

"That makes two of us." Greg said as he turned to sit down. "I'm still not convinced Winfield is all that anxious or willing to help."

"He can be a difficult man, that's a given."

"I understand difficult, and I even told him so, but I can't curb this feeling that he either wants to be an obstacle or he is involved somehow."

As Greg finished his line, Richard Ingraham knocked on the open door.

"Nice roomy office." He said with a serious look but more than a hint of sarcasm in his voice.

"Sorry," Greg apologized, "we could meet in the cafeteria I suppose but it wouldn't be as private."

"No, I like this." Ingraham replied, "private and intimate." Richard's dry humor broke the tension.

There was a momentary pause. John broke the silence. "Tell me about the new one, the young girl."

"Nineteen, Hispanic, perfectly healthy and much too young to be a mother." Ingraham said.

"Who has the baby?" Greg asked.

"Still in Maternity right now. Discharge planning is working with DSS for a long-term plan." Ingraham replied.

"What about next of kin, Richard?"

"The girl was here by herself. She is new to the country and very new to the area. No immediate family. Well, she did have a cousin, but he threw her out and he has a tribe of his own to feed." Ingraham stated with the callousness he was known for.

"Richard, was there any sign of what killed her?" John interjected.

So far, Greg's plan to sit and listen was working well.

"Like all the rest John, zippo! She had been gone a long while before they called the code. The notes up to that time indicate she was doing well, with the exception of some abdominal pain. She was scheduled for a CT scan in the morning. Latest labs all looked ok."

"What about medications? Any chance of an adverse reaction?"

"I don't think so John, a little saline and Ringer's. Nothing out of the ordinary."

"Ok, how about needle marks? Puncture wounds?"

"Nothing like that John." Richard added. "It's a mystery. The only odd finding was the petechiae. Her eyes looked as though she had been strangled. They were quite red from the tiny, broken vessels."

Greg spoke up. "Any ligature marks on the neck?"

John and Richard looked at each other.

"Spoken like a true investigator Greg. No ligature marks." Ingraham said. "Greg, what do you have so far?"

"I wish I could tell you I had some solid leads, but that would be a lie." Greg sounded apologetic. "I have some ill feelings about some circumstantial oddities, but nothing concrete. For example, Winfield exudes some level of involvement, but I have nothing to back it up. Just a few moments ago, I was walking near the cafeteria and heard the loading dock door close. When I looked around, no one was there. Several minutes later, I opened the door to have a look outside and I could see taillights pulling away.

I must have triggered an alarm because the security guard showed up and gave me the third degree. I would expect that, but I think he was responding to the first person to open the door, not me. I asked if they have a security camera on the dock, but "Barney Fife" wouldn't tell me.

Here is something else. I was headed home for the day and stopped at the diner just outside of town. I pick up the local newspaper and while viewing the obituaries, I notice that all of our victims are reposing at the same funeral home."

"Mease Mortuary?" John and Richard said simultaneously.

"Yes. Mease Mortuary. I'm guessing by your response, it's the only one in town?"

"Not at all." John replied. "There are actually a few parlors in town, it just so happens that Mease is the most popular. Why would you find that odd anyway Greg?"

"I don't know, that's the whole problem. In this line of work, you sometimes need to rely on gut feelings. I'm usually right about these things but even I think this one is a stretch."

"Mease is a straight shooter," Richard added," in fact, I think he's still on the board here, isn't he John?"

"The last I knew, he was. Seems like a fair enough guy." John said.

"Can we go back to the physical findings for just a minute?" He asked politely.

"The petechiae may be a common factor here. I've noticed it in the other cases I was involved in as well."

"What does that mean, John?" Greg asked with a touch of controlled excitement in his voice."

"Probably nothing Greg. The blood vessels in the eyes become dilated during asphyxiation. It can be very prominent in strangulation cases, but it is also found in many natural deaths as well, although to a lesser degree."

"But Richard just said there weren't any ligature marks. No signs of strangulation."

"That's true Greg, he did say that, but he means not outward signs. Ligature marks, bruising, burns and a broken hyoid bone can be outward signs of strangulation. There are more subtle signs as well, one being petechiae."

"I still don't understand" Greg said apologetically. "How does strangulation occur if the person isn't physically choked?"

"Pathological." Richard interjected with authority.

"Yes, it could be pathological or," John paused, "it could be chemical."

"Are you saying these people were poisoned John?" Greg asked with disbelief.

"I'm saying it's possible. I think we need to consider it. Pathological strangulation can occur when the air supply is cut off through physical obstruction such as getting something caught in the trachea or by a tumor mass in the thorax. Chemical asphyxiation occurs when an irritant, usually inhaled, ingested, or injected causes the lungs to stop exchanging oxygen. The heart will continue to beat and pump blood until it is deprived of oxygen itself. Because the blood is poorly oxygenated, the vessels try to expand to increase the amount of blood delivered to an organ. It is outwardly noticeable in the eyes. There are other signs as well such as cyanosis."

"Wouldn't these signs be evident at autopsy?" Greg asked.

"They would, and my guess is they were." Ingraham added. "I haven't seen the written reports yet, but I have to believe Kyle would have picked up on that and noted it. The difficulty here is that these signs may be notable in half of all deaths. It would not draw specific attention on its own merit."

Greg thought about this for a long moment. Something was triggering his internal instinct to raise the red flag.

"I can understand brushing over signs of strangulation as coincidental in a random death but after several deaths?" Don't you think that would warrant special mention?"

"I think you're right Greg. Perhaps we can ask Kyle about that personally."

"I'll do it." Greg said. "I plan to attend the autopsy on Lorena Nunez tomorrow, and I'll ask about the petechiae."

"It seems unlikely," John continued, that all these patients would have a common pathology and if they did, Kyle would certainly pick it up at post. That leaves us with some sort of chemical reaction."

"A reaction to medication?" Greg asked.

Richard took this one. "That would be the most obvious and logical Greg, but it could be almost anything. The chance that four patients of varying age, sex and diagnosis would be taking the same medication would be minimal, unless of course it were something very generic like acetaminophen or ibuprofen. If that were the case, nearly every patient in this hospital should be dead. A more likely culprit would be something environmental like food, air, water etc."

Greg's mind was racing, trying to put the pieces together. This dialog was interesting and would probably prove helpful but so far, they were no closer to solving this mystery.

"If it were a chemical reaction, we should see that in the results of the blood tests from the state crime lab. Right? Greg asked.

"I'm no toxicologist Greg but I would assume you're correct." Ingraham said. "When are those results due back Greg?"

"I should have them sometime tomorrow. It usually takes a few weeks, but I cashed in a favor. If I don't have them by the end of business tomorrow, I'll make another call."

"Well, it sounds like we need more information. I suggest we call it a night and see what the crime lab and Dr. Seike can tell us tomorrow." John suggested.

"That works for me," Richard added, "but don't hesitate to call me Greg anytime you think it's appropriate. I'm glad to help any way I can."

"I appreciate that Dr. Ingraham. I appreciate both of you taking the time to meet with me tonight. Just to make you aware, I have asked that I be contacted immediately should any more deaths occur and that the room is treated as a crime scene. I have also asked to review all the deaths in this hospital for the past twelve months.

Tomorrow, I will witness the autopsy and I will request video tapes from any security cameras installed throughout the facility." Greg caught his breath and continued. "I am also requesting copies of the posted departmental work schedules for the preceding two weeks to look for consistencies between the deaths and personnel."

"It sounds like you have your work cut out for you." John said. "I too will make myself available Greg. You know how to find me."

Greg thanked the gentlemen once again and they all stood up to leave. After a quick handshake, the two doctors disappeared in a flash and Greg was left standing alone in the office. Tomorrow would be a busy day and Greg still had some homework to do back at the hotel. Mary wasn't going to get a call tonight.

Chapter 57

Maury's pulse was finally coming down. He was fairly certain he wouldn't be disturbed again tonight. The body of Lorena Nunez was lying naked on a gurney in the center of the procedure room. It was approaching 7:20pm, time to check the door.

Just inside the right side of the door frame, Maury found the tiny electrical wire leading to the infrared sensor. Pulling the red wire back about one eighth of an inch, he could disarm the alarm momentarily, allowing his clients to come and go undetected by security.

He adjusted the wire with the agility of an experienced thief then opened the door. Josh was waiting off to the side of the loading dock as instructed. He followed Maury into the morgue without a word. Once inside, he inspected his prize.

"How would you like her?"

Josh was silent. Before him lay a young, beautiful Hispanic woman. Maury could sense his surprise. "Everything alright Josh?"

"You outdid yourself this time P.O. Man. She is gorgeous. She is also so young."

"Young is good, right?" Maury asked with a positive inflection. He suddenly felt like a car salesman about to lose a deal. "Is she everything I promised?"

"She's all that and more. She's actually too much. I feel very sorry for her."

"Hey, I feel sorry for her too but it's not like you killed her!"

"I understand that, but I just don't know if I can do it."

"I'll tell you what. I'm going to leave you alone for a few minutes. Maybe the urge will hit you. I'll just be in the other room. If you need help, call me."

Maury left. He couldn't believe it. "*Was everybody going soft?* "He thought to himself. This is the second one he lost in as many days. At this rate he was going to need to find another sideline. Ten minutes passed but he heard nothing from next door. He opened the door a crack and Josh was still standing there in the exact same place. Maury entered.

"What's up buddy?"

"I'm sorry man, I just can't do it. I'm really sorry."

Maury could sense the sincerity in Josh's voice, but he was still pissed.

"Look, I'm taking a great risk here. I can't just have people bail on me man."

"Don't worry, I'm going to pay you anyway." Josh said, never moving his eyes off Lorena's face. "I had a daughter once. She would be about her age now. You keep the money. I'm out of here. Please don't call me again." Josh turned and walked out.

Maury just stood there with the cash in his hand. He could hear the loading dock door close. He thought about having this one for himself, but he was too irritated to get excited. He wrapped Lorena's body back in the plastic shroud and moved her back to the cooler.

He locked the door to the morgue, replaced the wire to the alarm and walked to another, unmonitored exit. He had the money but lost the client. He focused on the money.

Chapter 58

The phone rang shortly after eight o'clock. "Hello." One word followed by several moments of silence. He knew the voice instantly but waited for the next move.

"I am concerned. This fellow from the State, what does he know?" The killer asked.

"I can only speculate but I don't believe he can be certain of anything. Perhaps you should back off for a while."

"That wouldn't be good for you, or me now, would it? If we back off now, it will only draw more attention and allow them to focus on the recent cases. No, I think we do just the opposite. Tomorrow shall bring two new victims. As long as I have a supply, the occurrence rate will increase."

"Look, I like the extra cash, but we're getting in a bit deep here. These are very dangerous waters right now."

"Save me the lecture. We have been doing this for quite a long while now. I would say we have the situation under control. I am concerned only enough to be more careful, not less active. Find out what this inspector knows. I'll call again in a day or two."

The killer hung up the phone and returned to the television monitor. He re-ran the video. The man just stood there looking at the body. He was amazed at the willpower this man displayed. "A pity really," he thought, "such a waste of a perfectly good body although she did just deliver a baby, wouldn't be the tightest ride."

He turned off the monitor, closed and secured the locker and walked out. *"Tomorrow is another day, time to make some plans."* His voiced echoed in his head. He realized he was becoming very proficient at his work. The hours were very long but he didn't feel the stress he had initially. He knew all too well that the stress from this was much easier to deal with than the stress of a personal financial struggle.

Chapter 59

"Couple in the next room bound to win a prize, they've been going at it all night long...well I'm trying to get some sleep, but these motel walls are cheap, Lincoln Duncan is my name and here's my song...here's my song..." a tune that had been running through Greg's mind non-stop since about 2am when he finally checked into his room. He stayed behind long after Shand and Ingraham left his make-shift office around 8:30 last night. By the time he did a little research and put his plan together for the following day, Greg left the hospital a little after 11pm.

His hotel shared a parking lot with an all-night Denny's, so he stopped for a bite. He couldn't believe how busy the place was this time of night. He decided to sit at the counter.

"Yes sir. What can I get you?" said the middle-aged waitress who had way too much energy for this hour.

"I guess I'll need just a minute or two to look over the menu." "Take your time pal, I'm here all night. You might think about the blueberry pancakes, they seem to be the big seller tonight. Make you sleep like a baby."

"I'll take that under advisement" Greg answered with nowhere near the same enthusiasm. "*she's probably right*" he thought, "nothing like a good carb overload to make you crash." He didn't even open the menu, he was going with her suggestion. Greg looked around the place while he waited for her return.

He wondered what was going on in each of these lives to bring them all here at this time, but then he realized this was the first stop off the Thruway exit. These people were most likely traveling and either needed a break from the road or had decided to check in at the motel.

"Come to any conclusions?" Greg turned himself around and found he was staring right at the waitress's name tag.

"Well... Laura, I'm going to take your suggestion and go with the blueberry hotcakes. Can I get some bacon as well?"

"Anything you want mister. I'm here to make you happy."

"Just like Mary" he said under his breath as Laura grabbed the menu and ran off. *"Another L name" he thought. "What are the odds?"* The thought triggered more thoughts and that brought him to his list of things to do tomorrow. *"Perhaps this is all just circumstantial"* he questioned himself *"but then why do Ingraham and Shand have the same gut reaction?"*

Greg shook it off and went back to perusing the room. He had forgotten how distracting people watching could be. In no time, Laura returned with a huge stack of steaming pancakes with extra crispy bacon. The aroma was overwhelming.

"Thank you dear, this looks amazing!"

"They're just pancakes" Laura quipped, "I'm amazing." She never cracked the slightest smile as she said this, and Greg realized that she probably was.

Chapter 60

By the time Kathy arrived at her desk at 8am, Alex Winfield already had 2 hours under his belt. He was always early but especially so today. "Kathy!" she heard him yell before she even had a chance to set her purse down.

"Good morning Mr. Winfield."

"Kathy, I need to have an emergency meeting with the board of directors this afternoon. Set it up for 3pm." Kathy sensed that he was even more agitated than usual.

"Of course, Mr. Winfield. What should I tell them?"

"Tell them the Administrator requests their presence! That's all they need to know."

"Wow, a lot more agitated" Kathy thought. "I'll get right on it sir." Kathy tuned and hurried toward her desk.

About halfway there, Winfield yelled again, "I need Barry Miller there as well."

"Yes sir."

Winfield could feel his pulse quickening. He sensed he was losing control, and nothing made him angrier. Alex sat in his chair and gripped the arms with such strength that he thought he could rip the leather right off.

He closed his eyes and envisioned himself beneath the barn floor yet again. It was both fear and a sense of protection. He could smell the wood, the hay and the decaying food surrounding him. It was quiet and dark. He let the sensation engulf him, hold him. Now his mother's sweet voice signing on the far away breeze.

He could feel the tension in his arms release. The muscles in his back begin to unwind. The sweet fragrance of apples, the lingering hint of long removed barn animals. The temperature of the cool earth beneath him calming his emotions. He once again took control. He opened his eyes before he would hear the sound of the rifle.

Alex relaxed back into the comfort of his chair just as the phone rang. The display told him it was Kathy calling. He harshly grabbed the receiver. "Yes!"

"I'm sorry to bother you sir. Barry Miller is on the line for you."

"Put him through." He heard the call connect. "Barry?"

"Good morning, Alex. Hey, listen, about the board meeting...I have another important appointment at 3 today, any way to move that back a bit, say 4:30?"

"I'm sorry Barry but it needs to be at 3pm. You'll need to move your appointment."

"What's the urgency Alex? Is something up?"

"Yes, something is up! The DOH is here investigating a few coincidental, untimely deaths and word has gotten out. At least to one of the board members."

"What does this have to do with finances Alex? I mean, what is it that you need from me?" There was a brief but noticeable silence on the other end of the line.

"I need to give them some good news Barry, something that will instill confidence." Now, it was Barry's turn to pause.

"What would that be Alex? I mean our revenue numbers are down a bit on the inpatient side. Sure, we're making it up on outpatient visits but the DRG's have us by the short hairs."

"Okay Barry, so here's what we do. I mention, very casually of course, that we have had one or two unexplained deaths. We are looking into it, and we have asked the DOH to participate. Then, you talk about moving forward with the new outpatient facility in Herkimer.

Present some numbers on our projected increase in O.P. revenue, increased market share, all that bull shit. Talk about how the new market share will increase admissions, restoring our margin."

"Alex, you know as well as I do our inpatient volume is fine. Our beds are mostly full. The real issue is length of stay. Patients are staying too long."

"Yes, of course I know that, Barry. I also know that just because I have had a winning balance every year I've been here, it doesn't make me a shoe-in forever. And what about you? I had to fight with this board to get them to back my plan to make you Chief Financial Officer and Chief Operating Officer. Do you know how rare that is?"

"I'm fully aware how rare that is Alex. I'm also aware that my salary and a half is still saving this hospital over a hundred thousand dollars each year by combining the two titles. Do you realize how hard I work, how many hours I put in?"

"I know Barry, I'm sorry. I'm just saying what is good for the goose is good for the gander. You watch my back and I'll watch yours. A little financial stroking will go a long way right now. Let's just keep the board off our backs for a little while until this investigation thing blows over."

"Alright Alex. I'll put together some dog and pony show for the board. You're not giving me much time to prepare though."

"It will be alright Barry, pull out some old graphs, they will never know the difference." Alex hung up the phone. He felt a little better. Barry had to hurry.

Chapter 61

Maury awoke ahead of the alarm going off, or at least he thought so. The morning was overcast, and the room seemed unusually dark. Thinking it was the middle of the night, he reached lazily for his cell phone on the nightstand. The glow from the screen blinded him momentarily.

Once his eyes could focus, panic set in. 6:45am. Even on a bad day, Maury was out of his apartment by 6:35. He needed a shower and coffee fast, but he knew he would never make it on time. He opened the phone again to his favorites and dialed the main hospital number. Calling in wasn't so bad, he would ask for Nursing Service and speak to the receptionist. The bad part was the harassment he would take from Lynette if she found out. She always found out.

Maury didn't sleep well which contributed to his not hearing the alarm. When he finally fell asleep around 3am, he was out cold. The events of the previous evening frightened him, but he wasn't sure why. He has come close to being caught before, but it never bothered him for long. He had lost clients before. People chicken out, freak out or don't show and he always took it in stride. It was a part of doing business. He didn't like it, but it happened. Something about this was different. Perhaps it was the guard showing up at an off time. Perhaps it was the sound of more than one voice.

"Nursing Service, this is Marsha. How may I help you?" Maury loved Marsha's voice. She was a looker too.

"Good morning, Marsha, It's Maury Slater."

"Yes Mr. Slater. How are you this morning?"

"I'm afraid I overslept Marsha. I'm running about 30 minutes behind."

"Yes Mr. Slater, I understand. I will pass this information along to Ms. Kuchar's secretary. Will that be all Mr. Slater?" She was obviously in a hurry,

"Yes Marsha, that will be all. Thank you."

"You're welcome Mr. Slater. Drive carefully now. Goodbye." If only the rest of his day would be this easy...

If he took a shorter than usual shower, he could still swing by Donovan's for Joe to Go. Just a small, local bakery/deli but he really liked their coffee. Once he arrived at work, he would check the log for last night. Perhaps there would be something to redeem his faith in his business plan.

Chapter 62

"Good morning, Laura. Are you still here?" Greg was astonished. "You bet ya, I'm always here...or at least it seems so." She still had the same energy level he witnessed last night. "That's one long shift" he said. "Yes sir. 11pm to 11 am, 3 days a week. Not so bad once you get used to it. Wouldn't you like 4 days off each week? He had to think for a moment. "I guess I would but not if I was so tired, I couldn't do anything!" "Nonsense. I get my seven hours sleep and I'm good as new. Up and at 'em. I work every other day, so it works out really well unless you like 2 days off together that is." "Well, it sounds exhausting to me Laura." "Hey, every day I'm on the right side of the dirt is a good day." He couldn't argue with that. Greg finished his coffee and set down enough money to cover his bill and a generous tip.

When he was back in the car, he dialed the office. "New York State Department of Health Investigative Division this is Ms. Sumanski. How can I help you?"

"Good morning, Christine, it's Greg."

"Good morning Mr. Webster. Are you playing hooky again today?" Christine had a great, playful way about her.

"Now Christine, you know I would only play hooky if you were involved." Greg shot right back at her. It was apparent that Greg and Christine were fond of each other and liked to tease each other but that was as far as it went.

"If only that were true Greg." She replied in a broken-hearted voice. "Actually, I'm calling for Tom. I ended up staying out here in High Falls last night and I may need to be here a few more days. Is he in the office yet?"

"Is she anyone we know Greg?"

"Funny Christine." A little giggle on her end. "Tom just walked in. Let me put you through."

"Thanks Christine."

"Spider!" "Hi Tom."

"Where are you?"

"I'm still out here in High Falls. Spent the night here." "Intentionally?" Tom joked.

"Funny. Yes intentionally. Tom, there is something going on here. I can't put my finger on it quite yet, but something smells funny."

"Might be the Mohawk!" Tom joked again.

"Man, you are on a roll this morning Tom. While I appreciate your attempt at humor, this thing is pretty serious." Greg's voice now indicated the stoic nature of the pursuing conversation.

"Ok Greg, let me have it."

"Well, the first 2 death have been followed by 2 more. That's four in as many days. I have reviewed charts, procedures, and conducted interviews. Hell, I even interviewed a patient who was a roommate of one of the deceased. So far, nothing."

"Any autopsies performed?"

"Yes, three previously one of which I witnessed. The fourth will be done this morning. In fact, I'm on my there now. I have spoken extensively with the Pathologist, Dr. Seiki and with the Hospitalists involved. Seiki is stumped so far and Shand and Ingraham share the same uneasy feeling I have."

"What about toxicology Greg?"

"Waiting for the results. I called Russ Lang to see if he could expedite things. He's my next call."

"Is it time to send out an environmental team?"

"I thought about it but no one else is reporting any symptoms. I really don't want to cause undue alarm."

"I guess you're right. So, what do you need from me?"

"I guess just some latitude for now. I'm hoping a couple more days will do it. Oh, and if you get a complaint at all, take it in stride if you can."

"I've got your back Greg. Take the time you need. Give me an update periodically and keep all your receipts. I'm sure you'll figure it out. If not, don't come back! Just kidding Greg."

"You get funnier by the minute Tom. Thanks for your help." Greg hung up the phone and drove off in the direction of the hospital.

Chapter 63

Barry Miller was already having a busy day. He was usually in the office by 7:45 A.M., but even earlier if there were early meetings scheduled. The people who worked for Barry thought he was a fair guy. Tough at times, but fair.

With his dual roles of CFO and COO, he had leadership responsibilities for most of the departments in the hospital. There were of course department heads, and in some cases, assistants who managed the day-to-day operations and reported to Barry. All in all, he managed around 30 departments.

When the previous COO retired, Barry made a proposal to the Board of Directors asking for the dual title. It wasn't that he didn't have enough to do. Managing the finances of even a smallish hospital like City, was a major task.

Along the way, Barry had learned to recognize and appreciate good talent. While some leaders are reluctant to employ people of caliber similar to their own, for fear of being outdone, Barry took comfort in having associates who could step in for him at a moment's notice. This was particularly true in the fiscal services department.

Alex Winfield always felt threatened by Barry. Not that Barry would want his job, but because he needed to trust Barry to make him shine. Alex knew what he wanted, and he knew which direction he needed to take the hospital, but he didn't possess the operating knowledge to make it happen. Barry did.

Knowing the strengths Barry had and his own weaknesses, he allowed Barry a great deal of latitude and supported his proposal for dual titles. It didn't hurt that the board's approval would save the hospital one-half of the COO's salary plus another 25% allocated for benefits for an additional employee. As part of the deal, Barry also worked in some contract language that would provide a bonus if Barry and his team could reduce patient length of stay by 20%.

Barry Miller was the one who negotiated reimbursement rates with the payers so he was keenly aware that dwindling reimbursements could only be offset by shorter lengths of stay. His plan to accomplish this was based on getting the cooperation of the admitting physicians. Not an easy task, and one that would have to wait for another day. Right now, his focus would be pulling together a presentation that would take the boards mind off the recent unexplained deaths.

Chapter 64

Mark's phone rang a few minutes after eight in the morning. "Mark, don't speak, just listen. The plan has changed. I need the goods in the locker within the hour." Mark was silent on the other end. He knew he had the Propofol, and he knew there was no way to get out of it. "By 9am Mark. Please confirm." "Of course, doctor. I'll deliver that myself." There was a click on the other end. Mark thought that tomorrow would be a good time to take that trip to Minnow Lake with the family. He would need to clear the time off with Bob.

Chapter 65

Greg was not even seeing the road as he drove back toward City Hospital. His mind was juggling a dozen tasks at once. At the top of the list, was another meeting with Alex Winfield. So many things to talk about, but he would need a few minutes to organize his list before walking into his office. He had a pen in his jacket pocket, but his note pad was in his briefcase on the back seat. He needed to find a place to pull over.

After a couple minutes, the shoulder of the road widened enough for his to get the car safely on the shoulder. He put the shifter in park, unbuckled his seatbelt, check his side mirror for oncoming traffic. All good. He turned on the emergency flashers and stepped out. He opened the back door, retrieved his briefcase, and returned to the front before a single car passed. He reached into the briefcase and found his note pad.

With the flashers still on, Greg began jotting down his thoughts in no particular order. He could prioritize them after they were all written down. He needed to get the schedules for all the departments. While he was at it, he would ask for the timecards of all clinical employees for the days of the deaths.

He would ask for an appointment with the security supervisor to talk about surveillance records and videos. He added a note to call the state lab again just in case they were ahead of schedule. If he had a few minutes, he would meet the daytime lab tech Lenore, and ask a few questions. As for Alex, it was time to talk about other avenues of investigation, perhaps the CDC and or EPA. He wasn't planning to attend the autopsy for Lorena Nunez, but he would follow up with Dr Seike when it was concluded.

Greg set down his note pad, looked in his rearview mirror, turned off his flasher, turned on his directional, and pulled back on to the highway. Just as he pulled back into to town, he glanced across the road and saw the Mease Mortuary.

He wondered if there was maybe more than coincidence that connected the funeral home with the deaths. He couldn't imagine what it could be, but it wasn't his job to imagine. It was his job to investigate. He would add that to his list.

Chapter 66

Pulling off 2 deaths today was going to be difficult at best. He had selected the victims that made the most sense. They were both on the second floor which houses medical surgical patients as well as the ICU. The post-surgical patient was in 2117, very close to the locker room. This one should be easy. The difficulty will be the coma patient in the Intensive Care Unit.

He would need to create some sort of distraction. The ICU is staffed by 3 RN's. If he injected the patient in 2117 first, one ICU nurse would respond to the code. That would leave two. The ICU is equipped with remote monitoring located at the nurses' station in the main hallway. He would not be able to just walk by the desk without being noticed. If he were able to come up the back staircase, on the far side of the unit, he could set off an alarm in the first patient room, hopefully drawing the response of both nurses. Once they were distracted, he could move around the back of the desk and disarm the monitor for his victim. Without disarming the monitor, alarms would sound as soon as he closed off the intravenous line.

This whole operation would require precise timing and a little bit of luck. It would be risky, but the only way to keep the DOH investigator off his trail. He would begin just before 9:30 which is when the first nurse takes her break. With some luck, that would leave one nurse on break, one responding to the code in 2117, and one responding to the other diversion. Almost time to go to the locker. The stuff had better be there.

Chapter 67

Maury parked his car at around 7:45. He didn't feel the need to rush like most days because they were expecting him to be late. He grabbed his coffee and his lab coat, locked the car, and headed toward the employee entrance. He was no sooner in the door when he heard his name being paged. Lynette.

He walked to the nearest phone and dialed the number for 3 West. "Hi, this is Maury returning a page. Is Lynette around?" he asked with a total lack of enthusiasm. "She's here somewhere, hold on a minute." Maury heard the handset thud against the counter. In the background, he could hear the typical, early morning chit-chat of the other nursing staff. "This is Lynette." Her voice sounded a bit more chipper than he expected.

"Hey Lynette, what's happening?" "Good morning, Maury. I was wondering if you could stop up a little later, maybe around 9:30? There is something I need to talk to you about."

Maury felt a cold chill run down his spine. *Why would she want to talk to him?*

His mind was jumping all around. *What does she know? Did someone see him the other night?* He composed himself. "Sure Lynette, I have a few things I need to do then I'll see you around 9:30.

"Great!" she spoke. "See you then." And the call ended.

Maury went to the nearest Men's room, splashed his face with cold water, dried it with a paper towel and put on his lab coat. His heart was racing as he made his way to the receptionist's desk to look at the morgue log. More disappointment as there were no new bodies.

Chapter 68

It was about 8:15 when Greg walked into the administrative suite. As always, Kathy was there to welcome him. "Good morning, mister Webster." Greg noticed something different about Kathy today. She appeared to be a little less formal somehow. A little less protective of her space perhaps.

"Good morning to you Kathy."

He must have had a surprised look on his face which prompted Kathy to ask, "are you alright Greg?"

Wow! Now he was really confused. She has never called him Greg, even when he asked her to. "Yes Kathy, I'm fine, thank you. I was wondering if I could have a few minutes with Mr. Winfield. It shouldn't take too long."

"It looks like he's on the phone right now, I'll pop my head in and see how long he will be."

Kathy stood up to go to his door and Greg couldn't help but notice that she was wearing a skirt that was substantially shorter than any he had ever seen her in. "Kathy," he said, with a noticeably stunned voice, "you look great today." He wanted to take it back as soon as the words left his mouth. He was afraid he had offended her.

"Well, isn't that sweet of you to say. I feel great today, Greg. Thank you!"

Greg felt as though he was in some parallel universe. Kathy cracked the door open and whispered something to Alex. She closed the door and walked back toward Greg.

"Mr. Winfield will be with you momentarily. Make yourself comfortable. May I get you anything?" Greg envisioned several comments he could make to that open-ended question, but he held his tongue.

Alex Winfield was pissed. Barry Miller was not answering his phone, the board meeting was just hours away and now, the pain in the ass from the DOH is going to suck more of his precious time. He opened his door. "Kathy, track down Barry Miller and tell him I need to see his ASAP! Mr. Webster, please come in." Greg looked at Kathy. She just rolled her eyes a little and picked up the phone. Greg followed Alex into the office.

"Have a seat, Greg. I'm afraid I don't have too much time for you today. There is much going on and I have an important board meeting this afternoon that I'm trying to prepare for."

"I understand," Greg responded, "I'll make this as quick as possible. This death yesterday, Lorena Nunez, is a bit of a deal changer. Unless you can provide me with a reasonable explanation, I have no choice but to expand the investigation."

"What does that mean exactly Greg?"

"It means bringing in some other agencies to assist. Right now, I'm thinking the CDC and EPA. Depending on what they find, we may need to consider others. If there appears to be suspicious intent of any kind, it could mean getting the FBI involved."

"Greg, you can't do that. Not right now. I have called a special Board of Directors meeting for this afternoon specifically to divert their attention from these events. Any word of more agency involvement will freak them out!" Greg noticed that Alex was becoming quite agitated.

"Alex, we already discussed this possibility, it shouldn't come as a surprise."

"You said you could hold off a while, that you could close the case if you didn't find concrete evidence."

"Yes, and I also said if there weren't any more suspicious deaths! We cannot just let this pattern continue. To let it go unchecked. I cannot be complacent about this, I won't!" Now Greg's temper was escalating, and it felt good.

There was silence for a few seconds, then calmly Alex said, "Greg there must be some way to postpone this."

Greg just stared at him, thinking quietly. "Here is the best I can do. The autopsy on Ms. Nunez is being performed this morning, if there is no obvious reason for her death then it's out of my hands. I have a few other leads I'm following which should take me into the afternoon. After that, I'll meet with Kyle Seike, he should be done by then. It looks like you have the morning to prepare for your meeting with the board."

Greg stood. "Just so you know, I plan to meet with a bunch of your staff today. I will let you know who when I'm done."

"Now you listen to me," Alex shouted, "I will tell you whom you can speak to and when! Who do you think you are?" He would have continued but Greg cut him off.

"I'll tell you who I am Alex, I am the new Sheriff in town, and I'm done taking orders from you! There is some serious shit going on here and I'm going to find out what it is."

"I'll have your job for this, you incompetent pain in the ass! I'm calling your boss right now!"

"Here, let me dial the number for you! In fact, I'll give you the governor's direct number as well. Do you really think they're going to fire me for doing the right thing? For doing my job? You make that call and you'll have every state and federal agency in here with their guns drawn, and you fucking know it.

Alex shut his mouth. He felt like his head was going to explode. He knew Greg was right. Greg stood up and walked out. His face was a little red too. Kathy was staring straight at the door when it opened, and Greg came thundering out. He looked at her and gave her a serious wink.

Chapter 69

Greg had no sooner left the office when Alex yelled through the open door. "Kathy, come in here!"

"Yes sir," she answered before she even left her seat.

"Where is Miller?"

"His secretary said he had left the office but didn't say where he was going."

"Page him Kathy, I need him here now!"

"Right away sir." She turned on her heels and headed for her phone.

"Barry Miller, please call extension 202, mister Miller, extension 202." Kathy waited for the phone to ring. And waited. And waited. "Kathy, did you get him?"

"Not yet sir." "Well, page him again!"

"Barry Miller, please call extension 202 immediately, mister Miller 202."

Nothing. "Mr. Winfield, he's not responding. Perhaps he needed to step out of the building."

"Then call him on his cell phone. I want him here now!"

"I'll try sir."

Chapter 70

Barry Miller heard the pages and felt his phone vibrate in his pocket. He knew it was Winfield calling, and he had no intention of answering right now. He was deep in thought, preparing for his day. If Alex wanted his presentation this afternoon, he needed to cut Barry some slack. Perhaps in another hour or so, he would be able to take a break. He would call back then.

Greg was on his way to the laboratory when he heard the pages. It sounded like Barry was in deep shit with the boss. He doubted there was any place in this building that someone could hide from Alex for very long. Poor bastard.

Chapter 71

As soon as Bob Kline walked into the pharmacy department, Mark ran over to meet him. "Hey Bob, I was wondering if I could have a few minutes of your time."

"Sure Mark, come into my office. Have a seat." Bob went behind his desk, pulled his lab coat off the rack, and put it on. "Is everything alright Mark?" He said as he took his chair.

"Yeah Bob, were all okay, just a little burned out. It's been a tough year so far."

"I Know it has Mark, and I feel for you. What can I do to help?"

"I think I need some time off, you know, maybe get the family away from here for a change."

"I think that's a great idea, Mark. When were you thinking about?"

"I was hoping to start tomorrow. It would just be three or four days. I know it's short notice."

"No, it's alright. I understand. Let me just make sure I can cover your shifts. I'll give Ed a call. He's only schedule for about 16 hours this week, I'm sure he would like the extra time. I'll give him a call but barring any problems, consider yourself off."

"That's great Bob, I really appreciate it."

"Happy to help. Do you have any place in mind?"

"We're thinking about getting a cabin at Minnow Lake. Nothing exciting but it's a really peaceful place. I think we could use that right now."

"I know you like it there. That sounds like an excellent plan. Enjoy it!"

Chapter 72

Greg was still buzzing from the adrenaline hangover from his meeting with Alex. It showed in the pace of his walk. He felt as though he was almost running. As he approached the laboratory door, his phone buzzed in his pocket. He recognized the number.

"Good morning, Russ. Tell me you have some good news."

"Well, that depends, Greg, what would be better news, if I found something, or if I found nothing?"

Greg needed to think about that. What was he hoping for in this investigation? Yesterday, he would have been happy if all of this was just a huge, unexplainable coincidence. Today, he would like to hang Alex Winfield up by his balls.

"I guess I'm not really sure, Russ but it is what it is. The truth is always best, right?"

"Good answer, Greg. Let me begin by saying that none of the samples submitted from the autopsies provide any solid signs of foul play. There is also no common thread between the patients, except, that they are all common threads!"

Greg was lost. "Are you trying to play me here Russ, because if you are, you're really doing a good job."

"I know buddy, sorry about that. Let me explain. There is nothing in any of the samples that stick out as an abnormal common thread. The problem is that the consistency across the samples is questionable. For example, if you look at the sodium, potassium, glucose levels, they are exactly the same."

Greg paused a moment. He was not chemistry major, but he knew enough to see the absurdity. "Do you think some samples were cross-contaminated Russ?"

"I don't think so Greg, if that were the case, we would see some really weird numbers. The numbers are fine, there just all the same. I think they are all from the same patient. Perhaps there was a labeling issue in the morgue or the lab?"

"I guess that's possible Russ, but the chances seem awfully remote. Let me ask some questions around here. Perhaps the lab has saved a back-up of the patient's blood. I was heading to the lab as you called, I'm right outside the door, Can I call you back?"

"Of Course, I'll kick this around here a little more, see if can break the code."

"I appreciate that, Russ. We'll talk soon." He put his phone back in his pocket and opened the door to the lab.

Chapter 73

"How may I help you?" Asked the woman behind the counter. Greg was in the same place he met Loretta just the other night. The place looked very different during the day shift. "My name is Greg Webster; I was hoping to see Lenore. I understand she is scheduled for duty today."

"Is she expecting you sir?"

"No. I'm sorry, I'm an investigator with the New York State Department of Health." Greg said as he offered his ID. She looked it over carefully.

"Perhaps I could direct you to the lab manager, Mr. Johnson," she said as she picked up the phone.

"No, thank you" he interrupted," that won't be necessary just yet. Lenore is the one I need to see."

"I'll see if I can find her for you." She walked out of the accessioning area and disappeared into the back. After a few minutes, she returned. "I'm afraid Lenore has been called away for a bedside draw. She should be back in ten to fifteen minutes. Would you like to wait, or I can take your number and have her call you when she is finished?"

Greg handed her his business card. "I'll be around, she can reach me at that number. Thank you." Before Greg left, he looked around the counter at all the vials of blood waiting to be analyzed. Each tube had a computer printed label with the patient's name, location, unique patient number and a bar code. He wondered what would need to go wrong to mislabel the vials. Maybe Lenore could help him understand. He left the lab and headed down the hall toward security.

Chapter 74

It was time. He opened the locker and found what he was looking for. Mark had delivered. He placed 2 vials of propofol, a small vial of lidocaine, 2 large syringes, 1 small syringe for the lidocaine and the vent spike in the pocket of his lab coat, closed and locked the locker and went into the men's room.

He loaded the small syringe with the lidocaine. He only needed one to use for both patients. Propofol was a good choice for the task for many reasons, particularly because it is readily available in the hospital. It also worked quickly and when preceded by a little lidocaine, caused little pain. He could have the patient scream in the first few seconds.

Propofol was also a pain in the ass to inject because it is an emulsion. The addition of soy oil allowed it to permeate the tissue and cross the blood-brain barrier extremely quickly. It also was more viscid than most injectables making it harder to withdraw from the vial and administer. He got around this by using a vent spike to allow air into the vial as he pulled the fluid out. He also used a wide bore needle. It wasn't like he had to find the patient's vein, he knew they would all have at least one intravenous line established,

He returned the empty vials and the vent spike to the locker and secured it. Target number two was just a couple rooms away from the locker room, but first, he would make his was to the ICU.

He took a deep breath, blew it out and thought about his past. The memories gave him the strength he needed to do this. He opened the door looking quickly to the left and the right where the hallway ended just 40-50 feet away. To the left was the long corridor leading past the nurse's station which was situated in the middle of the length of the hallway. At the far other end, was the ICU.

He knew that walking the entire length of the hallway was out of the question. The risk of being seen was just too great. The stairwell was just on the other side of the locker room. From there he would go up to the third floor where being seen wouldn't be an issue. It would place him someplace other than the murder site thereby creating his alibi. He would walk slowly, greeting some of the staff, and then make his way to the opposite stairwell, the one that came out in the ICU on the second floor. He would need the code to the door but that didn't present a problem for him. He knew that the door would alarm when opened from the inside, but not when the code was entered from the stairwell.

Into the stairwell and up the stairs he went. Reaching the top, he opened the door and turned left. This end of the hall was pretty quiet. By this time, baths had been done and morning meds have been passed. Patient discharges would begin around 11am, after the doctors made their morning rounds.

Looking ahead, he could see a few of the staff gathered around the nurse's station. He couldn't yet make out who they were, but it was of little concern. "Good morning, folks!" His voice was friendly and relaxed. "How is everyone doing today?" There was a variety of responses; "good morning, sir, morning chief, good to see you." "Keep up the good work now, you hear?"

By this time, he was on the other side of the station and headed for the opposite stairwell. There were seldom other people in this stairwell because all the exit doors were alarmed, unless of course, you possessed the code.

He descended slowly down the stairs, catching his breath, and steeling his nerves. He checked his pocket one more time. This would not be the time to realize you forgot something. He paused for a moment at the door. Looking through the fire safety glass window, he was able to see straight down the main hallway of the ICU. He didn't see much activity. He checked his watch, 09:35. One nurse should be on her break. That left just two. After entering the four-digit code, he heard the lock release and quietly pulled the handle.

Chapter 75

Greg found his way to the security office. Just before he entered, his phone vibrated again. It was a number within the hospital. "Greg Webster."

"The Spider Webster from Union College?"

"Hi John, I didn't think you remembered." "How could I not remember, you're the reason I'm married!"

"Wait a minute, I'm responsible for the beer and pizza only, your marriage is your own fault!" They were both laughing.

"You're right, that's why I'm calling. Sara asked me, not true, Sara told me to bring you home for dinner. I don't really have to bring you, you can drive your own car, but I do need you to come. Sara will not take no for an answer, and I would love to have some time to chat."

"Oh John, I would love to but I'm up to my eyeballs in crap over here."

"When you say over here, I'm guessing you mean the hospital. Look, I get it, but what are you going to accomplish after seven o'clock? You'll be in that building all by yourself at that time. Come over here and we can figure it out together. What do you say?"

"You make a good point. Alright, seven it is. What can I bring? "

"Well, unless your wife is with you, all we need is you. Pizza and beer okay? Just kidding. We will see you at seven! Have a good day buddy!"

John was gone so Greg put the phone back in his pocket and entered the security office.

Chapter 76

The woman in the outer office greeted him, "what can I do you out of?"

Greg's sense of humor got the best of him. Smiling broadly, he replied, "I had a little run in with Officer Belden last night and I was told to speak with his supervisor. Would he be around?

He may be, and who do I have the pleasure of speaking with?"

"The name's Webster and investigatin' is my game." He tried to pull off a little western draw, but he fell short.

"Listen pardner, that was pretty awful. Does Webster have a first name, and a title maybe to go along with it?"

"Sure does ma'am." He handed her his card. He could see her face begin to flush as she read the information. "Don't sweat it honey, that was fun! What's your name?"

She smiled appreciatively as the color began to fade. I'm Sandy, Mr. Webster. Let me get Mr. Dillon for you."

"You Have got to be kidding me! Don't tell me, his first name is Matt."

"Nice try Mr. Webster, it's Bill.

Chapter 77

Room 2401 was the first door on his left. He approached slowly. The door was open. He peeked in through the-all glass front wall and saw his target, but no one else. He reached for his pocket as he walked into the room, retrieved his gloves, and put them on. Sharon Simmons was on a ventilator, age 40 with a post- surgical infection from a ruptured fallopian tube. The same state she had been in for a little over a week.

This was going to be tricky. He pulled the small syringe containing the lidocaine from his pocket. He uncapped the needle and set it on the bedside table. He did the same with the first syringe of propofol. He would need to disarm the IV pump first, then inject the lidocaine. While that was numbing her arm, he would turn the ventilator alarm off. Any oxygen reaching her lungs would counteract the propofol so he would also shut the ventilator down.

With the sequence all worked out in his head, he began. IV alarm off. He piggybacked the lidocaine in the IV, pinched the line and pushed. He recapped the syringe and put it in his other lab coat pocket. He turned off the alarm for the ventilator, uncapped the propofol and piggybacked it. He needed to push it fast so it could take effect quickly. Then, he could turn off the ventilator. If he turned off the ventilator first, the patient would try to breath on her own.

He started to push with one hand. After 10 seconds, he reached over with the other hand and shut down the ventilator. He recapped the syringe, placed it his pocket and headed back to the stairwell door. He punched in the code and opened it. Nobody saw him. He didn't know how long it would take before a nurse noticed anything wrong.

He knew all the ICU rooms had closed circuit TV so the nurse at the desk could watch each patient when necessary. He also knew this would not be a concern today. This time, he took the stairs down to the first floor. He paused while he pulled out his PDA and earplugs. "It looks like the post on Lorena Nunez is about to begin." He said to himself. He entered the code on the door and opened it. That was when he heard the code blue being announced.

Chapter 78

Bill Dillon was just the opposite of Officer Belden. He stood about 5 feet, six inches tall and couldn't weigh more than one-fifty. He appeared to be in his early sixties.

"Mr. Webster," he said, as he walked out of a door behind Sandy. "I'm Bill Dillon, head of security."

"Howdy Bill, Greg Webster. Nice to meet you. I appreciate your time."

"I think you already met Sandy."

"I sure did, she made me feel right at home."

"Are we talking about the same Sandy? This one right here?" She's usually as ornery as a junkyard dog."

He smiled and Sandy stuck out her tongue at him.

"I see you guys have a lot of fun around here. I like that."

"Oh, we can be serious enough when we need to, and I guess it's time we do just that. Come on into my office. How do you take you coffee?"

Before Greg could answer, he heard the code being called.

Bill said "4201 is ICU."

"Bill, don't ask questions, just show me the way there."

"Follow me" Bill Said, "we'll take the back stairs, it's only one flight up."

The two men reached the stairwell unaware that the killer had just come through the same door. They ascended.

Chapter 79

Maury had arrived at the second-floor nurses' station at 09:37. Lynette was sitting at the counter.

"Good morning, Maury" she greeted him, "You are almost on time!"

"Here we go" Maury said, under his breath. "Hey Lynette, what's up?" Before she could answer, the paging system was blaring out the code.

"Code Blue, room 4201; Code Blue, room 4201; Code Blue, room 4201."

ICU was just at the other end of the hall. Lynette shouted "we'll do this later" as she sprinted down the hall.

Maury waited just a moment, thinking. *"they're going to page me for a cart in about 30 minutes, I'll bet. I think I'll get a coffee first.* Before he left, he looked at the room assignment sheet for 4201. Female, age 40. Maury had work to do.

As he walked back toward the elevator, he crossed paths with several responders coming the other way. He just put his back against the wall and waited for the stampede to pass. Waiting by elevator, he thought he saw Barry Miller coming out of the stairwell at the end of the hall. The door opened and Maury stepped in.

Chapter 80

The killer had made his way all the way across the building on the first floor and back to the opposite stairwell. He didn't believe anyone noticed him. When he exited the stairwell on two, he took at left toward the locker room and entered 2104.

All the activity was down at the other end of the hall. He reached his destination, unnoticed. The target was in a private room. He entered and closed the door. "Ms. Meadows, I'm doctor Slater." He didn't know if she could hear him. Lacey Meadows was an accidental drug overdose. She was only 19 years old.

He walked to the far side of the bed, where the IV pump rested. He pulled on his gloves, removed the syringes from his pocket and set them on the bedside stand. The patient was still and breathing slowly. The IV bag was labeled with Ringer's with a propofol additive. He was aware that this was not uncommon, just a small, maintained dose to mildly sedate. Too much for too long could have detrimental long-term effects, but he didn't think she needed to worry about that.

He silenced the alarm on the pump and injected the small dose of lido-caine. Lacey didn't move. He then uncapped the large syringe, stuck it in the piggyback site nearest her wrist and began to push. Her eyes opened and she tried to take a deep breath. She was looking at him. He watched as her skin color changed and her eyes began to glaze over. He pulled the empty syringe, recapped it, and placed everything in his pocket.

After checking the IV to make sure it was still running, he walked toward the door. He opened it, checked for traffic, and moved one door down to the locker room. He unloaded his supplies, took off his lab coat and secured the locker. In the lavatory, he took a leak and washed his hands. He checked his PDA, Seike was well into his examination of Ms. Nunez. It was time to catch up with Alex Winfield.

Chapter 81

Greg and Bill Dillon raced up the steps to the second floor. Bill punched in the code, the lock released, and he pulled the handle. Just inside the door to the left, they could see a crowd gathering in room 2401. Greg recognized Richard Ingraham who appeared to be running the code. It looked like a well-oiled machine. Organized chaos.

The ECG tracing was flat except for the regular spikes coinciding with the external chest compressions. From outside the room, Greg couldn't really see the patient. There were too many people around the bed. He turned to Bill. "How do these stairwell doors work. I noticed you entered a code to release the lock." Bill confirmed with a head nod.

"These are emergency exits and are supposed to be for emergencies only. Each floor has two, one at each end. There is also an all-purpose stairway toward the middle of each floor, near the elevators where the doors are not locked." Greg took a moment to digest the information.

"If these doors are for emergencies, do you need to enter the code to get out?"

"No, that would violate the fire code. You would need the code to get back in on another floor though. Except of course for the first floor, where you should be going in case of a fire or other emergency." I see, said Greg.

"So, anyone can go out any of these doors, but they need the code to get back in."

"That's correct. However, each time the door is opened, an alarm will go off, unless you enter the code first. We discourage routine use of these exits so only certain staff would have the code."

"Okay," Greg said," would the alarm be audible here on the floor or in the security office?"

"It would be audible here. We would have a visual alarm in security. Basically, it's a light panel superimposed over the floor diagram. There is one for each floor."

While Greg was preparing his next question, he could hear Dr. Ingraham calling off the code.

"That's it everyone. I'm calling it. Time of death 10:05 am." Greg and Bill waited silently and watched as the staff began removing the equipment. When Richard came to the door, Greg approached him.

Richard, what happened here? "Hi Mr. Webster, Mr. Dillon. The patient was in full cardiac arrest when I arrived about 2 minutes after the code was called. The nursing staff had already begun CPR. We did what we could, but she was never able to maintain any rhythm on her own."

"Anything unusual about this one?" Greg inquired. "It's hard to say at this time, Greg. The only this I know now, is the nurse said the ventilator had been turned off when she arrived."

"That seems significant."

"Yes, it does. Listen, how about giving me an hour to do some paperwork and think this thing through, and I'll meet you for coffee. Call me in an hour."

"Of course. Thank you, Richard."

When Richard was gone, Greg stepped into the room and made an announcement. "Attention everyone. My name is Greg Webster and I'm with the New York State Department of Health. I am here under the full authority of the State and with the approval of your administrator. I ask that you do not touch the patient any further until I have an opportunity to examine the room and the patient. I'll need just 10 minutes, then you can return to your duties. Thank you."

"Bill, can you stay for a few minutes?"

"Be happy to."

Greg walked around the bed to the outdoor window side of the room. Here, the ventilator sat idle on the left side of the bed. There was also a bedside table. He walked back around the foot of the bed where the IV pump and waste backet were. Hanging on the bed rail on this side was a catheter bag. He looked at the bag containing the patient's urine.

The urine appeared to be green. "Probably just the light" he thought to himself.

He put on some gloves and looked through the waste basket which was nearly full of the discarded wrappers of all the syringes and needles, alcohol prep pads and gauze, etc. He didn't see anything suspicious. He looked at the whiteboard at the foot end wall. There was the patient's name along with her doctor's name, nurses name, the date and day of the week.

"Sharon Simmons, age 40" he said to Bill. "So young. Bill, why do you suppose her ventilator was turned off? And the nurse was apparently surprised by that."

"I'm not really a clinical person, Mr. Webster. I wouldn't really know the first thing about that. Now, a mechanical malfunction, I may be able to help with but that doesn't seem to be the case."

"You know about mechanical things Bill?' How does that equate to security?"

"I worked 10 years in the maintenance department before they offered me the job in security. Back then, we did many of the minor repairs in house. Today, they have outside contractors for all that stuff. They say it's cheaper in the long run, but I'm not so sure."

"I would tend to agree with you Bill."

"Code Blue room 2104; Code Blue room 2104, Code Blue room 2104."

"Other end of this floor," Bill said hurriedly. "Follow me!"

Chapter 82

Barry Miller entered the administrative suite and walked right to Alex's door. On the way by Kathy's desk, he gave her a wink. He opened the door without waiting for an invitation.

"Alex, I hear you've been looking for me."

"I'll call you back" Alex said to someone and hung up the phone. "Where in Hell have you been? Kathy's been trying to reach you for two hours!" Alex was really pissed.

"Well, for starters, I've been working on that homework assignment you gave me at the eleventh hour. Aside from that, I had a few errands to run. It sounds like you have bigger trouble going on right now."

"What are you talking about?"

"What am I talking about? You have more blue light specials going on than Walmart! What are all these codes about lately?"

"I'll be God damned if I know," Alex replied. "What I do know is it's the last fucking thing I needed today, especially with the board meeting coming up this afternoon. On top of that, this Webster guy from the State is going to be crawling up my ass about it."

"What are you going to do?"

"There's nothing I can do. He's going to insist on strengthening his investigation and he's already threatened to bring in the CDC, EPA and even the FBI."

"Why the FBI? Does he think something criminal is going on?"

"Barry, people are dropping dead left and right, Young people! He doesn't know what to think. Hell, I don't know what to think."

"What does he know? Does he have any evidence at all of criminal acts?"

"As of the last time we spoke, no. But he doesn't need evidence to bring in the CDC, he can just make a call and they'll come running."

"Okay, so what? They come running, do a few tests, look at a few records, don't find anything just like he can't find anything, and they go home."

"It will be in the newspapers, on the TV for crying out loud! That's so what!"

"Alex, let me have a chat with him. Perhaps I can persuade his to move a little more slowly."

"What makes you think you can do that if I can't?"

"Because Alex, I'm me and you are, well, you're you. Look, you have a way of getting a little over excited, a bit defensive. It's going to take somebody calm, cool, collected. Just let me have fifteen minutes with the guy. What harm can it do?"

"Yeah sure. Anything to get him off my ass for a few minutes."

Chapter 83

Seike and Jim had just heard the second code blue of the morning being called. "What is going on?" Jim said. Kyle Seike had his arms inside the open cavity of Lorena Nunez's abdomen.

"It's a hospital Jim, it's not the first time there's been more than one code in a day, and I'm sure it won't be the last. It could mean we're going to have a busy week though, are you up to it?"

"Of course, I'm up to it, I just hope these patients aren't as young as what we've had lately. Hitting a little close to home, That's all."

"Think of how I feel!" Kyle responded.

"You should feel relieved, you're way older than any of them" Jim said jokingly.

"Funny my boy, now hand me some tools for getting fluid samples." Seike had been at it for almost an hour now and was close to being done. Obtaining some specimens for the lab was about the last step before closing the body.

Jim handed him a variety of vials, cups, and syringes. "Jim, while I'm working on these, print some labels and leave them on the counter over there. I'll finish up here while you take your morning break. We had an early start today and I'm sure you're ready for some breakfast."

"I'm good Doc, we only have another twenty minutes or so."

"I'm aware Jim but there's nothing much you can do to help me until I'm done here. By the time you're back, she'll be ready to be moved off the table. I insist."

"Alright then." Jim was confused but he wasn't going to argue. Seike has always won every argument and Jim knew it was a waste of time to continue trying. "I'll be back in twenty, can I bring you anything?"

"No thank you, young man. I am fine for the time being."

Jim removed his gloves and apron, walked over to the stainless-steel utility sink, and washed his hands and arms thoroughly. Then, he was off to the cafeteria.

As soon as he was gone, Kyle degloved, put on a fresh pair, walked over to his briefcase, and retrieved the replacement samples that would be sent to the lab. He placed the real samples back in the briefcase, closed and locked it and returned it to its place. Now, he was free to place the bag containing Lorena's organs back in her abdomen, tie off the carotid and femoral arteries for the mortician and close the incision.

Chapter 84

Maury was almost right, it was closer to forty minutes, but he did get the call to bring up the morgue cart. The call came while he was taking his break of course. It was a short walk from the cafeteria to the morgue. He knocked on the morgue door. "Yes, come in." It was Dr. Seike's voice.

Maury opened the door. "Ah, Mr. Slater, what brings you here this fine morning?"

"Hey doc, I need the transport cart to make a pickup. I thought I'd try knocking before going up to get the key. You know, one less trip."

"I do indeed know of which you speak. Help yourself, as you can see, I'm just finishing up with this young lady." Maury looked at the corpse lying on the steel table. Dr. Seike was rinsing her body with the flexible hose mounted above the body. He could see the large sutures or staples in the shape of a Y on her chest and abdomen. This did not look like the same girl he felt yesterday. Her skin was a pale grey. Autopsy changes a person he thought, and then laughed inside at the absurdity of it.

"Are you going to stand there and stare or get the cart." Seike said.

"Right. Sorry doc. Caught me off guard." He moved toward the cooler room.

"Surely, you've seen your share of dead people, have you not? Between the funeral home and here, I'm sure you've seen dozens if not hundreds." Seike questioned him.

"Yes, I've seen plenty, more than enough actually. It seems different somehow. I can't explain it."

"No need to Maury, it's alright. It still catches me off guard occasionally. Not an easy business. I remember the first time a cadaver raised his arms. Frightened the daylights out of me even though I was fully aware of the science behind it and the possibility of it happening. Go about your business young man, I'm sure someone is waiting for you."

Maury retrieved the cart and headed toward ICU. He passed Jim Larkin in the hallway. "Incoming?" Jim Asked.

"You got it." Maury replied. "Hey Jim, are you going to be here when I come back in say, fifteen minutes? If you are, I could use a hand getting her in the cooler. I may need the cart again today."

"I should be here. It will take me at least that long to clean up."

"Excellent! See you in a few."

Chapter 85

Déjà vu. Room 2104 was the same scene, with the same people that Greg and Bill saw just twenty minutes ago. Richard Ingraham was in charge here as well. Meds were being delivered, chest compressions were being administered, a male nurse or perhaps a respiratory therapist was pumping life-sustaining air via an Ambu bag. The noise was disharmonious and agitating, and people were running in and out of the room.

"People!" Ingraham shouted above the din." "Let's act quietly and quickly but controlled. When was she found like this?"

"The nurse's aide found her at 10:02." One of the nurses stated. "And before that, when was she last seen?" Ingraham wanted to know. The nurse holding the patient's chart stated "the last rounding on this patient was documented at 09:45. A routine check for input and output. The patient was asleep and breathing normally."

"Alright, let me have sone epi and a syringe with a long needle." She could have stopped breathing up to seventeen minutes ago, but her color still looks okay. Keep going with the CPR."

At that, Richard Ingraham picked his spot between the ribs and made the injection into the heart. A few had seconds passed when he said, "stop compressions." He looked up at the monitor and felt for a femoral pulse. He thought he felt something, but it was very weak. The ECG tracing verified that there was some activity, but faint and irregular.

"Let's have the paddles." Some moved the defibrillator cart closed to the head of the bed. A nurse applied the conductive gel to one paddle, then rubbed them together. She then handed the paddles to Dr. Ingraham. "Charge to 300." He watched as the needle on the gauge moved to 300 joules. "Everyone clear!" The staff surrounding the bed all took a small step back, making sure they were not in contact with any of the bed frame or the patient. Click, thud. Lacey's body rose off the sheet as if drawn to a magnet. Everything was still, while Richard watched the monitor. There was a faint tracing, but still no rhythm.

"Once more!" he ordered. "400 this time." The nurse adjusted the output to 400 joules. Clear!" Click, thud. Again, the body lifted. Again, Richard looked up at the monitor. Several seconds passed. There was a moderate increase in the activity of the young girl's heart. She was holding her own rhythm.

"Alright, we may be back in the game here!" Richard said with a little enthusiasm." Let me have a number 9 endotracheal tube, a laryngoscope and somebody call for a respirator. I want a liter of D5W with added sodium bicarb." People began moving quickly. "Oh, someone get the family on the phone for me."

Chapter 86

Greg and Bill had arrived at room 2104 at the beginning of the code. Richard Ingraham had arrived at the same time. They watched in awe as Dr. Ingraham took control of the room and orchestrated a miraculous retrieval of a soul bound for the outer limits. Greg looked on intently at all the different players and their roles, making mental notes of things he would need to follow up on later.

"Hey Bill," Greg said, "I'm going to stay here for a few minutes, but I'd like to ask if you would mind helping me? "

"Whatever I can do, Mr. Webster. I am at your disposal."

"Thank you, Bill. I would like you to begin checking any security footage you have for the last week, both inside and outside the facility. Take note of anyone you see more than once during that time. Also, if you have security logs for the rounds made that week, that may be helpful as well. I'll catch up with you later today but I'm not sure when, I'm already hours behind on my schedule."

"No Trouble, I'll stay as long as you need me."

Greg stayed behind, hoping to get a few minutes with Richard Ingraham. The room was quieting down now that the patient seemed to be somewhat stabilized. Ingraham was still there, along with a nurse, the respiratory therapist and me. Richard was checking completing one more evaluation of the patient. When finished, he came over to Greg.

"Have you seen enough of these to join or response team?"

"I know I've seen two more than I ever thought I would!" Greg answered.

"Walk with me Greg. Page me if anything changes" he said to no one in particular.

The men left Lacey Meadows to the remaining care team. Greg followed Richard to a small private room behind the nurse's station. There were two young women wearing scrubs sitting at a small round table. "Good morning, ladies, Ingraham greeted them, may we have the room for a few minutes please?" The women just stood and left, no conversation.

"What do think Richard?" Greg opened. Ingraham had his elbows on the table with his hands pushing back through his hair repeatedly.

"I don't know what to think. I do know that I can't keep up this pace." Richard seemed tired, beaten. Six young people in less than a week, Greg. Something is not right.

"I agree. Does this feel like the same thing as the others? The same vagueness?"

"On the surface, yes." Richard replied. "No outward reason for their deaths, but not entirely the same. The woman in ICU has been on the respirator for a while, which can by itself, cause complications. This last young girl was an attempted suicide so who knows what could have happened. There is however, one commonality between them."

Greg was cautiously excited. He didn't let it show, but inside, he was. "What would that be?"

"It is probably nothing, but both of these women were receiving small maintenance doses of propofol."

Greg thought for a moment. "Propofol, isn't that an anesthesia medication?"

"That's right Greg, it's actually the preferred anesthetic. It doesn't last too long, not many short-term side effects and the patient makes up pretty easily and quickly. On top of that, it's readily available and inexpensive." When used for quick, minimally invasive procedures, there is no need for additional anesthetic agents, like gases."

"It sounds like the perfect drug. How is it related here, Richard?"

'In addition to its value for surgical procedures, it is also used for patients on ventilators because it keeps them sedated enough to not want to breath on their own. Hence, less fighting against the ventilator."

"So, that explains Sharon Simmons. What's the connection with Lacey?"

"Excellent question. You see, propofol, in low doses, can also be used to treat anxiety. Lacey was being treated for post-suicide anxiety. Manage the anxiety, save the patient. Sometimes."

"Sometimes?" Greg dug a little deeper.

"Yes. There can be long term serious side effects with continued use. These can range from kidney disease to total organ failure and death."

"Do you think that could have happened here, Richard?"

"Without toxicology reports, we wouldn't know for sure," but I do know that Sharon's output, her urine, was green."

"Richard, I thought I noticed that too. I tried to blame it on the reflection of the light in the room."

"Amateur mistake Greg. Just kidding. With a large dose of propofol, the liver can't clear the chemicals fast enough, so the kidneys try to excrete them. The result can be green urine. Get a big dose at once, it's lights out for good."

"Richard, if you can make sure some samples are sent to the State lab, I can call and have the analysis and result expedited."

"I can have the lab draw Lacey right now. If we catch Sharon

Simmons' body, we can draw that too. Hey, speaking of results, have you received any from the other patients?"

"I'm glad you asked" said Greg, I received a call from my buddy at the lab. He said the results were all normal, but he also said they were all the same."

Richard looked confused. "What do you mean all the same?"

"That's what I said. I was told that it appears all the samples were from the same donor. I offered to check with the lab here, on my end. In fact, I was in the laboratory first thing this morning but then all hell broke loose."

"It sure did. It sounds like a labeling foul up to me. If that's the case, were screwed on the others unless the laboratory here has a backup."

"Backup? Does that happen."

"Sometimes. The lab will often hold a specimen for a couple days just in case an ordering physician wants to add a test to the panel. For example, I order a CBC for a patient and one of the results comes back low or elevated. Now, I may need a more specific test that breaks down one of the superficial, categorical tests that I ordered in the first place. If the lab still has the specimen and it is still within the window of viability, they can run the test without having to draw the patient again."

"That's great!" Greg exclaimed. "Now I know what questions to ask when I meet with the lab." Just then the door opened, and a nurse walked in.

"Dr. Ingraham, I have the family of Lacey Meadows on line two."

"Greg, I need to take this."

"Of course. Thank you, Richard, I'll let you know what I find out."

Chapter 87

Maury was on his way to 2401 with the morgue cart. As he passed by the desk, Lynette came out to meet him. "Hi, Lynette."

"Mr. Slater, keep walking, I'll go with you to pack up Mrs. Simmons."

"Okay, thanks Lynette. Hey, you wanted to speak to me before. What's up?"

"Oh right. Yeah, I just has a question for you, but I already found the answer. Thanks anyway Maury!"

They continued down to 2401. The room had been cleaned except for where the bed was. The furniture had been moved out of the way and the body was already wrapped. As they were about to move Mrs. Simmons on to the gurney, an aide came through the door. "Lynette, Dr. Ingraham would like fifty milliliters of blood drawn from Sharon before she is taken away."

"Did he say what for?" Lynette inquired.

"He didn't give any details, he just one fifty ml. vacutainer would be sufficient."

"Okay, thanks. Alright Maury, we need to unwrap her again."

Maury could feel himself getting a little excited. It always felt like a striptease when he first unwrapped a corpse. They found the end of the wrap which was under Sharon's left shoulder. They pulled to untuck the plastic, but they needed to turn her on her side to free her arm. With another quarter turn of the sheeting, her left arm was bare. Along with her left breast. Maury could feel a sudden rise.

Lynette caught Maury staring at Sharon's breast. "Hey Maury, do you know what necrophilia is?"

Maury felt his temperature rising a little. Embarrassment, guilt? He couldn't tell.

"I worked in the death business for a lot of years Lynette. I'm familiar with it."

"Can you believe that men actually have sex with dead people?"

"Well, from what I've heard, it's not just men. I've heard stories from people who should know that women have sex with dead men as well. Been going on for hundreds of years too."

"How is that even possible? I mean how is intercourse possible with a dead guy?"

"Are you familiar with rigor mortis, Lynette? It can happen."

"Well, I've never seen it and I've wrapped a lot of dead men in my time." Lynette snapped back.

"How long after death are you wrapping them?"

Lynette thought about her answer. "I would say twenty to forty minutes, usually."

"Well, that's the problem, visible signs of rigor usually don't show up for three to six hours, depending on the temperature."

"So, you're saying that after being dead for three hours, a guy can have an erection?"

"I'm saying that all muscles experience rigor at some point. No telling which muscles when, but eventually, yes."

Maury was enjoying this now. He actually knew more than Lynette about this topic. This was the first time he felt smart in front of her. It may be the first he felt smart, period. "It works its way down Lynette, starts with the eyelids, facial muscles, neck, etc. Full rigor can take a day or more. that's why embalmers prefer to get the body asap, it's a lot less work for them when they begin the process before full rigor sets in."

"This is very interesting Maury! You seem to know a lot about it."

"If you're around enough, you can't help but learn."

"Have you ever done it Maury?" Now he was getting nervous. *Was she truly interested, like double date interested or just fishing like "give me some rope to hang you with?"*

"Have I ever done what, Lynette?"

"You know, slept with a cadaver?"

"Gee Lynette, I lived in a mortuary! I've slept with hundreds of cadavers! If you're asking if I had sex with any of them, the answer is no." He wasn't angry, he wasn't loud. Just covering his tracks.

"Well, that's too bad! I would have thought it cool if you had, you know, had sex with them." Maury thought she genuinely looked disappointed.

"Are you just screwing around with me Lynette? Trying to catch me at something else you and your friends can use to make fun of me? If you are, I'm done playing this game."

"I swear Maury, I really find the topic, and you, interesting. As for my so-called friends, I have never joined with them in making fun of you. I may have questioned you about your tardiness, but that's all. I'm sorry if I ever hurt you."

She looked like she may cry. Maury felt awful. "I'm sorry too Lynette. I guess I'm not used to someone being nice to me." Now they both looked sad.

"Maury, can we go out for coffee sometime?" Maury couldn't find his voice.

"Really Lynette? You would go out with me? I mean, have coffee with me?" Lynette met his eyes,.

"I think it would be nice, so yes, I would like to go out with you. That's why I asked you to come up earlier. I was going to ask you out but then everything went crazy and when I finally saw you, I lost my nerve."

"Can we do it soon Lynette? I mean, can we go out soon?

"I knew what you meant Maury" she said with a girlish grin, how about tonight? Maybe a burger and fries instead of coffee?"

"That sounds great Lynette. Can I pick you up somewhere?"

"How about meeting at the park downtown at six o'clock? I'll be on the bench by the statue."

"Awesome. I'll see you there." Lynette had collected her sample and was pulling the plastic back over the body. "One last look before I finish Maury?" She gave him a flirty smile.

"No thanks, I'm too excited already!"

Maury wheeled the cart out the door and down the corridor toward the elevator.

Chapter 88

Greg was on his way to the lab once more. He had two questions that needed answering. How does a labeling error happen? And do they keep backup specimens? When he was at the entrance to the lab, his phone vibrated. It was John Shand.

"Good morning, John."

John could tell he was flustered. "Hi Greg, are you alright?

"Sure, I'm fine. Why do you ask/"

"You just didn't sound like yourself. Rough night?"

"No, my night was fine, more like a rough morning. Two more patients coded this morning, about a half hour apart. One died."

"Oh Greg, that is a rough morning. Anyone I know?"

"Both were on the second floor, one in ICU and one in room 2104."

"2104, is that the young girl, Meadows?"

"That's the one, John, the one in ICU was Simmons."

"I'm familiar with them both Greg. The Simmons woman was post-surgical complications, the Meadows girl, Lacey, I think, tried to do herself in. I was on the night they brought her in. I thought she was doing well."

"By all accounts, she was, until this morning. I was at both codes. Bill Dillon and I were meeting in his office to talk about security when the first code was called. He took us up the back way to ICU. We watched the team try to revive her, but it was no use. They no sooner pronounced her dead, when the second code was called at the other end of the hallway. We raced down there and arrived at the same time as the response team. Richard Ingraham was at both. He and his team did a remarkable job bringing this young girl back from the brink."

"Listen Greg, I want to hear about everything but I'm in the middle of morning office hours and I need to get back. We're still on for tonight, right?"

Greg paused. With all the excitement already this morning, he had forgotten about dinner with John and Sara. "Oh man, I'm not sure John, I mean, I would love to, but I have no idea what the rest of this day holds for me. I only know that I'm already two hours behind."

"Greg, I know this sounds counter-productive to you but You're going to need to eat, and a few minutes away may give you a fresh perspective. Besides, Sara really wants to see you. What do you say?"

"I always thought she liked me better," Greg said. "Alright, it's a date."

"Terrific Greg. I promise we'll only keep you as long as you feel you can be here. I'll talk to you later." He was gone.

Greg didn't even have time to place his phone back in his pocket before it began buzzing again. "Greg Webster."

"Hi Mr. Webster, this is Kathy from Mr. Winfield's office." Greg could feel his spirit lift. He remembered how nice she looked the last time he saw her. She was back to calling him Mr. Webster, perhaps he lost some ground.

"Hi Kathy, how can I help you?

"Mr. Miller has asked me to set up an appointment with you. He was wondering if you could meet him in his office this afternoon around 4:00pm."

"I'm sorry Kathy, who is Mr. Miller again?"

"Barry Miller is our Chief Financial Officer and our Chief Operating Officer."

Greg wasn't connecting the dots. "He must be one busy guy. What is the nature of this meeting, Kathy?"

"He wasn't specific about the topic but I'm sure it has something to do with your investigation. As COO, he is in charge of most of the departments you have been questioning. Perhaps he would like an update on your progress? I'm just guessing really."

"It may be difficult getting together today, there has been a lot going on and I'm already several meetings behind schedule. Could you please let him know that I will try to make it? Could you also give me a call around three? I'll let you know if I've caught up enough to break away."

"That sounds like a plan Greg. I'll call you at three. Thank you!"

"Thank you, Kathy." Back on a first name basis, Greg thought. Now, if he could just get through that laboratory door. He put his phone in his pocket and pulled the handle.

Greg stepped to the counter, introduced himself and asked to speak with Lenore.

"I'm Lenore" the young lady said.

"Hi Lenore, I am so happy to finally meet you!" She looked at him like he was crazy. Loretta had told Lenore that the inspector from the health department wanted to speak with her, so it wasn't a surprise, but she didn't expect him to be so happy about it. Or for that matter, happy period.

"It's just that I have tried walking through that door all morning, but

I've been interrupted multiple times. Anyway, is there a place we can sit for a few minutes, maybe grab some coffee?"

"I haven't had my break yet this morning" she replied, "would you like to go to the cafeteria?"

"That would be perfect, I'll even buy, he offered."

"Allow me to let someone know I'm leaving, and I'll meet you right out in the hall." She said as she walked away.

Greg exited into the hallway and waited with his back to the wall. Looking left from the laboratory, he could see the security office and beyond that, the cafeteria. To his right and down the hall a way, he saw the entrance to the morgue. At the end of the corridor, was the exit door to the loading dock that he heard close that night.

"Here I am. Are you ready?"

"Lead the way, Lenore." Greg and Lenore started to walk off toward the cafeteria when he heard a door close, down the hall behind him. He turned to see a young man in a white lab coat leaving the morgue.

"Hey Lenore, do you who that man is?"

"Yes, that is Maury." She said it like everyone would know that.

"He is an um" she paused, trying to find the word. "I don't know what his title is. Maybe an aide? Patient escort perhaps?"

"Does he also assist in the morgue, like Jim Larkin?" Greg inquired.

"To my knowledge, his only role in the morgue is to bring the bodies of patients who expire down there." Lenore answered as they rounded the corner into the cafeteria.

Greg and Lenore went through the line. He placed a blueberry muffin and two empty coffee cups on the tray that they shared. Lenore asked for scrambled eggs, bacon, and a slice of unbuttered toast. When they reached the cashier, Greg paid as promised. They proceeded to the coffee center and filled their cups after which Lenore led them to a table near the back, where it was less congested.

"Thank you for breakfast, Mr. Webster. You didn't have to do that."

"It was my pleasure, Lenore." He smiled and she reciprocated. She was young, about twenty-four or five he guessed, and quite pretty, in a young and innocent way. "Did Loretta tell you what I wanted to speak to you about?"

"Yes, she said it had to do with the death of Lorena Nunez."

"That's correct. But I'm also looking at some other unexplained deaths, including one this morning. Anyway, based on the time stamps for collection, processing and resulting Lorena's last draw, I believe you may have been the last person to see her alive." He left a little dead space before he continued. He could see she felt a little nervous. "Don't worry you are not implicated in this at all. I just wanted to know if you noticed anything unusual about the situation and if you could tell me what condition she was in, and or what her mental status was."

Lenore was measuring her response. Well, I didn't notice anything unusual. She was alone, alert and seemed very happy to have her baby. She was having some abdominal discomfort, but it didn't seem severe during the time I was with her, which was just a few minutes."

"Did the two of you converse?"

"I introduced myself as I always do, told her why I was there, assured her it wouldn't hurt, and I told her how beautiful I thought her baby girl was. She responded, and I remember this vividly,

"She is a gift, and I will give her the life I never had."

Lenore paused and let her head drop forward just a little, shielding her eyes from Greg.

"It's okay, Lenore, I'm sure this is difficult for you."

"It's just not right, she was so young and what will become of her baby now?"

"I agree with you and I'm not sure what will happen to the baby. My guess is they will try to find the father, or a blood relative. If they are unsuccessful, the baby will most likely be placed in foster care until an adoption can be arranged."

Trying to change the subject a bit, Greg said, "Lenore, I was hoping you could tell me about the proper procedure for labeling collection tubes and specimen cups. More specifically, how could they be mislabeled? Again, nothing you did wrong and no direct correlation to this case. Just a general curiosity."

"I guess there could be several ways for that to happen although I think it's rare. The process begins at patient registration. Every visit, whether inpatient or outpatient, generates a unique registration number. For inpatients, that number will remain the same for the entire stay. Outpatients are issued a new number each visit."

"Lenore, is this number randomly generated by the system.?"

"It's not random, but it automatically assigns the next sequential number. The system will not allow the issuance of duplicate numbers."

"So, this in an account number and not a patient specific number."

"Yes and no. It is an account number but specifically liked to that patient by cross reference to the patient's profile. The system looks for date of birth, gender, address, and social security number if applicable. This is all done behind the scenes. For example, the SS number does not display every time an account is pulled up."

"Okay, I'm with you so far. What happens on the lab side once the patient is registered? In this case, let's make it specific to inpatients."

"When the order is placed in the computer on the floor, that order flows from the nursing module to the lab module. At this point, it shows up on our to do list. It tells us the name and location, as well as the tests ordered. Each test, or group of tests require a specific number of tubes to be drawn of each size and color."

Greg paused just a moment to make sure he was going to phrase the next question correctly. "So, each tube size is based on the test being ordered. One may require a 3ml tube and another, a 5 or 10ml tube?"

"That's correct. The color refers to the rubber stopper at the top of the tube. The difference is mostly determined by the additive within the tube. Each test may require a unique protocol. Some require a preservative. Some require spinning in a centrifuge. Other require immediate refrigeration.

Having the system tell us how many of each color tube is required, the phlebotomist, the one doing the collection doesn't need to calculate all that. We just grab the right number of tubes and head off for the collection."

"And that brings us to labels" Greg steered her toward a conclusion.

"You know where you're going, who the patient is and what collection equipment to bring. What's next?"

"Once we've reviewed the information in the system, we send a command for labels to be printed. We will receive one printed label for each tube required. The label will specify the date, patient name, account number and ordering physician. Once the labels are printed, we place them in our collection basket that we take to the floor. When we arrive, we ask the patient their name and date of birth. We then scan the bracelet that the patient was given on admission to verify we have the correct one."

"Then you apply the labels to the tubes." Greg interjected.
"Not yet," Lenore replied. We draw the patient's blood. Once all tubes are filled, we label them."

"Why not label them before?" He quizzed her.

"Because shit happens." Greg found that funny coming from her, and he chuckled. "These tubes are very reliable, but not perfect. Every now and then, one malfunctions, usually due to the tube losing is vacuum. If we already labeled it, we would be short one label, which means a trip to the nurse's station to reprint the label or worse, a trip back to the lab. We are not going to stick the patient twice, so we draw an extra tube and label it later. That creates a point of failure, and we don't like that."

"I don't like that either," Greg said.

"Lenore, did everything go smoothly the day you collected Lorena's blood?"

"Yes, perfectly."

"What about labs drawn in other departments? Does it work the same way?"

"It should. In order for a result to flow back to the ordering physician or department, the information needs to be entered in the same manner, through the ordering module."

"You did a great job explaining that Lenore! I have one final question for you. Are you familiar with backup specimens?"

"I am. We sometimes hold surplus blood for 24 to 48 hours to avoid having to redraw a patient if the doctor wants to add a test. It also comes in handy if a tube is dropped and shatters or the specimen is compromised somehow."

"Give me an example of how a specimen becomes compromised."

"Most of the time, the reason is temperature related. Perhaps it was not placed in the fridge right away or sometimes the courier is late with specimens from one of our offsite clinics. They use coolers with ice when they transport, but if they're caught in one of our famous snowstorms, the cooler cannot be relied upon to accurately maintain the proper temp."

"Where do you see yourself in five years? Ten? Do you aspire for greater things?"

"I think about it. I'm still young and I really love what I do, but I don't see myself here ten years from now. Maybe I'll work at the health department someday," she said jokingly, "you never know."

"If there is ever anything I can do to help you, don't hesitate to call me. I mean it," he said as he handed her his card. "Does forensics interest you at all? I have connections there."

"Something to think about." She said." I had better head back before I lose the job I have," she smiled.

"Not while I'm here." Greg reached out to shake her hand.

Taking his she said, "you're pretty cool for a health department inspector."

"Thank you, Lenore. I think you're pretty cool as well. As they stood to leave, Greg realized that spending just a few minutes with someone like that can change your outlook on life. At least for a while.

Greg was heading to security when his pocket buzzed. He pulled the phone out and looked at the screen. Home office calling.

"Greg Webster," he answered.

"How is your affair going out there, Greg? Is she pretty? Tall? Redhead?"

"Good morning, Christine. Did you just describe yourself? If so, you left out a few things, but I'm not going to say them on the phone. You never know when the governor is listening."

"Well, you'll just have to whisper them to me the next time you're here. When is that going to be, by the way?"

"Not soon enough, I'm afraid. The bodies are piling up faster than I can count."

"Sounds serious, Greg. I had better put the boss on the line. I enjoy the sexual banter but now, you're a bit of a downer." Hold on while I transfer you.

"Hey Spider, how's the fishing out there? Caught any of those big, scary carp that haunt the Mohawk?"

"You're a funny guy, Tom. Ever think about leaving the department for stand up?"

"And leave you? Never! In all seriousness, how is it going?"

"It's getting worse, Tom. I feel like I'm stuck in a run-on chapter in a novel. No end in sight."

"Tell me about it, Greg. More deaths?"

"Another one this morning, I thought it was going to be two, but they brought the other one back. Ages 40 and 19. That makes 5 people under age 58 and those are just the ones we know about! I witnessed both codes this morning. I can say that I am impressed with the emergency response team. They seem to be doing a great job."

"Every dark cloud. Isn't that what they say?"

"Sure, that's what they say until the dark cloud turns into a tornado. I planned a full day of interviews today, but the codes have set me a couple hours behind."

"Well, I don't want to stand in the way of progress, not that it sounds like you're making much."

"You just can't help yourself. Can you?"

"I do what I can, Greg. Trying to keep it light. Holler if you need anything."

"Thanks Tom. Hey, can you transfer me over to Russ Lang in the lab?"

"What, I'm your secretary now? I need to start wearing short skirts and making coffee?"

"Oh thanks, now I have to live with that image in my head! Hey, don't talk like that in front of Christine, she keeps a knife in her desk draw."

"She showed it to me, several times already. Hold on, I'll get you over to the lab." Greg could hear Tom yelling, "Christine! How do I transfer this call?

Greg couldn't keep from smiling. He had a great boss.

"Forensics, Russ speaking."

"Good morning, Russ."

"Hey Spider, I'm glad you called. I have something!"

Greg could feel a nervous excitement in the pit of his stomach. "Excellent, let's have it."

"Well, it's not really something yet, but it could be soon."

Letdown. What a day!

"How about you tell me what you don't have?"

"Okay, but first, tell what you found about the labeling. Any explanation for the uncanny similarities of the specimens?"

"Not yet Russ. I did get the lowdown on the procedures, and I must say, they are pretty tight. Accidental mislabeling doesn't sound likely. I have some other ideas that I'm trying to work through. I just need the time. So, what about you?"

"Nothing further on the blood, I still think they all came from the same donor. However, the breast pad you sent me directly may be turning up something. We noticed some odd compounds in the patient's secretions. We know that there is an oil-based component involved. The other chemical analysis may take a while. It could be medications the patient was given but we don't have the breakdown yet."

"It sounds like it has potential though, right? Could the oil be of a topical nature, like nipple cream?"

"Sure, it could be. Once we break down the actual chemical ingredients, we'll know. Maybe another few days."

"Any way to put a rush on it? I know you're already skipping this ahead of other projects, but I have very few solid leads here and the numbers keep going up. By the way, you will be receiving some new samples for another patient, actually, two patients. You should receive those by the end of the day. They are labs drawn on two patients who experienced cardiac arrest just minutes apart. One succumbed, but the other was resuscitated. I'm looking for similarities. Both were on a maintenance dose of an anesthetic called propofol at the time of arrest. Are you familiar with it, Russ?"

"I'm familiar with the name Greg, I can't say that I've had any direct experience with it. I'll look into it though."

"Thanks, Russ. Let me know if you have a breakthrough on the pad. If I have anything else for you, I'll call."

Greg hung up the phone, put it back in his pocket and took a deep breath. He had no reason to feel any closer to a discovery, yet deep down, he had a feeling he could only describe as hope.

Chapter 89

Maury was on cloud eight, or was it nine? Whatever cloud people go to when they're really happy, he was there. He had a new spring in his step and a strange feeling deep inside.

When he arrived at the morgue after leaving Lynette, Jim was there to help him move the body off the cart and into the cooler. "What's the story with this one?' Jim asked.

"A forty-year-old lady in ICU bought the farm, I guess. Almost had another one at the other end of the hall just a few minutes later. They brought her back."

"It's nice to win one now and again." Jim said.

"It sure is Jim, it sure is."

"Maury, are you alright? You seem different, happy."

"I guess I am Jim. Not something I'm really accustomed to. Feels kind of good!"

"Well, I'm happy for you, Maury. Everyone deserves happiness, I guess. You tend to forget, especially working in this department."

"You've got that right, Jim, dead people don't make the best company. Although sometimes, that's all the company I need. Alright, I will be on my way. I appreciate your help, Jim. Catch you later."

Maury walked out into the hallway and headed toward the cafeteria. He thought about Mrs. Simmons in the morgue. She looked good and the timing was ok. He could surely find a taker in his little black book. Not tonight, I have a date.

Chapter 90

"What do you mean, he may or may not meet me?" I'm the COO, not some pissant he can turn his back on, this is my hospital." Barry was not quite calm, cool, or collected as usual.

"I'm sorry Mr. Miller, I'm just passing on what he said. It appears he is running behind today. Off to a bad start, I guess."

"Alright Kathy, I apologize, I didn't intend to take it out on you. I guess we are all under a tremendous amount of stress right now. By the way, did you have a chance to talk to him?"

"Not yet. He stopped by early this morning, and I think I grabbed his attention but then he was off and running. I was planning to give him a call a little later, see if I could entice him in a little lunch, so to speak."

"Yes, clever idea. We need to find out what he knows. Working together, we should be able to do just that. I'll be over around 2:30 to get ready for the meeting. Please make sure I.T. has a projector ready in the board room for me."

"I'm on it." Kathy said and hung up.

From the privacy of his office, the killer just finished watching the scene from the morgue. He couldn't believe what he saw, and he knew he had to find a way to stop it. Something or someone was distracting Maury. He needed to find out what or who.

Chapter 91

Greg was chatting with Sandy in security, waiting for Bill Dillon to show up. He didn't have an appointment, so he wasn't upset about waiting, besides, Sandy was a hoot.

"So, when d'you spose Marshall Dillon'll be gittin back?" Greg said with his best western drawl. "Did he need to run over to the OK Corral to stop a shootout?"

"I think you have your westerns mixed up, Mr. Webster." Besides, Marshall Dillon just went to the local watering hole to wet his whistle. He should be pretnear back by now." She mimicked his attempt.

Bill walked in. "Howdy Marshall!" Greg yelled out. "Where you figure a man can find a spittoon roun' these here parts?"

"You're an odd one, Webster."

"Hey, it's her fault," he said, looking around at Sandy, she started it."

Bill just shook his head and walked into his office. Greg followed him in.

"Did you find anything Sheriff?" Greg asked.

"Which is it now Greg, Marshall or Sheriff? Here's an idea, how about Bill? Seems easy enough."

"Yeah, sorry. Just finding a way to escape the reality of my day." Greg apologized.

"Try whiskey" Bill said in his deadpan way, "seems to work in the movies."

"I may try that tonight."

"Excellent. I haven't found too much. A lot of people come and go here, and we have barely scratched the surface of our surveillance video. There is one thing that sticks out as odd. This guy here." Bill was pointing to a freeze frame of a video from outside the building. "Guy's name is Maury Slater, works in the nursing department as a gopher mostly. Transports people around, takes supplies between departments, that sort of thing."

"I saw this guy just a few minutes ago," Greg chimed in, "He was coming out of the morgue."

"That would be him. One of his jobs is escorting the deceased to the morgue. Never been any trouble really, seems to slack off from time to time, otherwise, an okay kid. Came to us a few tears ago from a funeral home. The owner sits on our board, he got him the job."

"So, what is odd about him being on camera outside the building?"

"Well, it wouldn't be except that we have several clips of him, from different days, during times he's not on the schedule. We haven't found anything else thus far."

"I'm sorry Bill, back up just a second. You said his name was Slater?"

"Yes, Maury S-L-A-T-E-R. Is that raising a red flag for you?" Bill asked.

"I interviewed a patient who was a roommate of the gentleman that died. He said a man came into the room and introduced himself as Dr. Slater. We checked the physician rosters here and the surrounding hospitals, but no one fit the description. Probably coincidence. Let's move on." Greg made a mental note to talk to Mr., Slater.

"That's all I have Greg. We'll keep checking the tape and I'll let you know if something comes up."

"I appreciate it, Bill." Greg walked around Sandy's desk and toward the door. "See ya Miss Kitty!"

As soon as Greg hit the hallway, his phone vibrated yet again.

"Greg Webster," he answered.

"Hi Greg, this is Kathy, I know you're having a rough day so I was wondering if you would like to have lunch with me. I'll have food brought in from the cafeteria and we can eat privately right here in the small conference room. We will be all done in thirty minutes, and I'll try to answer any questions you have about City Hospital. Maybe I can help you."

Greg felt a small tingle of excitement. He was going to eat something, somewhere, it may as well be with Kathy.

"What time are you thinking Kathy/"

"Does 12:15 work for you?"

"It sure does. I'll see you then."

That still left Greg about an hour. Time to see Kyle Seike.

Chapter 92

Greg completed the short walk to the morgue in under thirty seconds. The door was open. Jim Larkin was arranging supplies in one of the cabinets. The autopsy room was spotless.

"Mr. Larkin," Greg called from the door, trying not to startle him.

"Come in. Hi Mr. Webster, just cleaning up a bit. How can I help you?"

"Good morning, Jim. I was hoping to speak with Dr. Seike, is he here?"

"I'm afraid not sir," he said he needed to run a few quick errands outside the building. I expect him to be back before lunch though. Can I have him contact you when he returns?"

"Sure, that would be great, thanks. This place sparkles today. Did you do all this cleaning?"

"Oh, thanks. I can't take credit for all of it, housekeeping washes and waxes the floor, but I do the rest."

"Nice job! Is housekeeping allowed in here by themselves, Jim?"

"No, Dr. Seike doesn't want anyone in here unless he or I am around."

"I see. What happens if a patient dies after your shift? Do they hold the body on the floor until morning?"

"Well, no, I guess there is one exception to the rule. In that situation, either a nurse or an aide would transport the body down here and place it in the cooler room over there." Jim was pointing to the adjoining room that is accessible from the autopsy space as well as from a separate door from the corridor."

"I'm curious" Greg said, "is there some sort of log you keep here for people entering after hours?"

"There is a log" Jim responded, "but it is not kept here. Whoever is bringing the body down must first stop at the main reception desk to log in and pick up the key. When finished, they return the key and log out."

Greg mentally filed this information away for retrieval later.

"Jim, do you mind if I look around some while we talk?"

"No sir, make yourself at home."

Greg walked slowly around the room, not really looking for anything, but noticing everything.

"How long does a body stay in the morgue?"

'That depends, sir. If they're just awaiting pickup by a funeral home, they could be here from less than an hour to several hours. If it's a weekend or a holiday, they may be here overnight. If they're schedule for a post, that would be an autopsy, it may be two to three days. Three is unusual. Dr. Seike prefers to do his posts as quickly after death as possible.

He has no problem working weekends, trust me, I know. I've even been called in on holidays to assist with autopsies."

"Jim, what's your take on these recent deaths? Do you have an opinion?"

"Wow, that's way above my paygrade, Mr. Webster. That's a question for the doctor."

"I'm not asking for your medical opinion Jim, just your gut feeling. And please, call me Greg."

Jim paused a moment assessing any possible ramifications of answering.

"Honestly, it concerns me. I don't have any real reason to think something is going on, but it bothers me that so many young people have died over the last year. I mean there must have been thirty to forty of them in the last twelve months!"

"Thirty to forty? How does that compare to last year?" I would say double, and that was double from the year before that."

Greg would need to review those records today.

"Can you think of anything different about the hospital over the last two or three years that would correlate to the increase in young deaths? Any changes in staff, physicians, administration?"

"I don't know, I'm not too involved in the day to day, I'm sort of secluded here. I get out to the cafeteria a couple times a day, and I pick up supplies in materials management and the laboratory but that's the extent of my travels."

"Have you heard any chatter at the lunch table about changes? Anybody complaining?"

"Let's see" Jim's wheels were turning. "I know we haven't had a raise in a while, which makes some people complain. We have had a few staff meetings about it. They call them focus meetings and they're mandatory for all staff. I guess we've had three or four in the last year."

"What is the crux of these focus meetings, Jim."

"Usually money, or I guess the lack of, would be a better description."

"Who leads these meetings?"

"There always the same. Mr. Winfield opens them with a pat on the back for a job well done, then Mr. Miller drops the reimbursement bomb."

"What's the reimbursement bomb?"

"I don't understand it all too well, but it sounds like the insurance companies keep trying to pay us less for our services. Doesn't make sense to me because my premiums keep going up. If the insurances companies are making more money through premiums, why do they need to cut back on their payments?"

"What does the administration expect the employees to do about it, Jim?"

"There are two things that come up every time. We need to reduce the length of stay and, we need to find more business on the outpatient side. We seem to have the funds to keep opening primary care clinics and expanding lab and imaging outreach, but there isn't any money for raises.

I suppose I can be a voice for promoting our outreach services but what am I supposed to do about reducing length of stay? My patients are already dead when they get here! And we get them out as fast as we can."

"Not much more you can do about that Jim. Who talks about the length of stay at these meetings?"

"That would be the new guy, Barry Miller. He's always saying it's everyone's job. Quicker appointments, faster results, shorter procedure times, no social admissions. Heck, why don't we just kick these people out to the curb?"

"You just said Mr. Miller is new. How new?"

"Well, he not really new, he's been here quite a while but in the last couple, three years, he was named COO as well as his original position of CFO."

Greg shut down for a minute going totally inside. He knew there was something in this conversation that was critically important, but the pieces were not fitting together. That seemed like a lot of power for one person to hold. The financial officer and the operating officer are often on opposite sides of the table, one represents the employees and material needs and the other controls the purse strings.

"Jim, I want to switch topics for a moment. What's your procedure for sending specimens to the state lab? Specifically, how are the labels generated and who does the labeling?"

"Okay, the labels are computer driven. We find the correct patient in a lookup; select the tests we want to order and push the print button. The labels print on that laser device over there and we adhere them to the tubes, cups, or bags, we place all the specimens in a leak proof container with a chain of custody seal and ship them off."

"Sounds like the same procedure the lab uses, with the exception of the chain of custody. Who labels the specimens, Jim?"

"He does!" Another voice just joined the party.

"Dr. Seike, I'm glad you're back. I wanted to discuss the results of the post on Sharon Simmons, that is if you have a few minutes." Greg looked over at Jim. He sensed that Seike was not happy that Jim was talking to him without his presence. Judging by the flushed appearance on his face, Jim believed he was in trouble.

"I would be happy to discuss the results, Mr. Webster. Let me just set my things down and we can sit over there." He was pointing to two stainless steel swivel stools next to the autopsy table. "Jim, why don't you take a break for a while. I can see how hard you've been working. You deserve it. Oh Jim, close the door on your way out."

Chapter 93

He fired up his wireless device and checked in on the morgue. Seike had completed his exam of the body and Jim was just cleaning and restocking. Then he heard the other voice. It was Webster. Where was Seike? He didn't like that Jim was alone with him.

Oh boy, the inspector was asking too many good questions. Too many incriminating questions. He needed to find Seike now. He picked up his phone and dialed the number. Several rings but no answer. He tried again with the same results.

Jim expressed his concerns about the rash of deaths. He said they have been increasing for years. This was going to bring a lot of heat from the

State. He picked up his phone again and hit redial.

"Yes" the voice said.

"Where have you been? I've been calling."

"I can see that" Seike replied. "I've been busy. What's the urgency?"

"The urgency is that fucking inspector! He's in your space right now with your boy! And your boy is talking a blue streak!

"Alright, I'm just about there. I'll handle it."

"I hope so."

The killer hung up. Maybe one more mishap would confuse them, take them off the trail for a while. Time to look at the patient roster again.

Chapter 94

Seike set his briefcase down near the counter and placed his hat atop the coat rack. He was putting on his lab coat as he spoke.

"I'm sorry to keep you waiting Mr. Webster, have you been here long?"

Greg thought the apology was just an excuse to go fishing. Fine with him.

"Not long, about 30 minutes give or take." He exaggerated. "Jim is a fine young man, seems like he has a good head on his shoulders."

"I agree" said Seike, "I enjoy working with him. He is a very insightful assistant. And what did you learn if I may ask?"

"I learned all about the logbook for the morgue, who has access, how they gain access etc. I was just learning about the processing of lab specimens when you walked in."

"And what did you learn exactly Mr. Webster?"

This guy is a lousy fisherman, Greg thought.

"I learned that the process is quite the same as in the main lab. The only difference it seems, is the use of the chain of custody bag."

"Quite right. I guess Jim did a good job."

"When you walked in, I was asking Jim who labels the specimens and you answered, he did. Is that always the case? Is there ever an occasion where someone else, say you, would need to print and adhere the labels?"

Judging by the look on Seike's face, Greg was raising his hackles a little.

"Jim always prints and applies the labels. You see, the process needs to be started and completed in one step, otherwise we leave room for mistakes to take place. If he is witnessing the chain of custody by placing his initials on the bag, he is assuming responsibility for the accuracy for what is inside. This is not just a clinical act, but a legal one as well."

"I understand, let's move on. What information did you extract from poor Sharon Simmons?"

Greg believed Seike was hiding something, but he wasn't going to figure that out right now.

"Sharon Simmons was septic. She had a fallopian tube rupture and a subsequent infection. Before this occurrence, I believe she was in good shape. The surgeon performed a hysterosalpingo-oophorectomy so there was nothing left of the reproductive organs.

I did find a small laceration to the colon which is likely the source of the infection. The laceration may be directly related to the surgery, a mistake if you will, or indirect, a result of the infection. Difficult to specify."

"So, death due to sepsis. Any other significant findings doctor?"

"No, that was clearly the cause of death."

"It must be nice to have one you can solve for a change!" Greg was aware his comment could be misconstrued as sarcasm.

"Most are that way, Greg; we've just had a recent run of bad luck."

"I suppose you're right. Hey, is Sharon's body still here? I'd like to take a look at her." Greg had no real reason to look at her, he was just testing Seike's reaction."

"I'm not sure, let's have a look, shall we?"

Seike led the way to the cooler. He unlatched and opened the thick stainless door. He stepped inside and motioned for Greg to follow.

"Step in if you would Greg, we need to close the door to keep the temperature stable."

Greg stepped in and Kyle closed the door behind them. It made a considerable thud when it closed. Greg was sure it was done for emphasis.

The room was mostly void except for the two empty gurneys. The nine steel doors in the far wall reminded Greg of the side of an ice cream truck, the kind that go door to door. Only one door had a tag on the front.

"There she is, number five, right in the middle." Seike said as he moved toward it. He pulled on the latch and the door swung to the right. Greg could see the feet; one had a toe tag. Seike grabbed the end of the tray with both hands and pulled hard. Again, for effect Greg assumed. The tray slid effortlessly out of the wall. When the entire tray was extended, it clicked into place.

Sharon's body was totally naked except for a thin sheet from her head to her ankles. It struck Greg that just a few hours ago, this woman was alive." Life is fragile," he whispered. Kyle moved to the left side of the body, so Greg went around to the right.

Kyle reached up for the head end of the sheet, pausing and looking at Greg. Without looking away, he quickly pulled the sheet of in one motion like a magician making something disappear. It didn't have the desired effect. His effort to intimidate Greg fell flat. Seike was disappointed, Greg was pissed.

"What now Mr. Webster?" Do you wish I stay or would you to prefer to examine her on your own?" Greg looked up and down the body. Pale on top but a little color toward the bottom. Eyes closed, mouth open about halfway. The textbook Y incision not sutured closed extending from both shoulders to the sternum and then down to the pubic bone.

"I'll only be a moment, why don't you stay?" Kyle didn't answer nor did he move. Greg started at the face and looked closely at her body, slowly following her contour. Neck, shoulder, chest, abdomen, arm, the hand, across her pelvis and then back up the other side. Kyle took a couple steps back to allow Greg passage up Sharon's left side. Hand, elbow.

His eyes fixed on the elbow now. The antecubital space, the front side of the elbow where blood is drawn, and intravenous lines are place was very discolored. The skin appeared almost burned especially next to the pallor of the rest of her.

"Kyle, what causes this discoloration?"

"Excellent question Mr. Webster. Mrs. Simmons had been receiving a maintenance dose of propofol. This, I'm afraid, is the downside of an otherwise remarkable drug. Prolonged use of propofol can have many adverse effects, necrosis of the injection site is just one."

"She was receiving the drug because of the ventilator."

"That's correct Greg. Someone had done their homework!"

"Dr. Seike, I think I'm done here. Thank you. We can put her back now."

Greg retrieved the sheet from the floor. He and Kyle each took a side and pulled it back over Mrs. Simmons.

"Thanks for your time, Kyle that was very insightful. I must be going now, yet another meeting awaits. Please tell Jim I'm appreciative of his time as well."

"Any time young man." Kyle said as Greg walked out the door.

Chapter 95

Bob Kline was sitting in his office with his feet up on the corner of his desk listening to an oldies rock station. He was just about to pack it up for lunch when his phone rang. He recognized the number, but he wasn't sure he wanted to answer. In fact, he would prefer not to.

"Pharmacy, this is Bob."

"Robert, long time, no speak. I trust you are well. And your lovely wife, I hope she is well also." Bob didn't say anything.

"Listen Bob, I have been trying to reach Mark without success and I really need to speak with him. Is he in the building?

Bob really did not want to have this conversation.

"No, I'm sorry, Mark is out of the office for a few days." There was a long pause.

"That answer disappoints me."

"I'm sorry to hear that but that is the case. He should be back soon though."

Not soon enough for me, Bob, it looks like you will have to do."

"No, I told you before I cannot be directly involved. I can't help you."

"Oh Robert, enough of the drama. I suppose I could pay a visit to your lovely wife and share some of the information I'm privy to. I'm quite certain she would find it, shall we say, revealing? Bob knew what information this guy had, and he also knew that his wife finding out would end his marriage and his career.

"What do you need."

"That's better. It's a small task really. I think a vial of 50 should do it for now. The locker, end of the day. There will be a present for you. Perhaps you can buy your wife a little gift. Something revealing?"

"Done. Don't call again please. Bob Hung up.

Chapter 96

Bill Dillon was working on his sixth cup of coffee since he arrived this morning. The only thing more exhilarating than his coffee intake, was his coffee output. "Sandy, back in five." She was well aware of his bathroom habits.

"Piddle break Sheriff?"

"Leave it alone, Sandy."

Bill had just started a stream when his phone rang. *"Oh Great. I can't answer the phone and hold my Johnson at the same time."* He said to no one. *"Tried it once, wasn't pretty."* He flushed, zipped, washed, and dried his hands, then checked his phone which had stopped ringing. It was Sandy.

"Where's the fire, Sandy?" He said as he walked in. I was only gone three minutes.

"Boss, you need to see this." Officer Belden had been reviewing tape as well as the printout from the lock security log from the second floor." Look at these entries from this morning. Someone entered the passcode on the west stairwell door at 09:36, just before the first code. The passcode was then entered at the east stairwell at 09:44 just before the second code."

"Someone from the emergency response team?"

"Doesn't make sense boss, the code wasn't called yet."

"Who else has the passcode, Belden."

"As far as I can tell, aside from the response team, the fire department, security, the CEO and the COO."

Bill tried to process what this information meant. If it meant anything at all.

"At the moment, we don't know if any of these events are suspect. Let's sit on this for a bit. Good work Belden. Keep at it."

"Sandy, did you throw out my coffee?"

"You drank it." She yelled back, then rolled her eyes.

Bill had a thought. He called the maintenance supervisor.

Chapter 97

Greg had about four minutes to make to administration for lunch. Would have been plenty, then his cell phone buzzed. Headquarters.

"Greg Webster," he answered.

"Hey Greg, sorry to bother you, Tom said you were fishing."

"You too?"

"Yeah, couldn't resist, sorry. I've got news!"

"Real news Russ or made-up crap that you and Tom came up with?"

"Real news. You did it buddy, you gave me the key that opened the door!"

"What key Russell?"

"The oily substance Greg, It's propofol!"

Greg wasn't following, "one step at a time here partner."

"Okay, listen. I did some research on propofol. It contains ten percent soy oil. The oil is what makes it work so well. Once we realized it contained oil, we just cross analyzed a sample of propofol against the chemicals on the breast pad. Bingo!"

Greg was shaking. He was speechless. He immediately knew that his worst fears had been realized. This was no longer coincidence, bad timing, misaligned planets. This was most likely murder.

"Hey Greg, you still there?"

"Yes, I'm here Russ. Hey listen, great job. I need to run right now, I'm late for a meeting. I'll call you back."

Greg was now a few minutes late. He kept walking toward the admin department blindly. He could see but he would never remember the walk.

"Hi Kathy, I'm sorry I'm late. It's been one hell of a morning."

Kathy rose from her desk and walked toward him. She straightened his tie and said, "it's all good Greg, take a deep breath. She took his hand and led him into the conference room.

The table was set with fine China, better silver than they use in the cafeteria, glasses that looked like crystal and a fresh bouquet of flowers. There were only two settings, one at the end of the table and one right next to it on the corner.

"Wow! Is our state senator joining us?"

"I hope not. This is just you and me. A little, relax and get to know each other time. Sound okay to you?"

Greg didn't know what to make of this, but he wasn't minding it.

"Um, yes, sure, sounds perfect."

"Excellent. Here, lean forward and I'll help you out of your jacket." Kathy stepped behind his chair, rubbed his shoulders for a few seconds, then pulled the jacket down. She took one sleeve, then the other, removed the jacket and folded it on the chair on the other side of him. From behind, she bent to place her lips close to his ear and whispered, "better?"

He could smell her perfume, it was alluring, but not too strong. She walked back around his chair to take her own. As she slowly sat, she smoothed her short skirt beneath her. He could just barely make out the top of her sheer black stocking beneath the grey fabric of her skirt.

"Would you like me to serve you Greg?"

He just looked at her, frozen in time. *Was she thinking what he was thinking?*

"Is chicken cutlet, okay?"

She was not thinking what he was thinking.

"Sounds delicious," he stuttered.

She slid the serving platter between their plates and removed the dome top. He could swear she was showing more cleavage than there was this morning. He felt it getting hot in the room.

"I hope you like breast."

Oh boy, really hot in here now. "I love them! It, I love it."

"I'm glad, I love it too. I don't think there is anything quite as enticing as a hot, juicy breast!"

She has got to be kidding me! He thought. He felt like Tim Conway with Mrs. Wiggins. They each had a portion of chicken, broccoli and a twice baked potato resting on their plates.

She poured water from an ice-cold cut crystal pitcher into our glasses. Sweaty, nearly frozen droplets of water were dripping from the bottom as she poured.

"It's wet" she said.

Greg was caught between bursting out laughing and ripping her clothes off.

"So, Kathy, this is very nice. I appreciate all the trouble you went through. You thought you may be able to answer a few questions for me?"

"Oh, of course," she said disappointedly. "What questions do you have? If you prefer, we can start by you telling me what you have discovered so far, and I can try to fill in the blanks."

Greg felt a little befuddled. He felt like he was being played. *Did Alex have her set this up, to set me up? He wondered. That would explain the absurdity.* He decided to play along for a while.

"That sounds fair. So far, I have nothing concrete. I have some ideas and I have a few clues, but I'm still following up on them. I have interviewed lots of fine folks here, and I have several more to go. Which leads me to my first question.

Who is Barry Miller, and why does he want to meet with me? I know what you told me on the phone earlier, but why now? He must know that I've been here all along, why the urgency to meet today?"

"Well, I think he has been busy too and is just getting around to it." It may also have to do with the board meeting this afternoon. Perhaps he wants an update to take to the board."

"Alright, what time is the board meeting?"

"That's scheduled for 3 pm."

"And my meeting with his is at 4 pm. How does that help him?

Kathy suddenly looks like the cat that ate the canary. With longer legs and nicer breasts. Much less fur too.

"I guess maybe I'm wrong about that. She sighed, "I'm not sure why he wants to meet you, but I had to tell you something! I'm sorry. I really like you Greg, I'm sorry I lied."

"Let's call a truce and start over. Okay? From the moment I met you, I thought you were professional, intelligent, and capable. I didn't imagine you as an over aggressive sex kitten. Well, maybe I imagined some of that. Anyway, while I enjoyed your attention and energy, playfulness and of course, award winning acting, it's just not you. So, here is the sixty-four-thousand-dollar question. Who put you up to it?"

"I'm embarrassed and I feel like a fool." This is not who I am. I am all those things you said before, I'm just in a tough spot."

"Do you want to talk about it? I'm a good listener."

"I'm sure you are, but I really can't."

"Okay Kathy, I'll respect that, but hear me now, I am talking to you as a friend. There is some serious shit going on here and I think it's going to hit the proverbial fan soon. Heads are going to roll. If you know something, say something. To know and not say, will make you an accomplice. You have my card; you have until tomorrow morning. After that, I won't be able to help you. This was fun, thank you."

Greg stood and grabbed his jacket. "You're a good kid, Kathy." With that, he gave her a child-like kiss on the top of her head, then walked out.

Chapter 98

Alex heard the door to the conference room open. A moment later, Greg Webster poked his head into the office. "Good afternoon, Alex, getting ready for the board meeting?"

This was the last thing he needed right now. "Yes Mr. Webster" he said politely. "I was just preparing my remarks about your presence here. Do you have an update for me?"

"It would be premature to share any specifics with you, Alex but you may consider opening with a quote from Chicken Little; the sky is falling!"

Greg pulled his head out of the doorway.

"Not funny Webster!" Alex yelled into the hallway.

"You have no idea!" Greg shouted back.

"What am I going to do now?" Alex thought to himself. He picked up the phone and dialed. "Morgue, Jim speaking."

"Where the hell is Seike?

"I'm sorry, who's calling please?"

'This is Alex Winfield, I need Kyle Seike immediately!"

"I'm sorry Mr. Winfield, I believe Dr. Seike has left for the day. I can try to get a message to him if you would like."

"I'll tell you what I would like young man, I would like people to do the work they're hired for! I'll find him myself! Click.

Jim heard the call disconnect. "Yes Mr. Winfield, eat shit Mr. Winfield, you suck Mr. Winfield! Jim gently placed the phone back in the cradle.

Chapter 99

The killer didn't need to wait for the next delivery, he knew he still had plenty in the locker. He hadn't planned to have to kill the Meadows girl again, one dose of that size should have been more than enough. This time, he'll try a little more. It's still the lunch hour, the floor should be lightly staffed but he needed to hurry. He headed for the locker.

Lacey Meadows had been relocated to the ICU as a result of her near-death experience. She was now comatose and on a respirator.

"Mr. and Mrs. Meadows?" "I'm Lynette, one of the nurses on this floor. I'm covering for Lacey's regular nurse who is currently at lunch. Is there something I can get for you? Coffee, some lunch perhaps?"

"No thank you dear, we arrived just a short time ago, we're fine for now."

"Alright, I'll be at the station if you should need me." She handed Mrs. Meadows the remote control. "This red button is the call button. It will alert us at the station when pressed. Please don't hesitate to use it. I'm just going to pull this curtain closed so you can have some privacy."

"That's very kind of you dear." Thank you.

With that Lynette left the room.

The killer knew Lacey was moved to room 2401, the same room Simmons was in when she died. He had stopped at the locker and gathered his tools and supplies. He walked nonchalantly along the first floor, nodding, and waving to employees as they passed. When he reached the stairwell, he opened the door and ascended.

At level 2, he looked through the safety glass, past the nurse's station and down the hallway. It was clear. He entered his code, heard the lock release, and opened the door. The curtain was drawn inside 2401 preventing his from looking inside. He stood still and listened, no voices, just the rhythmic pace of the respirator breathing for Lacey.

He walked quietly into the room until he reached the end of the curtain. He turned the corner, around the edge. To his surprise, a man and a woman were sitting at the bedside. They appeared startled as they quickly turned their heads around.

"Hello?" she said.

"Good afternoon, I'm sorry if I frightened you. I'm Dr. Slater. I've come to check on Ms. Meadows. are you her parents?"

"Yes, were her mom and dad."

"I see. I'm very sorry about the current situation, we are hoping for some improvement soon."

"Improvement? You think there is a chance for improvement, Dr. Slater? That is not the impression we were given by Dr. Ingraham. He told us she was barely hanging on, that we should expect the worst." Are you both speaking of the same patient? Our child?" Mrs. Meadows was now crying, her husband's hands on her shoulders.

"Perhaps if she didn't get greedy with illicit drugs, she wouldn't be here sucking up valuable resources and wasting our money!" The killer thought to himself.

"We physicians tend to look at things differently sometimes. I prefer to see the glass half full."

"What is your specialty, Dr. Slater?" asked Mr. Meadows.

The killer was caught off guard. He paused. He pulled out his phone. "You will have to excuse me; I need to take this."

He left the room quickly, pausing just long enough to peek into the hallway. No one visible, he pushed through the exit door. He heard the alarm. He forgot to enter the code. Think quickly, he said under his breath. Up, you must go up. Everyone will expect you to go down, you must go up.

He climbed to the third floor, maternity. Too much security here, he went up another flight. Long term and palliative care center. This would have to do. He entered the code and pulled the door. It looked clear. He would walk straight down the hallway to the central staircase.

Just before he reached the exit door to the unsecured stains, the elevator door opened. He darted through the door and held his back to it. He turned to look through the safety glass back toward the elevator. Richard Ingraham was just getting off. Too close.

Chapter 100

In ICU room 2401, Mrs. Meadows pushed the red button. A moment later, Lynette appeared.

"How can I help you?" She could see that Mrs. Meadows was crying. Her husband said, "There was a doctor in here, just a moment ago, he was acting strange and telling us that there was hope that Lacey would recover. The exact opposite of what Dr. Ingraham had told us not more than an hour ago!"

"I'm sorry," Lynette offered, I didn't see a doctor on the floor. Did he give his name?"

"Yes, it was Slater. Mrs. Meadows exclaimed, expressing her agitation. He had a lot of nerve offering up false hope to desperate, vulnerable people."

"Did he introduce himself as Doctor Slater or mister slater?" asked Lynette.

"He definitely said Doctor. He said he was here to check on her, but he didn't look at her chart and didn't go near her bed."

"Can you describe what he was wearing?"

"It looked like a dark suit with a lab coat over the top."

"Did the lab coat have a name embroidered on the left, over the pocket?"

"No, said Mrs. Meadows, there was no name on the coat."

"How long ago did he leave?"

"We asked what his specialty was," Mr. Meadows said, "but he didn't answer. He pulled out his phone, said he had to take the call, and ran out the door. That was about one second before the alarm sounded."

Lynette knew he went down the stairs, setting off the alarm.

"Can either of you describe him?" she asked.

Mrs. Meadows answered, "six feet tall, dark hair, greying at the temples, medium build and light colored or rimless glasses."

"You sound sure about that?"

"I notice things." She replied. "it's a gift.

"Except when it's a curse. followed Mr. Meadows.

Lynette was sure it wasn't Maury. She was relieved.

In the security office, Bill Dillon was notified of the alarm. The west end of the second floor. He ran to the exit and climbed the steps. He didn't pass anybody suspicious on the first floor and he didn't encounter anyone in the stairwell.

When he returned to his office, Sandy was on the phone. "A nurse in ICU has a description of the person that set off the alarm. He was in the room with Lacey Meadows."

"You know where I'll be," he said and headed toward the door.

"Men's room?" Sandy said.

He just looked at her.

The killer was in his office now. He locked himself in, he was sweating profusely. He still had the meds in his lab coat pocket and needed to return them to the locker, but he couldn't risk it now. He couldn't be seen on the second floor for a while.

Chapter 101

Greg felt like he had been working twelve hours already. He couldn't ever remember having a day that was back-to-back excitement for a long period of time. His day wasn't even half over.

It was a perfect summer day, sunny and warm. He wasn't much of a fan of winter, but it was the price that had to be paid for perfect summers. The snow running off the mountains to the north and south, made the long journey down gently sloping hills to small streams, to bigger streams and then to the Mohawk River.

The days of commerce on the river were long gone. From the days of the barge canal to the waterside carpet and leather mills that drew power from the endless flow of natural energy, the river was now destined to be enjoyed by boaters, campers, and those picnicking at a riverside park.

Occasionally, a large pleasure boat would make its way through the chain of locks that connected to the Hudson. From there, you could make your way to anyplace on the eastern seaboard.

Greg grew up here, went to college here and worked here for all of his life. He had little desire to travel to foreign or faraway places, he was convinced he lived in the best place on the planet. A sentiment not necessarily shared by his wife.

Mary was much more open to the idea of being somewhere else. A place where winter existed in story books and Christmas movies, where green grass was only found in inner city parks and where underground trains and cabs were the preferred mode of transportation.

She was prepped for a big city life, but then family happened, and he became the hunter-gatherer and she the mother-housewife. It wasn't by choice really, more necessity. He knew she was disappointed that she missed out on a career.

His long hours away from home didn't help. A topic for another day, he told himself as he pulled into the driveway of the Mease Mortuary. He made a mental note to call Mary later in the afternoon.

The place looked like the typical, small town, family run funeral home of the Northeast. A large main building that appeared to have three finished floors built on a full basement. The three plus car garage to the left of the house and set back considerably from the road was noticeably added or expanded after the property was no longer a primary home.

To the right side, when facing the house from the street was a parking lot. There were two long, slowly inclined ramps, one on either side that led to the back of the house. He guessed that one was for handicap access and the other, for caskets. There was a large porch that covered the length of the house in the front, adding a certain warmth to an otherwise cold atmosphere.

Greg parked his car in the lot to the right. There was a sidewalk the cut through the lawn, Close to the porch. There was maybe 10 feet between the porch and the walkway, just enough to offer a little well-manicured landscaping. He stepped up onto the first step of a staircase that felt much wider than it looked. Greg realized this house was much more than he envisioned from the street.

It was six steps to the porch floor which was all of twelve feet front to back. A very welcoming feel. A song by the Eagles began playing in his head, *"you can check out any time you like, but you can never leave."*

He reached the door and rang the bell. He expected to hear a loud gong or maybe a haunting Halloween laugh but instead, he was pleasantly surprised by the 2 note, high-low ring of a classy, and most likely expensive chime.

He waited. Big house, he thought, may take a while.

Things to do, can't wait forever. Maybe looking through the glass will speed things along. He was just reaching for the doorbell again when he heard the inner door open. A gentleman, probably in his early sixties, opened the door. He was shy of six feet tall, on the thin side, dark hair and wore a half smile that said, "I'm sorry for your loss, how can I help?"

"Good afternoon, may I help you?"

"I'm sure you can. My name is Greg Webster and I'm with the investigation division of the New York State Department of Health." He handed the gentleman his card. "Would you be Harold Mease?"

"That would be me, what can I do for you Mr. Webster."

"I was hoping I could ask you a few questions?"

Mease didn't hesitate at all.

"Certainly, Mr. Webster, won't you please come in?"

He held the door wide and let Greg pass through.

Greg stepped into the generous foyer. Ahead and just to the right, was a central wide staircase that was roped off at the bottom. Straight ahead was a hallway leading toward the back of the house and to the right and left were wide open entryways into viewing rooms.

Each room had a pedestal with a visitors' book and a box for prayer cards. There was a brass floor stand, about thirty-six inches high, in the center of each opening. At the top of each brass stand was a fourteen-inch square frame with black fabric inside. The fabric was ribbed to hold those white plastic letters with the names of the deceased.

From where he was standing, he could only see the front to middle of the rooms, but he was sure they continued most of the depth of the first floor.

"If you'll follow me, please, we can chat in my office."

"This is a beautiful place Mr. Mease."

"Thank you," he said as he kept walking. Again, the Eagles, *"there were voices down the corridor, I thought I heard them say ay, welcome to the Hotel California."*

At the other end of the hallway, he noticed additional doors that opened to each of the viewing rooms. Near the back wall of each room were the supports for the caskets. There weren't any caskets present but the kneelers were already in place. On each end of where the casket would be, were the pink and white marbled torchiere lamps that reminded him of Washburn's strawberry marshmallow ice cream he had as a child.

There were three doors at the back end of the hall. The one to the left was the Ladies Room, to the right, the Men's Room and straight ahead, the Office. He opened the office door and held it for Greg.

"Thank you," Greg offered."

"My pleasure, Mr. Webster. Please have a seat." There was a large cherry desk ahead with two burgundy leather chairs facing it. Behind the desk, a high-back chair finished in the same burgundy leather with brass nails all around the edging.

Once seated, Mr. Mease opened the show.

"You have questions, Mr. Webster. I'm happy to assist you if I can, however, I'm afraid I don't have much time this afternoon. I have an important meeting off premises and a few things to tidy up here before I leave. If the time we have is not sufficient, you are welcome to return at any time."

"That's fine Mr. Mease, and I apologize for showing up unannounced. I was attempting to check one task off my over-abundant list in between other meetings that I have. I'll try to be succinct.

Mr. Mease, I've been conducting an investigation at City Hospital this week that involves several unexpected and so far, unexplainable deaths. This is going to sound odd, and I apologize. I was having a meal at a diner here and I noticed that in the newspaper I was reading, that nearly all the obituaries listed Mease Mortuary as the host funeral home. This is going to sound crass, are you the only show in town?"

Mease gave him a more than a mortician's smile. "We're certainly not the only show in town as you say. There are several funerals service companies in High Falls and the surrounding area. I like to think that providing quality, compassionate after life services makes us the leader in our field.

In an area this small, referrals are the best way to build and maintain a business. Collectively, our business does not spend much on advertising. No one wants to see ads about death, I don't want to see ads about death! This is a very personal matter. Every funeral we host, is our calling card. It self-perpetuates, the more you host, the more referrals you get. It's really that simple. Do a good job and people will notice."

"Mr. Mease, are you also on the board of City Hospital?"

"I think you already know the answer to that question, or you prob-ably wouldn't be asking it. Yes, I have proudly served on the board for over twenty years now. A hospital in a community this size requires special guidance to survive, especially in this day and age. Many hospitals our size have gone out of business in the past ten years, some of them were our neighbors. We have to be smarter, sleeker.

"Mr. Mease, how would you say the average age of your clients in the last twelve months, compares to previous years. I haven't done the math, but my perception is our average age is much lower than it has been in a while. You may not think so, but that bothers me as much as you. I would rather see everyone live to be 100. It gives me no pleasure to prepare a young person for burial or cremation. The young take the greatest toll on undertakers."

Mr. Mease, I understand that an orderly at the hospital used to work for you."

"Yes, that would be Maury Slater. He worked with me for about five years."

"What can you tell me about him?"

"If I could have a son, he would be it. He didn't work *for* me. I've had plenty of employee like that. Maury worked *with* me. He started out performing menial tasks like everyone else, but he learned quickly, and he excelled. By the time he left, he was my assistant. He helped me prepare clients, he hosted viewings, he directed processions, he sold caskets and supplementals. There wasn't any part of the business he couldn't do."

"Why did he leave?"

Harold Mease paused, he saddened. "I didn't want him to, I wanted him to go to mortuary school, to become licensed. I couldn't afford to pay him what he was worth without being licensed. He wasn't sure he wanted to spend his life around death. When he couldn't commit, I got him the job at the hospital. The pay was just a little more than I was paying him, but the benefits were much better. He needed to have a normal life and I wanted to help him have it."

"Is Maury capable of murder?"

Harold's eyes got as big as baseballs.

"What? Are you insane? Listen, Maury had a difficult childhood. His father deserted him and his mother was insufficient in many ways. As a result, Maury seemed a little slow, and was picked on for it all through school. But I'm telling you, Maury Slater is a bright, sensitive kid.

He always showed compassion around here and he was an asset to this business. He wouldn't hurt a fly. I would take him back in a heartbeat, if would go to school. If he did that, he would be the future of Mease Mortuary."

"Thank you for your time, hospitality, and your honesty. I have just one more question for you. Is the body of Lorena Nunez here?"

"Yes. She is being prepared now which is why I must go soon."

"I understand. I know this may seem unconventional, but may I have a look at her."

"It's not only unconventional Mr. Webster, but also against the law."

"It's not against the law for me to see her. I am a duly authorized agent of the New York State Health Department of which you are a licensee. You can call my office if you need further clarification. Please, I am looking for something very specific."

"Tell me and I'll check on it." Mease countered.

"I'm sorry but I need to see this with my own eyes."

Harold Mease thought long and hard about this.

"Very well, but we must move quickly."

He stood and moved to the door at the back of the office.

"This way."

Outside the door there was an elevator to the left, a door to the outside and one more door to the right. Harold opened the door to the right, and we descended down a curved flight of stairs. At the bottom, an open door led to the preparation room. The was a body on the table partially covered by a sheet.

They approached the body. Lorena Had a large IV line hooked up to an artery in her chest. She also had what looked like a half inch steel tube stuck into her abdomen. Greg moved to her left side. He pulled the sheet back to look at her arm.

"Mr. Mease, this nasty area in the left antecubital, can you tell me what caused this?

"It appears to be a chemical burn, probably from IV medications. I couldn't be sure as the type of chemical."

"Does she still have blood in that arm?"

"Probably not, she has been hooked up to the formalin for a while now. If there was still blood, it would be contaminated."

Greg thought for moment.

"Gail Shapiro, did she have a similar mark on her arm?"

"You know, I believe she did. In fact, I've been noticing that same ugly bruise on many of the young clients."

"For how long now? How long have you been noticing the bruises?"

"Well, bruises are not uncommon in clients coming from a hospital, but these severe bruises, I would say at least a year or two, maybe longer."

"Did you ever report them?"

"Mr. Webster, it is the job of the coroner or pathologist to report on any suspicious details of the body. When they arrive here, the investigation is over."

"Okay. I need a sample of the skin from that area."

"Again Mr. Webster, I am not authorized to" Greg cut him off.

"I am authorizing you to do it. It is part of a formal investigation and if you refuse, you can be cited for obstruction. Please Harold."

Mease took a cup out of a cabinet and a scalpel from a drawer.

"How much do you need?"

"Just a half inch square, but make sure to include all the layers of the skin."

Harold filled the request.

"Thank you, Mr. Mease. I'll let myself out."

Chapter 102

"Christine, I need to speak with Tom right away."

"This sounds serious, Greg,"

"Dead Serious" she knew this was not going to be a playful moment. "I'll put you through."

"Greg, what's going on?"

"I need help Tom; I need someone to come out here and help me." He sounded desperate. "Of course, Greg, whatever you need."

"I need two people to go through some records and I need them today. I think if we pull an all-nighter, we can have this issue resolved tomorrow."

"That's great Greg. I can have two clerical agents out there by 4pm. Will that do?

"Yes Tom, that will work."

"Who should they report to when they arrive?"

"Have them go to security and talk to Sandy or Bill. They'll know what to do. One more thing Tom, we 're going to need the State Police on standby. Oh, and one more thing, I need a courier to come out here and pick up a specimen that needs to get to Russ ASAP."

"That was two more things Greg. Just saying. Do they get the specimen from you?"

"Sandy in security will have that as well."

"Okay Greg, let me get the wheels turning. Are you safe?"

"I'm fine Tom. Thanks."

Greg hung up and called Sandy to get her onboard.

Next, he called John Shand. He was in the office.

"John, it's Greg. I need your help."

"Sure Greg, what is it?"

"Can you meet me at the hospital at 5pm? I know it's short notice and I wouldn't ask if..."

"Greg, I'll be there. Are you okay?"

"I'm fine. I'll see you in my office. Oh, please apologize to Sara. Dinner tomorrow, I promise!"

Greg hung up. He was getting close to the hospital. He had one more call to make.

"Mary, it's me."

"I thought I recognized the number. Hey, Greg, we need to talk."

"I know babe, but I can't right now. I'm just calling to tell you I won't be home tonight or tomorrow."

"Oh, come on Greg! What the hell is so important that you need to be there every night? I'm tired of raising these kids alone!"

I know Mary, I'm sorry. After tomorrow, this will be all over and I'll be home and we can talk. This is critically important Mary, I can't leave just yet."

"Do what you need to do Greg, you always do."

She was gone. He felt lousy but what was he supposed to do? *Let more innocent people die?*

He was back in the parking lot. It was almost 2:30pm, he had a few more loose ends to tie up before his 4 o'clock meeting with Barry Miller.

Chapter 103

Alex had finally tracked down Dr. Seike after trying for what seemed like hours. "Where are you? I need you here, the board is about to arrive, I haven't seen Miller, this idiot Webster, seems to know something and I am in the dark."

"Relax Alex, everything will be alright." He always had a way of calming Alex.

"Where have you been?" Alex was almost pouting.

"I had some business to take care of Alex, just routine business that needed to be done during business hours. I'll be back soon. I'll meet you after the board meeting. Just remain calm and you will be okay."

Alex could feel his anxiety begin to wane.

"Yes, of course. I can do this. I'll see you later."

Alex hung up the phone. He sat back in his comfortable desk chair and took some deep, slow breaths. He remembered being under the floorboards, the earthy aroma of the barn. Deep breaths, darkness, peace.

Kyle was not nearly as relaxed as Alex. He knew the lid was about to be blown off of this thing and he needed to prepare. The day would come, he didn't try to fool himself. It actually lasted longer than he believed it ever would.

Greg Webster was a worthy adversary. He didn't seem so at first, but he quickly proved otherwise. The truth would soon be told, and the best Kyle could do was to be prepared. There was no longer any way to stop it. He would rest contently knowing his plans were set and he would soon be returning home.

Chapter 104

"Miss Kitty!"

"Mr. Webster, Bill is waiting for you, go right in."

"Hi Sheriff, you got something for me?"

"Greg, sit down. The was a probable attempt on Ms. Meadows again."

"What do you mean possible, Bill."

"We got a call from a nurse who was covering in ICU during the lunch break. She said a man claiming to be a Dr. Slater entered the room and came upon the girl's parents. It appears the curtain was closed so he wasn't able to verify the patient was unattended until he had already made himself known.

According to the parents, the man was acting strangely and then left abruptly. At that time, security received a notice of the west end stairwell alarm being triggered. The nurse did not see anyone in the hall after the alarm sounded. She is certain he exited via the stairwell.

I ran to the stairwell when the alarm went off. I went to the second floor, but the stairwell was empty. I didn't see anyone suspicious on the first floor either."

"Were the parents able to describe the suspect?"

"Yes, they were. Male, six feet, medium build, dark hair greying at the temples and clear or rimless glasses. He was wearing a dark suit under a lab coat. The coat was not monogramed."

"That's a pretty good description. Anyone we know?"

"We're checking the tape now."

"This must be our guy. We need to stop him."

"Do you have evidence that indicates foul play?"

"We have pieces of the puzzle; I need another twelve hours to put them together. Which reminds me, what's everybody doing tonight? I hate to ask you to do this but"

"No need, we're here as long as you need us." Bill said. Sandy nodded her head in agreement.

"Excellent," Greg replied, "This is going to be our operation center.

Bill, we're going to need eyes on the perimeter. Can you spare a couple guys?"

"We can do that."

Sandy, I would like you to be my point person with my department. You may be getting calls from Christine, Tom, and Russ. If any of them call, I need to know right away. There will be two agents arriving around 4pm, their job involves chart review, so I'll need you to coordinate with Medical Record. Make sure they have everything they need. If anyone has questions, call me.

One last thing Sandy, I need you to give this cup to the health department courier who will be here shortly. He's been told to ask for you. Okay, Bill, I need to see you privately for just a minute."

Sandy left Bill's office and closed the door behind her.

"Bill, I am going to meet with Jim Larkin and then I'm going to Barry Miller's office. We will reconvene here around 5pm. If you need me for anything, call me. Even if you don't need me, I want you to call at 4:15. You won't need to speak, I just want Miller to hear what I'm saying to you."

"Got it, 4:15."

"Bill, I want to thank you for all your help. Also, there is a good chance some State troopers will be coming around tomorrow. Just wanted you to know."

"Be careful out there, cowboy. Call if you need anything. I'll send Sandy to help you."

Greg smiled as he left.

Chapter 105

The door to the morgue was open, so Greg just walked in. Jim was sitting at the counter, staring at nothing.
"Hello Jim, do you have a minute?" Jim didn't move.

Walking toward him, he repeated, "Jim?" Greg placed his hand on his shoulder.

"Hey, Mr. Webster."

"Why don't call me Greg? I think we know each other well enough now."

"That's very kind of you, thank you." Jim answered.

"You seem down, Jim, is everything okay? Where is Dr. Seike?"

"I don't know where he is, he left right after he finished the autopsy this morning. He packed up a few things, put them in his briefcase and walked out."

"Did he say anything?

"Goodbye Mr. Larkin. That's it."

"Is that unusual for him?"

"He has never used the word goodbye. See you, until tomorrow, have a good evening, but never goodbye."

Jim, the other day when we were talking about the recent deaths, you were concerned. Aside from the ages of the patients, do you have specific reasons to be concerned?"

"Just some things that don't feel right."

"Jim, did Seike lie to me this morning when he told me you always print the lab labels?"

Jim didn't answer right away. It was clear that whatever his concerns were, he was more disappointed by the way Seike left. He looked like a kid who recently lost his father.

"Jim, what else doesn't feel right?"

"Last week, I was stocking that cabinet over there when I noticed a hole in the wall just to the side of it. I didn't remember seeing it before even though I stock it once or twice each week. I mentioned it to Seike and soon after, he sent me on a break. When I returned, we got busy, and I didn't have a chance to check it again. The next morning, the hole was gone. It was patched and painted.

I figured I was seeing a shadow or something. So, I just let it go. But there have been several times lately that Sr. Seike had sent me on errands or asked me to do him a favor. Get him aspirin, tea, coffee, the newspaper, supplies. Every now and then, he would offer to label the specimens himself. It was more than an offer; it was a command.

One day, I returned from one of the errands a little too quickly and

I witnessed him taking vials of blood out of his briefcase and placing the labels I printed on them. He didn't know I was there, but I realized why he was sending me away. I don't think the specimens submitted, were the correct ones.

Another thing that bothered me was the fact that he never found much on the autopsies of the younger patients. If I asked about it, he would use some medical jargon to explain it away.

"Jim, I appreciate what you're telling me. I'm sorry you were placed in an uncomfortable situation. I am going to ask you a question, and I need you to think carefully and answer truthfully. After that, I need to leave. Do you understand?"

Jim nodded his head affirmatively.

"Alright. Of the unexplained deaths in which you assisted Dr. Seike, how many had a noticeably ugly bruise of the antecubital region of either arm?"

Jim began tearing up. Greg put his hand back on his shoulder.

"I knew it wasn't normal, I should have said something."

"Jim, it's not your fault. How many?"

"All of them."

"Jim, are photographs taken during autopsies?"

"Yes, sometimes, but he never took photos of the arms. He always described them as normal bruising from intravenous administration of meds."

"Jim, I need to go. I will want to talk to you late tomorrow. If you need anything, call me. The information you have shared with me, is going to save lives. You need to know that and believe it. You are a good man, Jim Larkin!"

Greg needed to get moving. He had just a few minutes to get to Miller's office and on the way, he needed to make another call.

Chapter 106

Alex Winfield was a nervous wreck. He tried not to show It, but Kathy knew him too well. Most of the time, Alex made sure he was in control, but every now and then, he behaved like the sky was falling.

"Administration, Kathy speaking."

"Kathleen, please tell Mr. Winfield I'm all set up in the boardroom and I'll be there momentarily."

"Of course, Mr. Miller, I'll tell him right now."

"Go ahead, I'll hold. Let me know when he has left the office, I need to speak with you."

"Yes sir, let me put you on hold for a moment."

She placed Barry on hold and rang Alex.

"Mr. Winfield, Mr. Miller is all set in the boardroom, he will join you there momentarily."

"Thank you, Kathy."

She waited until Winfield left the department.

"Thank you for holding, how may I help you?"

"Did you have a nice luncheon, my dear?"

Just talking to him was making her skin crawl. She had embarrassed herself with Greg Webster and for what? She didn't love Barry, not even close. They had dated a few times, he liked to show off by taking her to nice places and buying her pretty things, but he was egocentric, judgmental, and just generally not much fun to be around. Lately, she was thinking she should just call it off, even if it meant losing her job. She wasn't sure why she agreed to act as a spy for him, perhaps she welcomed the opportunity to flirt with Greg.

"Lunch was fine."

"And did you extract the information from his?"

What an ass. "He doesn't appear to have any solid information. He said he has a few things he needs to follow up on. He didn't act like he had anything threatening."

"That's good news Kathleen. You're a good girl and we appreciate it. I better run now; I wouldn't want to keep the board waiting."

"Okay, goodbye,' Kathy said, and hung up.

Chapter 107

"Christine, it's Greg."

"Everything alright?"

"Yes, moving along on our end. Any news there?"

"The courier has picked up the specimen and is on the way back. Russ has been notified and will take care of it as soon as it arrives."

"That's great. I need another favor, Christine. I want to give you some names and I want you to find out everything you can about them. I need the information this evening. Is that possible?"

"I will do my best Greg."

"I know you will, thank you. I am going to be in meetings the rest of the afternoon and early evening, if you have trouble reaching me, call Sandy in security, she will be staying all evening."

"Is Sandy your special girl, Greg?"

"Come on Christine, you know you're my special girl, Sandy is just a placeholder."

"That makes me feel better, I love you too!"

"Hey, I'll email the names to you. Thanks again!"

Greg had one more stop to make before meeting Miller at his office.

He headed toward the Nursing Services office.

"May I speak with Charlene Kuchar, please?" he asked a young gentleman at reception.

"May I say who's inquiring?"

"Greg Webster, Department of Health," he handed him a card. "I'll let her know you're here, would you care to have a seat?"

"Thank you." Sure, *I'll have seat, he thought, for about 20 seconds, then I'm going in.* Every second of inactivity was becoming difficult to handle.

"Mr. Webster, nice to see you again. Please come in." Greg walked in first, she closed the door behind them. How can I help you?"

"Charlene, od you a doctor by the name of Slater?"

"There is a Doctor Slater at Higgins Hospital in Utica, but certainly not on staff here. You're asking because of the episode in ICU just a while ago. I was informed about that. The staff is very anxious."

"Do you know anyone in this hospital who would impersonate a doctor, or who may have access to medications?"

"I can't imagine anyone I know impersonating a doctor, although we have had a few over the years that seemed to be pretending. Access to medications is another story. Most of the clinical staff handles medications every day, but they are tightly controlled. Each department has a medication vending machine that stores the drugs that are typically required on that unit."

"Who has access to the vending machines?"

"Well, pharmacists of course, they keep them at par level. Registered nurses have access as well, they retrieve the meds when requested by the physician."

"Do the physicians have access?"

"They don't need it; the nurses do that for them."

"How do the nurses access the drugs?"

"They are assigned a unique password by the pharmacy department. They enter their password then they enter the patient's information by scanning a bar code. The system then knows not only who retrieved the meds, but whom the meds are intended for. When the nurse arrives at bedside, they verify the patient by scanning their bracelet. They also scan the code on the drug packaging which matches the drug dispensed to the drug given to the order."

"Sounds like a fail-safe system."

"It's as close as we know how to get right now."

"Who checks the pharmacy, Charlene?"

"They have their own internal procedures which I have no direct knowledge of. You would need to ask them."

"One last question. Who is Maury Slater?"

"Maury's official title is Orderly. He helps wherever he is needed, so he floats between departments. He is a good employee, not the sharpest tack in the box, but he tries. Keeps to himself mostly, kind of shy, not always punctual. He has been with us for about five years I would say."

"Is there a reason you ask?"

"Just the name. Trying to find a connection."

"To think that Maury could be involved in something nefarious, would be to over-estimate his capabilities."

"Thank you, Charlene, you have been very helpful."

"My pleasure Mr. Webster."

Greg needed time to speak with the pharmacy director. He knew who could make that happen.

Chapter 108

Alex Winfield was getting ready to call the meeting to order. There were sixteen chairs around the large table in the boardroom plus another ten lined against the walls. Most of the gatherers were still standing when Alex spoke.

"Ladies and gentlemen if you would find a seat, please, we are ready to begin. Mr. President, please call the meeting to order."

Alex sat at the head of the table, the board president to his immediate left. The only other designated seat was at the opposite end, on the corner. A laptop computer was positioned on the table, awaiting the presence of Barry Miller. The chair at the end of the table was relocated to make room for the projection screen the dropped from the ceiling.

The president opened with a few cursory remarks then turned the floor over to Alex. He looked around the table at the dozen or so member who were present. To his left, about halfway down the line was Harold Mease.

"Good afternoon, friends, thank you for coming. I apologize for the short notice today, there are a few important circumstanced that justify this impromptu gathering. Barry Miller will be joining us shortly to give you a financial update. While were waiting, I want to tell you about an issue that has been going on this week."

He paused and looked around the room again, taking measure of the friends versus foes in the room. He figured it was an even split.

"Some of you may already be aware of a prolonged visit by the State Health Department. While D.O.H. visits are a routine part of any hospital's operations, this one is a little different.

In the past week, we have witnessed an above average number of deaths involving younger than average age patients. The six deceased patients range from 21 to 57 years old."

Members around the table began to make comments to each other. Alex needed to reign them in.

"Please folks, we can open the floor for questions and comments later."

The room quieted.

"All hospitals are required to report any suspicious death to the health department. We followed that policy and reported the first. After the second report was generated, the D.O.H. investigative division sent an agent to perform an inhouse review.

Since he has arrived, there have been four additional deaths and one young girl who is hanging on by a thread. A suspicious death is one that is unwitnessed, and for which follow up review does not demonstrate a reasonable cause.

In each of these cases, the patients were unaccompanied when they died. In each case, an autopsy was performed by our pathologist, Kyle Seike. While there were underlying medical issues in each case, there didn't appear to be sufficient evidence to support a cause of death."

Alex paused again to evaluate his audience.

"The agent on board is Greg Webster. He and I have spoken every day, several times each day in fact. The last we spoke; he had no concrete evidence of any culpability on our part. If the episodes were to end for a while, I strongly feel Mr. Webster would end the investigation.

Our major concern in all of this, is community perception when this goes public. And it will. We will all need to work together to ease the community's fears and apprehension. We need to downplay our streak of bad luck and tout the many strengths that continue to make City Hospital the premier healthcare provider in this area."

He rested again, then "I'll take some questions while we wait for Mr. Miller who I am sure, has good news on the financial side.

Chapter 109

"Hello Kathy." Greg said as he entered the administrative suite. She looked up from her desk with obvious embarrassment.

"Greg, I've thought about what you said. I don't have a lot to say, but I am ready to speak up."

"Okay, I was here to ask a question but let's go with your idea. What's on your mind?"

"First, I want to apologize for my behavior earlier."

"You already did that Kathy, let's put it behind us."

"Barry Miller and I have dated in the past. Nothing serious, at least as far as I'm concerned, anyway, it was Barry that put me up to it. He asked me to seduce you to get information from you. He wanted to know what you know."

"Did he put pressure on you, threaten you in any way?"

"Not directly. You don't know Barry, he yields a lot of power, but he does it quietly. He and Winfield are always battling each other for control. I don't know what it is all about, but I do know something isn't right. It creates a poisonous work environment for everyone. I'm often drawn right into the middle of it.

I don't know how, but I have a gut feeling Barry is somehow involved in this. Lately, he seems obsessed with what he would call free-loaders, patients who don't have insurance. He has no sympathy for people who can't make their own way.

He has made statements in the past that make me ashamed to even know him. He wasn't always that vocal, there were even time when he could be somewhat charming."

"Kathy, do you recall when he started to change?"

"It was subtle at first, just an odd statement here and there. Little by little it got worse. I would say it started about three years ago. About a month ago, he was meeting with some of the physicians to encourage them to discharge patients their patients more quickly.

When the meeting was over, one of the physicians hung back to speak with him privately. The doctor was asking what he was supposed to do with a patient who needed post discharge care but had no place to go. Barry said if were up to him, the patient would go into the dumpster."

"Wow, that's cold. Kathy, I would like to talk with you some more, but I need to get moving. I would like you to do something for me. Can you schedule a meeting for me with the head of pharmacy? I won't be available until 4:45 but it really needs to happen today. Please persuade the manager to wait for me."

"That would be Bob Kline, but he's usually gone by 4pm, I'll see what I can do."

"Kathy, I have witnessed your power of persuasion, I have faith in you!"

She smiled. Greg's phone rang.

Chapter 110

There were just a few questions from the board members which Alex managed to bullshit his way through. Barry Miller had an even better brand of bullshit than Alex. He made a point of showing up late which the board believed was a result of his hard work and over-taxing schedule. Barry was a master at choreographing his entrance to look like the hero.

He presented slide after slide of the progress being made in controlling the market in hospital sponsored primary care and ancillary services.

"Bringing our services to the community by putting primary care in their neighborhoods assures our place as the preferred surgical, maternity, and inpatient hospital in the area. Control the doctors, and you control the patients.

The inpatient numbers paint a different picture. It's not just about controlling the patient's choice we must also control the length of stay for every admission. As you know, we have struggled with this historically.

When I took over as COO in addition to my fulltime responsibilities as CFO, our average length of stay was approaching seven days! Now seven days is fine if it is warranted as determined by the insurance companies, and we will be paid accordingly. If not, we will be paid based on a diagnosis that may only cover two days.

You have heard this time and time again, I know. This time, I have a better report for you. Over the course of the last three years, I have been working with physicians, our coders and discharge planners to coordinate our efforts to make sure our patients get what they need and what they deserve, but nothing more.

It was slow in the beginning, but commitment and persistence has paid off. As of this month, our average length of stay has gone from 7 to 4.4 days! That creates a positive swing in our bottom line of nearly five million dollars!"

Lots of compliments coming from the board members now. Alex was not only surprised by this sudden turn-around, but he was also pissed that he wasn't informed ahead of the meeting. Alex was the hero-apparent once again.

There were many questions asked by the members, many detail oriented that required Barry to speak longer than anyone wished. Then Harold Mease raised his hand.

"Yes, Harold." Barry called.

"Barry, how have you handled timely discharge of our less fortunate patients? The ones without insurance or poor paying insurance and the ones who are here because they have nowhere else to go?"

Barry hated the question and disliked Harold Mease. *This guy thinks he can question my methods after I just saved the hospital five million dollars,* he was fuming inside.

"Harold, that's a good question and I'm afraid there is no concise answer. With your permission, I would like to respond to each of the board members in writing. I have an important meeting in just a few minutes with the gentleman from the health department. I'm sure Alex brought you up to date on that story. I don't want to keep him waiting. Thank you all for your time."

Barry packed his computer and left the room quickly. He didn't want to face any more questions today. Besides, he had a meeting.

Chapter 111

Greg and Barry arrived at Barry's office at the same time.

"You must be Greg, I'm Barry Miller, thanks for coming."

"Nice to meet you Barry, I've heard a lot about you."

"Really? From whom?"

"Oh, Alex, Kyle Seike, Bill Dillon, Kathy, some staff on the nursing units. It seems everyone I talked to had something to say."

"You've been a busy boy, Greg!"

Little smart ass, Barry thought. He won't feel so smart when he goes home empty handed. Greg looked at his watch, 4:04pm.

"Are you in a hurry, Greg. I hope I'm not keeping you from something."

"No, I'm good Barry, just expecting a call from the office. So, what did you want to meet about Barry? Kathy didn't seem to have much information for me."

"I like to keep things on a need-to-know basis, Greg. Kathy is a good girl, but she doesn't need to know."

"Oh, I get it," Greg replied, "But I guess I'm more of a like-to-know-where-I'm- going kind of guy. I like being prepared for my meetings." Greg was looking Barry right in the eyes and smirking just a little.

"I see. If there was something specific, I wanted to talk about, I would have given you time to prepare." Barry responded sarcastically.

"Fair enough, Barry. So why don't you get this party started."

Greg was looking around the office while Barry was getting ready to answer. It was a modest office in a building across the street from the hospital, that housed all the finance offices as well as Information Technology.

There was a large desk in front of a very large window, a credenza along one wall and a long table on the other wall that held several electronic devices. It didn't appear that Barry had a closet in the room but there was a coat tree, behind and to the side of his desk.

"Greg, I'm going to be up front with you. I think your investigation here is a waste of taxpayers' money and a waste of my resources. People die, sometimes at a young age. It happens here, and everywhere else. You're not going to find anything wrong with our procedures or our policies. I think it's time you wrap it up and call it a day."

Greg was listening but he was also staring at the coat tree. There was a cap on the top hook, a sweater on a hanger balancing on a side hook and the suitcoat Barry took off when he entered the office.

"Well gee Barry, all you had to do was ask me nicely. Your opinion regarding my presence here is noted. Your concern that I am wasting your resources and your hard -earned taxes is noted, but I really don't care.

I'm doing my job and I'm going to keep doing it until the job is finished. I'm the one who decides when it's done. Not Alex Winfield and certainly not you. I'm here to protect the people of this state. The same people who pay taxes and insurance premiums so that you have a job."

Greg's phone rang. It didn't buzz or vibrate this time, He wanted to be sure Barry heard it ring.

"Greg Webster." He knew Christine was on the other end. He knew she wouldn't say anything, as instructed.

"Yes. Yes. Uh huh. That's great news. Yes. That's right, I sent the other specimens early this morning. Thank you, that sounds like a real break. I'll be here if you come up with anything else. Yes, thanks. You too."

He hung up. While he was conducting his phony phone call, Greg continued to look at the coat tree. There was something hanging under the suit jacket, He couldn't see much of it, but it appeared to be white.

"Sounded like an important call, anything you can share?"

"Yeah, that was the call I was waiting for. Good news, progress."

"Can you share it with me, it is my hospital?"

"Your hospital? You are an employee here Barry, this is a community hospital, you don't own it. You may have a contract to perform certain duties, but you are employed by the board of directors."

Barry was pissed and it showed. He stood and began to pace back and forth behind his desk.

"What are you, six feet?" Greg asked.

"Six one, but what does that have to do with anything.? I asked you to share your information with me. You are investigating my facility and I have a right to know where the investigation is going!"

"You have the right to a fair and thorough investigation. You have a right to a full and complete report, Greg paused, "actually, you don't, but the board does. I have the right to protect sensitive information during an active investigation. You are on a need-to-know basis Barry, and right now, you don't need to know."

Greg's turn to stand up. As he did so, he looked over at the table with the electronics. He noticed a small, pocket-sized video display device. Looking back at the coat tree, he strained to see what was under the dark suit jacket. He realized what it was.

"It was lovely chatting with you Barry, perhaps we'll meet again sometime. I need to go now."

"My meeting, I'll say when it's over!" Barry yelled.

"Wrong again, Barry. See ya."

Greg turned and walked out. He had a good time. *This Barry is an okay guy. Not!*

Chapter 112

On his way to meet Bob Kline in the pharmacy, Greg made a call to security.

"Security, Sandy."

"Sandy, it's Greg. Can you put Bill on please?"

"Sure, hold on."

"Hey Greg, what's up?"

"Bill, we're going to have a meeting in your office at 5:15 but first, I need you to do something."

Greg told him what he wanted, hung up and continued on to the pharmacy.

It looked like most of the pharmacists were gone by the time Greg got there. As he walked in, Greg could hear a faint alarm ringing somewhere in the back of the department.

A short, balding guy in an island print, open collar dress shirt appeared from a back room.

"Mr. Webster, I'm Bob Kline. You asked to see me?"

"I did Bob, I'm sorry if you had to wait around just for me. This was the first break in my schedule, and it was important that I see you today."

"I'm happy to help. What do you need?"

"I had a long chat with Charlene Kuchar today, she explained how medication acquisition happens once the drugs are on the floor. The missing link is what happens on the pharmacy end."

"Okay, it begins when we place an order from one of our supply sources. This could be a pharmaceutical company or from a group buying arrangement. Once the drugs arrive, they are checked into the materials management module. This lets us know the total drugs on hand at any time.

We make rounds as needed throughout the day to stock the vending machine located on each unit. Because each transaction is captured real-time, we know the level of each drug, at each location. A withdrawal from the machine requires a personal password as well as specific patient data.

We know who got what, when, and by who. Nice and clean."

"Impressive! I imagine you perform manual inventory as well. How is that handled?"

"Yes, we check our physical inventory against our electronic count every morning, Monday thru Friday. We don't have the staff to do it on the weekends."

"Who performs these manual verifications, Bob?"

"My assistant, when he's here and when he isn't, I do it. We are never off at the same time."

"So, I guess fishing together during the week isn't happening." Greg joked.

"Fishing nor anything else."

"Bob, who checks for outdated supplies?"

"Good question. My assistant oversees that, unless he is off, then it's up to me."

"Can you explain that process to me?"

"Sure, at the end of each month, we check all of our inventory here and on all the units. Anything that has an expiration date in the next 30 days, is removed and replaced. That allows us a full thirty-day window without risk of an expired drug being administered.

The soon to expire drugs are returned here and disposed of according to current regulations. Many are returned to the supplier for credit, but others are disposed of here either by dilution or incineration."

"Who signs off on the returns or disposal."

"I sign off on all of my assistant's disposals and he signs off on mine."

"Bob, have you found any missing drugs recently?"

"No, it's been quite a while since we have had any issues. Occasionally, we will have a portion of a dose go missing but that's usually an issue on the unit. The nurse draws 1ml out if a 2ml vial, disposes of the rest but forgets to document it. Nothing major."

"One more question Bob and we're through, what is your assistant's name, and will he be here tomorrow?"

"His name is Mark Hilton, and he won't be back until next Monday, He took his family on vacation. His little girl has been ill this year and he felt they needed some time away."

"I'm sorry to hear that. I hope she gets better soon. Thanks for your time, Bob."

Chapter 113

Barry was pacing around his office, wondering what to do next. Webster was not the pushover he expected. He still didn't believe there was anything to worry about, but he couldn't sit idle either. His phone rang.

"Kathleen, nice to hear from you."

"Mr. Miller, please hold for Mr. Winfield." She didn't wait for a response.

"Barry, I asked for a little dog and pony show, what happened in there! You totally undermined my, my authority, that's what happened! You never told me about these new figures on the length of stay. It would have been nice if I were aware of that before the meeting."

"Why, so you could take the credit for it? You haven't lifted a finger toward improving those numbers. You didn't have the balls to deal directly with the physicians, I did all of that. I made the numbers go down and now, I am going to be rewarded for it."

"Rewarded for what? That's your job! You wanted the extra title of COO, so it became your responsibility. You have been rewarded for the last three years, or have you forgotten about that huge bump in pay?"

"This is not about salary Alex; this is about the bonus money for bringing the length of stay down. My take, according to my contract, equals about one million dollars. I'll be asking the board to approve that next week."

Alex was silent on the other end. He went to his safe place. Shallow, sustained breaths. The smell of the barn.

"Barry, when did you work that into your contract? How did you do that without me knowing it?"

"Are you kidding me Alex, you saw today what the board thinks of me. I'm the strong one Alex, I'm the one they trust to do the tough things. I'm the one who manages the money while you handle public relations. You're a fucking glorified party host Alex."

"Well, we will see what happens Barry. I'm not going to take this lying down. If you want a battle? I'll give you one!"

"Aren't you forgetting something Alex? You have the health department breathing down your neck. You can't handle them without me. I don't know what you've been allowing to go on around here, but it sounds like Webster has proof of it. You better worry about the fire in your own kitchen before you try to put mine out."

Barry hung up. He needed a plan.

Alex was hell bent on upsetting Barry's plan for a bonus. He would need help from the board, but he may have just enough friends left to do it.

Chapter 114

Greg was on his way to security when he noticed the light through the open door of the morgue. He continued slowly toward the light. As he approached the door, he could hear voices, at least two.

He stood still trying to listen but then he heard footsteps behind him. He turned to look back, "hello Greg." His heart pounded in his chest. "Holy shit Bill, you scared the life out of me."

"What are you doing way down here, Greg?"

"I was coming to your office, but then I saw light and heard voices coming from the morgue."

"Come on," Bill said, and walked through the door. These guys are from maintenance, they're looking for that hole in the wall that you asked me to check out."

"Find anything fellas?" Bill asked.
"We moved the cabinet out of the way and with the right lighting, it does appear that the wall was recently repaired." Bill and Greg looked at the area the man was pointing out. "Anything else," Greg asked.

"Yes. When we moved the cabinet, we heard something move. We opened the doors but didn't find anything. However, on top of the cabinet, we found this."

The guy handed a small black box to Bill.

"It looks like a camera," Greg said.

"It is" replied Bill. "It looks like a wireless video camera, but why would they have one here."

"I don't think it's supposed to be here. Jim never mentioned it. I think someone planted it. I think someone wanted to see what was going on in this room," Greg said. "We need to put it back. If someone is watching, we don't want to tip them off. Hopefully, no one has noticed yet."

Greg and Bill walked back to security.

"Miss Kitty," Greg said as he entered the outer office.

"How's it going cowboy?' she replied.

"Let's just say it has been one interesting day. Any word from my office?"

"No word Greg," but your agents are here. I got them set up in Medical Records. They're reviewing all charts of deaths in the last three years.

"Excellent!" Greg said, "Bill, we're going to need to use your conference room, I'm expecting at least one other person to show and we're going to need some room to spread out. Dr. Shand should be on his way, while we're waiting, I'm going to make a call."

Greg stepped into the hallway and dialed the home office.

"Good evening, Christine" he didn't wait for her to extend the usual greeting.

"How did you know I would answer?" Do you really think Tom would answer? I think it was a safe assumption." Greg quipped. "Speaking of Tom, may I speak to him please?"

"Sure, hold a second."

"Greg, I was beginning to think we were just going to sit here all night. What's up?"

"It's time for the troopers, Tom. We will need two of them in plain clothes."

"You've got it. Should we pull from local barracks?

"Sure, I don't see any potential conflicts. I'm fairly certain this is going to go down tonight. I have a suspect but not much in the way of direct evidence. I think our best bet is to catch him in the act."

"You won't be putting anyone in harm's way?"

"No. Everyone will be fine. Tom, I need to speak with Christine again."

"Okay, hold on. Christine, how do I transfer this thing?"

Greg shook his head. *"Some things never change."* He said to nobody.

"Yes Greg."

"Christine, do you have any information on the names I gave you?"

"I thought you would never ask!" she returned. I do, and you're not going to believe what I found!" She gave Greg the information, then at his request, transferred his call to Russ Lang in the lab.

"Russell, how are things coming along?"

"Greg, I just got the results from the tissue sample you sent. I hope you're sitting down."

Chapter 115

Bob Kline did not have a good feeling. In fact, he was terrified. *"How could the timing be this bad?"* he thought, *the one time he was directly involved.* He had intentionally avoided it all this time.

Bob had prided himself on being a straight shooter, truthful, tough but fair. Mark found himself in a jam after incurring all the expenses surrounding his daughter's medical care. Then he got the call that day, from the unfamiliar voice, telling him he could help Mark without being involved. All he had to do, was look the other way.

Bob told the caller he wouldn't do it, that he was not about to put his license, his career on the line. He wanted to help Mark but not by doing something illegal and unethical. Then, the caller said something that made Bob shiver, "I have some pictures."

There was only one event in Bob's life that he regretted. *"Was it possible this guy had proof of that?"* he wondered. It was years ago; he and his wife Carla had tried to have children but were not successful. They did all the testing, nothing was wrong with either of them, it just didn't happen. As they grew older, they made a decision to accept their fate and move on.

There was always something missing. They both had great jobs, lots of expendable cash and they were in great health. Friends of theirs at the time, were experimenting with partner swapping. At first it didn't appeal to them but as time went by, and the excitement in their lives dwindled, they became more open to the idea.

It didn't happen right away, but eventually they decided to try it. The party was going to be at a friend's house, and there were rules. The most important being that everyone wore full facial masks from the time they arrived until the party was over. Secondly, couple paring was random. Each male and female guest was given a number. The numbers were then drawn from one of two bags, a bag containing female numbers and the other, male.

Couples were assigned a room, and no one was allowed to move from room to room. A timer was set for one hour. At the end of the hour, numbers were re-drawn, and the clock would begin again. After two sessions, it was over.

No one was supposed to know the guest list except for the hosting couple. As r as Bob was aware, no one else in the group worked at the hospital nor at the bank where his wife was employed. The evening went as planned and without incident. Or so Bob thought.

A few weeks went by before Bob received a few photos at work. One of the men who partnered with Carla, had managed to take pictures of her, not only naked but without her mask. Bob never said anything to Carla. He never questioned her about how it happened, but he did remember she wasn't feeling well, and was very tired when they left that night. He assumed it was a from all the activity.

Bob knew that if these pictures showed up at the bank or the hospital, both their careers were gone anyway. He thought it was best to just play alone, hoping it would never be exposed. Now he had a choice to make, he knew he couldn't do anything about the pictures, but he could go back to the locker and remove the drugs. With Mark away, Bob would be the obvious fall guy, if he removed the drugs, he would no longer be directly involved. He could still lose his job, by the wouldn't go to jail.

Barry Miller had calmed slightly but was still trying to formulate a plan of what to do next. He grabbed his PDA and turned it on. After a moment, the screen lit up and the view of the morgue appeared, but something was different. The angle didn't look quite the same. He could still see most of the room, but he was sure the camera had moved.

He didn't hear any sound, but that wouldn't be unusual. He theorized that the camera must have been displaced by movement of the cabinet. He anticipated having a view later as Maury moved the body of Sharon Simmons into the autopsy room to accommodate a client. He admired Maury for his entrepreneurial spirit.

Barry pulled out his patient roster for the current day. Shaking his head as he went down the list, *"I see several that don't belong here"* he said *quietly* to himself, *"we live in a world of bleeding hearts. If you don't work, you can't pay, you don't deserve it. healthcare included."*

"Ah, look at this one," he grinned, *82 years old, widowed, no children, been here for 13 days waiting for placement in a nursing home. We could be waiting another month for this guy to get out. No one would even miss him. Perhaps we will do him a favor. After all, the night is young, as they say."*

Barry moved his suitcoat to the side and grabbed his lab coat.

Chapter 116

Greg had all the pieces he had asked for, now he needed to put them in place.

"Welcome everyone and thank you for coming. I've asked you all here to assist me and the health department in solving a serious and mysterious issue. I am hopeful that by the end of this evening, we will have not only identified the scope of the issue, but also the perpetrators. This is not a normal DOH investigation and it will require atypical methods to address it. Let me go around the room and make some introductions.

Bill Dillon is the Head of Security and our host. He has been working non-stop today to put things in place for tonight's events.

Sandy is Bill's assistant and is working closely with my office to coordinate our joint response.

Dr. John Shand is here at my request to help me review pertinent medical records to see if we can determine a pattern and reason for the unexplained deaths.

Dr. Richard Ingraham is also a physician on staff who happens to be on duty tonight so he will be available in a limited capacity but will also be our eyes and ears on the units.

We also have two agents reviewing charts in Medical Records to determine how long ago these occurrences started.

There are a handful of associates in our office in Albany, working angles that will assist us. In fact, they have already provided us with several facts that have brought us this far.

Last, but not least, please welcome Sergeants Otosky and Lawrence of the New York State Police who are undercover and will be helping us when necessary.

Bill will act as the coordinator tonight. He has some of his men and women stationed around the facility as we speak. We have several wireless headsets that we will use to communicate. He will provide instruction on their use, right now.

Dr. Shand and I will be in Medical Records, should you need us. Everyone will check in with Bill on the quarter hour, sooner if there is something urgent to report.

Thank you again. Let's get started."

Greg, Shand and Ingraham went out together. In the hallway, Richard said, "what do you know so far, Greg."

"It looks like we can link at least two of the deaths and the attempt on Lacey Meadows to propofol overdose."

"Holy crap!" exclaimed Richard. "That explains the failed attempts at resuscitation. Could they be post anesthesia?"

"Well, we thought about that, both Meadows and Simmons were on small, maintenance doses of propofol, but Lorena Nunez was not."

John then asked, "how did you make the connection Greg?"

First, I picked through the trash in Lorena's room after she died. Most of the waste was from the code, but I found a breast pad that had some discolored discharge. I'm not even sure why I thought of it, but I sent to our lab for analysis. Initial tests only confirmed that there was an oil component. By then I had learned that Simmons and Meadows were receiving propofol, so I asked our lab guy to research it. Sure enough, the discharge on pad proved positive."

"That's a great find, Greg. I would have missed that for sure." John said.

"It gets better, on a whim, I went to visit Mease Mortuary, I saw his ad in a paper at the diner. Nearly all the deceased were reposing at that funeral home. We had a nice chat and I asked if Lorena's body was still there. He was still embalming her. I convinced him to let me have a look at her. I couldn't get a blood sample because she was already half juiced with formalin, but I was able to get a tissue sample of her antecubital fossa where the IV had been, which was grossly discolored and necrotic.

When I pressed Mease, he told me that all the recent, young bodies he received from the hospital had that same discoloration. That's when I knew for sure."

"So, how do you prove all that?" Richard asked.

"That is what we are doing here tonight. We are going to get our proof. John, are you ready to look at some charts?"

"You guys go ahead" Richard said, "I'll be around if you need me."

There weren't many staff left when John and Greg arrived. Greg recognized his girls seated at a table in the middle of the room. He wasn't sure of their names, but he had seen them around the office.

"Hi, I'm Greg and this is Dr. Shand."

"I'm Julie," the first said, "Hi, I'm Michele."

"Thank you both for coming, Greg said, what have you found so far?"

"Well, we've only been at it for a little over an hour, but we've gone through three months of charts for people who died while here. There is a wide range of ages, both male and female. A few were elderly, end of life types like heart attacks or stroke, and there were a few that were previously diagnosed with serious ailments, like cancer.

There were, however, an equal number of patients who didn't have any pre-existing conditions that would put them at risk of dying while they were here."

"Thanks Michele," Greg said. Have you separated the suspicious ones out?"

She handed Greg a stack. "Here they are."

"Excellent! John, let's sit over there and go through these." He pointed to a smaller table about ten feet away from the girls. There looks to be about twenty charts here, we'll split them up. We're looking for any similarities like, diagnosis, age, gender, recurring visits, insurance type, and length of stay. Let's also look at the attending physician, which unit they were on and whether they had IV's running. I'll work this pile of charts starting from autopsy, lab results, imaging studies etc. Then we'll switch stacks."

"Sounds good Greg" John answered.

The room was quiet. No phones were ringing, few people were coming in or going out. It felt nice. Greg opened the first chart and looked to see if an autopsy was done. It was. The results were quite normal, a mention here and there of signs of smoking, obesity, early cardiovascular changes. He looked at test results, all normal.

He made a note then pulled the next chart. Everything was normal. Then another and another, all the same, normal autopsy, normal labs. Greg went back to the previous charts and checked specific test results. He jotted down the numbers for like tests. Every test he compared, was within one or two percent of the others.

"John, what do you think of these?" Greg showed him his notes with the side-by -side numbers. "What are the odds?" John looked them over, then he checked each chart for gender."

"Too close." He said, "it would be one hell of a coincident, especially given that two are male and two are female."

"My thought exactly," Greg said. "Keep going John, I'll be right back. Double check the post-mortem results with the results when the patient was alive."

"Got it," John said.

Greg walked out and headed toward the laboratory. While he was walking, he checked in with Bill for the second time.

"Bill, this is Greg, over."

"Yes Greg."

"Anything happening ,Bill?"

"The only movement we've seen is Bob Kline going to the men's locker room on the second floor. Probably using the bathroom. He was there less than five minutes and then walked back down to pharmacy."

"Did he use the stairwell by any chance?"

"No, and he shouldn't have access anyway."

"Ten-four. I'm heading toward the lab. Talk to you if fifteen."

"Ten four, Greg. Out"

Greg entered the lab and found Loretta sitting behind the counter. "Just the person I'm looking for!"

"Good evening, Mr. Webster, how can I help you?"

"Loretta, I need your assistance. This is not a comfortable question, but it is a vital one. Should you agree to do it, you will need to keep it just between the two of us. Is that alright with you?"

"Mr. Webster, you are the law around here and more importantly, I trust you! Whatever you need, if I can do it, I will."

"Thank you. I need to see the most recent lab results for a patient. The name is Kyle Seike." Greg watched as the color left Loretta's face. "I said it was a big ask."

"You're talking about Dr Seike, correct."

"Yes, Loretta, that is correct."

She paused, took a deep breath, and then turned to the computer. After several keystrokes, she said, "The most recent results I have are from three months ago, will that do?"

"Absolutely! Could you print them for me?" The words hadn't left his mouth when the printer come to life.

"Is there anything else I can do for you Mr. Webster?"

"Not that I can think of right now, Loretta. "You are amazing! Thank you."

Greg grabbed the papers and started heading back to Medical Records. "Greg, it's Bill, come in."

"Greg here."

"Hi Greg, Sandy has Christine on the line for you. Over."

"Ten-four, keep her on the line, I'm heading your way. Greg out"

Security was just a short walk from the laboratory. Greg made it in about twenty seconds.

"Line 2, Greg." Sandy announced when Greg entered the office.

"Thanks Sandy." He picked up the phone "Christine?"

"Hi Greg, Kyle Seike just purchased an airline ticket to Austria. It leaves Albany at 9:20am, connects thru JFK at 11:10am."

"The son of a bitch is trying to run," Greg said. "Nice work Christine, we need to stop him, but not in Albany. Get a hold of security at JFK and alert the New York State Police at the barracks nearest JFK. Tell them to wait for our word.

We are also going to need a search warrant for his home, wherever that is. Can you track it down?"

"What do you think? she asked.

"Right, pardon me. Thanks Christine!"

He went back to Medical Records. As he walked in the door, John greeted him. "I've gone through several more charts Greg, there are more unanswered deaths than I could have imagined."

John, let's compare all the similar autopsy lab results to these," he said, holding out the papers."

John took the papers and sat down. He set the results from Kyle Seike down next to the list he compiled from the charts. His eyes scanned up and down, side to side. He checked again from the top of the list. He set his pen down and looked up at Greg.

"No."

"No? Are you sure?"

"I checked them twice Greg, not even close!"

Greg began pacing, thinking. "What am I missing?" He said aloud but to no one in particular. "I was sure it would be a match." Then it occurred to him. "John, bring your sheet and come with me."

"Where are we going?" John asked.

"Back to the laboratory."

On the way Greg said, "What else do we know?"

"We've gone through a little more than half the charts. So far, all the patients who died had intra-venous lines. That goes back a year and a half Greg."

"Alright, when we get back, we focus on how he is selecting his patients. There has to be a common denominator."

They reached the laboratory, and luckily, Loretta was still there. "Hello again Mr. Webster, Hi Dr. Shand," she greeted them excitedly.

"Hi Loretta," John replied.

"Loretta, I have another favor to ask of you. I need results for two more people, Barry Miller, and Alex Winfield."

Loretta looked stunned. "Mr. Webster, I could get in a whole lot of trouble for doing this. The people in I.T. monitor our access of patients, especially other employees. I could lose my job."

"I can assure you Loretta, your job is safe. We will not use the data you share as part of any criminal prosecution if it comes to that. We will subpoena any reports we need through the proper channels when the time comes. We just don't have the time right now. You have my promise and the power of the State of New York behind you. Your action may also save lives."

Loretta paused a few seconds the replied, "I said I trusted you and I meant it." Once again, she did her magic on the screen. "These results go back a little longer. About six months for Mr. Winfield and closer to a year for Mr. Miller."

"That will be fine," Greg said. Loretta pressed a button, and the printer sprang into action.

She handed the results to Greg. "John?" Greg said as he handed the sheets to him. John looked over the sheets, comparing the results to his hand-written spreadsheet. First, Miller and then Winfield. "We got it Greg!'

Both men thanked Loretta and left the lab. When they were outside, in the hall, Greg asked, "which one?"

"Take a guess," John said.

Chapter 117

Maury arrived at the park early. He was too excited to hang around at home. It was a nice evening, with low humidity, and the air was cooling with the setting of the sun. He sat on the bench where they planned to meet and looked around nervously.

There was moderate crowd for this time of day, many taking advantage of the nice weather. There were a few remaining restaurants downtown, unlike the period from the 1940's to 1960's when downtown was the nucleus of every American city.

High Falls suffered from urban spread much like the rest of the cities and towns in and around the Mohawk valley. Strip malls and big block stores located on the outskirts replaced the family-owned businesses of downtown. The park Maury sat in was a result of many empty, dilapidated buildings being torn down.

At 5:53pm, Lynette arrived. Maury knew this because he looked at his watch every thirty seconds for the last fifteen minutes. He could feel his pulse quicken as she approached. "Hi Lynette," he stood to greet her.

"Good evening, Maury, it nice to see you. You look different without scrubs and a lab coat. You look nice!"

"You look great too Lynette! Hey, would you like to walk around for a while before dinner?"

She smiled at his and said," you read my mind."

So, they walked around the outside of the park and back through the center, talking about work and fellow employees and lots of other topics. The time passed quickly and before long, it was dark.

"Are you getting hungry Lynette?"

"I guess I am, I've been so content just walking and talking, I haven't really noticed," she answered.

There was still a pizzeria downtown, take out mostly but they did offer seating for about ten people.

Maury said "I know we talked about burgers and fries, but would you settle for Italian? If not, I would be happy to drive out to the highway."

She didn't hesitate, "Italian sounds perfect!"

They headed off toward the pizzeria and Lynette reached for Maury's hand. "Do you mind?" she said.

"Not at all." Maury couldn't believe what was happening. Everything felt so comfortable, so right. He wasn't his usual awkward self, he felt confident, calm. The arrived at the restaurant, found a small table near the window, and ordered dinner.

Chapter 118

Greg and John were back in Medical Records reviewing more charts. "Greg" John said, "What do you think it all means?"

"I'm not sure yet, John, I have to say I was surprised by the lab results. Not what I had expected, which changes the way I need to think going forward. I do have a feeling that we are running out of time."

"You think the killer is going to attack again soon?"

"I do, John. I'm not sure why other than to rub our noses in it. But I feel it strongly. We need know how he chooses his victims. We get that and I think we get him or them, as it may be." Greg, walked to the other table to check on the girls.

"Ladies, anything I can get for you?"

"No thanks Greg," said Michele. "I'm fine." Julie followed."

"Have you found anything new" Greg asked.

"More of the same, we're more than two years back now and the vast majority of these deaths could be labeled suspicious. I do think I'm seeing a patter though," claimed Michele. "I'm making notes on patients who died post-surgery and it seems that they all got thru the surgery fine. Then, either infection set in, or some other complication that delayed their discharge. It appears that one to three days after surgery, they were gone."

A light went off for John and Greg at the same time. "Michele,' John said, have you done the same comparison for non-surgical admissions?"

"Not yet Dr. Shand."

"Okay," Greg exclaimed. "We are changing our focus, forget about looking any further back, we can do that later, for now, let's go through the same charts, non-surgical admissions only. We need to know when the routine admission became something other than routine.

Write down the admission date, diagnosis and expected length of stay. Look closely at any admission that exceed the expected LOS. For all of those, look for the reason it changed. Did the patient fall out of bed? Did they have a stroke? Did they require physical therapy? Were they waiting for placement outside the hospital like a nursing home bed or extended care facility bed? Was there no one at home to care for them upon discharge? Any reason you can find, write it down. If you need help or have any questions, call me. As soon as you have identified a trend, let me know.

John, let's take a walk."

"You know where this is pointing, don't you?"

"Yes Greg, they are tied to length of stay."

"That's what I'm thinking. We need to get a copy of the patient roster for today. Where can we get that John?"

John thought for a moment. "I know each unit will have their own but that could take hours to obtain and review. Who would have a master?" he thought aloud.

"The nursing office!" John exclaimed."

"Of course, they would have to and so would discharge planning, right?

"That's right John, but are we going to find anybody in those departments tonight?"

"Probably not" John said, "but the evening nurse supervisor would have access."

"John, track that person down and get the roster for today. I'm going to check in with Bill. Call me when you have something."

They men parted ways, John to find the nurse supervisor and Greg to Security.

Chapter 119

Sausage and mushrooms, they even agreed on that. They shared a large pizza and a picture of diet coke. They joked a lot, mostly about people they worked with. And they talked about themselves. The conversation wasn't rushed, and they both listened intently to each other, careful not to interrupt.

Lynette, Maury had found out, grew up with a single parent, just as he had. Her mom had died when she was in her teens. Her father worked much of the time, so Lynette was the primary caregiver while her mother was ill.

After a few months, her mother passed. Lynette tried to balance school with household chores and tried to keep her father happy. The first year was hard but they got by. Then her father started to drink.

He would stay out after work, hitting one of the local watering holes and then, come stumbling into the house. Most nights he would pick at the dinner she had prepared then fall into bed. It was the other nights she dreaded. The nights he expected Lynette to take his mother's place.

She saved Maury the details, but he didn't need them. The picture was an easy one to paint. He felt horrible that she had to endure such trauma. His own experience wasn't hostile, but the sexual tension seemed familiar. He could empathize with her, and he told her how.

She listened to his story with as much interest and caring as he had hers. They realized that perhaps they could sense the other's pain even before tonight. That unspoken darkness that is palpable between victims of similar fate. They talked about that.

"Lynette, I have never felt this close to any one in my life. I mean my mother and I were close but in a dysfunctional sort of way. The only person I could say made me feel comfortable and cared for is Harold Mease. He always treated me like a son."

I may be making a big mistake by telling you this, but I hope that you will understand. If understanding is beyond reach, maybe you can forgive me and still give me a chance.

You asked me earlier today if I had ever had sex with a corpse."

Maury went on to tell his story about history with Mr. Mease and about his little black book. He tried to be as non-graphic as possible, but he made sure she knew the truth. She didn't run away, and she didn't look frightened. She reached across the table and held his hands while he described his sordid life.

When all was said, after tears flowed on each side of the table, Maury and Lynette walked back to the park. They told each other how wonderful the night had been, how happy they were to have someone to talk to and how much lighter they felt having shared their darkest secrets.

"Maury?" Lynette said, taking his hands in hers, If I left my car here for the night, would you give me a ride home? Would you hold me tonight?

Maury didn't answer, he put his arm around Lynette and walked her toward his car.

Chapter 120

"Bill. Greg here."

"Loud and clear Greg, over"

"Gather the troops, I'm on my way."

"Ten-four."

When Greg entered the security office, the players were all there, except for the security detail out on the floors. "My gut tells me we should be seeing some action soon. We should be able to put a plan together shortly after Dr. Shand returns. "Dr. Ingraham, how does it look up above?"

"It's been a peaceful night so far, Greg. A couple admissions from the E.R. but nothing major. Evening visiting hours are winding down and I expect a quiet night."

"How is Miss Meadows doing?"

"I checked on her a little while ago. She's still here, which is amazing. Her parents have been with her all day."

"Bill" Greg asked, "You have someone stationed near her room just in case she is the intended target?"

"Affirmative" Bill said.

"Sergeants Otosky and Lawrence, your time is coming. Bill will go over the details with you soon.

"Are there any questions? Greg asked."

Sandy spoke up, "How you are holding up, cowboy?"

"It's been a long day, a long week I guess, but the adrenalin has kicked in I feel good. I'm no more tired than any of you, I'm sure. Thanks for asking Sandy."

The door opened and John walked in holding the patient roster up over his head.

Greg stood to meet him. "Is that it, John?"

"This is it, Greg. The nursing supervisor was happy to share it with me."

"Anything jump out at you John?"

"There are a few that stand out when you apply our criteria. The first is a female, 61 years old with end stage renal failure. She was admitted four days ago but isn't expected to last more than a day or two.

The second is also a female, 72 years old with Non-Hodgkin's Lymphoma. She was admitted twelve days ago but had been responding well and is scheduled for discharge tomorrow.

The last one is a male, age 28, motorcycle accident. Admitted three days ago, in ICU, Strong heart but little brain activity. This is the type of admission that could last for a month or more before either the family gives up or they find a bed for him at a critical care facility."

"Richard, what do you think?"

"It looks like the first two are going to resolve themselves, wouldn't be worth the risk."

"John, how about you?" Greg asked.

"I agree with Richard. The gentleman is the most likely candidate."

"History tells us he prefers females, but we're not sure why. My gut tells me he is going for a male this time, if for no other reason than to mix things up a bit. Okay, we need to get moving. Bill, get everyone in place, quickly!"

The team began moving. "John, come with me for a moment."

John and Greg walked down the hallway toward the morgue.

"John, I want to thank you for all your support. We couldn't do this without you."

"It is my pleasure, Greg. This wouldn't be ending if not for you. Who else in your department would be this devoted to finding the real answer? This is way beyond the expectations of a health department investigator. The physicians here and the hospital owe you a great debt."

"Thank you, John, between you and me, I think nearly everyone I work with would try to do the same thing. We get a bad rap sometimes, always looking like the protagonist, but we really do have the public's interest at heart."

"You're right, but I have a new perspective and you have a new supporter!"

"Thank you, John. There is one more thing I want to discuss with you, but we can do it tomorrow at dinner. Make sure Sara knows I'm coming this time."

Chapter 121

The killer put on his lab coat, placed the PDA device in one pocket and checked the other pocket for his tools. He had two 50cc syringes filled with propofol that he had prepared earlier in the morning for his failed attempt at Lacey Meadows. He left his room and walked confidently toward the hospital.

There wouldn't be many people around tonight, visiting hours have ended and the evening shift is staffed very lightly compared to the day shift. He didn't need to stop at the locker, but he would, just to be sure Bob Kline kept his end of the bargain. He would hate to have to play one of his cards now.

That was a fun night, he remembered. It wasn't his first sex party and he doubted it be his last. A friend of a friend invited him and his guest to join. He had a difficult time talking Kathy into doing it but eventually, she gave in.

What were the odds of him being selected along with Bob's wife for the second round? Fortune favors the brave. There were always flutes of champagne at each bedside, sort of an icebreaker before the real action began. It was easy for him to slip the medicine into her glass while she wasn't looking. It was even easier to obtain the medication. Membership has its benefits.

Wouldn't it be lovely if Bob was aware the drugs his wife consumed the night those pictures were taken, came from Bob himself? Talk about adding insult to injury. First, I screw his wife and then he drugs her. The irony.

He felt a cool draft on the back of his neck, as he crossed the street. The sun had set. Time for business now. He pulled the collar of his lab coat up, wouldn't want to catch a cold.

Chapter 122

"Greg, Bill here, come in."

"Ten-four Bill, over"

"We have movement. The suspect has just entered the building. He's heading toward the east stairwell. Everyone, hold their positions."

Several ten-fours were spoken followed by many seconds of silence.

"Suspect has entered stairwell. He has entered the code and is on the second floor. He just ducked into the locker room. Position four, can you hear anything? Over."

"Position four here, it sounds like he's fiddling with a locker. Yes, I just heard the door slam. Wait, he's coming out. He went back into the stairwell."

"Roger, position four, we have him." More silence.

"Position one here."

"Go position one."

"The suspect is on the first floor heading west. Over."

"Bill, Greg here."

"Go Greg."

"He's heading for the west stairwell. This must be how he did it before without being seen."

"Roger Greg. We'll pick him back up at the west stairwell."

A long minute of silence.

"Position five here."

"Go position five."

"We have him, headed our way."

"Roger that position five."

"Suspect has entered the west stairwell, Position five, over."

"Position six, be ready."

'Position six, roger."

He could hear the code being entered and the lock releasing.

"Position six, suspect is on the unit, walking east."

"Roger, six. Position seven and eight. He's coming your way. All others, take your positions. Quietly."

The ICU was silent except for the gentle beeping of equipment. Piece of cake he thought. Room 2403 was the third room on his left, just two doors down from where he failed to end Lacey's life just hours before.

As he approached the room, he could see that his victim had a room-mate. The curtains were open, but he would handle that. At least there weren't any visitors. As he walked by the first bed, he pulled the curtain with him.

He could see his target, a young man on a respirator. He walked past the respirator, to the far side of the bed. He placed the syringes on the bedside table, checked the IV and turned toward the respirator. He silenced the alarm.

He held the IV line in one hand, down near the piggyback site. He uncapped the needle and held the syringe tightly. He pierced the piggyback with the needle, turned off the alarm on the IV pump and drew back a tiny bit. A little blood raced into the line.

He closed off the line above the bifurcation and pushed. Not too hard or the vein will blow, too little and the patient may respond. He continued to push while he watched the monitor. The patient didn't move. The ECG tracing didn't vary. Highly unusual. He reached for the other syringe, uncapped it, and stuck it in the piggyback. He began to push.

"All units, GO!"

The curtain flew open, the killer turned his head quickly to look at the commotion. Sergeant Otosky jumped out of the other bed holding his revolver, aimed at the killer's chest. Several of Bill's men were standing inside the door along with a few more state troopers.

"Barry Miller, meet some of my friends." Greg said from behind the officers.

"Put the syringe down Barry, it's over." Barry looked around the room.

"You little pissant," he said to Webster, "You don't know the first thing about running a hospital.

"Put the syringe down Barry." Officer Otosky repeated.

No one moved. The patient hadn't moved a muscle the entire time.

"It's not supposed to end like this," Barry said quietly. "I'm supposed to be the hero, I'm the one who wins. Do you think you can change things, Webster? Do you think this changes anything? Do you really think healthcare will be better for what you've done here today? It's broken and you can't fix it."

"Barry you will have plenty of time to fix it from your prison cell. Killing innocent people isn't the answer. Now, put the syringe down."

"Innocent my ass! Barry shouted. All losers looking for handouts. Can't carry their own weight!"

"Mr. Miller, you have one last chance to place the syringe back on the stand and step away from the patient."

Barry knew it was end game, he no chance of escape. Moving easily, he pulled the syringe out of the IV line. He held it in his hand, looking at the creamy white fluid, a droplet paused on the end of the needle.

Suddenly, he moved the syringe to the patient's throat, the needle ready to puncture the skin.

"Step back," he shouted, "everyone put their guns down or I give your buddy here a big stab in the neck. I'm right on the jugular, he would be dead before you could pull the trigger. You are going to drop your guns, kick them over here and walk away."

"We can't do that Miller," Otosky said, his gun still trained on Barry's chest.

"You will do it and you will do it right now.! He will not survive this needle stick."

"Okay Barry, we'll try it your way. Everyone, drop your weapons. Easy, on the floor."

"Yeah, easy does it," Barry said. "One at a time, kick them over here." He was putting more pressure on the tip of the needle, Greg could see the skin, taut and ready to puncture. The guns slid across the floor, one at a time. Barry kicked them into the corner under the bed.

"Alright now, I want everyone to back out of the room. I'm going to give your friend here just enough to make him drowsy, then I'm going to put him in that wheelchair and he and I are getting out of here.

The men began backing out of the room slowly.

"Not you Webster!" he shouted. "You're staying with me. You do what I say and your friend lives." Greg stayed behind as told. Everyone else was outside the room.

"Now smartass, watch and learn as I use modern technology to get me out of here. They all believe I'm just going to dope the guy up a little. That shows you how foolish you all are. Why do I need him? I have you and all the guns."

He started to apply more pressure to the needle, Greg could see the skin turning red under the point, a droplet of blood beginning to form.

There was a sudden sound! Not very loud but obvious. Greg looked up at Barry Miller just in time to see the bullet enter his forehead. He fell back against the wall and then disappeared under the bed.

Sergeant Lawrence threw back the covers and sat up, a trickle of blood running down his neck. The pistol with the silencer still in his hand. "Otosky," Lawrence yelled.

Otosky turned the corner. He looked at Lawrences neck, "what happened?" he sked.

"Damn hospital razors" Lawrence replied, "dull as shit."

The others rushed into the room. "It's over." Greg spoke. "Bill, can you take charge here, I need to make a phone call." He didn't wait for an answer.

"Greg" John said, "are you alright?"

"I believe I am, John. I believe I am. Let's meet in Security in thirty minutes to wrap up.

Greg walked out of room 2403 toward the exit to the west end stairwell. On the way he passed Lacey Meadows' room.

He peeked in the door, no one was there besides Lacey. He crossed the room to her bed and stood at her side. The ventilator was still breathing for her, and the ECG monitor still showed a heartbeat.

He placed his hand on top of hers. It was warm and soft. "Hang in there Lacey, I'm sorry I couldn't help you. Greg's eyes welled up with tears. He thought of his own children back at home and he had a sudden longing to be with them, to hold them, to protect them.

He wiped the tears away and started to withdraw his hand. Lacey squeezed it, weakly but surely. He squeezed back and whispered "I'll come back to see you again. Soon, I promise."

Greg left her room and walked slowly toward the main staircase. He removed the phone from his pocket and dialed the office.

"New York State Department of Health, Christine speaking."

"Hi Christine, it's over. Time to put the rest of the plan in place."

"Greg, she spoke, Are you okay?"

"I will be Christine. Tell everyone to go home and get some sleep. And please tell them I said Thank you. Tomorrow will be a busy day. I'll call in the morning."

"Goodnight, Greg."

"Goodnight, Christine."

Chapter 123

Greg woke up at the hotel around 6:15am after a restless night's sleep. The wrap up meeting in Bill's office took closer to an hour than thirty minutes. There were, of course, many questions asked, some he could answer and others that would require the light of day to expose.

By eight o'clock, he was on the phone to Tom at headquarters. "Good morning Greg," Tom said excitedly. "I hate telling you this, but you're somewhat of a hero around here!"

"Hero?" Greg replied, "how do people even know about it? It's only eight in the morning!"

"Bad new travels fast, I guess." Tom joked.

"Has Winfield been picked up yet?" Greg asked.

"About 6:30 this morning. We thought it would be best to nab him before he went to the hospital. It will give us time to get a subpoena to search his home and office."

"And how about Seike?" Greg pushed.

"Troopers are waiting for him at JFK. They will wait until he boards, and then pull him off. We need to be sure his intent was to flee."

"Who knows at the hospital Greg?"

"Good question. We tried to minimize staff involvement last night but there were still a few that knew something was going on. It hard to say how busy the rumor mill has been this morning. I guess a few flags will be raised when Alex doesn't show up for work. I guess I'll head over there now and talk to some people."

"That sounds like a good idea Greg. Make sure you're near a TV at 10:00am, the Albany, Utica and Syracuse news will be covering JFK live. It won't be rumor after that."

"Got it. I really need to get moving then. Tom, can we hold off a day or two before doing any interviews? I need some time to wrap things up here, then I'll need a day at home to patch things up."

"You've got it Greg! If you need help today, call someone who cares."

"You're a funny guy, Tom."

"Trying to keep it light buddy."

"Thanks, Tom"

Greg made his way to the hospital and headed directly to administration. Kathy was at her desk, crying. He stood at the doorway. "Hi Kathy," he said compassionately. "I'm sorry for your loss."

"Greg" she said, "what happened? There are all these stories going around and I don't know what to believe."

Greg crossed the aisle to her desk and sat down. "Should we start at the end or the beginning?"

"Let's start with last night."

Greg thought about it, what impact this conversation was going to have on Kathy. She knew Barry intimately, at least at one time.

"Fair enough" Greg replied. "We had information that supported the theory that the killer either was an employee or had an inside source. We had evidence that Kyle Seike was sending fraudulent specimens to the State lab. We found evidence that identified the drug used in the killings. We just didn't know why."

"How long did you have this evidence, Greg? Could some of the killings had been prevented?"

"This all came together yesterday. If we had known sooner, we would have done everything in our power to protect the patients. Until 7pm last night, we were still in the dark. But we had a notion that the killer would make another attempt. When we finally discovered which patients were being targeted, we came up with a plan to catch him."

"So, it's true that Barry Miller was the killer."

"Yes Kathy, I'm sorry."

"For how long Greg? How many people?"

"I can't disclose many details because this is still an active investigation, but I can tell you that it's been going on a long while, and the numbers are frightening."

"Kathy, we need to talk about next steps. Has anyone contacted the president of the Board of Directors?"

"I've been told that the V.P. of Human Resources has taken care of that. When will Mr. Winfield return?" she asked.

"I guess that depends on whether he is charged with a crime. That decision will be left up to the Board and the District Attorney."

"What should I do now, Greg?" Kathy asked sadly.

"You're probably going to receive a lot of phone calls; my advice would be to let Human Resources or Public Relations handle them. If I were you, I wouldn't make any comments to anyone. You're a smart girl, you will know what to do. I'm sure an interim CEO will be appointed soon."

Kathy hesitated, and then asked, "Did Barry have to die?"

"No. He chose to die."

Greg left Kathy's office and continued to make his rounds. He stopped by to see Loretta in the lab. He wanted to reassure her that nothing was going to happen to her employment and to thank her once again for her help.

From there, he walked just down the hall to Security. "Hi Cowboy" Sandy said when he entered.

"Howdy Miss Kitty, wanna meet me at the saloon later?"

"Not tonight cowboy, I have a hay date."

Greg had to think about that for a minute.

"Oh! Headache, very good Kitty! Where's the Sheriff?'

"He's coming in a little later. I guess he was up half the night with the State Police."

"Yella belly!" Greg joked.

"Got that right Cowboy."

"Sandy, I want to thank you and Bill, and your helpers, for everything you have done for me. I can never repay you."

"No need, Greg, we should be thanking you. I can't image anyone else caring enough to do what you did. It was the most selfless thing I've ever seen. And I've been round these here parts for a long while now! Sandy winked. "You take care, Greg."

"Thank you Sandy."

Greg had just one more stop before going over to John Shand's for lunch. John had called early this morning to change the dinner to lunch. After the late night and all the excitement, John decided to reschedule his afternoon patients.

Greg made his way to the main stairwell and walked up the one flight. He made a left at the top of the stairs and headed toward the ICU. He nodded at the staff as he passed the nurse's station on his way to 2401. He looked through the window and found the curtain drawn around the bed. He took a deep breath before entering. He knocked lightly on the door. A woman's voice said "come in."

Greg stopped at the edge of the curtain, took another breath, and pulled it slowly.

He was surprised to find several people standing around the bed. Dread filled his thoughts. "I'm sorry to interrupt," he said. The people all turned to look at him. There, stood Richard Ingraham, Charlene Kuchar, two nurses he didn't know by name and a couple he hadn't met.

They began to quietly applaud. In the middle of the group, Lacey Meadows was sitting up in bed. Her eyes were open, and she had a small, but genuine smile. She was still hooked up to the respirator and was unable to speak but she didn't need to. Greg knew everything she was saying by looking in her eyes and watching her smile.

He moved toward the bed and the others parted to give him access. Reaching the bed, Lacey held out her hand. He took it in his, and they both began to cry. After several moments, the couple came toward him. "Mr. Webster, we're Lacey's mother and father, we want to thank you for all you have done. Greg couldn't speak, he just reached out to hold both of them. "Thank God, it's behind us, he said."

"Richard Ingraham approached Greg and held out his hand. "Greg, all of us owe you our deepest gratitude." Greg grabbed his hand and Richard pulled him into a hug. Greg could swear that the stoic Richard Ingraham was teary.

"Richard, it is you and your staff, and Lacey's parents who are responsible for her recovery. I am impressed and humbled by your knowledge and compassion. It was an honor to meet all of you. I must be going now, but I would like to ask permission to give your daughter a kiss."

"By all means, Mr. Webster.

Greg said his goodbyes and walked a little taller toward the front entrance of City Hospital.

Chapter 124

Greg drove toward the diner with one eye on the fading City Hospital in his rearview mirror. He wanted to see the 10am news but not around hospital people. That cut was new, deep, and painful, his presence there would magnify that.

The diner was the same one he stumbled upon where he found the newspaper with the obituaries. He thought about how much value there can be in partaking of local eateries and a small town's sixteen page newspaper. It seemed like a hundred years ago.

The place was pretty empty now, perhaps it always was, he pondered.

The television was mounted behind one corner of the counter. The volume was down so he asked the waitress if she could turn it up on her way to get him coffee. She obliged without comment. When she returned with the coffee, he said, "would it be possible to change that to the 10 o'clock news?"

"Anything's possible, they tell me."

He didn't know who "they" were, but he was glad they told her. She fished around for the remote for a minute then found it. She blew the dust off it while he thought *"what are the odds the batteries still work?"* To his surprise, they did. She clicked through several channels, finding the news just as the banner came across the screen.

"Man shot and killed at local hospital."

LIVE REPORT! Bethany Swart

"We're now going out Live to High Falls where a man has been killed at a local hospital."

"Shannon, residents, and employees are shocked by a deadly shooting last night in the ICU of City Hospital. While the hospital is not making any public statement prior to completion of the investigation, News at Ten has interviewed several employees of the hospital.

While we wait for an official announcement, we have been told that the deceased is Barry A. Miller, current CEO and CFO of City Hospital.

We have not talked to any direct witnesses, but word on the street is the shooting took place in the Intensive Care Unit and the shooter or shooters were undercover members of the New York State Police. A possible reason for the shooting can only be speculated at this time.

What we can currently only call rumors, other hospital executives may be involved."

"Mary Beth, we have breaking news from our New York City affiliate WNYN, please stand by."

"That's correct Robin, State Troopers from one of the downstate barracks have made a statement that Kyle Seike, MD the lead pathologist at City Hospital in High Falls, New York has been removed from a scheduled flight to Vienna, Austria and arrested.

Shannon, we are told that an executive of that hospital was shot and killed last evening in the ICU. State Police on the seen are not releasing any motive for the arrest. Back to you Shannon."

"Thank you Mary Beth Hildreth form Affiliate WNYN. We're now going back to Bethany Swart in High Falls for an update. Bethany?"

"I'm here Shannon, we just received information that Alex Winfield, long time CEO of City Hospital has not reported for work this morning. Hospital officials are simply saying he is unavailable. A source from the county D.A.'s office is telling us Alex Winfield was picked up for questioning in the early morning hours at his home. Our source is not saying if he has been charged with any crime."

"It looks like there may be a lot more to this story, Shannon. This is Bethany Swart reporting exclusive, live coverage from High Falls."

"Thank you Bethany. Wow! Stay tuned, there's more to come on News at Ten, after this from your local advertiser."

Greg just stared at the TV for a while, thinking about everything that had transpired in the last 24 hours.

"Warm up?" The waitress asked. Greg had hardly touched his cup.

"No, thank you. You can turn that off now if you prefer."

"Seems to me like you saw that coming," she added, "News like that will keep the pot stirred for quite a while around here."

"No doubt," Greg said. "He placed money on the counter and headed out.

Chapter 125

The drive to John's house was relaxing. The time, the mindless hum of the pavement and the view of the river valley, brought his busy mind to a crawl. John and Sara's house was located on a hill, south of the Mohawk. As he climbed, he could see the river on his right, and the rolling, green hills of farmland on the other side.

According to John's directions, Elmwood Avenue was the next right. The house was set back into a thinly wooded area with a big front yard. There was an old Weeping Willow tree that shaded a good portion of the grassy area. There was a picnic table underneath, adorned with a red and white gingham tablecloth and three place settings.

He turned into the driveway and pulled up near the house. The outside was painted a pale grey that blended in nicely with the forested background. The cream colored trim amplified the sun's reflection perfectly. A welcoming, wrap-around front porch screamed "sit with me a while."

As Greg approached the porch, Sara came hustling out to meet him.

"Welcome Greg, it's so nice to see you again! Come on up!" she said from the top of the steps.

"Hi Sara," he said as he hugged her, "what a beautiful place you have here!"

"Thank you, Greg, it really is heavenly. Please have a seat." She pointed to a wicker sofa that was accompanied by a love seat and an oval table, all wicker as well. In the center of the table, there was a tray with a pitcher of iced tea and several glasses. The pitcher of tea was loaded with ice and was sweating in the heat of the day.

"John will be joining us shortly; he is on the phone with a patient" she said as she poured a glass of tea.

"I'm in no hurry, Sara, in fact, I don't think I'll ever leave! What a difference compared to where I live, new houses, young trees, not much yard. I'm not complaining really, we like it there, that's just the sacrifice that has to be made to live near your work."

"Big city suburbs are like that" she said, "it's different around here."

"Good morning, Greg" said John as he opened the screen door onto the porch. I'm sorry, I was held up for a minute with a patient. Rigors of the job!"

"Not everyone can have a cushy job like me!," Greg joked.

"I don't think that accurately describes your last few days " John reminded him.

John was right, Greg's week wasn't even close to cushy, but there is the sunshine and shadow, the stress was diminishing.

"You boys had a busy night!" Sara said. "I'm so proud of you! Who knew back in the day that a couple average, beer drinking, pizza eating undergrad students would end up being heroes? Together no less!"

"Not me" said John.

"I always knew I'd be a hero" Greg clowned, but him?" He pointed a John.

They laughed for a few minutes. It was a release.

"Greg, I'm still missing a few details regarding what led up to last night's madness. Would you mind helping me out? I understand if it's too soon for you to talk about."

"It's fine John. Where do I start? Let's see, well, I never had a good feeling about Alex Winfield. He always seemed somewhat defensive, even paranoid at times. The more I spoke with him, the more it bothered me.

Kyle Seike seemed very likable at first, and, very knowledgeable. At our first meeting though, when I asked about his credentials, he became noticeably agitated, like, who was I to be questioning his credentials. It didn't take long to doubt his ability, I mean the guy never found anything substantially wrong during autopsy. He was either deficient or lying.

"I was interviewing Jim Larkin, his assistant the other day, nice guy, very helpful. We were discussing the procedure for securing and labeling specimens, and I had just asked Jim who applied the labels to the containers. Seike walked in right at that moment and said, "Jim does." I thought it was odd that he would answer when I clearly addressed it to Jim. I looked at Jim and he was quite uncomfortable.

I didn't push it then, but I went back and spoke to Jim again. He told me Seike had changed in the last couple years and that he would often send Jim on an errand or coffee break when it was time to label the specimens.

It was around that same time that we realized the samples we received at the lab were too similar for comfort. I believed Seike was swapping the patient's blood with someone else's. Larkin said Seike carried his brief-case with him all the time, I figured he was bringing in samples to make the exchange.

That's why I had the samples we received analyzed and compared to Seike's. When that theory proved wrong, I realized that one of the other suspected players may be involved. So, we pulled results from Winfield and Miller and compared them to ours. Bingo!

Alex was the donor for all of the specimens sent to the State lab. That way, there was never any evidence found in Seike's evaluations."

"So, what is the extent of Winfield's involvement, Greg?" John asked.

"We don't know yet," Greg answered. "He obviously contributed the blood but whether he knew about the killings is inconclusive. But, it's still early, who knows what they'll discover moving forward."

Sara asked, "without the lab results, how did you know that propofol was involved?"

"That was just luck, Sara. When I examined the room after Lorena died, I found a breast pad in the trash. I wasn't even sure what it was at first, then I remembered Mary using them when she was breast feeding the kids. Anyway, the pad had a greenish discharge on it. I don't know why, but I wrapped in a paper towel and put it in my pocket to send to the lab.

As it turned out, that was the one thing that wasn't tampered with. It required a little time and a little more luck, but we proved it was propofol. Now we knew how, but not who or why."

"The why was answered last night in Medical Records," John said to

Sara, "Greg had some of his staff reviewing charts alongside of us looking for factors that tied the victims together. The common denominator was length of stay. It should have been more obvious, Barry Miller has been hounding physicians for years now to cut back length of stay. He would want us to discharge early, even if it meant the patient dying on the way home."

"It just comes down to the greed of some individuals. Without doubt, the system is broken in some ways, and we can all do better, but not when people consider the issue, in terms of their personal financial wealth." Greg said.

"You're exactly right Greg," John added, "we need to focus on the best interest of the patient without prejudice. We need to create a system that is fair for patients and the medical providers. Someday perhaps."

"So, that leaves just the killer," Sara said. "When did you know it was Barry Miller?"

"I didn't know for sure until I saw him in the room with that syringe in his hand.

I had a gut feeling, that's why I asked Bill to put a tail on him. I met with Barry around 4pm yesterday. He asked for the meeting through Alex's secretary, Kathy. He didn't say why he wanted to meet, he just expected me to be there.

At first I thought "who is he and why do I care?, then things got weird. Kathy invited me to lunch in a private conference room. There was fancy food, and she was behaving oddly. About five minutes into it, I realized someone put her up to it, so I called her on it. First she tried to explain it away, but then she told me the truth. Barry wanted her to find out what I knew.

That placed me on guard when I met with him later. We were in his office and in two minutes, I knew that I was in the presence of the most arrogant man I would ever meet. Let's just say the meeting didn't go as he had planned.

While he was giving me a lesson in arrogance, I was looking around his office. I was drawn to two things, the number of electronic devices he had, and what appeared to be a lab coat underneath his suit jacket that hung on a coat tree.

Twice in the investigation, I was told about a Dr. Slater being at the bedside of a victim, wearing a white lab coat. One was a gentleman who died early in the week and the other was at the attempt to kill Lacey. I put two and two together and I formed my suspicion. Shame on him for insisting on meeting with me."

A car turned into the driveway of the house. "Are you expecting anyone John?" Sara asked.

"Not me" said John.

"I believe they're here at my request. Excuse me for a moment." Greg said. He stood and walked down the steps and out to the car. A woman stepped out as he approached and that chatted for a few minutes. She went around to the trunk of the car while Greg got something out of the back seat.

They fiddled there for another moment then they both started walking toward the house. John and Sara sat there, just a bit confused. As Greg and this woman got closer, it appeared the woman was carrying a basket of some sort with a towel over the top.

"Sara and Greg Shand, I would like you to meet Jo Langdon."

"How do you do Ms. Langdon, please come join with us." Sara said politely.

"Thank you," she replied, "Mr. Webster has told me so much about you."

"Really," John said and looked at Greg.

"John, Sara," Greg began, Jo and I have an issue we want to discuss with you." Jo reached for the basket.

You see, perhaps the greatest victim of all in this tragedy is right here in this basket." Jo lifted the baby from her resting place. "I know how hard and for how long you have tried to have a baby." Tears were already filling Sara's eyes, "you are under no obligation of course, and if I've overstepped, I apologize, but I wanted you to have right of first refusal."

Jo handed the baby to Sara. John was looking over her shoulder at her.

"This is Lorena Nunez's daughter, Maria. Lorena didn't have any next of kin and the father is unknown. Maria needs a foster family until adoption can be arranged. If you were to agree, you would be first in line for adoption."

"John, she is beautiful." Sara said.

"Yes, she is," he agreed.

"I know this a lot to consider, and you should take your time." Jo said. "Maria will be kept at the hospital for a few more days. After that time, we will need to find a temporary foster family. You have some time to think it over."

"How did you manage to get her over here?" John asked.

"Jo and I go back a way, and I pulled a few strings at the health department. The reality is this, it is very difficult to find stable foster homes for infants. It will take a few months before she is cleared for adoption, for which time she would reside in an orphanage."

"John" Sara said, "do you know how long it takes to find a newborn through an adoption agency? If we wanted to do this, and I'm not speaking for you, this is something we both need to agree on, one hundred percent, but we could be on a waiting list for years."

"Honey," he responded, I want her, I don't need time to think about it. There is a reason this happened here. We couldn't save Lorena, but we can certainly save Maria."

Jo spoke again, "Lorena told the social worker at the hospital that she moved here from the city, because she wanted a better life for her daughter. It was the most important thing to her. I think you would make a great family, and honor Lorena!"

The afternoon went on at a casual, comfortable pace. Jo stayed through lunch before retuning Maria to the hospital. Sara held Maria the entire time.

Greg stayed well into the late afternoon. He and John and Sara had a wonderful time sharing stories of the past and plans for the future. Greg opened up about his relationship at home, acknowledging that at times, it wasn't great. He also stated that this experience had given him a new appreciation for his family, and he vowed to do everything in his power to bring them all back together.

Sara told Greg that he could start by bringing his family back to High Falls the following weekend for dinner.

Epilogue

It was one year to the day that the horrors of City Hospital concluded. Much has happened since that time and Greg decided to take the morning to visit the riverside park and reminisce. It was late summer again, and he loved this spot by the water.

He hadn't spent an unusual amount of time rehashing the events, he wouldn't allow it. But he did take anniversaries seriously, and he believed there were opportunities to grow, but this was such an epic event, he didn't know where to begin.

He started by thinking about all the people he had met. In his life, he had never met so many, in so little time. The first who came to mind, were the deceased, all of which he met after they were gone. He remembered all the names, wondering if he would ever forget, or even if he wanted to. He said a silent prayer for them.

He also prayed for their families, some of which he had met after the incident was over, mostly at the legal proceedings. They seemed to seek him out, finding some small comfort in meeting someone who was on their loved one's side. It always made him feel sad that he couldn't have done more, but he accepted their comments with humility.

Alex Winfield popped into his head. He wasn't really sure at the time what the extent of his involvement was. Based on some of the work Greg's office, primarily Christine, had done exposed information that was surprising. At his request, Christine ran background checks on Alex, Kyle Seike and Barry Miller.

Some of the details resulted in being able to stop Seike before he left the country. The most interesting discovery was that Alex was born in Germany, to a Jewish family. His name was Allis Wienfeld, and he had a brother Sigmund. Their mother was killed while trying to sneak the boys out of the country. Alex, knowing his mother was dead and fearing the same result for his older brother, slithered his way to the Austrian border as his mother had instructed.

When he made it the across the border, he was met by an uncle who had escaped earlier. Along with the uncle, was Sigmund. He had escaped as well. The brothers were raised by the uncle in Austria until shortly after the war ended at which time, they all moved to the U.S. It was here that their names were changed to Alex Winfield and Kyle Seike.

The uncle didn't want them to be traced back to their roots. They were in a new country so they would begin anew. He stressed the importance of them protecting each other without anyone knowing they were related. He sent them to separate schools and different colleges. He instilled upon them the strength that came with money and the necessity of frugality. They learned well.

They were able to hide behind that façade for nearly five decades, working together and protecting one another. Alex did not know that Seike was concealing the results of the autopsies. His brother wouldn't let him know. Alex was just the guy who furnished his own blood samples. Seike would never tell him why, and Alex would never ask.

Seike was found guilty of Conspiracy to commit murder, after the fact, and sentenced to 25 years, without the possibility of parole. Alex was convicted of aiding a felony crime and sentenced to eighteen months. Both men lost their licenses forever. They are doing their time in different prisons in New York.

Barry Miller was apparently just greedy. It seemed to be more about power than money, but he found it hard to have one without the other. Having been a long term executive at City, he had his sights on being CEO, replacing Winfield, whom he despised.

Had he not died that night, he would have faced one-hundred-twelve counts of murder in the first degree, which would have earned him the title of history's most prolific serial killer, an honor he may have been proud of. His estate will be divided amongst the families of the victims.

It was found that Barry had installed the camera in the morgue. The PDA in his possession was connected by a live feed from the camera. The intended use could only be speculated, but most think it was to keep an eye and ear on Seike. The device did not have recording capabilities.

The locker in the second floor men's room was key evidence in the case. Many empty and full vials of propofol, along with syringes, needles, and other paraphernalia were found. All had Barry's fingerprints and some of the needles had blood in them which were DNA matched to several victims.

The supply chain was linked to the pharmacy department. Bob Kline was indicted for accessory to a felony for which he pleaded guilty. Because he was coerced by the use of threat by Barry, the jury showed some leniency. Bob was forced to resign his position and his license was suspended for three years. No one else in the department was charged.

Dr. Shand and Dr. Ingraham were key witnesses for the prosecution. They are both still busy at the hospital, Richard as part-time hospitalist, and John Shand is the new Medical Director. He brought in a new physician and a nurse practitioner to take over his practice so that he could devote his time to the new job.

He is now home most nights for dinner with the family and is only on call for managerial issues at the hospital. Maria took her first steps last week. She and her parents, and of course Uncle Greg, spend lots of time together.

As for Greg's life, he had become somewhat of a local hero. His name was known, not only around High Falls, but in the Capital District as well. He spent a lot of time at the trial, both observing and testifying, and was interviewed by regional and even national news stations because of his role at the Department of Health.

His friend and mentor, Tom, was considering retirement and Greg's name was tossed around as a worthy replacement, but he wasn't sure what he wanted. Life at home had improved significantly, partially due to Greg's greater presence, but also because he was really making an effort to be more available for Mary.

He was spending more time with the kids, giving her a bit of her old life back, and she was not regretting giving up her career quite as much.

When Greg spoke with her about a new opportunity he was considering, she listened intently and promised her support of his decision.

He was contacted by Harold Mease in his role as the newly appointed board president of City Hospital. Harold had also testified regarding the unique bruising of the arms of the victims. Harold mentioned to him that Maury had decided to come back to the mortuary part time and enroll in school. He had a girlfriend who seemed very supportive. In fact, she was a nurse at City. Harold would finally have someone to assume the business when he was ready to retire.

The hospital was in need of an interim CEO and Greg's name was suggested by several people inside the hospital and out. It would mean a better salary than Greg was getting to work for the state and, he wouldn't need to travel as much.

He talked it over with John and Richard and they both supported him whole heartedly. He agreed to interview with the board. He was nervous, it had been a long time since he interviewed for a job.

The meeting went well, many things were talked about, and the board made a very generous offer. He thought about it and told them he had a few stipulations. First, he wanted to have a team approach to running the hospital. Second, there would be transparency everywhere, meaning no hidden agendas and no power struggles. Finally, he would be paid only one dollar more than the next person in line and he would only receive the same percentage pay increases as the rest of the staff.

As Greg looked out at the water moving downstream, he became aware of how quickly our lives go by and how the ripple effect of our decisions can change the lives of those around us. He was ready to go home and see his family and then visit with his neighbors, the Shands.

Other books by this author include:

Buried Ethics: Digging Up Bones
(Book 2 in the Greg Webster/Ethics Series)

Twisted Ethics: How Thin the Line
(Book 3 in the Greg Webster/Ethics Series)

A Tale of Two Fishermen
(An illustrated children's book)

Why Do We Have to Move?
(An illustrated children's book)

www.gerardmichaelmcallister.com

Gerard Michael is an author, musician, gardener, saponier and paintographer. He resides in the Mohawk Valley region of upstate New York with his best friend and partner, Marilyn.